COLD SNAP

COLD SNAP

TONI ANDERSON

Cold Snap

ALSO BY TONI ANDERSON

COLD JUSTICE® SERIES

A Cold Dark Place (Book #1)

Cold Pursuit (Book #2)

Cold Light of Day (Book #3)

Cold Fear (Book #4)

Cold in The Shadows (Book #5)

Cold Hearted (Book #6)

Cold Secrets (Book #7)

Cold Malice (Book #8)

A Cold Dark Promise (Book #9~A Wedding Novella)

Cold Blooded (Book #10)

COLD JUSTICE® – THE NEGOTIATORS

Cold & Deadly (Book #1)

Colder Than Sin (Book #2)

Cold Wicked Lies (Book #3)

Cold Cruel Kiss (Book #4)

Cold as Ice (Book #5)

COLD JUSTICE® – MOST WANTED

Cold Silence (Book #1)

Cold Deceit (Book #2)

Cold Snap (Book #3)

Cold Fury (Book #4) - Coming soon

"HER" ROMANTIC SUSPENSE SERIES

Her Sanctuary (Book #1)

For Kaylea Cross – for being a fabulous friend and wonderful person. And, also, for letting me borrow her dog's name to use as Brynn's fictional boyfriend.

1

JANUARY 22

Fri., 8:00 a.m. FBI HRT morning briefing

FBI Hostage Rescue Team Operator Grady Steel leaned back in one of the hard plastic chairs with his arms crossed and his legs stretched out under the table as he listened to the big boss debrief them on their last op in the Arizona desert two nights ago.

Grady had been there on the ground, and his teammates had filled him in on anything he'd missed. He already knew the details. Gold Team had been lucky overall, luck earned by training their asses off on a daily basis, but lucky, nonetheless. No deaths. No serious injuries. Lots of bad guys neutralized, one way or the other.

Meghan Donnelly and Seth Hopper had both suffered minor injuries. Hop had fractured a bone in his foot, but the guy had limped in here this morning with a grin the size of Texas on his butt-ugly face.

Grady glanced at his buddy and rolled his eyes.

Shook his head.

Love made people stupid.

"We found a defect in Operator Donnelly's chute that was responsible for the malfunction at lower altitudes. We're conducting a review of all the equipment to make sure the other chutes are fully operational so nothing like this happens again."

Grady glanced at Donnelly as she sat there stony-faced. The defect had made her smash into a canyon wall after a nighttime HAHO jump. She could easily have died or broken her neck, but, thankfully, aside from being winded and suffering some nasty bruising, she'd been unhurt. Grady suspected the life-threatening danger and minor injuries weren't what bothered her most.

She might not show it, but Grady knew she was feeling relieved and vindicated that there was tangible proof it hadn't been *her* fault.

Donnelly was like him.

She'd scrapped to get through Selection with every ounce of grit and determination she possessed, and then, afterward, when she'd finally made it, she was still not a hundred percent convinced she deserved to be here. Donnelly was the first female operator to make it onto the Hostage Rescue Teams, which meant she'd worked twice as hard as everyone else to get here. The pressure not to fuck up must be intense.

Especially when she doubted herself.

It was hard to explain that unsettling mix of bone-deep self-confidence walking secretly hand-in-hand with a perfectly disguised and well-hidden sense of insecurity. It kept you on your toes, that was for damn sure.

The two of them shared an equipment cage, and he was slowly getting to know the taciturn operator.

She was solid.

He liked her.

But she, like him, in a small corner of her brain that she would never admit to, probably feared that at some point, someone would realize a mistake had been made and throw her off the teams. It was his recurring nightmare, but he was finally starting to believe.

That this was real.

That he belonged.

Daniel Ackers cleared his throat.

The director of the FBI's Hostage Rescue Team didn't join the daily team briefing very often, but when he did, he liked the sound of his own voice. "Given the events of January so far, we want to make sure everyone talks to psych. Schedule a meeting within the next two weeks, or we will do it for you."

Ackers met Grady's narrowed gaze before flicking to Cowboy. Ryan Sullivan was openly scowling.

"This is mandatory," Ackers continued.

Grady kept his expression neutral and his protests locked behind his teeth. He hated shrinks. They all did. The fact the assigned shrink was a pretty blonde was the only saving grace. Still, Grady would rather do cold weather exercises in the high Arctic than have his head examined.

Aaron Nash, an assaulter on Gold Team's Charlie squad, glanced at his watch. "Less than ten days of January left. The sooner this month is over, the better."

A-*fucking*-men.

Grady swallowed the thick knot in his throat that wanted to garrote him with grief. He refused to let it.

He'd learned long ago that any show of weakness was punished. He was alive. He was healthy. He had his dream job, where jumping out of helicopters and blowing things up was all part of a day's work. He was fortunate, and he didn't intend to fuck it up. He planned to enjoy it for as long as he could and then retire to join a fugitive task force in one of the big cities, chasing bad guys and kicking ass until he couldn't keep up anymore. He had no idea what he'd do after that. Buy a boat and sail around the world? Set up whale watching tours the way he and one of his childhood friends had once dreamed? As long as it didn't involve Florida or golf, he'd figure it out.

He covered a yawn.

They'd been working nonstop for weeks.

Grady was looking forward to spending the weekend sleeping. Except, he'd offered to take Grace Monteith's kids to swimming lessons on Sunday morning. The widow of his friend and former teammate was pregnant with her third kid. The team had rallied in general support, but Grady knew from experience it was practical help that made a real difference. There were plenty of people to hold her hand. He'd be the one painting the walls and driving the kids around whenever he was home.

Ackers finally wound down—no new information regarding Kurt Montana's ill-fated flight out of Harare—and Gold Team leader Payne Novak took over the briefing. A knock on the door had Novak pausing.

Grady hiked a brow. *Weird.* No one interrupted the daily briefing unless it was life and death.

The door opened and two FBI agents in business suits stood with their badges out, sour expressions on their unsmiling faces. One of them held a piece of paper.

Uh oh. Someone's in trouble.

Everyone shifted as the words "arrest warrant" floated above the urgent whispers.

Someone had definitely fucked up.

Grady didn't shift, but he frowned. Either a member of HRT or the field agents had made a big mistake. Still, the field agents had some balls serving the warrant like this, in front of everyone on the teams.

Grady stretched his neck and stared at the ceiling. More drama. He hated drama.

The two agents made their way along the side of the room, weaving through the bristling bodies that stood along one wall. Everyone was holding their breath, wondering who the hell had screwed up.

Then Grady caught Novak's worried gaze and an icy wave of fear flooded every cell in his body.

No. No way.

A moment later, he sensed the short, white, blonde female agent stop behind him and dread crawled up his spine and expanded into his mouth.

"Grady Steel," she said. "I'm Agent Ropero. This is Agent Dobson."

What the fuck?

She removed her cuffs from her pocket. The big Black agent beside her watched him nervously.

"I'm arresting you on—"

Grady bolted to his feet. "The fuck you are." He glanced around at his teammates, looking for the tightly controlled amusement that would say this was some sort of elaborate joke they'd constructed for his birthday tomorrow. "Is this supposed to be funny?"

His teammates looked anxiously uncomfortable.

"This is not a joke, Operator Steel. We have reason to believe you were involved in a hit-and-run incident a few days ago that left a senior citizen dead."

Grady reared back. He had no clue what the hell they were talking about. No way would he fail to report an accident or to assist a person who'd been injured. He glanced around in confusion, and some of the operators refused to meet his gaze.

Did they genuinely believe he'd killed someone with his truck and then lied about it? Bitterness soured in his stomach.

Ryan Sullivan came over. Gripped Grady's arm. The two of them often butted heads, but they were good friends. "We'll get this sorted out. Don't say a fucking thing until your attorney turns up."

"I don't have an attorney." A cold steel bracelet wrapped around Grady's wrist and cinched tight as his hands were drawn behind his back.

Agent Dobson removed Grady's firearm, and Grady gritted his teeth to stop from smashing the other man in the face. The agent was only doing his job—poorly, but whatever.

Grady was innocent. Resisting arrest wouldn't look good no matter how wrong and unfair this all was.

"I'll make a call and get someone with you ASAP." Ryan grabbed his shoulder and stared hard into his eyes. "Do not say a word, understand? I know you didn't do this. There's been some error, but don't say a word without legal counsel."

Grady nodded, but he was so thrown by what was happening he didn't have a clue as to what the next step might be.

He met Novak's piercing gaze as he walked from the room. Was that belief or condemnation written in his boss's eyes?

Grady's entire world was burning to the ground before him. Everything he'd ever dreamed of was slipping out of his grasp and fuck if he knew why.

2

Shame seared Grady's insides as the two agents marched him past his silent colleagues. He held his chin at a belligerent angle. No one would see him crawl.

He wanted to lash out but knew that would end with him being reevaluated as a team player. No, he had to suck this up and treat it like a training exercise he had no intention of failing.

It wasn't the first time he'd worn cuffs.

Donnelly broke the screaming tension. "Don't worry, Grady. We know this is a mistake. We'll sort it out. You'll be back in no time."

Her public support made him want to choke up, but he hid it behind an expressionless mask. Noise erupted behind him, but he was led away too quickly to hear if he was being defended or crucified.

Despite his training, sweat broke out down his back and made his thin black t-shirt stick to his skin.

They didn't stop to pick up his gear, not even a jacket. His phone buzzed like a bee in his side pocket.

The two agents put him in the back of a Bucar and drove him to a building on campus that had been used last week as taskforce headquarters during the hunt for a vicious serial killer.

Dobson opened the car door and let him climb out on his own. Crows flew overhead through the branches of the winter-bare trees, disturbed by the sound of gunfire from a nearby FBI Academy shooting range.

At least there wasn't anyone around to witness his humiliation.

Ropero tugged him by the arm and hustled him inside. Grady could have smashed her against the wall and disarmed her, even while wearing cuffs, but he wasn't sure he could take them both without someone getting shot.

Whatever his self-delusion, this wasn't training. This was real. To them, he was the bad guy and he had nowhere to run except to his own doom.

He needed to keep his cool, no matter how much he felt like a caged animal.

A brief thought about his father flitted through his mind but he pushed it away. That asshole deserved everything he'd received. This debacle wasn't justice. This was a mistake of epic proportions. He just needed to prove it.

They escorted him upstairs to a place that looked very much like an interrogation room. Table screwed to the floor. Three chairs.

"I want a lawyer. I'm not talking to you guys without a lawyer."

The big guy closed the door and stood in front of it with his arms crossed and his expression troubled. The blonde pulled out her handcuff key and unlocked Grady's cuffs. Grady rubbed his wrists as he stared in surprise at her serious face.

"You don't need a lawyer, Operator Steel," Agent Ropero stated.

Grady bristled because only an idiot would talk to law enforcement without legal representation. He opened his mouth to argue.

Agent Ropero cut him off. "You're not under arrest. You're not wanted in relation to any hit-and-run. You are free to leave at any time."

Grady frowned. "Is this some sort of joke?"

"No joke." Ropero glanced at her partner then walked slowly around the table and sat. "We needed to talk to you."

"Ever heard of cell phones?" He slipped his out of his pants pocket and put it on Do Not Disturb.

Part of him wanted to test the truth of her words and get the hell out of here. Curiosity kept him rooted to the floor.

Ropero opened a folder and slid out a headshot of a man in his early thirties. It was a photograph Grady saw every day at work.

"What we're about to say to you is top secret and mission sensitive. You cannot share this with your friends."

Friends? He'd be lucky to have any after this fiasco. Grady still wasn't convinced this wasn't some elaborate prank the guys had set up. If these two started stripping, he was going to lose his fucking mind.

"We need your help to catch one of the FBI's Ten Most Wanted Fugitives. Someone the Bureau has been chasing for twenty-seven years."

His stomach started to settle. Grady craned his neck to see what else was in her folder but the contents were hidden. "Eli Kane?"

Ropero looked surprised. "You know the case?"

Grady snorted. "Everyone knows the case."

Kane was a stain on humanity and the Bureau's greatest failure and shame.

His sweat cooled on his skin. Deliberately, he sat next to the female agent rather than opposite, crowding her so that she narrowed her gaze at him in annoyance.

Welcome to the club.

Dobson locked the door, came over and sat down heavily.

Grady glanced at the cameras.

"They're not recording. We're the only people in the building."

Ropero didn't look happy with him, and the feeling was entirely mutual.

He picked up the photo of Kane. "Why the theatrics?"

Ropero exchanged a look with her partner. Her mouth tightened. "We're sorry about the necessity for that, but we need for everyone to believe you've been suspended from the FBI and essentially disgraced."

Anger burned along his nerves. "So, you walk into a Hostage Rescue Team briefing and destroy my reputation in front of everyone I work with because there's been another bogus sighting of a man who disappeared twenty-seven years ago? Do you have any idea how long and hard I trained to get into HRT?"

Her eyes flashed. "I know exactly how hard you worked. I know every damn thing there is to know about you. I told Agent Dobson this wasn't going to work and that you wouldn't be interested in putting the Bureau's needs above your own."

Anger morphed into resentment. The hell she judged him from nothing more than what was written in his personnel file—while simultaneously screwing up his life as if his desires and feelings meant nothing. But he had a feeling she was playing him, and he wasn't that same youth who'd been so handy with his mouth and fists, not anymore. His training surpassed Ropero's in spades. Didn't make him a better agent necessarily, but he'd learned to leash his inner demons and use them to catch the bad guys.

"Wouldn't be interested in what?" he asked calmly.

Her eyes flashed. "That's privileged intel for agents assigned to this case."

Grady pushed back his chair. "You are out of your goddamn minds if you think I'm gonna sign up for some bullshit secret mission at the cost of my career without any information—"

"Hear us out for five minutes." Dobson took over, obviously sensing Grady was done with their games. "You probably know that over the years Eli Kane has been sighted all over the US and all over the world. Just last year, the Bureau sent a group of agents to the Australian Outback to surveil then detain a man fitting

Kane's description after a tip off. All the pieces fit. Age, height, eye color, facial characteristics. His basic life history. FBI thought they had their guy. *We* thought we had our guy. Unfortunately, we failed to get DNA no matter how hard we tried."

"It isn't easy hiding out in a town in the middle of nowhere with only a couple hundred people in it," Ropero put in. "Where everyone knows one another." She eyed him coolly.

He eyed her back.

"Australian cops eventually brought the suspect in for questioning at our request. He wasn't talking, and so they let us have a crack at him. He wouldn't budge. Then one of the local cops leaked who we were looking for to the press, and the back-of-beyond became a goddamn three-ring circus." Dobson relaxed back into his chair. "The publicity turned out to be a blessing in the end. A photo of the suspect appeared in the newspaper and was enough for a woman in Sydney to recognize him as the assailant who'd raped her ten years prior. That provided probable cause for the locals to get a DNA sample and compare it to that collected in the woman's unsolved case."

"Needless to say, it wasn't Kane." Ropero took over. "It was a serial rapist who'd immigrated to Australia from the US twenty years ago who had a good reason not to wanna talk to the cops or give his DNA."

Grady tapped his fingers on the tabletop. "This is all you guys do? Hunt Eli Kane?" He narrowed his eyes at these people who'd so cavalierly dragged him into their half-baked quest. "Twenty-seven years is a long time to be sitting on the FBI's Most Wanted list. He's probably dead in a ditch somewhere."

"He might be. But we don't think so." Ropero blew out a long breath, clearly hesitant about sharing whatever information was stuck up her butt. She stared him in the eye. "What I'm about to tell you cannot be shared, not even if you refuse to help us."

"I work with Top Secret information daily. I know the drill. But what exactly am I supposed to tell the guys? That this was all some stupid misunderstanding?"

"Tell him," Dobson urged.

Ropero shot her partner a look. "Ten days ago, there was a bank robbery. A locally owned Savings and Loan in a small, tight-knit community in the US. While dusting for prints in the safe deposit room, local ERTs pulled fingerprints that they ran through IAFIS."

The Integrated Automated Fingerprint Identification System was part of the FBI's Next Generation Identification system that combined fingerprint identification with facial recognition technology and other biometric data.

"And?" Grady demanded impatiently.

"The print belonged to Eli Kane."

Grady shifted in surprise.

Dobson took over. "The hit was flagged to us but sent back to the local cops as an unknown."

"Did Kane rob the bank?" Grady asked.

"We don't know the identity of the bank robber at this point, but we do know he wore gloves and appears to be slightly shorter and younger than Kane would be. Security footage only goes back a few days prior to the robbery. Analysts have been unable to identify Kane on it."

"We assume he had surgery. No way he'd have remained at large for so long without some sort of facial reconstruction." Dobson crossed his legs and tapped his finger slowly on the scarred table. "A two-million-dollar reward is enough reason for the general public to turn him in—if they could easily identify him."

"Prints on metal potentially last for years," Grady pointed out. "You've no idea when that fingerprint was laid down."

"We're aware of that." Everything about Ropero was tight and gritted.

Which certainly made him feel better. The iron around his chest had loosened further.

His life hadn't been destroyed.

These bozos could find someone else to work with, someone

who specialized in undercover work—not an elite tactical operator. He'd worked too hard to destroy his career, but he was curious about the case. Kane was part of the Bureau's imperfect history. Like Waco and Ruby Ridge, like Hanssen and Stone.

Today they strived to do better, but mistakes were still made. And Kane deserved to be punished for his heinous crimes.

Dobson frowned at Ropero. "The bank claims the outside metal of the boxes is polished on a regular basis which suggests the fingerprint arrived sometime in the past few months." He sighed. "As embarrassing as it was, Australia taught us an important lesson. The chances of us sneaking into a small town and asking questions without catching Kane's attention and him immediately disappearing are next to none."

"You guys don't exactly blend in." The agents looked like G-men. Even in casual clothes their demeanor and behavior screamed law enforcement. "He probably left as soon as he heard about the bank robbery." Grady spoke with a slice of maliciousness he wasn't proud of. But they'd dragged him into this whether he liked it or not. He wasn't going to roll over and let them rub his belly and say all was forgiven. Grady wasn't the forgiving type.

"We realize that, too," Dobson said patiently.

"Why'd the evidence tech run prints in the first place if the robber wore gloves?"

A smile curved Dobson's lips. "Damned if I know. A slow day? Or serendipity finally bending toward justice?"

Grady ran his nail along a scratch in the table, giving himself time to think. The information was intriguing.

"What does any of this have to do with me?" Anyone in HRT would be pleased to take down the former agent who'd cold-bloodedly murdered his wife and two young boys before disappearing, but Grady wasn't sure why these agents were talking to him alone, nor why they'd marched him out of the team briefing like a common criminal.

Another silent exchange between the two field agents as they decided whether or not to trust him with their precious intel.

Dobson spoke. "The bank that was robbed…was located in Deception Cove, Maine."

Grady stilled.

Blinked.

Swore.

"According to our records," Dobson held his gaze, "you not only grew up in the town, but you also have an account at the bank with a safe deposit box in that building, and you own property and have family there."

Grady closed his eyes and stared up at the ceiling tiles. To clarify, he gritted out, "You don't think I have something to do with this asshole, do you?"

Dobson shook his head. "No, but you know people. You're a local."

Grady pushed to his feet. "I hate to break it to you, but I don't know shit about the people in that town. I haven't lived there in nearly fifteen years and haven't visited in eight." The last time had been for a funeral.

"You have family there and local knowledge. You can collect data and evidence…"

Grady scowled. He had a sister. She hated him. "For how long exactly?"

Ropero bristled. "As long as it takes."

"Fuck you. You storm into my life with a half-assed plan and expect me to give up the rest of my career for your crusade—"

"You go where the FBI sends you," Ropero snapped with a mean twist to her mouth.

"The fuck I do," Grady snarled back.

Dobson's shoulders slumped.

Grady looked at them. "This was the best plan you could come up with? Me returning alone to my hometown with my tail between my legs after I'd been thrown out of the Bureau for vehicular homicide, in the hopes that someone would magically reveal a secret that Kane has spent nearly three decades success-fully concealing?"

Ropero shrugged. "We thought that if you understood the seri-ousness of the situation—"

"I understand the seriousness all too well." He struggled not to raise his voice. "It's you two clowns who seem to be struggling."

Ropero threw up her hands, thrust to her feet, and stalked away in disgust.

"Fine." Dobson leaned forward. "What do *you* suggest?"

3

TWENTY-EIGHT YEARS AGO

Winter

S pecial Agent Eli Kane sat in a paper-thin gown on a doctor's examination table. He wasn't Eli Kane today though. He was using one of the many aliases he'd set up for his undercover work.

Some the FBI knew about.

Some they didn't.

No way in hell did he want *this* getting back to his ASAC.

Getting an STD at his age was mortifying. He needed to tell his wife, but he was working a case that meant he wouldn't be home for at least another week, and he didn't want to tell her over the phone. He'd tell her when he got back. Suggest it might be a good idea for her to go for a checkup, just in case she hadn't had any symptoms. He'd watch the boys.

That last party had been wild.

His fingers shook a little as he pressed them into his thighs.

Too wild.

Unnerving flickers of memory flashed through his mind. Pain that had quickly morphed into something different.

He swallowed tightly.

Yeah. Way too wild.

Better not to think about it.

He'd been at an orgy, for Pete's sake. What had he expected? Sobriety tests and hand-written invitations?

He'd worn a condom most of the time, but not for blowjobs and…well, he wasn't sure about *every* time.

It was irresponsible with AIDS going around. He knew better.

But it'd been hard to think straight when there'd been so much booze, drugs, and pussy floating around like some debauched Roman feast. And how he had feasted, especially after trying an experimental pill that had promised to have his dick hard for hours. Boy, had that ever worked.

He'd fucked and been sucked off so often he'd been sore.

But the women he'd had…

The men he'd let screw his beautiful wife…

They'd been lining up to have her. She was so freaking gorgeous.

Two kids and she still had the body of a goddess. Smile of a siren.

Thinking about watching her have sex with another guy, even sitting in this cold sterile environment which was about as sexy as a refrigerator, gave him a semi.

One big, good-looking guy had taken her twice, once on the dining room table laid out amongst the food like a succulent roast. Then, later, up the ass over the arm of the couch.

Lisa never let him do that to her, but he figured she'd been as high as a kite the same as him. She certainly looked as if she'd enjoyed it. She'd caught his gaze during the first act. Smiled as if he was the only one in the room. Until the guy had rammed hard enough to move the table and brought her attention back to him.

They'd looked magnificent together, Eli could admit. As if they'd both walked out of a porn movie to entertain the rest of the mortals in attendance.

After watching her come like a rocket the second time, he'd gone and followed a little blonde to a bedroom and done to her

TONI ANDERSON

what his wife wouldn't let him do to her. The blonde had been young and sweet, but not too young—they wouldn't have allowed her into the party if she hadn't been of age. The organizers were very strict with their admission policy.

The woman had enjoyed it, too. She'd screamed with pleasure as she'd come and urged him to keep going, to hurt her. He'd slapped her ass until it was red, and she'd loved every fucking second.

And if the Bureau ever found out he was toast.

He wiped the sweat from his brow.

Getting turned on from fucking other women and watching his wife fuck other men was his dirty little secret.

Christ.

Lisa was so prim and proper most of the time. Didn't even swear. It made him laugh thinking about it. Thinking about her. He loved her. He loved her to the point of insanity even when she spent all their money on things they didn't need and couldn't afford.

Fuck.

He wiped his brow.

He might need to start moonlighting or urge Lisa to go out and get that job she'd been talking about. Maybe if she was working, she wouldn't be spending cash they didn't have.

But he liked to indulge her.

The parties had been her idea, and he'd balked at first because the suggestion was both so unexpected and so fucking tempting. But he'd used his expertise, so he wasn't too worried about their identities being revealed.

The first one he'd gone to he'd recognized a judge, a millionaire, and a senator. If they could do it, why shouldn't he and Lisa?

Who the hell had the right to tell him what to do? As long as he wasn't breaking any laws.

During this last party, the judge's wife had let him come between her breasts and then she'd lapped him clean like a goddamn dog.

She was the one who'd shared a line of cocaine with him. He'd never done coke before. It had fucked him up good, but, at the time, he hadn't felt as if he could say no. After that things had become a little hazy.

Those memories flickered again... Weight. Pressure. Pain. Pleasure.

Heat burned his cheeks as the doctor walked into the room.

His heart hammered and his hands shook as the doctor asked him to move the gown higher so he could examine the encrusted tip of Eli's sore penis. The doctor stared intently and then indicated Eli could pull the gown back into place.

Thank God.

"I have good news and bad news. The results are back on the sample you brought in last week, Mr. Fullam. They confirmed Chlamydia."

Shit.

The doctor pursed his lips. "You're single, correct?"

Eli scratched his brow, hoping the doctor wasn't going to go all puritanical on him about having sex outside marriage. "Yeah."

He and Lisa probably shouldn't go to another party, or maybe just one more, knowing it was the last time and make the most of it.

The parties were too big a risk. He loved his job. Needed his job. Being a G-man was everything to him. But the sex... Man, the sex was unbelievable. Better than cocaine.

"The good news is that I think the antibiotics are working, but we'll extend the course by another ten days."

Eli laughed awkwardly. "And the bad news?"

The doctor pursed his lips. Stared down at his notes. "You have a very low sperm count."

Shock rushed through Eli. What did that mean? "Because of the Chlamydia?"

The doctor shook his bald, shiny head. "I don't believe so. I suspect your sperm count has always been low. It's nothing to be ashamed of," the doctor reassured him. "A medical condition like any other."

The words buzzed around Eli's brain pinging off his skull.

"Perhaps advancements in modern medicine might someday allow you to father a child. And there is always adoption to consider…"

Eli just sat there. He laughed then, a little confused. "What if I told you I already had children?"

"I'm afraid I'd say that is very unlikely. Very unlikely indeed." The look on the doctor's face wasn't disapproval. It was pity. He climbed to his feet. "But miracles happen every day. Pick up the prescription from the desk. Good day to you, sir."

4

PRESENT DAY

I t was 10 p.m. on a Saturday as Grady pulled into the driveway of the achingly familiar clapboard house that had once belonged to his grandparents and was now, technically, his.

It looked in good shape. Better than it had when they'd been growing up.

His sister and her husband had grudgingly kept an eye on it for him and took care of repairs and maintenance. And, he'd discovered, they were making the most of it.

Grady climbed out of the Jeep he'd borrowed from Grace Monteith and stretched out his limbs after hours of sitting. The air was damp and cold. Snow lay piled into mounds where the sun didn't reach this time of year. Ice coated the driveway and wooden steps, although they'd been treated with sand.

The lights were off.

He braced himself and walked slowly up the steps he'd pounded every day after school. His grandmother had often sat on the veranda and waited for him to come home, a smile on her face but worry in her eyes.

He hadn't made it easy for her.

That was probably his biggest regret in life. Causing her a moment of concern.

He fitted the key in the lock, almost surprised it still worked. Inside, he glanced around at the modern-looking renovated space with its white walls and uncluttered appearance.

A breath shuddered out of him.

Hell.

It had been eight years since he'd last been here—for his grandma's funeral. Around the same time his application to join the FBI's New Agent in Training program had been approved. It felt like a lifetime ago.

He'd always dreaded the thought of returning. His grandma had been the single joy of his childhood, the one good thing in this life. His grandfather had died a few years after Grady had lost his mother. Gran had been left to raise him and his older sister alone.

The idea of being surrounded by his grandmother's things without her being here had scared him more than any jump off a Navy frigate or confrontation with a gun-wielding radical.

That's why he hadn't come back, plus the fact there was nothing here for him anymore.

He'd needed to get away. Needed to escape. Needed to prove himself.

But Gran wasn't here anymore, and the loss hit him all over again.

He glanced into the living room where he'd spent many long afternoons lounging in front of the TV and craned his neck to see into the connected dining area where he'd worked on his homework as his grandma had alternately encouraged and threatened, depending on her mood and his. Getting a decent education had been her one line in the sand. She always forgave him for getting into scrapes, fights, and fuck ups, but never for turning in a late or rushed assignment.

He owed her everything he was today.

Everything he'd achieved. Every arrest. Every rescue. Every moment of joy or satisfaction in his life. All because she'd pushed him to achieve rather than apathetically follow the footsteps of his loser father.

A wave of guilt and shame slammed into him that he'd been so terrified of coming back and facing his past. Nothing remained of her essence except some of the furniture he recognized that had been stripped down to the bare wood and French polished.

Why had he imagined things would stay the same?

Why did it hurt so much that they hadn't?

The lump in his throat was like a boulder. She was gone and would never know exactly how much he'd loved her.

He dropped his heavy kitbag on the refinished hardwood and headed along the corridor to the kitchen. He grabbed a clean glass out of a gleaming white cabinet before running the tap. He drank deeply and scrubbed a hand over his face.

He was exhausted. He was pissed. And beneath it all was this thin layer of grief he'd spent years trying to avoid.

The sound of the front door opening had him turning slowly.

"Grady?" His sister, Crystal, hovered near the kitchen door. They hadn't seen each other in eight years, but she didn't step forward to hug him, nor he her.

Her husband, Bob Grogan, stood behind her like a silent shadow. Grady assessed Bob for a long moment, and then met his sister's angry sky-blue eyes—the exact same shade as his own.

"What are you doing here?" Her accent was thick with the burr of the East Coast. Grady had lost the accent around the same time he'd ditched the town.

He took his time finishing the water before answering. He wiped his mouth with the back of his hand.

"Pretty sure this is my house, Crys. Nice to see you've been taking such good care of the place." He didn't bother to hide his sarcasm.

His sister's lips pinched. She'd never liked him—not even when they'd been little kids and it had been the two of them against the world.

23

She crossed her arms over her chest. "If it had been up to you, it would be a mouse-ridden dump. Derelict. Condemned."

He flinched at the last word. He was going to have to get used to it.

He leaned back against the counter, faking casualness. "If it had been up to me, I'd have sold the place when Gran died. Now I see why you persuaded me to hold onto it, and it wasn't because I might change my mind and come back to live in Deception Cove." That had been her argument in the days after their grandmother's funeral. Don't rush a decision. He might one day want to come home.

A flicker of guilt crossed her features then was doused by long-standing rancor and resentment. "Unlike some people, we couldn't bear to see it rot." She shrugged inside her thick winter jacket. Maine in January was a frigid bitch. "Bob and I did all the renovations and furnished the place. We rent it out occasionally to cover the cost of repairs."

His lips carved into a grim smile. It was a well-rehearsed story, but she forgot one thing—he knew the truth.

"I seem to remember sending you many thousands of dollars over the years to cover the 'cost of repairs.'" Plus, he paid the property taxes. "You've been conning me all this time and using this house for rental income."

"It should have been mine!" his sister screeched.

Christ.

"Gran left the house to me." Grady pressed his lips together to suppress the only words that could truly hurt her. Because their grandma, the woman who'd raised them both when their mom had died and their father had gone to prison, had loved Grady more than she'd loved Crystal. And Crystal had never been able to deal with it.

Maybe it wasn't fair, but Grady had never rubbed it in. Right now, God help him, he wanted to.

She gathered herself and inhaled a long, calming breath. They'd both had issues with their tempers as kids, and he'd worked hard to curb his. Being a Hostage Rescue Team operator funneled that energy in positive ways—if you counted close-quarter battle training and rescue simulations with live ammunition positive. He wasn't sure how he was going to cope without that release.

Hot sex with a willing woman?

Fat chance. He hadn't had the time or energy for romance lately. His mood had been consumed by the loss of his teammates and the desire to find those responsible.

Grueling runs in bitter weather were probably in his near future.

"How long will you be staying?" Crys made her voice sweet as her hands anxiously rubbed her forearms. She needed him more than he needed her right now. At least, that's what he wanted her to believe.

He straightened from the counter. "I'm back, possibly for good."

Crystal's jaw dropped in horror. Then her expression turned scornful. "They fired you, didn't they? The FBI fired you. What did you do? Steal something? Kill someone?"

Grady lifted his chin. *Suck it up, buddy.* He was going to have to get used to humiliation and shame, like roadkill being pecked at by sharp beaks.

Sounded a lot like his childhood.

"They finally figured out you were a no-good piece of crap and kicked you out, didn't they?" She took a step forward, shaking her fist.

Bob stopped her with a hand on her arm. "Crys. Leave him be."

She shook him off. "Why should I?"

"Because he's your *brother*."

Grady eyed the big man again. He'd been in Crystal's grade at school. If Grady remembered correctly Bob had a stepfather who'd adopted him as a little kid. That guy was in Eli Kane's age range.

"I realize I'm more fatted calf than prodigal son, but you're going to have to say goodbye to your golden goose until I get a misunderstanding sorted out."

Crystal wasn't amused by his mixed metaphors. "You can't do this."

"I believe I can." He picked up a laminated "Welcome Sheet" on the kitchen counter. "Something tells me you're going to have to get online and cancel a few bookings until I figure out my next move."

"If there are any refunds they'll come out of your pocket." Her voice rose.

His sister's tone set his teeth on edge. He narrowed his gaze, wondering how she'd turned out so mean. Was it growing up poor, or was greed part of their DNA? Like the father they'd disowned years ago who'd killed a man for his wallet. "I'll cover any refunds for the next two weeks, Crys. After that, you're on your own."

She was damn lucky the house wasn't booked tonight, or he'd be noisily evicting people right now and ruining Crystal's perfect host rating. It would expose her for the fraud she was, renting out a house she didn't own, but he wasn't sure it would gain him any points with the locals or aid his cause.

She licked her lips, probably calculating how much more she could squeeze out of him. "There's a long-term lodger in the base-ment unit. She's no trouble. Helping family in town for a few months."

Grady was about to open his mouth and say "no way" when his sister's next words stopped him.

"Brynn Webster, do you remember her from school?"

Grady frowned. He vaguely remembered the name.

"She's a good few years younger than us—her husband ran off and left her a couple of years ago. Poor thing." His sister's tone didn't sound sympathetic. "Her parents own the Sea Spray Café."

He nodded slowly. He remembered her now. Brynn must be

five or six years younger than he was. A painfully shy kid who'd blushed every time someone looked her way.

He rubbed his jaw as he thought about the Sea Spray Café. It was a popular hangout for tourists and locals alike. Maybe it would be worth cultivating a connection there.

"Why can't she stay with her parents?" He pushed because he didn't want Crystal getting suspicious if he capitulated too quickly.

"Her mom is sick and doesn't want anyone to see her struggling. Cancer. Can't see her lasting long, poor soul. They live out on Pikes Turning, and you know how treacherous the roads are this time of year. Brynn wanted a place in town as she's at the café all hours of the day and night—she's managing the place." Crystal wrung her hands together. Then her lips firmed. "And I assume you're going to need an income of some sort to keep from starving to death, unless you're the one who robbed the Hearst Savings and Loan Bank week before last."

Grady schooled his features to surprised interest. "Someone robbed the bank?"

"Yeah. Got away with over five hundred thousand dollars and a bunch of safe deposit boxes were broken into and ransacked. The security guard was shot in the leg—you remember Saul Jones?"

Grady nodded. He and Saul had been best friends in high school, along with Darrell York, who'd taken on his father's mantle as Montrose County Sheriff. At the last census, Montrose had a population of 10,000 that swelled to easily twice that in the summer months. Deception Cove was the largest of a string of small towns spread along the peninsula's rocky coastline and the county seat where the sheriff's office was located.

Grady doubted the new sheriff would be all that glad to see him.

"He got out of the hospital a couple of days ago and is staying with his ma again—his wife divorced him last year and forced him to sell the house." Crystal seemed to relax into the familiar routine of gossip. There wasn't much else to do in a small town beside church, fishing, and catering to tourists…except stealing other people's houses apparently. "Now everyone's wondering what people were hiding in those safe deposit boxes." She snorted.

Grady had hated the lack of privacy when he was growing up here. Hated the fact everyone knew about his shitty childhood and asshole father. But as Ropero and Dobson had suspected, it might prove useful.

"The downstairs unit is self-contained," Crystal pointed to the lockable door that led down from the kitchen. "Brynn's no trouble. At the café twelve hours a day except Monday, when they're closed. Visiting her mom the rest of the time. You won't even know she's here."

Grady raised a brow. Brynn Webster obviously paid her rent on time. Otherwise, Crys wouldn't be quite so enthusiastic.

"She can stay for now," he agreed grudgingly. "Any more inhabitants I need to know about before I hit the sack?"

His sister and her husband both shook their heads.

Crystal's features settled into bowed unhappiness. Bob stepped forward and held out his hand. "Good to have you home, Grady. It's been too long."

Grady shook the man's hand.

Not long enough. And he was stuck here for now.

Happy fucking birthday.

5

Brynn Webster was currently existing in her own private version of Hell.

All the years away at college—learning, training, then building her own business from scratch—and here she was, back cleaning tables in her parents' small restaurant in Deception Cove, Down East, Maine, while her mom battled cancer.

At least she was alone for her pity-fest.

The chef had gone home about an hour ago after he'd prepped for opening tomorrow. Angus Hubner was an exceptional cook and had been with her mom almost since the beginning. Brynn had known him for as long as she could remember. She hoped he didn't decide to retire any time soon.

The Sea Spray Café was her mother's pride and joy. The pale wooden floorboards and white-washed walls created a clean open space with just the right amount of rustic nautical charm. The furniture was bare wood or painted a blue like the ocean. It was beautifully put together and a testament to her mother's good taste. Original paintings that were for sale by local artists adorned the walls.

Her parents had gutted and renovated this space years ago

and turned the café into one of the classy go-to eateries Down East. It was busy all day long, even in winter when the locals got to enjoy it in relative peace. In summer, they opened up the large deck outside that was crammed virtually every day. Situated between Rockport and Bar Harbor, they had plenty of passing traffic even though they were well off the main highway.

Brynn turned off all the lights except for the string of fairy lights that outlined the huge picture window overlooking the rear deck. The window framed a spectacular view of the harbor that was one of the main draws of the café. The image was quintessential Maine waterfront complete with a lighthouse on the nearby headland. It was beautiful and evocative. And she'd never felt more out of place.

She eyed the liquor bottles behind the small bar and contemplated a nightcap before she headed back to her one-bedroom rental apartment. But she was too tired to appreciate a good single malt, and the thought of being spotted drinking alone made her decide against it. She loved this town, but she did not love the busybodies who delved into everyone's business.

After Aiden left, whispers and gossip followed her every time she visited from Boston. But here she was, back in Deception Cove, until—

She shoved the thought aside. Refused to think that way.

Instead, she went over to the coat rack, dragged on a sweater, grabbed her scarf, and wrapped it around her neck, then slipped into her deep blue woolen coat before pulling her cute gray winter hat out of the pocket and dragging it over her head. She checked the kitchen one last time, because, as tempting as it was, the last thing she needed was the place burning down. Then she bolted the front door and slipped out the back onto the deck that overlooked the harbor.

She double-checked to make sure the door was locked as it tended to stick a little in winter. The wood was slippery underfoot so she moved carefully. She'd need to remember to sand these steps and the front walkway when she came back tomorrow morning.

The night air was chilled, but the sea was calm and the reflection on the water mirror perfect. The smell of the sea calmed her the way it always did, but the sense of being trapped here, in a life she didn't want, threatened to drag her down like a lead weight around her heart.

Then she thought about her mother's chemo and pushed away the self-pity. Brynn would do anything for her parents, even suck up running the restaurant until her mom recovered her strength, or they found a permanent manager, or they sold the place—which she kept encouraging them to do.

It would break her mother's heart, but Brynn couldn't stay forever. She'd sublet her Boston apartment for six months and moved her personal belongings into storage. Would it be long enough for her mother to beat this?

Her fingers curled into fists in her pocket.

It would be. It had to be.

Brynn was exhausted, and her feet ached. She'd been at the café since eight a.m. without a proper break after one of the servers called in sick. Thirteen hours later, her brain buzzed, so she decided to walk down to the water to clear her mind like she often did before heading back to her rental.

She desperately needed to recruit more wait staff.

Her breath frosted on the exhale, and she shivered inside her coat as she snuck down the narrow alleyway between businesses in a shortcut she'd been using since she was a kid. A noise had her jerking around.

Unease crawled up her spine. What the hell was that?

She couldn't see anything except deep shadows and dirty snow.

Was someone there?

It wasn't the first time she'd felt as if someone was watching her...

Nothing moved.

She held her breath, feeling the darkness for any clue.

Suddenly a cat leapt up onto the top of the fence and hissed at her. Her heart stopped.

The stray ginger tom who lived under the deck of the neighboring shop bared his sharp teeth.

"You little freak! You scared the shit out of me." She'd been feeding him scraps from the kitchen, but he was too ornery to get close to.

Brynn shook it off. What had she expected? A serial killer hanging out like in some teen slasher movie?

She snorted.

Nothing interesting ever happened in Deception Cove—except for that bank robbery, which still had the whole town agog. Years of living in the city must be rubbing off on her and making her jumpy.

Gravel scuffed under the soles of her sensible work shoes as she continued down the steep slope. She concentrated on not breaking her ankle. They'd had fresh snow last weekend followed by a couple of unseasonably warm days that had melted most of it to an ugly gray slush.

Another storm was in the forecast.

This part of the world, this time of year, there was always another storm on the horizon, but this next cold snap looked as if it was going to be brutal.

Brynn came out of the narrow space at the bottom of the hill and released a breath. Thanks to the damn cat, her heart beat faster than usual, and she put her hand on her chest to settle herself.

Sometimes she hated being a woman. She bet men didn't worry about rape or murder every time they went somewhere alone.

She crossed the quiet street and began walking along the wharf where the tethered fishing boats swayed gently on the high tide, their tackle tolling softly against their masts.

The scent of brine filled her nostrils and she inhaled a damp, fresh breath that blew away the lingering cobwebs. She loved this little harbor with its raucous gulls and the slight, ever-present odor of fish.

She huddled into her coat, walked to the end of the short pier, and stared into the inky depths of the water. A gull took off from the mast of one of the sailboats and she started.

"Damn." She gave a self-conscious laugh. She never used to be such a scaredy cat.

She spotted a figure in the distance, walking quickly in the other direction. Head down. Too far away to tell who it was.

She went to turn away and head home to bed but paused as something broke the surface of the water.

A seal?

She frowned. No. A plastic bag? Or a tarp that had blown away from its moorings? Her eyes slowly discerned the outline of a long narrow object like a log. Then she spotted branches, outstretched in the water.

No, not branches, she finally realized. Arms.

"Help! Someone help me!" she yelled as she pulled off her coat, scarf, socks, and shoes, curling her toes instinctively against the wicked temperature. She looked around but there wasn't anyone nearby. She gritted her teeth before she jerked off her sweater and flung it on top of her pile of clothes.

She looked hopefully around again. "Dammit."

She braced herself and leapt into the water, holding her breath as she hit. When she resurfaced, she sucked in a shocked lungful of air as the icy water clasped her bones.

She coughed and spluttered. "Oh, my fucking god."

She shook off her reaction to the cold and struck out. She wasn't the world's strongest swimmer, but the harbor was sheltered and calm. The outer breakwater protected the town from the fiercest storms, and tonight even the mighty Atlantic was slumberous.

Her teeth chattered. She thought she saw the figure move and then watched in horror as they began to roll and sink beneath the surface.

"Stop. Wait!" She kicked harder and reached the spot where she'd seen them go under. There was no sign of them now.

She dove, reaching out in front and to the side as she kicked forward. She opened her eyes, but it was too dark to see anything so she closed them again and used her hands to search the water around her. She encountered nothing and began to wonder if she'd imagined everything?

Her lungs were bursting with the need to inhale, and she stretched out her arms another inch to the left. The back of her fingers brushed against something soft. She arrowed after it and grabbed hold. A sleeve. She gripped tightly to the arm within the sleeve as she kicked upwards, dragging the person with her.

Breaking the surface, she inhaled hungrily.

"Help!" She couldn't tell if the person she held onto was breathing or not, but they weren't responding. How long had they been under?

She spat out a mouthful of what tasted like dead fish and diesel fumes. She wasn't skilled enough to perform mouth to mouth while floating, so she started tugging the person to the pier.

Suddenly there was someone in the water beside her, grabbing the other arm of the victim and helping to tow them back toward the dock.

"Are you okay?" the man asked.

Shivers shook her so violently she could barely speak. "Y-y-yes."

She felt the stranger's eyes on her face. He seemed to take her at her word because he suddenly powered away from her and dragged the victim quickly to the nearest ladder. She spotted another person on the side, who reached down and helped haul the unconscious victim out of the water and up onto the pier.

Brynn's fingers were numb from cold, her whole body one giant, convulsive shiver, but she kept doggedly kicking and inching herself back to dry land. It took forever, but she finally reached the dock and realized the stranger had waited in the water for her. Probably worried he'd have to rescue her, too.

"Think you can climb out on your own?" he asked.

She was too cold to speak now so she nodded and wrapped her stiff fingers clumsily around the metal rungs of the rusty ladder and pulled herself out of the water, feeling as if she weighed a thousand pounds. The frigid air temperature hit her sodden flesh like a whiplash, and she wanted to weep.

God help her, the water was warmer than the night air that cut through her like a blade.

The stranger was right behind her. As soon as they were both safely out of the freezing water, he ran to where the drowning victim was laid out on the wooden planks.

Caleb Quayle—a young man who often came into the café with his loud friends to hit on her youngest waitress—stood over the prone form. Caleb and the stranger stared down at the drowning victim but made no effort to start CPR.

Do I have to do everything?

Brynn stumbled forward. "Is he breathing? Does he have a pulse?"

The stranger looked at her, oddly. His stern features looked vaguely familiar under the harsh glow of the streetlights, but she couldn't place him. Caleb's expression was stricken, mouth agape.

She stepped forward then stared down at the person she'd helped rescue.

Oh, god.

Milton Bodurek.

Manager of the Hearst Savings & Loan.

His face was milk-white and his features slack—probably because of the small circular hole that glistened in the center of his forehead rather than the fact he'd been in the water too long.

She stumbled back a step. She couldn't believe what she was seeing.

Dead.

He was dead.

Someone caught her arm and placed her coat around her shoulders. "You need to get warm. What's your name?"

Brynn couldn't answer. All she could do was stare at the man on the ground.

"She's Brynn Webster. I heard her scream for help when I was coming out of the bar. Ran straight down here."

"Who're you?" the stranger asked.

"Caleb." Caleb sounded resentful now, which was his usual tone. "Caleb Quayle."

Her fellow rescuer grunted. "You have a phone on you, Caleb?"

Caleb nodded, looking suspicious.

"Call the sheriff's department while I escort Ms. Webster back to her place before she succumbs to hypothermia. Don't touch the body," he said sharply as he pulled on his socks and shoes.

"No chance of that." The young man glanced around warily as if suddenly worried for his own safety. "Hey, how do I know you didn't do it?"

"How do I know you didn't?" the stranger countered.

Brynn glanced up and took a step away from both men. *Good question.*

"Look, Caleb, we could stand here all night playing *Clue*, but Ms. Webster and I both need to get dry and warm. Someone else —that would be *you*—needs to guard the body until law enforcement arrive." The man's expression turned bitter. "Tell Sheriff York that his old friend and colleague Grady Steel is seeing Ms. Webster back to her apartment. Tell him he'll need to call the medical examiner. Darrell knows where to find me."

That was why he'd been so familiar, Brynn realized. Grady Steel.

He was six years older than she was, and she hadn't seen him in years. He'd hung out with Darrell York and Saul Jones back in the day. The three of them had been magnets for trouble. Then they'd surprised everyone by joining the Montrose County Sheriff's Department after they'd left school.

She stamped her bare feet and looked around for her socks and shoes.

Caleb swore. "Bob Grogan told us you were back. Said you were fired from the FBI. We looked it up on the web, and the news said you killed someone in a hit and run."

Brynn gasped in shock.

Grady raised his chin another notch but didn't meet her gaze. "I'm an FBI agent accused of a crime I didn't commit. I'm on paid leave while an official investigation takes place."

Caleb's lip curled. "We're supposed to believe that?"

"I don't give a shit what you believe. Make yourself useful and call the damn sheriff."

Brynn was so cold she could no longer feel her extremities.

Caleb took a bullish step forward. "Maybe you killed Milton."

"Why the fuck would I shoot Milton?" Grady sounded exasperated. "Where's the motive, Einstein?"

Caleb frowned, clearly confused by the question.

Grady Steel picked up her scattered belongings and his own jacket and wallet. "If I'd killed someone, he'd be wearing two bullet holes not one, but that's just me and years of training, asshole."

Caleb raised a meaty fist. "Someone should teach you a lesson."

"Get in line, hotshot."

Grady didn't appear bothered by the younger man's threats.

He went to wrap his arm around her shoulder, but she angled away, dragging her coat closer around her frozen torso.

Grady Steel paused then waved her in front of him. "After you, ma'am." Then he yelled over his shoulder. "Don't touch the fucking body, Quayle, else you'll be third on the Sheriff's suspect list."

Brynn's teeth chattered as she asked, "W-who are one and two?"

Grady looked her straight in the eye as if to gauge her reaction. "You. And me." The amused curve of one side of his mouth caught her off guard. "Probably not in that order."

6

"Want your socks and shoes?" Grady asked the pretty woman who was barefoot and blue from cold.

She stopped and took her things from his hands, careful not to touch him. She wobbled as she dragged them on, but he refrained from offering help. She seemed scared of him, and he couldn't blame her under the circumstances.

"Edith will be distraught," she muttered.

Milton's wife.

While with Ropero and Dobson at Quantico on Friday, Grady had started a list of men in the local area aged fifty to seventy-five, men who could conceivably be Eli Kane. The case agents were conducting background checks on all suitable targets.

Milton was on that list.

He'd been one of the stalwarts of the community, but he'd only lived in town for twenty-five years. He'd claimed to be the grandson of Abraham Bodurek, and was, like Grady, related to one of the town's founding families who'd settled here in the late 1700s. Milton's father had moved away more than forty years ago, and Milton had inherited the bank as his grandfather's closest living relative.

Could Milton have been Eli Kane?

Unlikely, but not impossible. It would have been a bold move on Kane's part.

It couldn't be a coincidence that the bank was robbed and two weeks later Bodurek turned up dead. What had he known? Why had someone murdered him?

"Did you see him go into the water?"

"No." Brynn Webster finished pulling on her clothes and started walking at a fast clip toward her house. *His* house.

"Did you hear anything?" Grady followed her.

She shook her head.

"What were you doing down there?" Could she have had something to do with Bodurek's murder?

She swung around to face him, outrage in her pretty eyes, clearly hearing the suspicion in his tone. "I was getting some fresh air before I went home to bed."

He grinned, and she blinked at him. She was cute when she was mad. "You do that a lot?"

"Yes. Yes, I do." She nodded then frowned. "Since I've been back, anyway. It helps me wind down after a long day waiting tables." She huffed out a breath and hurried on. The house wasn't far. Nothing was in Deception Cove.

"Ever seen Milton Bodurek down there at night before?"

"No, but I've only been back a few weeks. He keeps his fancy sailboat down there. He was probably on that." She shot him a narrow-eyed glance. "What about you? Did you see anything?"

"Not a damn thing. That was the first time I've seen Milton Bodurek since my grandma's funeral eight years ago."

"How come *you* were at the harbor?" she asked him.

He didn't miss the healthy dose of suspicion in her tone. Fair under the circumstances. Smart even.

"Heard someone yelling for help."

"Me."

He nodded. He made her nervous though he was trying not to.

"Ar-aren't you freezing?" she asked.

Grady spent a lot of time in uncomfortable circumstances and found it easier to deal with by pushing it out of his mind. "The sheriff will probably be by to talk to you, soon."

Brynn Webster grunted in a very unladylike manner.

He tilted his head. "Normally, I wouldn't have let you leave the scene, but hypothermia is a definite possibility for both of us. Go grab a shower and a hot chocolate or something."

Her fine dark brows rose. Clearly, she didn't like being told what to do.

They were approaching his white clapboard house which sat three streets back from the harbor.

"You were brave going in after him," he offered, searching for some sort of neutral territory.

"I must have lost my mind." She hunched her shoulders and curled into herself. "I appreciate you jumping in after me. I'm not convinced I could have towed him to shore on my own."

He pressed his lips together. She'd been braver than most civilians would be. "It's my job—or at least it was, until very recently."

"Was Caleb telling the truth?" A crinkle appeared on her brow and she caught her blue-tinged bottom lip with her teeth. "About the hit and run?"

Cold was so deeply embedded now he could barely feel his legs, but he kept them moving forward regardless. "FBI put me on paid leave while they check my truck and various surveillance cameras in the area for evidence. It's standard procedure. Media and gossips never really care too deeply about the facts, do they?"

"Isn't that the truth?" Bitterness dripped from her words like the water dripped from her wet clothes.

"There's no evidence of any wrongdoing as I didn't have anything to do with the incident. I'm confident the FBI will be able to clear me shortly."

She didn't comment on whether or not she thought he might be guilty. Why would she believe the word of a man she didn't know—except, possibly, by dubious reputation?

She pointed. "This is me, here. I'm staying in your sister's downstairs rental."

He snorted.

"What?" she asked.

He shook his head.

"What?"

"Nothing." He put his hands in his pockets. "I'm upstairs."

She stopped walking. Her lips formed a perfect circle. "Oh."

She hesitated, obviously uneasy at the idea of sharing a house with a stranger.

The outside security light came on, and he got a better look at her. Long wet hair was plastered to her skull. Big, dark eyes blinked up at him.

He reached out and hooked a damp strand off her cheek.

Her skin was shockingly cold.

He waved her ahead of him down the driveway. He wanted her on his side. He could use her. That's what he told himself as he watched her walk along the side of the house to the basement apartment door.

"Get out of those wet things ASAP."

"Screw the hot chocolate. I'm gonna take a whisky into the shower with me."

"Good idea. By the way…" He waited until she turned to look at him. "You might want to start locking your doors."

Her eyes widened as if he'd issued a threat. Then realization dawned. "You don't think Milton killed himself, do you?"

No doubt in his mind Milton Bodurek was a victim of a homicide. "I've never seen a suicide victim shoot themselves between the eyes."

She flinched. "Have you seen a lot,"—she gulped—"of dead bodies?"

"Too many."

He left her and climbed the steps to the main house. He locked and bolted the door behind him, something he didn't remember ever doing growing up. He carried his gear up the stairs and hesitated outside what had been his grandparents' room. He swung the door wide and swallowed hard. The space had been completely remodeled and now included a small ensuite bathroom.

Pain lanced through him as bittersweet memories of the only person he'd ever truly loved swept over him. Her existence had been wiped away with fresh paint and new furniture.

He shook it off.

He wasn't a kid anymore. He was an FBI HRT operator working undercover for the next few weeks to catch one of the most notorious criminals ever to carry a badge.

He dragged the case inside the room and dumped it on the bed. Removed his weapon and wallet along with his leather jacket. Then he walked into the shower, fully clothed. He turned the water on hot. Braced his hand against the wall and wondered why someone had placed a gun between Milton Bodurek's eyes and pulled the trigger.

7

Brynn stepped out of the shower and wrapped herself in a thick fluffy robe. A second later, someone started hammering on her front door.

"Coming," she yelled.

The hot water had made her feel human again, but the sight of Sheriff Darrell York standing on her doorstep in full uniform, complete with broad hat and heavy parka, brought everything that had happened back into sharp focus.

"Brynn," the sheriff said slowly, "I hear you had a bit of an adventure down at the harbor tonight." He gave her a nod but couldn't stop his eyes from running down her frame. Ironic, as he hadn't noticed her in the years she'd been growing up when she'd had a giant crush on him.

She'd gotten over the crush a long time ago, assisted by a couple of dates with the then Deputy Darrell York shortly before she'd gone away to college.

Before Aiden had cut out her heart.

"I wouldn't exactly call it an adventure." She forced herself to soften her tone with a smile. "Can you give me five minutes to get dressed? Your old friend Grady Steel is upstairs. If you want to talk to him first."

Darrell ignored her suggestion.

"Mind if I wait in the warm?" He stepped inside without waiting for an answer but, as he was here in an official capacity, she couldn't exactly leave him standing on the doorstep.

She headed for the bedroom and closed the door firmly between them.

She dressed quickly in soft black leggings and thick socks. She dragged on a warm yellow sweatshirt from her Yale days, a maybe not-so-subtle declaration she wasn't from around here anymore.

She tied her damp hair back in a short ponytail.

In her small living room, Darrell stood staring at the bookshelf, which was full of local guidebooks and whatever paperbacks vacationers had left behind.

He turned as she came into the room. His eyes skimmed over her again, and she didn't know if it was attraction or because that's what law enforcement people did. Looking for weapons, drugs, lies.

"Can you walk me through what happened tonight, Brynn?" he asked gently.

She gritted her teeth in irritation. She wasn't sure why she was reacting to him this way. She'd become cynical of men since Aiden, and sometimes it was hard to pull back from that bitterness.

She opened her mouth to tell him how she'd found Milton when there was another knock on her door. She went over to answer it and was surprised to find Grady Steel leaning against the doorframe.

His gaze rose over her shoulder. "Saw the patrol vehicle out front. Figured I'd save the sheriff time and come give him my statement."

"Why not?" Brynn stood back to let him in. Whatever people said about Grady Steel, he'd actively helped her tonight and not stood on the sidelines watching her struggle. Plus, she had a sheriff in her front room, so she wasn't exactly in danger.

Easier to be brave with backup—one of her father's many sayings made her suppress a smile.

"Not sure how the FBI conduct interviews, but we usually question witnesses separately." Darrell rested his hands on his belt and tipped his head to one side. His gold star glinted dully on his chest. "Been a long time, Grady."

The edge to the sheriff's tone suggested it hadn't been long enough.

"I thought you two were friends?" she said with a certain amount of amusement. They'd certainly been tight in high school.

"Grady became too good for us once he joined the FBI, didn't you, Grady?"

"The Bureau keeps me pretty busy, *Sheriff*."

Brynn didn't miss the dangerous glint in the man's benign expression.

"Who wants a drink?" she asked brightly, heading into the small kitchen. If a couple of alpha males wanted to take potshots at one another that was their business, but she wasn't going to hang around to watch the show.

She was done being a bystander in her own life.

"I'll take one," Grady raised his voice.

"I'm on duty, Brynn. Maybe next time."

Next time?

Darrell's warm tone suggested a deeper relationship than they actually had.

She sighed as she uncorked the bottle of eighteen-year-old Highland Park she kept for special occasions and emergencies. Today definitely counted as the latter.

She pulled out two highball glasses and splashed two-fingers worth of whisky in each. She carried the glasses back into the living room and handed one to Grady. He'd taken the armchair in the corner and cradled the glass in both hands as he leaned his elbows on his splayed knees.

He raised the glass. "*Sláinte*."

She blinked.

Had she ever really noticed his smile before? She didn't think so.

She'd never thought of Grady Steel as being particularly attractive back in school, but when he sent her a lazy smile, she was suddenly aware that he was ruggedly handsome.

Her realization took her by surprise. She hadn't noticed anyone's looks in a couple of years.

Darrell's brow furrowed in disapproval.

She didn't care. She took a large swallow, and the burn of the liquor down her throat made her cough. At least it helped to get the taste of dead fish out of her mouth.

"How about I begin?" Grady offered. "I arrived in town shortly after ten p.m. Check with Crystal as she was over here about thirty seconds after I walked in the front door. Figure she has some sort of camera set up so she can monitor people going in and out that you can check." His lip curled. "Something I plan to rip out tomorrow."

Brynn's brows stretched high. Why would he rip out his sister's security system?

"I'll ask her for the footage." Darrell nodded as if it had been his idea.

Grady gave the guy a humorless smile. "When Crys arrived we, ah, *chatted* for a while."

Darrell smirked. "I bet you did."

It was no secret the siblings didn't get along.

"Was she expecting you?" asked Darrell.

"I wasn't expecting myself." A self-deprecating smile played on Grady's lips.

Brynn's heart gave an unexpected flutter. She shoved the feeling aside.

"Circumstances have changed over the past thirty hours." Grady sipped his whisky. "Nice scotch." His tone was warm with appreciation.

Would the FBI have really suspended him if they had no evidence he'd been involved in the hit and run? She vaguely remembered a few incidents growing up. Car and property damage with Grady behind the wheel. Another reason everyone had been so shocked when the then sheriff had offered him a position as deputy after graduating high school.

"I decided to head out for a walk and stretch my legs after being on the road all day." Grady glanced at her as if he could hear her thoughts.

She looked away, a little ashamed. She was no better than the gossips in town.

"Anyone who can verify your movements?" asked Darrell.

Her eyes swung back to Grady. It hadn't crossed her mind he might be here with someone else.

Grady's gaze locked with Darrell's. "My cell phone and Jeep. Both have GPS capabilities." He rubbed the back of his neck. "I bought gas a couple of times. It's a long way from Quantico."

"That it is. That it is." Darrell tipped back on his heels and his expression soured. "One way trip?"

"Definitely not." Grady stared at the glass in his hand. "The Bureau can't afford not to suspend me until they run tests on my vehicle. It's standard operating procedure. The FBI generally uses physical evidence to clear crimes, not hearsay."

Darrell looked away. "Guilty until proven innocent?"

"Innocent, period." Grady's expression had taken on a hard edge. "*I'm* not a liar."

Darrell sneered. "Doesn't make you innocent."

"I guess we'll let the Bureau figure that out, won't we?"

Undertones flowed between the two men that Brynn could only begin to guess at.

"Look, if you want to talk to me about the hit-and-run in Virginia, I can arrange a conference call with my boss at the FBI, or with my lawyer. Put the local sheriff's department at ease."

Darrell looked impatient. "Tell me about tonight. What happened when you went for a walk?"

"I headed along Main Street when I heard a female shouting for help."

"And naturally you ran to her aid?" The snide twist to Darrell's lip wasn't pretty.

Brynn wondered how she'd ever thought him handsome.

"Naturally." Grady took another swallow of the amber liquor.

"He jumped in the water to help me drag Milton back to the pier. I wouldn't have been able to manage alone." The image of the bullet hole in Milton's forehead flashed through Brynn's mind. She didn't think she'd ever unsee it. She took another sip then set the whisky aside as her stomach rolled. "I didn't realize Milton was dead. I thought whoever it was, was unconscious. I just saw him yesterday when he picked up a coffee and brownie on the way to work."

"What were you doing down at the harbor so late?" Darrell asked her.

"I wanted a breath of fresh air after being stuck inside all day. I cut down the alley at the side of the café to walk along the wharf before heading home." She frowned, remembering being scared witless by the cat.

"I was about to turn around and head home when I saw something floating in the water. It took a few seconds to realize it was a person." She covered her mouth. "I thought they—he—was alive. I thought I could save them." Her teeth started to chatter again and she picked up her glass and swallowed the last drop of whisky, concentrating on the smoky taste. "I don't know if I'd have dived in if I'd realized he was already dead."

She looked around. She knew how terrible it was when someone disappeared and you didn't know if they were dead or alive, and yet, she'd have hesitated to go into the water to retrieve a corpse. It was a heck of a realization about herself and not one she was proud of. "Is that terrible to admit?"

"No." Grady shook his head. "Human. Very human."

She contemplated pouring another drink, but she had to get up early again tomorrow.

"You see anyone else down there?" Darrell asked Grady.

"The young man, Caleb Quayle, arrived ahead of me."

"Brynn?" Darrell asked.

Brynn frowned. "I thought I saw someone walking north away from the harbor onto Abbot Street when I first got down there, but I couldn't tell who it was."

Had it been the killer? She shivered at the thought.

"Do you have any surveillance cameras in town?" asked Grady.

"Gee. I'd never have thought about checking into that," replied Darrell. "Good thing the ex-FBI agent is here to help."

"Not ex," Grady said firmly. "And I was simply trying to help."

Darrell hitched up his belt. "I don't tend to ask for procedural help from witnesses."

"I didn't witness anything. And it's not often one of the first people on the scene is a trained FBI agent." Grady climbed to his feet and stretched.

Despite herself, Brynn was drawn to the display of lean muscle and wide shoulders.

"*Suspended* FBI agent," Darrell insisted, "and trust me, I have not overlooked that coincidence."

Brynn's eyes went wide. Did Darrell really believe Grady Steel was a suspect? Did that mean she was, too?

"You have a weapon with you?" Darrell asked him sternly.

Brynn jolted.

Grady's mouth firmed. "Yeah."

"I'm going to need to take it for ballistic testing."

Grady blew out an audible breath. "You're not serious?"

"As a heart attack."

Grady slowly removed a lethal-looking black pistol with his forefinger and thumb from a shoulder holster that was hidden by an unbuttoned, soft-looking, red, plaid shirt. "You have an evidence bag or shall I get one from out of my luggage?"

Darrell pulled a bag from his back pocket. He'd obviously come prepared. Grady took a step forward and dropped it in carefully. "I need it back ASAP."

"Maybe while we're at it, we should do a GSR test." Darrell tilted his head to one side.

Grady sat back down. "I went for a midnight swim followed by a hot shower. Your window of opportunity for gunshot residue is already shut."

Darrell's expression darkened.

"And even if I did test positive for GSR, I shoot thousands of rounds a week for my work on the Hostage Rescue Team. Every pore in my body could and probably would test positive for gunshot residue. It would mean nothing in a court of law, and you know it."

"I think it's important to follow procedure, but you're right. By leaving the scene and by your own admission of taking a shower you've already potentially destroyed evidence."

Anger filled Grady's expression, but he didn't respond.

Brynn found herself coming to Grady Steel's defense. "It was that or both of us dying of exposure. The water was barely forty degrees. Are you planning to run tests on me, too?"

"Don't you worry none." Darrell moved to stand in front of her and she rose to her feet, not liking the height disadvantage. She knew it was a mistake when Darrell placed his hands on her shoulders and gave her an over-friendly squeeze. He tried to stare into her eyes but she looked away. She couldn't escape his words though.

"I'll need a written statement in the morning, Brynn. Come to the station when you have time. Keep your doors locked, and don't talk to anybody about what you saw tonight. Neither of you."

She hurried to the front door, deliberately breaking the contact. "I'm not sure what time. I'm expecting a lineup when I open the café in the morning so everyone can interrogate me in person. Forget church. The pews will be empty tomorrow."

"Well, don't mention seeing anyone else down there, okay?" Darrell insisted. "Right now, we're the only people who know that small detail."

"Do you really think it might have been the killer?" she asked, chilled again. "I didn't hear anything that sounded like a gunshot."

"We'll know more after the medical examiner performs an autopsy. He should be able to pinpoint time of death."

She opened the door. "You don't need to worry. I won't be talking about any of it to anyone." It had been a hell of a night. "Goodnight, gentlemen."

The men headed to the door. Darrell squeezed her arm as he passed, and she gave him a tight smile. Grady sent her a nod, and she noticed how incredibly blue his eyes were—like a cerulean sky on a cloudless day.

Without a word, she closed the door after them, flicking the latch and securing the deadbolt. She had no desire to notice anyone's blue eyes or honed muscles. The last thing she needed was to meet a man here when she had no intention of staying—and neither did he.

She didn't want a man in her life, period.

Not anymore.

And what if Grady wasn't as innocent as he claimed?

Milton Bodurek's bloodless face popped into her mind, and she shuddered. Just because she was home in Deception Cove didn't mean it was safe. Death and danger lurked everywhere.

8

"You're really gonna take my weapon for testing?" Grady asked as they walked down the side of the house to the front steps.

"Just routine, Grady. You know the procedure."

He did, but he didn't have to like it. At the bottom of the front steps, he pulled out his door key. "You going to test every 9-mm in town?"

"If I have to." Darrell lost his cockiness without the audience.

"How's Lorraine?"

Darrell shifted his gaze away. "Fine. Busy with the kids."

"How many do you have now? Two?"

"Three." Darrell's smile was proud. "You never settled down?"

It had been a while since he'd met anyone he even wanted to date let alone *settle down* with. He shrugged. "Married to the job, I guess."

"Not anymore." Darrell's eyes gleamed maliciously.

"You never got over it, did you, D?" Grady watched the other man closely.

"What?"

"The fact I got into the FBI and you didn't."

Darrell bristled. "I left Quantico voluntarily."

Grady crossed his arms over his chest. It was freezing outside, but he didn't intend to show that it affected him. Pride was one of his many flaws. "Only because you knew they were about to kick your ass out for failing an exam."

"Bullshit." Darrell sneered at him. "I'm sure you did your best to make sure they failed me. Anyway, I decided I liked it fine here, policing a community I grew up in and knew well. Not strutting around the country puffed up on self-importance." Despite the cold, sweat beaded on the other man's brow. "You never really belonged here so you never really understood."

"You and your father sure as hell made sure of that."

"You're the one who used blackmail to become a cop."

"You're the reason I needed to," snapped Grady.

It was a direct hit, and they both knew it.

Anger burned at the reminder of old wrongs. "Must be nice to have a daddy who handed you the reins to a sheriff's job—even if is for the smallest, least-populated county in the state."

The barb struck home with the precision of a HK PSG-1 sniper rifle, but Grady wasn't done. "I bet you didn't even have to get new signs made for your campaign. Just re-use the old ones." He laughed softly. "You sure people didn't think they were still voting for your daddy?"

"I earned this badge. The people voted for *me*." Darrell pushed his nose close to Grady's. "Anyway, having a sheriff for a dad beats the hell out of having a murderer as a sperm donor. I guess the apple didn't fall far from the tree, did it?"

On the outside, Grady didn't let the words rattle him. He'd heard it all before, a million times. He yawned. "You planning to arrest me for not bowing and scraping to the feudal king, or can I go to bed now?"

Darrell shook his head and took a few steps away. "I should arrest you. I fucking should just for leaving the scene."

Darrell wouldn't dare.

"You know I didn't kill Milton Bodurek, but if you need any help with your investigation…"

"You'll be the exact last person I'll call." Darrell threw up his hands and strode away. "You always were an arrogant prick. Let's hope the FBI wants you back, huh? Because we sure as hell don't want you around here."

Ouch.

Darrell wrenched open the cruiser's door and climbed into the tricked-out SUV with the Sheriff's logo painted on the side in green and gold.

Grady watched the man speed away down the familiar narrow streets. Did Darrell know anything about Eli Kane? Did he suspect that one of the FBI's Most Wanted criminals was hiding out in town? Grady doubted it. Darrell simply wasn't that smart.

What about the former sheriff?

Sheriff Temple York was eagle-eyed and intuitive and had never missed a trick. His son had been an entitled SOB, and his father did everything to protect him.

Darrell's parents lived in a fancy modern house up on the headland. Supposedly the money came from his wife's side of the family. Grady was gonna make sure the FBI dug into that. Just in case the money was a payoff to keep quiet.

Suddenly finding Eli Kane and figuring out who else in his hometown might know the truth had become an essential mission. What other lies hid beneath the surface of this quiet, tight-knit community that had always looked down their noses at him?

He was going to do his very best to find out.

———

Brynn struggled to get to sleep. Every time she closed her eyes, she saw Milton's glassy-eyed stare. A floorboard above her head creaked and her eyes widened as she remembered that only a door separated the basement apartment from the rest of the house.

Her heart started racing.

Did Grady have the key? Should she be worried?

He'd have to be the stupidest murderer in history if he intended to kill her and get away with it…but she'd still be dead.

She jumped out of bed and crept over to the short staircase that led up to the main house. She eased her way cautiously up the varnished treads, wincing as one of them groaned. She paused and then, when the house remained silent, slowly continued.

It wasn't as if she was doing anything wrong. This was her right to privacy as a tenant.

Had Crystal Grogan been spying on her? She guessed it wasn't unreasonable to have cameras on the entryways. But what if Brynn had wanted to take a lover for a night? Revulsion curled in her stomach at the thought of one of the town's biggest gossips knowing what was going on in Brynn's personal life.

At the top of the stairs, she carefully reached out and made sure that the two bolts were engaged, top and bottom.

She eased silently back down the stairs, almost embarrassed to be doing what was basic security. That was the problem with society—expecting women to be polite rather than allowing them to fiercely embrace their own safety.

She checked the front door again and slipped back into bed.

She grabbed her phone and searched Grady Steel's name online. The articles for the past twenty-four hours were numerous, and all painted a picture of a scandalous incident and disgraced agent. But they were extremely light on details. No victim's name. Simply a photograph of a black truck being towed away.

There were millions of black trucks in the US.

She remembered Grady's vehement denial. Surely if there was any physical evidence that he'd been involved in someone's death, even accidentally, he'd have been locked up already?

The FBI wouldn't just take his word for it though, they had a reputation to protect. It wasn't a small sheriff's department in some Podunk town. It was the *FBI*.

She plugged her phone back in and turned off the light. She was tired, and she needed sleep. The floorboard above her head creaked again.

Dammit.

Brynn clutched her pillow to her chest. Then she got up again, closed the bedroom door, and wedged a wooden chair under the handle. Back in bed, she opened the bedside table and pulled out her snub-nosed 9-mm pistol. She checked to be sure there was a bullet in the chamber before placing it within reach.

This time when she lay down, she let the tiredness drag her down into the depths of sleep.

9

Grady was up early the next morning, clearing the footpaths and steps of the thin layer of snow that had fallen overnight when he saw Brynn Webster emerge from her basement apartment.

"Morning." He tried to assess her mood.

The dark circles that shadowed her eyes suggested she hadn't slept well. Her voice was gruff with tiredness and suspicion. "Morning."

In daylight he could see her hair was a deep reddish amber, almost the color of sugar maple leaves in the fall. It peeked out from beneath a gray hat. Stormy gray-green eyes with thick dark lashes were emphasized by a sprinkling of freckles over a pert nose.

She was a lot prettier than he remembered in school, but he hadn't paid a lot of attention back then. A six-year age difference was a generation to a teenager. She'd been a kid when he'd been growing into a man.

Darrell York sure was paying attention nowadays.

Were they lovers?

For some reason, the idea left a sour taste in Grady's mouth.

It wasn't only the fact the guy was married. Darrell had

constantly cheated on his girlfriends back in high school. Grady doubted a wedding band would change the habits of a lifetime, and he pitied Lorraine. But she'd known what she was getting into.

He didn't understand how someone could fall for the good ol' boy charm and not see through to the moral decay beneath. While Darrell might not be overtly corrupt, he certainly wasn't an upstanding or particularly admirable citizen. He was a cheat and a bully and a liar.

Brynn hadn't seemed particularly friendly toward the sheriff last night, but the way Darrell had staked his territory suggested he was hoping that might change. She hadn't been particularly friendly toward Grady either. He needed to change that, but he could tell she was still, rightfully, cautious.

He propped the snow shovel against the side of the house, rubbed his bare hands together and blew into them. He had gloves somewhere he should dig out. "So, where's the best place around here to get a decent cup of coffee?"

She shot him a reluctant smile. "I'm not about to suggest anywhere in this town is better than my mom's place."

Which was the opening he'd hoped for. "Are you going there now, or are you off to church?"

"The café."

"Mind if I tag along?"

"We're not open to the public for another hour."

He let a smile curve his lips. Dusted off his rusty charm. "I won't get in the way, promise. I can even make the coffee myself." She looked startled by the idea. "I need to stock up with groceries, but the shops don't open for another hour, and I'm dying here without caffeine."

"Hah. If you can figure out the coffee machine without help, I'll give you a job on the spot." Brynn snorted.

"I like a challenge."

He ignored her surprised expression, then jogged up the steps to lock the front door. It wouldn't keep his sister out, but he had plans for that. He was back down the steps before Brynn had reached the end of the drive.

She frowned as he fell into step beside her. "Does Crystal really have security cameras set up?"

"She did." Grady grimaced. "I took them all down and will deliver them back to her this afternoon." He didn't want his sister watching his actions day and night. He stuffed his hands deeper into the pockets of his jacket. "As far as I can tell, they only covered the outside doors and garage. I assume it was for security rather than pure nosiness."

Brynn raised a cynical brow. "I think you're being kind."

"That's not something I'm accused of very often." He shot her a smile. He planned to erect his own camera system, but he'd give Brynn as much privacy as he was able.

He wanted to ask her what had happened with her husband but needed to worm his way into her trust. Something told him she wouldn't want to discuss getting dumped. Who would?

"What I don't understand is why she's letting you stay and why you feel it's okay to take down her cameras?" Her clever eyes were on him, searching his face for answers.

"If it was up to Crys, I'd be sleeping in my car." He stuffed his hands even deeper in his fleece-lined leather jacket and at Brynn's confused expression explained. "She's not letting me stay. It's my place."

"What?" She looked baffled. "You jointly own it?"

He shook his head.

"She ran the rentals for you?"

"Let's just say the first I knew about the rental situation was when I walked in the door last night." Agent Ropero had informed him Friday afternoon. Hadn't he felt like a fool.

Brynn's eyes sparkled with a cross between outrage and wonder. "Crystal told everyone in town it was her house."

Grady rolled his shoulders. Pulled a face. "In which case, for my own sanity, it would be better to let people believe she's doing me a favor, rather than the other way around."

Her brows creased and met. "I think you're being far kinder to her than she's ever been to you."

He shrugged away the unexpected sting of that statement. The fact his and Crystal's relationship was so irrevocably broken made him suddenly sad. And, although legally the place was his, guilt still festered that their grandma had made the choice she had.

"Maybe it's time one of us tried a little kindness or at least mercy on the other." A shaggy gray dog darted down a side street. It didn't have a collar, and he wondered if it had escaped or if it was a stray. It was gone by the time they crossed the street.

They approached the café and began passing other people on the sidewalk, many of whom he recognized. Grady held people's gazes and nodded, but they ignored him and said good morning to Brynn instead.

Resentment hardened inside him, but he pushed it aside. He'd made the decision to go along with this plan. It was practical and efficient. The unexpected hurt from the town's rejection was something he'd have to swallow. He should be used to it by now.

They reached the café, and she led him down the side of the building and up the wooden steps at the back.

She almost slipped, and he steadied her, ignoring the soft curves in his hands and concentrating instead on keeping the two of them from face-planting on the ice-encrusted deck.

He helped her grip the side rail. "You okay there?"

She laughed, and the sound rang out in the quiet morning. "Yeah. Thanks."

"Stay there." He hung onto the side as he skated forward and made his way to the wooden barrel full of sand that was on the deck beside a snow shovel. He tossed down a few scoopfuls and then sprinkled more over the steps while Brynn watched him.

"What?" he asked.

She shook her head.

He let a smile steal over his lips and recognized the stirring of interest in her gaze. "*What*?"

She hiked a delicate brow. "You seem awfully nice for someone with the reputation of a reprobate."

"Not to mention an alleged killer," Grady said bluntly.

Brynn flinched, and her face blanched, clearly remembering the bullet hole in Milton Bodurek's forehead.

"Shit. Sorry. I shouldn't have said that." He planted the scoop back in the barrel. Turned to look over the harbor which was gray in the early morning light.

He'd never imagined coming back to this town, this community, not after his grandmother passed. Being here filled him with a mix of longing and nostalgia he hadn't expected. The scent of the seashore, the scrape of the wind over his weather-beaten flesh, the screech of the gulls on chimney tops, the noise of boats bobbing gently on the water. Fog hugged the water but was burning off the rooftops like steam in the thin rays of the morning sun. It was atmospheric and ghostly and made a shiver shimmer along his senses.

Good thing he didn't believe in ghosts.

Brynn moved to stand beside him as they both stared down at the waterfront. Yellow tape cordoned off the marina where Milton Bodurek's sailboat was moored. Two sheriff's department SUVs were parked, blocking entry to the walkway.

"Do you think he was killed on his boat?" Brynn asked in a quiet murmur.

Grady rolled his shoulder and narrowed his gaze. "Probably."

"Do you think the murderer is someone from town, or some stranger passing through?"

He looked down and caught the worried expression in her gray-green eyes. "What do you think?"

She turned back to watch the deputies working the scene. "It's always easier to believe that killers are not the people who walk amongst us."

Grady nodded. "Easier, but not necessarily accurate."

She shivered. "Do you think it has something to do with the

bank robbery? Milton was the manager there, and this town is not generally a hotbed of crime."

He shrugged. "Maybe." *Definitely.*

She examined him, her gaze searching for better answers.

"Could the killer be a danger to anyone else?" She blew out an exasperated breath. "I know you don't have the answers, but you're in the FBI, and I'm worrying out loud."

He watched the dive team suiting up to go into the water and wished he was with them. He liked action, not sitting around on the sidelines waiting for clues to fall into his lap.

"I guess that depends on why they killed him. But there is one thing…" He met her gaze and hated how fear formed shadows across the back of her eyes. "I wouldn't be taking any more lonesome walks along the harbor at night. Not until this bastard is caught."

10

B rynn boosted the heating in the café to combat the chill that had clung to her bones since last night.

"I have defused bombs less complicated than this coffeemaker," Grady Steel growled as he stood with his legs apart, bending slightly from the waist as he concentrated on figuring out the sophisticated and temperamental machine her mother had imported from France twenty years ago.

Brynn tried not to notice the lean muscles as he stood there in a T-shirt and jeans, but she'd be lying if she said her mouth didn't go a little bit dry when looking at him. Maybe it was a good thing that she was finally attracted to another man. It proved she was truly over Aiden.

Grady swore again.

Brynn held back a grin because she liked the fact she wasn't the only one who was confounded by the damn thing. Her parents insisted that they'd paid so much for it that they would never replace it.

Suddenly, there was a hiss of steam, and the scent of good coffee permeated the air. The look on Grady's face was pure satisfaction that he'd solved a problem, even if the problem was only creating coffee.

"Hah ah!" His face lit up with glee, those sky-blue eyes shining with intelligence. "How do you take your coffee, Ms. Webster?"

She laughed and shook her head as she slid him two clean mugs from the dishwasher. It felt good to smile again after her experience last night and the worries about a killer being out there on the loose plaguing her sleep. Not a lot she could do about it. She was hardly a likely target, but she would take a few extra precautions until he—or she—was caught.

"Lots of milk for me. No sugar."

"Sweet enough, huh?"

Her toes curled at the warm look he threw her, and she told herself she was being ridiculous. Everything she knew about this man suggested he was surly and potentially dangerous. Not the sort of guy she should get tingles from looking at.

But perhaps the guy had changed. He was, usually at least, an FBI agent.

And didn't everyone deserve a second chance? Everyone except her ex, that was.

Grady was the polar opposite in looks and demeanor from her former husband. The dark and slightly dangerous aspect of Grady Steel contrasted sharply with Aiden's polite blond perfection. He'd been far too perfect, she realized. Like some fake Ken doll.

Dammit.

Thoughts of Aiden had her good mood disappearing.

Grady pushed the mug in front of her and she blinked her way back to the present.

She shook herself out of her painful memories and picked up the coffee and took a sip. "Oh. That's good." She took another sip. "Really good."

"Millions of dollars have been spent by the US government training me." The ecstatic expression that crossed his features when he took a sip from his own mug was amusing and sexy as hell.

"That, ma'am, is your tax dollars at work." He raised his brows. "I guess I have to be good for something, huh?"

Sympathy moved through her. She couldn't imagine this man leaving an injured person on the side of the road to die, and she knew exactly how painful it was to be accused of doing something you hadn't. "The FBI will figure it out."

He lifted his cup to his lips again and grinned. "Yeah, well, they better get a move on before I get a better offer."

"You'd be hired in a snap, but I'm not sure I can pay you what the federal government does." She checked the clock and frowned.

Grady noticed the action. "Something wrong?"

"No." She placed mugs on shelves and then started putting this morning's delivery of fresh locally made baked goods into the refrigerated glass display case. "Just that my server, Jackie Somers, was supposed to help me open. She called in sick yesterday, but I haven't heard from her today to say she isn't coming. She should have been here fifteen minutes ago."

"Is she usually reliable?"

Brynn pulled a face. "Not the term I'd use. She can be a little flexible with her timekeeping, but she's a good worker once she's here."

"Want me to help out until she turns up?"

"No, don't be silly."

"What's silly about lending you a hand when you need it?" His expression flattened. "I have nothing better to do right now. At least I'll have a front row seat to the Grady Steel roasting and get to hear what everyone is saying."

"Likely that you killed Milton Bodurek on his boat and pushed him in the water before running around to help me pull him out?"

"Is that what you believe?" His tone was serious.

A rush of unease slid across her shoulders. She refused to be charmed by good looks and nice manners. She wasn't that foolish, not anymore. "I honestly don't know."

She expected anger, but his gaze was sober.

"Fair enough. I'm essentially a stranger to you and my reputation precedes me. Plus, present circumstances are less than ideal. But I can tell you I've never hurt anyone in anger." His expression turned rueful. "At least not someone who wasn't actively trying to hurt me first."

He stared out the window toward the harbor, shifted, and looked at her again. "I love my job. I plan to be back in Quantico training with my teammates as soon as the knuckleheads running the tests on my truck clear me for duty."

The atmosphere had turned heavy, and she needed to lighten it for her own sake. "You have a Jeep *and* a truck? I definitely can't pay you enough."

"Jeep belongs to a friend who doesn't need it right now." He cleared his throat as his voice roughened. "My truck is getting the full treatment at the lab. It better work when the evidence techs are done with it."

"You're truly not worried?"

"I'm not worried about the investigation. I'm pissed." He took another long sip of coffee. "If I had hit someone, I certainly wouldn't have left the poor bastard to die on the side of the road. But you have no reason to trust me, and I get that."

Milton's face flashed into her mind again. She hoped he hadn't suffered.

"It must be frustrating that people are questioning your integrity." She understood that better than she wanted to.

"I'm used to it." He grinned, and she felt that flutter in her chest again.

Grady Steel was a deceptively attractive man, and she didn't appreciate that her eyes had been opened to that fact.

"Anyway, enough of this morass of self-pity, Ms. Webster. Let me help you out until your errant server arrives." He hooked his thumbs in the loops of his jeans and a line creased one cheek. "You can pay me in coffee."

Her mouth went dry. Maybe she could pay him with sex.

"Ahem." She cleared her throat at the totally inappropriate

67

thought. "Fine." She knew she was playing with fire but was done caring. "On one condition."

He cocked his head to one side.

She tossed him a clean apron. "Call me Brynn."

"Brynn." He rolled her name warmly over his tongue as he wrapped the black apron around those trim hips. "I always wondered...is it short for anything?"

He'd wondered about her name? She hadn't realized he'd even known she existed. She shook her head.

"I like it."

Her heart did that thing in her chest again. Maybe she needed to take a physical.

"Call me Grady."

"Not Beelzebub or Mephistopheles?" Brynn forced some humor into the conversation.

His grin turned wicked. "You can call me the Prince of Darkness if you want. Our little secret."

She laughed, then jumped when the back door opened, and Angus Hubner strode in.

The old man didn't say anything. His brows rose as he took in Grady standing behind the counter wearing an apron. Then he shrugged out of his heavy coat, hung it on a peg out of the way, and started pulling things noisily out of the refrigerator.

11

———————

Jackie Somers came bursting through the back door two minutes before opening, and Grady was strangely disappointed.

"Sorry I'm late!"

She was tall, gangly. Her long, dark hair was windblown, and her white cheeks had small patches of red high on the cheekbones. She was somewhere between sixteen and eighteen years old. Five ten. Blue eyes outlined with a heavy tinge of makeup and cynicism.

The young woman brought herself up short at the sight of him. "Who's this?"

"Your replacement." Brynn produced a humorless smile.

Jackie's mouth dropped open, and then she began to look angry.

"I'm kidding." Brynn was quick to give the kid a break. Grady wouldn't have been so understanding. "This is...Mr. Steel who kindly offered to help out when my server unexpectedly didn't show up on time for her morning shift."

Jackie scowled. "The roads were terrible—"

"You live a five-minute walk away."

"Fine. I was up late talking to Caleb on the phone. He said he

69

helped you pull the body out of the water last night. It shook him up."

Helped was a stretch.

Watched, maybe.

Brynn's expression morphed into surprise. "I didn't know you two were dating. Isn't he a little old for you?"

"He's twenty-one." Jackie glowered defensively. "Didn't realize I had to tell you everything that happened in my life. Thought you didn't like gossip."

Oh, the girl had attitude.

Grady settled in for the show.

Brynn shot him a glance, clearly aware he was listening to every word.

"You're right, I don't have any right to know about your private life, but I do expect you to arrive on time when you're fit for work."

The young woman seemed to belatedly remember she'd taken yesterday off because she'd claimed to be sick.

"Well, I'm here now." Rather than apologize, the girl pulled her lips into a sour smile. She hung her jacket and purse next to Angus's coat, then pushed past Grady to hit the restroom.

"I take it you don't need me anymore?" he asked Brynn with amusement.

Her expression quirked. She rose up on tiptoe to stare over the display counter at all the curious faces peering through the window of the front door. "I suppose not, but I think you might be good for business."

"Always leave them wanting more is my mantra."

"Is it now?"

The air shifted between them.

For a moment, her eyes shone with a glimmer of attraction, but she blinked it away. She pasted on a bright smile that didn't quite hide the shadows once again lurking in her eyes. "Maybe I'll adopt that mantra as my own."

Grady's lip twitched. "Maybe you already do."

Her eyes widened, and her mouth dropped open a little in surprise.

He was flirting, and he shouldn't be.

Another time, another place, he wouldn't have minded exploring that ripe mouth and curvy body, but right now he was undercover, and she was a distraction he couldn't afford. She was a means to an end. He needed to remember that.

She straightened, as if remembering it was time to open the doors for her ravenous customers. Still, she paused, and her voice grew soft. "Thanks for all your help today."

"No problem. I was happy to do it."

"Because everyone's secret ambition is to work in a coffee shop." She rolled her eyes and laughed. It was a nice sound. "Grab yourself more coffee and a muffin on the way out, Grady Steel. Consider it a bonus."

She turned and walked away.

He carefully picked up both of their mugs and emptied the contents into the sink. He glanced around and saw no one was looking. He hesitated for a moment, then, ignoring a stab of guilt, grabbed a paper sack and slid Brynn's mug inside along with a blueberry muffin that was calling his name. He spotted Angus's mug beside the gas hob but the man was standing right next to it.

Shame.

Not that this was strictly legal without a court order, but he couldn't ignore the opportunity to eliminate a few family trees when chance presented itself.

He opened the dishwasher and placed his own dirty mug inside. Then he rolled up the top of the bag and put it on the floor while he shrugged into his leather jacket.

Jackie Somers came out of the ladies and flounced past him.

The young woman didn't like discovering the fact she was so easily replaced. He could sympathize, but at least he always turned up on time, eager to work.

She shot him a glare, and Grady grinned. He was pretty sure

he remembered her mom, Julie, from high school, and recalled everyone had been scared of her back then.

Angus glared at him from the kitchen. Grady stared right back. Right age, height, and build for Eli Kane. Brown eyes rather than blue but easily changed with colored contacts. His expression gave nothing away. A heavy beard hid the lower half of his face. The man wiped his hands on a cloth draped over his shoulder and turned away to stir a pot.

Grady wanted Angus's DNA.

He picked up the paper bag and went to the back door with a last look at Brynn, who was smiling at the front door at the salivating horde as they came pouring in. She met his gaze, and he lifted a hand in acknowledgement.

He headed out the back door and stood on the deck, inhaling the viciously fresh air, as he watched police divers slide back into the murky waters of the harbor.

Looking for a weapon? Or something else?

He didn't fancy their chances and hoped they had metal detectors with them.

As if sensing he was being watched, Darrell York raised his head and looked up to where Grady stood against the railings.

His old friend didn't smile.

Did he really believe Grady had something to do with Milton Bodurek's death? Or was he looking for a convenient scapegoat?

Grady had no intention of being caught up in that tangled web. Hopefully the ME's time of death would provide Grady with a rock-solid alibi.

A growing rumble of voices from inside the café told him the place had filled up. Inquisitive gazes through the window scratched the back of his neck like cat claws, but he didn't turn around.

Was Milton Bodurek's death tied in some way to Eli Kane?

How?

Why?

It seemed like a stretch, but at the same time Deception Cove had one of the lowest crime rates in the country. Combine a murder and a bank robbery in the space of two weeks and things were heating up in the worst way.

Had Kane already run?

Seemed like the sensible thing to do. Kane hadn't survived as a fugitive this long without being anything except smart.

Grady's phone buzzed, and he checked it. Ropero wanted a meet.

12

E li Kane watched the heavy-set diver slip beneath the surface of the icy water as the idiot sheriff looked on.

Milton had been a good friend. A good man. Whoever had killed him had been looking for something.

Money?

Or him—Eli Kane. *FBI's Most Wanted*.

What a joke.

His instincts were screaming to get the hell out of town, had been since he'd heard about the bank robbery.

He kept flashing back to putting a hand on the wall of metal boxes. He closed his eyes at his own stupidity. He was usually so damn careful. He hadn't given it a second thought at the time. He'd gotten sloppy over the years but who in the hell imagined the Hearst Savings & Loan would ever get held up?

Fingerprints didn't last forever, and he knew Milton liked the bank to sparkle, so maybe there had been no trace left to suggest he'd ever been in that room.

According to witnesses, the robber had worn gloves. No logical reason for the cops to collect fingerprints—but the sheriff was more interested in the appearance of solving the case rather than using his brain to whittle down the suspects and save police resources. The evidence team had been inside the vault, and if the mess they'd left behind them was any indication, they'd definitely dusted for prints.

Eli had done a little snooping of his own. Figured he had a good idea who was responsible for the armed robbery. Maybe he'd pay them a visit and relieve them of the five hundred thousand they'd stolen. Always handy to have cash on hand even though he had money stashed all over the world in numbered accounts.

He watched the bubbles float to the surface as the divers swam a search grid and exhaled through their regulators. He was curious as to what they'd find, but not so curious as to try to insert himself into the investigation. His skin already felt as if it were full of ants.

Maybe he'd leave town. Maybe it was time. He didn't plan to spend the rest of his life in a cell.

He touched the handgun he wore under his jacket. He wasn't scared of dying. Not anymore. But he'd rather do it on his own terms, and in his own time.

When he was ready.

And he wasn't ready yet.

13

———

Grady drove to Bangor and parked along a quiet side street then walked to the Federal Building on Harlow. Agents Kelly Ropero and Noel Dobson met him at the door. The reception area was empty except for them because it was a Sunday. Without a word, they ushered him into a conference room inside the small FBI satellite office within the building.

An immediate blast of relief hit him at the sight of his boss, Payne Novak, flanked by four members of Echo squad—Aaron Nash, Cowboy, Malik Keeme, and Will Griffin. His Charlie squad partner Meghan Donnelly sat next to Griffin and sent Grady a curt nod. They were all dressed in casual clothes so as not to draw attention to their comings and goings.

"What happened last night? You're supposed to be keeping a low profile, not involving yourself in another suspicious death," Ropero snapped as soon as the door closed.

Grady ignored her.

"Good to see you without the handcuffs, Grade." Cowboy leaned back in his chair and gave the case agents a cool stare. Obviously, these guys had been briefed on the fake arrest which made the iron bars around Grady's chest further ease their grip.

"No kidding." He grinned as he dropped into the chair beside Novak.

After much resistance, Ropero and Dobson had agreed to work collaboratively with Daniel Ackers and HRT. Ackers had been pissed at the agents' actions but had approved the op. Grady hadn't known what form the support would take.

He couldn't have asked for better.

He wouldn't forget the people who'd supported him unconditionally in that moment when his world had seemed to be crashing down around him. But he frowned. "Who's taking Grace's kids swimming?"

"Livingstone volunteered. Yael's recovering well but is still in the hospital," said Cowboy. Yael Brooks had been seriously injured less than a week ago. "Kincaid and his fiancée are taking the kids to the movies afterwards so Grace can put her feet up. Birdman and Levitt were on house cleaning and yard duty yesterday."

"Okay. Good."

Eli Kane was important, but they couldn't let Scotty down by neglecting his widow or children. Gold Team had been cruelly reminded of their own mortality recently. They each needed to know their loved ones would be supported if anything happened to them.

Not that Grady had any loved ones outside HRT. His sister would probably throw a party if he died.

He forced the thought away. He needed to stay sharp. Focused. "Where's the rest of the team?"

"Quantico, until we have a solid lead." Novak sent a pointed stare at the case agents. "I'm afraid Red and Blue teams still believe you've been suspended."

Acid soured in Grady's stomach. "It's just the seven of us?"

"We need to keep this lead locked down tight," Ropero warned like they were all six-year-olds. "Having a full team of HRT agents staged nearby could tip off Kane."

"You don't think we'd take that into consideration?" Novak

asked in a deceptively mellow tone.

"I don't want to risk it." Ropero made a visible effort to calm herself. "This might be our last opportunity to capture him and make him face justice for his crimes. The number of cell phone cameras amongst the public means we must be extremely cautious of any activity out of the norm."

"We know how to be both covert and cautious," Novak stated. "This is not our first rodeo, Agent Ropero."

"The fingerprint hit came straight to us." Ropero stared around the room. That print had led the two agents to hatch their cunning scheme to make Grady a national pariah. "Except for the FBI Director, Assistant Director, HRT director, a couple of techs at HQ, the people in this room are the only ones who know about the possibility that Eli Kane might be living somewhere in or near Deception Cove. We can't afford to blow it."

"No one at HRT is going to leak information." Novak bristled at the implication.

Ropero flicked her ponytail off her shoulder. "I'm not willing to take that chance."

Novak glared at her. "But you're willing to risk my team by leaving us short-handed?"

Ropero's lips pressed firmly together. "My plan, SSA Novak, is for Operator Steel to set up surveillance cameras in areas we can't easily access without drawing unwelcome attention, to talk to locals, and to use his insider knowledge and contacts to help us eliminate people so we can quickly narrow down the suspect list and hone in on potential targets. Once we have a credible ID, we can assemble a full team and apprehend Kane."

Not a terrible plan considering it was illegal to lock down the entire community and go door-to-door with DNA swabs.

Speaking of illegal… Grady placed the paper bag on the table, forcing away the guilt he felt at the invasion of Brynn's privacy. More than anything he wanted her off the suspect list and he didn't want to think too hard about why that might be. "Managed to get the DNA of Brynn Webster, who is currently running the

Sea Spray Café for her mother who, according to my sister, has cancer."

Ropero crossed her arms. "It's not admissible in court."

"No," he said patiently. "But if we cross-reference families who had access to safe deposit boxes at the Hearst Bank with white males fifty to seventy-five, her father, Paul Webster, is on that list. The opportunity arose, so I took it." Grady stared at Ropero. He wasn't about to apologize for breaking a few rules when she'd stomped roughshod over plenty when she'd arrested him in the middle of a team briefing.

Ropero clearly hadn't forgiven him for not falling into her plans like a good little lapdog. Which made them even because he hadn't forgiven her for terrifying him with that stunt on Friday morning.

"Brynn Webster is twenty-eight," Dobson cut in, breaking the tension between them.

"Kane disappeared twenty-*seven* years ago." Ropero pointed out.

Grady yawned. He hadn't gotten a whole lot of sleep lately. "Maybe he already had a second family. He worked undercover for years. He was a master of disguise."

"A second family could explain why he's been so difficult to find," Novak agreed. "His backup plan was already in place. Maybe he was living part time in that other identity at the time of the murders."

Ropero didn't look convinced.

Grady crossed his arms. "I took advantage of an opportunity that presented itself. Wasn't that what we decided? Whittle down the possible suspect list until we can focus on the remaining few who fit the parameters? Anyway,"—he nodded toward the mug— "you don't have to run it."

Ropero tapped her foot and stared thoughtfully at the bag.

"You are correct, Operator Steel. That is the plan. Thank you." Agent Dobson ignored his partner.

"What happened last night?" Novak asked.

79

"Came home to a hero's welcome." Grady narrowed his eyes at Ropero. "My sister hates me, which wasn't news. You were correct when you told me she's been renting out the house I own without my permission for the past few years. She wasn't exactly happy when I showed up to turn off the money spigot." He tapped his fingers on the table. "I removed the camera system she'd set up and plan to change the locks so she can't snoop. Oh, and I have a lodger in the basement, but I can reinforce the inside lock to make sure she can't access the rest of the house should I need to."

"Who's the lodger?" Ropero asked.

"Brynn Webster."

"Is that how you obtained the DNA sample?" Ropero asked archly.

Grady narrowed his eyes at the woman. "I took a used mug from the café this morning after helping her open. The Sea Spray Café is a major hub in the town and a great potential source of information."

Ropero relented. "You're right. Sorry, I'm tense. I keep visualizing Eli Kane climbing into his car and driving over the border, never to be seen again."

Grady understood. Eli Kane was a monster.

"Brynn is the person who jumped in the water to retrieve the body of Milton Bodurek last night." Grady filled them in on what had happened.

"*Brynn*?" Cowboy queried with a suggestive smile. "You knew her before?"

"Not like that, you pervert. She was a kid when I left. I remember her though."

"You want to use her?" Ropero's tone suggested that was more acceptable than befriending someone. "What do we know about this Webster woman?" She turned to her partner.

Dobson sat and began typing, presumably requesting a criminal background check on Brynn.

"How do you know this woman didn't shoot the dead guy

and push him into the harbor?" Nash asked. They called Nash "The Professor" because he was whip smart and excelled at looking at a situation from all the angles.

"I don't," Grady admitted. "But why bother rescuing him after she shoved him in—especially if no one noticed the gunshot? I certainly didn't hear it. Once Milton Bodurek was in the water he would probably have floated out to sea on the outgoing tide. Next stop Bay of Fundy. No one would have known what happened to the guy except the shooter."

"Which presumably was the point of pushing him in the water in the first place." Novak held a report that sat in front of him. "Are local law enforcement dredging the harbor for the murder weapon?"

Grady's lip curled despite himself. "Yeah."

"They find anything yet?" Ropero asked.

"Not that I know of, but I don't have any useful contacts inside the sheriff's department."

"Didn't you used to work as a deputy there?" Ropero pushed.

"For about eighteen months fifteen years ago." Before he'd joined the State Troopers out of Bangor and gotten his criminology degree by studying part-time. He'd known he needed to get out of Deception Cove to have any chance of succeeding. Needed a clean slate. "But the fact I was suspended while the FBI investigates whether or not I killed some poor innocent on the side of the road hasn't exactly endeared me to local law enforcement." The words slid out like glass shards. "Plus, the current sheriff is a guy I hung around with in high school. His dad was the former sheriff and offered us both jobs as deputies after graduation."

"Nepotism at its finest," Ropero derided.

It hadn't been that neat or tidy, but Grady didn't disagree.

"Let's just say Sheriff York and I have a history. Not a pleasant one."

"Is he any good at his job?" asked Novak.

Grady considered for a moment. "He knows how to hire

people who will make him look good. He's adept at sweet talking people, especially women."

Ropero and Meghan Donnelly both rolled their eyes.

"I'm just saying it as I see it." He recalled how Darrell had been overly attentive to Brynn last night. "I think he was planning to hit on Brynn Webster when he interviewed her about finding Milton Bodurek's body. I invited myself to the party as it was in my basement, and I wanted to know what else she might have seen—which was someone walking away from the harbor as she arrived. She didn't see a face or recognize them, but it would be worth checking any surveillance cams in the area north of the harbor."

Dobson made a note on the pad at his side.

"The sheriff used the opportunity of a witness interview to hit on someone who was presumably traumatized?" Cowboy asked with a derisive curl to his lips.

Grady nodded. "Brynn Webster didn't seem that impressed either."

"I can see why," Donnelly remarked.

"He's married, isn't he?" said Novak.

"Yep. Three kids. I didn't bother with a sample of his DNA as his father was the sheriff for ten years before Eli Kane went missing. It's not him. I'd appreciate a look into the former sheriff's finances though. He lives in a nice big house on the bluff." Grady tapped a pen on the table. "Temple York is a smart guy. If Eli Kane showed up in town, he should have noticed."

"Unless he was paid not to?" Dobson queried, easily following Grady's line of thought.

"Or Kane has had so much surgery he's completely unrecognizable." Grady raised one shoulder. "It's another thread to tug."

"You say the dead guy was the manager of the bank that was robbed?" said Nash.

"Yeah. You should test his DNA so we can rule him out, too. He arrived in town about twenty-five years ago. Kane could have taken over Bodurek's identity, but it's not likely. Not with that large of an inheritance." Grady spotted a coffeepot and walked over to pour himself a cup. He took a sip. Not as good as the one he'd made in the café this morning but better than most police sludge.

"Assuming Milton Bodurek is not Kane, could Eli Kane have killed him?" Nash asked.

"Motive?" asked Novak.

"Maybe during the robbery investigation, the bank manager uncovered evidence Eli lived in town and tried to blackmail him?" Nash suggested.

"A dangerous plan considering Kane's reputation," said Dobson.

"Well, the guy *is* dead," Grady responded.

"Maybe Kane was simply seeing *if* Bodurek knew whether or not the FBI had found anything to link him to the bank?" Nash mulled. "Killed him afterward so he couldn't ID him."

"Hardly laying low." Grady wasn't buying that angle.

"The manager didn't know anything about the investigations." Ropero leaned against the edge of the table.

"Kane wouldn't know that Bodurek was ignorant," said Nash.

"If it *was* Kane who killed the bank manager, he sure as hell knows now," Cowboy said laconically. "Bodurek swears he doesn't know what Kane's talking about, so Kane decides it's safe to stick around—after Bodurek is dead. Throws him in the water. Cops might connect the robbery to the murder, but as long as no one brings up Kane's name, he isn't too worried. He's living under the wire. No one suspects him."

"Any evidence of torture on Bodurek?" Nash asked.

"Not that I saw." Grady looked askance at Ropero.

"I'm waiting for the ME to conduct the autopsy. Apparently, he doesn't work on the weekends." Ropero seemed deflated at the delay. "But torture doesn't have to be physical. It could be a gun to the head or the photo of a loved one. An implied threat. It would take a cold heart not to succumb to that kind of pressure."

Eli Kane's heart was a block of ice.

14

——————

B rynn looked up as her mom's best friend and long-time server, Linda, arrived in a whirlwind of winter parka and shopping bags. Her shoulder-length, wavy, strawberry-blonde hair was windblown despite the cute cranberry wooly hat she wore.

Linda kissed Brynn's cheek then hung up her coat and tied her black apron around her waist. "What's this I hear about you pulling poor Milton Bodurek—God rest his soul—out of the harbor last night?"

"Just another day in boring old Deception Cove," Brynn said wryly.

"This town isn't boring." Linda shook her head. "I think this town is bursting with goings on. You're the one who complains it's boring."

"I think it's boring, too." Jackie came behind the counter and loaded a stack of dirty dishes into the dishwasher. She was probably the only person who hadn't grilled Brynn on what had gone down last night and that was probably because they'd been too busy to even catch their breath, plus Caleb had likely already recast himself as the hero in his version of events.

"You're seventeen. You think everything is boring." Linda

dropped her voice into a whisper so only Brynn could hear. "Except sex or alcohol."

Brynn suppressed a grin. Linda was incorrigible. "Do you think Mom and Dad heard?"

Linda hooted. "I'm surprised they aren't here making sure their sweet baby is okay."

"Mom had a treatment scheduled." Melancholy wanted to roll over Brynn, but she forced it away.

"On a Sunday?" Linda frowned. "Chemo's a bitch."

"Not if it works," Brynn argued.

"Even then." The other woman had gone through her own breast cancer fight three years ago. "But if it works you don't care as much."

That's what they were all praying for. That it worked. That her mom went into remission.

"I suspect Dad decided to keep her in the dark until she's finished at the hospital. Otherwise, she might blow it off and track me down."

"Your daddy wouldn't let her do that."

"Exactly."

"You really jumped in the harbor?" Jackie turned from the dishwasher, interest gleaming in her black eyes.

"I really did." Jackie had been hostile all morning, and this was the first sign she'd thawed.

"I couldn't believe it when Caleb told me. Was the water gross?"

The taste of rotten fish still lingered in Brynn's mouth, and she made a face. "Very."

"I suspect realizing Milton Bodurek was already dead made it ten times worse." Linda's mouth compressed into an upside-down smile.

Brynn's stomach gave a little squeeze. She pressed a hand to her midsection. "Thanks for the reminder."

"As if that lot would let you forget for a moment," Linda

scoffed. She stood on tiptoe to inspect the clientele. "Jesus, it's packed. Jackie, table three wants their check."

Jackie grumbled and headed off with the payment machine.

Linda caught Brynn's arm. "You sure you're okay?"

Brynn nodded.

"What time did you leave last night?" Linda clearly wanted all the details.

"Late. It was probably close to ten thirty by the time I locked up."

Linda grimaced. "Sorry I couldn't stay any longer. You know how Kent gets."

Linda's second husband wanted Linda to quit. Linda refused while Brynn's mom needed her. It was another in a long list of reasons for her parents to sell this place.

Brynn had a feeling her mom was holding on to the café as a sort of symbol linked to her survival. Selling felt too much like giving up even though her parents had both earned every moment of a nice relaxing retirement.

Linda poured herself a coffee. Her shift didn't officially start for another ten minutes. "I found you another server."

"What?" Brynn's head shot around so fast she pulled a muscle. She clutched her neck. "Ouch. Way to bury the lede, Linda."

"Whiner." Linda put her cold hand over Brynn's and squeezed gently. "My niece, Prudence. Just got to town. She was working in a hotel down in Boston. Waitressed to put herself through college. Said she fancied a change in scenery and is living with us until she can find her own place. I'd have mentioned it sooner, but I didn't want to get your hopes up until I'd spoken to her."

"And she wants to work here?" Damn. This was the answer to a prayer. Brynn had barely had a day off since she'd arrived. She had her own work projects she needed to catch up on and hadn't spent nearly enough time with her mom.

"Yup. Told her to come in for an interview or you can talk to her on the phone. Do not mess it up." Linda shook her finger at her. As if Brynn wouldn't be willing to grovel for good help.

"Now go grab a break while Jackie and I are both here. Go out the back so people don't hound you."

"I love you." She flung her arms around the other woman's thin frame and squeezed her tight.

"I love you, too. Your mom is a fighter. If anyone can get through this…"

"I know." Brynn held on tight for another long squeeze then let go.

Linda waved her away. "Get out of here before you make my mascara run."

Brynn sniffed as she shrugged into her coat and tugged on her hat.

She sent Angus a big grin, and he nodded, barely dragging his attention away from the fish he was expertly filleting with a casual swipe of a lethal blade.

Brynn stepped gingerly onto the back deck that, thanks to Grady, wasn't slippery. The cops were still down at the harbor. A group of onlookers gathered nearby with anticipation to see what, if anything, they pulled out of the water.

A shiver formed between her shoulder blades as eyes drilled into the back of her neck. She purposely ignored the curious stares through the window behind her.

She headed down the steps and turned up onto Main Street wanting to avoid the harbor and the questions that were bound to arise. She didn't have anywhere to go but couldn't stand being in the fishbowl a moment longer. She strode aimlessly along the street. Too late she realized she was heading toward the sheriff's office and there was Darrell York climbing out of his big SUV, watching her.

She forced herself to keep moving toward him rather than cut and run.

15

It seemed like a good time for Grady to hit Ropero with more bad news. "I'm pretty sure I'm on the suspect list for Milton's murder. They took my weapon to run ballistics."

Novak swore. "I'll make sure they don't connect the results to your service weapon." Which Grady would have had to surrender if he'd truly been suspended. Novak bent to remove a subcompact SIG Sauer P365 from his ankle, along with the holster.

Grady protested. "I have a backup."

"Now you have two." Novak handed it over along with a couple of magazines of ammo. "I'll fill out the paperwork."

"How close are the locals to catching the actual bank robber?" asked Grady.

Ropero pulled a disgruntled face. "No viable leads. The vehicle used in the robbery was a black 2004 Ford Focus. Stolen two days prior from Augusta. It hasn't been found. Robber came in late in the afternoon, right before closing, waving around a 1911. We have a general description of a white male, 5'9", about one-sixty. Age, anywhere from twenty to forty. He deliberately disguised his voice. He got away with a considerable amount of cash as they were waiting on an armored truck to pick up the local businesses' weekly takings."

"That sounds like an inside job."

Ropero nodded. "Outer vault was open—someone was accessing their safe deposit box—so he rushed inside and had the manager open a few boxes. According to reports he stole some heirloom jewelry and gold. The locals put out a statewide alert to pawn shops in case someone tries to sell it. The getaway driver honked, and the guy inside immediately went to leave. The security guard chose that moment to find his balls and tackled the robber on the way out. Unfortunately, he was shot in the leg for his efforts but not badly hurt."

Grady nodded. "Good."

"In and out in five minutes flat. Guy climbed in the vehicle and essentially disappeared. No sign of the car on any of the interstates. No trace of the money either, although as the teller forgot to put a dye-pack inside the bag then maybe that isn't surprising."

"She forgot?" Grady queried.

"Could she be involved?" Novak asked quickly.

Dobson checked the report. "A Miss Fancy Lucette."

"Jesus, she's still alive? She was a friend of my grandma's." Grady snorted. "She was way past retirement when I lived in town."

"Could she be involved?" Novak repeated.

Grady pursed his lips and shook his head. "It's possible but highly unlikely. She knows everyone in town and is well liked. All the old-timers have accounts in the branch, and I can't imagine she'd be okay with her friends being robbed of their hard-earned money."

"You have an account there, right?" asked Novak.

"Yeah. I inherited a safe deposit box from my grandmother and keep the deeds to her house there." He didn't know why he hadn't closed the account years ago. Still subconsciously holding onto that link with his grandma, he guessed.

"I plan to visit the bank and check the box tomorrow so I can look at the setup and talk to people there. I need that list of everyone who rents a safe deposit box so I can start going through it in detail." He aimed the last at the case agents.

Dobson pressed a button with a flourish and a printer started spitting out pages.

"We've sent you the family trees we've constructed so far," Ropero added. "If you can categorically eliminate anyone, do so."

"If the robber did take something that could identify Eli Kane, then their life may be in danger." Nash tugged his bottom lip.

"I don't disagree but, again, it's hardly laying low, is it?" argued Grady. "I mean, I know he'd have no qualms killing, but each death brings heightened risk, more cops, more eyes on the area. If it gets out that the FBI believe Eli Kane is living in or near Deception Cove, all hell will break loose with the media showing up, and we'll have tips coming in from every direction to claim the reward."

Two million dollars was a heck of an incentive.

"Will the Bureau take over the murder investigation from the Montrose County Sheriff's Department?" Grady asked Ropero.

"Only if the locals ask us for help or if the bank robbery is suspected of being linked to other interstate crimes. We can't afford to do anything differently than what we'd do if we hadn't found Kane's print in the bank because he knows exactly how we operate." Her expression faltered. "I almost brought the local feds into the loop but…" Her eyes scanned the room. "The more people who know, especially those who live close by and may talk to friends or spouses, the more chance that Kane somehow gets wind of it and bolts."

And everyone in the FBI wanted to catch this bastard.

"You know that chances are he's already fled, right?" Eyes on Ropero, Grady took another sip of his coffee.

"We chase this clue until we are certain it leads nowhere," Ropero stated baldly.

Novak's chair screeched over the floor as he climbed to his feet. "You two can do that, but my team can't be on this exclusively for long. If a dynamic situation comes up that needs our skillset we're out of here, Grady included."

Grady ignored the warmth that spread through his chest.

"But until such a time, we keep looking." Ropero pushed back. "Agreed?"

"Be nice to catch this motherfucker," Grady murmured.

Novak nodded and gave him a look. "I don't like you being alone without backup."

He shrugged. "I grew up there. I can handle it."

"That's not why I don't like it. You're part of the Hostage Rescue Team, and we work together."

Emotion wanted to choke him, but he forced out, "Yes, Boss."

"What's the plan?" Ryan Sullivan asked impatiently. He looked like his Cowboy moniker today, dressed down in worn jeans, plaid shirt, and snakeskin boots. "Because if I have to sit in some shit-hole motel for days waiting for something to happen I may officially go insane."

"Pretty sure that train already left the station." Meghan shot him a snide look.

"Bite me," Ryan shot back.

"Not my type, remember?" Meghan raised her brow and tucked in her chin.

Ryan gave her a silent look that Grady couldn't read.

"Children," Aaron Nash admonished gently. "No fighting in front of the guests." Nash eyed the two case agents. He clearly didn't trust them yet. Neither did Grady.

Novak narrowed his gaze and took a long, hard look at Meghan Donnelly. "You know, Grady, I think I have an idea how to give you a little extra backup in Deception Cove without being too obvious about it."

Cowboy sat forward.

"How good an actor are you, Donnelly?" Novak asked.

The female operator's chin jerked high. "Good enough."

Her father had died early last week, and the memorial service had been rescheduled for later next week. The fact she appeared to be holding up even though Grady knew she was devastated by the loss suggested she was a very good actor indeed.

"You want me to go undercover as Grady's girlfriend?" she asked with interest.

For no reason at all, the image of Brynn Webster's stormy gray-green eyes appeared in his mind. He forced it away. This was an op, not a vacation.

Novak shook his head. "No, not Grady. I don't want to complicate his backstory or limit his options." He pierced Cowboy with a look.

"What? Me? As Donnelly's boyfriend?" Ryan Sullivan's voice sounded strangled. "You have to be kidding."

"I figure that with the number of women you date you should be able to act the part easily enough."

"Dating lots of women doesn't make them interchangeable." Ryan looked appalled by the idea.

"It's okay, Cowboy." Donnelly's grin was as sharp as an alley cat. "I promise I'll go easy on you, *babe*."

Ryan groaned. "Kill me now."

"Better be on your best behavior, Sullivan," Nash warned with a laugh.

"Damn straight." Grady crossed his arms and gave his buddy a death glare. "That's my partner you'll be cozying up to. We don't date teammates, remember."

Cowboy raised his face to the ceiling and closed his eyes. "Sweet Jesus. I promise never to complain about downtime again. Send Nash. I bet Donnelly likes him."

"Too late. I want you two in town ready to act as backup if necessary. You can scope out the locals in the meantime. Take photos for facial rec. Act like tourists." Novak stood, ending the discussion. "I'll get the backgrounds organized and bookings arranged. You guys are going to make a great couple and have a lovely time exploring Maine on the government's dime, and you won't be stuck in some shit-hole motel."

"I'm thinking about breaking my arm like Livingstone did," Cowboy announced with his eyes still closed.

"I'll help," Donnelly offered.

"Won't matter. You can do this op with a broken arm. You could do it with two broken arms." Novak smirked.

Donnelly nudged Cowboy. "Come on, Ryan. It'll be fun."

"Sure, it will. Bank robberies, dead managers, FBI fugitives. Winter in Maine. And now an actual fake girlfriend." Ryan shuddered and shook his head. "I'm not sure I'll survive this op."

"Nothing usually happens in Deception Cove." Grady scrubbed his face. He was in disbelief that he was working undercover in his hometown and that the place might be hiding the secrets of one of the biggest mysteries in FBI history. He pushed back his chair to stand. "I'm going to head back now."

"Yeah. Use your charm on this Brynn woman and see what she knows," Ropero stated.

Grady gritted his teeth to stop from snarling at his colleague. It might have been his original plan, but hearing her spell it out put his back up.

"There is one thing," he remembered. "Her husband left her a few years ago. I want to know what the story is."

"I'll start digging," Dobson offered. "What's your next move?"

Grady headed to the door. "I plan to visit another high school friend of mine this afternoon. Saul Jones, the security guard who was shot during the bank heist."

Ropero's gaze sharpened almost gleefully. "Maybe you'll prove useful after all."

16

Darrell York adjusted his sheriff's hat and gave Brynn the smile that had once enthralled all the girls in high school. But the dazzling brilliance of that classic young male quarterback beauty had faded. Overindulgence had led to a loss of muscle tone and his smile had become bitter with cynicism.

She could sympathize. "Sheriff."

"Brynn." He said her name warmly, as if they shared some kind of secret.

It was weird. He'd once pushed for more than she'd been willing to give, and he'd been pissed when she hadn't yielded. But now he acted as if that part of their relationship had never happened. Or maybe this was just one long continuum in a game designed to get her into bed. Boy, was he ever in for disappointment.

"You coming to make your statement?"

She'd forgotten all about that.

"Yes." She checked her wristwatch. "But I only have ten minutes. I figured it wouldn't take long," she said hopefully.

"I can always bring it by your place later…"

Her smile froze in place. She wondered where that iron-clad

self-belief came from. That if he kept pushing, he'd eventually wear down her resistance. Finally get what he wanted.

Was it a man thing? Or a cop thing? Or exclusive to Darrell York?

"That's not necessary. You must be incredibly busy with the robbery and Milton's death. If I don't get finished today, I'll come by tomorrow."

They headed up the steps and inside the square redbrick building that housed the Montrose County Sheriff's Department on one side and City Hall on the other. Darrell put his hands on his heavily laden equipment belt and looked down at her. "A murder investigation should take precedence over serving coffee, don't you think?"

She kept her face expressionless. She'd done her part last night when she'd retrieved Milton's body from the sea. She hadn't seen anything that could help catch Milton's killer, and Darrell knew it.

"As long as you're prepared for the riot that ensues in town when customers don't get their caffeine, then I can stay for a little while longer." She spoke lightly, but she did not want Darrell finding an excuse to turn up on her doorstep tonight.

He held the door for her, and she looked around curiously. She'd never been inside the Sheriff's Department before. Had never even received a parking ticket.

Darrell keyed in a combination for a door beside a wide counter protected by Perspex and waved her through. There were two people in the waiting room, and Deputy Jean Trout turned from dealing with one of them to smile brightly.

"Hey, Brynn. How are your mom and dad?"

"Doing great, Jean. Thanks. How's yours?"

"Mom is currently obsessed with K-Dramas, and Dad is miffed she's not paying him enough attention."

"Wait until she discovers K-Pop, then he'll really be in trouble. Give them my love when you see them next."

"Same." Jean looked serious all of a sudden. "We're all praying for Gwen. Just so you know."

Brynn felt the lump in her throat grow. "We appreciate that." Her mom was a sworn atheist, but no one in town seemed to hold it against her.

"This way." Darrell caught her attention again.

She followed him, weaving between desks where some of the deputies sat working and a couple stood around talking. She raised her hand to the people she knew. She'd gone to school with many of them and waited on the rest.

Darrell headed for his office, and she balked at the door. "I'm sure one of the deputies can take my statement. You must have more important things to do. You don't need to bother yourself."

"Nothing more important." Darrell gave her a smile that was way too warm and held the door in such a way she was compelled to go inside.

She could feel the deputies eyeing them speculatively as Darrell shut the door. He took off his wide-brimmed hat and heavy jacket and hung them on the coat rack in the corner. No doubt it had belonged to his father.

The frosted-glass-walled office with its old-fashioned wooden paneling was cluttered with thick stacks of manilla folders on the desk. The windows were high up, so it was hard to see anything outside except the currently cloudless sky, which was the same vivid blue of Grady Steel's eyes.

She thrust the thought out of her mind. Discovering that her libido wasn't dead was shocking. But maybe it wasn't a terrible realization. However, she had no intention of acting on it.

"Make yourself comfortable," Darrell insisted, indicating the office chair this side of the desk.

It was hot from the old-fashioned radiator that sat pumping out heat beneath the large window. Reluctantly she removed her own hat and coat. Looked like she was staying.

She clasped her hands together. Was she a suspect the way Grady had suggested? Should she call her lawyer?

Darrell pulled out a form from his file drawer and handed it to her along with a pen. He slid the stacks of folders across his desk to create space for her.

Then he propped himself on a corner close enough that his thigh almost touched her forearm. "Detail exactly what happened after you left work last night and mention if you noticed anything unusual yesterday. Anything at all."

"Unusual?"

"You know, any strangers at the café."

Seriously?

"We have strangers in the café every day. Wouldn't be much of a café if we didn't. We had a couple in today with Eastern European accents. You think the Russians sent a hit-squad to murder Milton?"

"It's not a joking matter, Brynn. The man is dead." Darrell was clearly disappointed in her.

She sighed. "Trust me, I'm aware."

She started writing, reliving the movements of last night step by step, uncomfortably aware of the way Darrell watched her as she wrote.

"Did you identify the person I saw walking away?" she asked.

Darrell grunted noncommittally.

"Any clue who might have had a reason to kill him?" She glanced up.

Darrell's mouth tightened, but he didn't respond.

"Oh." Realization dawned. "Grady said I'd be a suspect... I never imagined..." She hesitated. "Is that true?"

Darrell didn't meet her gaze. "Standard procedure to investigate anyone who finds a body."

"If I'd shot Milton, I sure as heck wouldn't have gone in the water after him." She shuddered at the memory of the bone-chilling cold. She tried not to think about the heavy dragging weight of the body she'd hauled to the surface, or the black unseeing eyes of a man she'd known since she'd been a little girl.

Darrell laid his hand on her wrist, and she started in surprise.

"I have to play this by the book, Brynn. We might be a small police department, but we do things right."

"Of course." She shifted to break the physical connection. "When was the last time we had a murder in town?"

Usually, the local cops only dealt with traffic offenses, drug addiction, and property theft—not bank robberies or murder. The low crime rate was one of the reasons people moved out here. It certainly wasn't for the taxes.

"We had a suspicious death a couple of years ago, but the Medical Examiner ruled natural causes in the end. We've had the occasional questionable missing person case—" He cut himself off when Brynn flinched.

She dragged a tired hand through her hair. "Yes, I'm familiar with how the world views unexpected disappearances. When Aiden first left, everyone thought I'd murdered him and buried him in the woods."

Darrell's lips pressed together in a tight line.

Brynn ignored him and carried on writing her statement.

"Milton was always pleasant to me. I liked him." He was a little obsequious maybe, but polite. Whenever he came into the café he tipped well, and his wife had a dry wit and a wry sense of humor that Brynn appreciated.

Darrell grunted. "Obviously, not everyone felt the same way."

"How's Edith taking it?"

"I went to see her after I left your place last night." He made it sound like they'd shared a hookup. "She was well and truly shook. Doc had to come over and give her something to help her rest."

"I can only imagine how awful that must have been for her." Brynn gripped the pen so hard her knuckles ached. The clock ticked on the wall, and she could smell the odor of the man beside her, not entirely unpleasant but something she'd rather avoid if possible.

"How are you doing, Brynn? Recovered from the shock yet?"

Darrell asked as she finished writing about her arrival back at the house with Grady.

The sheriff was reading as she wrote, which at least saved time.

She hunched her shoulders. "I'm okay. I guess. Still a little shaken. My first dead body." She grimaced, then looked up. "Do I date and sign it?"

"Yes." He stood and took the form from her.

"Can I go now? Jackie finishes at two, and Linda will be on her own. I can't afford to upset her—unless you know anyone who wants to work full-time at the café?"

He shook his head. "Not off the top of my head, but I'll think about it."

He sat in his chair.

Eager to escape she went to stand up, but he held up his hand.

Dammit.

"I need to sign it and then I can give you a copy." Rather than reading it through again though, he templed his hands on the desk and stared at her. "Brynn, I know it's been difficult since Aiden—"

"That man leaving me was the best thing that ever happened." She hid the painful throbbing wound beneath a rueful smile. "Pity he didn't do it before we tied the knot because the paperwork was brutal."

Having to pay to file for a divorce in absentia when the man had stolen all their savings to run off with some bimbo had been the final insult. She didn't even know if he knew they were legally divorced. He obviously didn't care.

Darrell shook his head and stared at her statement. "I never did take to the guy." He shot her a look from under his lashes. "He wasn't nearly good enough for you. You're a very special woman, Brynn, one I shouldn't have let get away."

What was she, a fish?

He signed her statement with a flourish and turned to make a quick copy on the printer behind him. Brynn realized he'd made her endure this entire episode simply so he could deliver his play like some sort of performance art.

"Well, it all worked out for the best. You found Lorraine and are blessed with such an adorable family. I enjoy them all when they come into the café, and that baby. He's gonna break a few hearts, just like his daddy."

Darrell opened his mouth, probably to bemoan the fact his wife didn't understand him, but Brynn didn't give him the opportunity. She took her copy of her statement from his hand.

"I can't wait for Mom to get better so I can get back to my boyfriend, Bowie." Damn, that was the name of her friend's dog, but it was all she could come up with in a pinch.

"You have a boyfriend?" His tone was amused, as if he didn't believe her. He leaned back in his seat. It creaked ominously.

Resentment grew so she doubled down. "Yes. Bowie. He's a little younger than me, but I find younger people so much more… malleable. Don't you, Sheriff?" She smiled brightly.

His eyes narrowed, and maybe she hadn't been subtle enough with her dig.

"As long as he's legal."

She blinked slowly. It had never crossed her mind that "Bowie" might not be a full-grown adult.

"Well, if you get lonely for a little company while you're here in town, or need a shoulder to cry on,"—his eyes were compassionate, and made a complete sham by every word that came out of his mouth—"you can always call me. I'm here for you."

Anger surged through her. That he had forced her to spell it out for him rather than him understanding the nuances of their interactions.

"I'm not looking to start anything with a married man, Darrell. Have a little more respect for me than that." She stood and grabbed her coat and hat off the rack. Rage made her veins feel hot.

Darrell caught her arm as she reached the door. She jerked away from him as she turned.

His eyes were hard and bright with anger of his own. "I was just being a friend, Brynn. You might appreciate having the sheriff on speed dial if you're ever in trouble."

"If I was ever in trouble, I'd hope the sheriff's department would help regardless of whether or not we're 'friends,'" she spluttered. No wonder her father had warned her not to date this guy when she was eighteen. "At least I have an FBI agent living upstairs. Perhaps he'll answer in an emergency."

Darrell expression tightened. "Watch out for Grady Steel. He knows how to turn on the charm to get what he wants, but he's not someone you should trust."

A bit like you.

But she didn't say it. Instead, "What happened between you two?"

"He only cares about his precious career, which he's gone and fucked up." Darrell's nostrils flared and his upper lip curled into something ugly. "He's a wily sonofabitch and only friendly when it suits him." His gaze slid down her body. "Don't you forget that."

She yanked open the door. "Have a good afternoon, Sheriff." She held her head high as she walked through the bullpen and let herself out of the side door, waving to Jean along the way.

Her heart pounded all the way back to the café.

17

Grady stuffed his hands deep into his jacket pockets and went for a walk, needing to clear his head.

Drawn to the majesty of the ocean he walked to the southern side of the headland and watched the waves roll in off the Atlantic to pound the white sandy beach with power and fury. The sky had clouded over. The brisk breeze filled his chest with the tang of the ocean, sharp as ozone, as elusive as smoke. The rush of love took him by surprise. Like unexpectedly catching sight of a former lover you hadn't realized you still had feelings for.

The wind had gotten up since last night, white crests forming far out to sea. The town was hidden and protected thanks to this spit of land reaching out and embracing the Atlantic. It wouldn't help the water visibility though.

Had the sheriff's department found the murder weapon during their search of the harbor today? Even on a good day it would be easy to miss in the silt and murk.

He stared out to sea.

He was an experienced diver. He'd have been happy to lend his assistance if they'd asked. The fact they hadn't, suggested he really was a suspect.

Grady hadn't heard a shot last night.

Either the killer had used a suppressor or Milton had been killed elsewhere and transported to the harbor to dispose of the body late at night when it was quiet. But why choose the relatively busy harbor as a body dump site when there were places all over the coast like this one, isolated and deserted?

No, Grady's money was on Milton being murdered on his boat then dumped over the side. The killer likely still had the murder weapon.

Grady caught movement out of the corner of his eye. The gray shaggy-coated dog he'd spotted earlier was sniffing along the sea grass that edged the beach. Beneath the filthy matted coat, the poor thing looked half starved.

He took a step toward it, but the dog raised his head warily then took off. Grady wished he had some food on him to use as a lure.

Maybe he'd come back in the Jeep. Tempt the dog with something to eat, catch it, and take it to animal control.

He turned around and headed back along the narrow road toward town. Lights were on in the Jones' small clapboard house on the edge of town—a house where he'd spent many of his teenage days hanging out in Saul's bedroom.

He climbed the front steps, noted peeling paint on the siding and a rotten board that needed to be replaced. He knocked on the door and waited.

It took a moment for anyone to answer, probably because people rarely waited for someone to answer the door around here. They simply knocked and walked in. But after so many years being away that didn't feel right. He had no idea what his welcome might look like.

Saul opened the door with a wary gaze, a crutch propped under one arm. A boot and removable cast encased his right leg below the knee. His expression cleared when he spotted Grady, and his eyes brightened.

His old friend grinned. The familiar features were a little older and broader, hair a little thinner on top, but still the same wry twist on his wide lips. "You don't call, you don't write."

Grady gave a half laugh, keeping his shoulders hunched, his hands dug deep in his pockets, reminiscent of the teen he'd once been. "I'm here now. How you doing?"

"Who is it?" A querulous voice called from inside.

"Want to come in?" Saul asked with a glance over his shoulder.

"Sure." Grady nodded.

Saul's mother sat in her old armchair in the corner, and Grady was immediately transported back half a lifetime.

"Mrs. Jones. How are you?"

The woman scowled. "I heard you were back. Heard a dead body turned up not long after." She sniffed and went back to her show.

Condemned and convicted.

Just like your father.

He heard the unspoken comparison loud and clear.

Didn't that encapsulate what this town thought of him? And maybe it wasn't so far from the truth. He looked enough like his old man to be his double and was certainly no saint.

His mood soured.

Saul grimaced and indicated they go into the kitchen. "Want coffee or beer?"

Grady remembered why he was here and yawned widely. "Shit. Sorry. I had a long drive followed by an eventful arrival. Didn't get a lot of sleep last night. Better make it coffee."

Saul snorted as he hobbled around the kitchen, filling the coffeemaker. "We must be getting old."

"Speak for yourself." The last thing Grady wanted was to get too old to do the job he loved. "I heard about the bank robbery."

Saul flinched. His hands shook and he spilled fresh ground coffee on the worn counter. He swore. Awkwardly wiped up the mess and turned on the machine. Clearly still traumatized from the event.

He propped up his crutches, leaned against the counter and crossed his arms. "You ever been shot?"

Grady shook his head.

"Fucking hurts, man." Saul laughed, winced, and looked away. Fear darkened his expression. "Asshole shattered my tibia and surgeon had to put in a metal plate."

"What happened?"

Saul ran his hand over his nose and chin. "Fucker comes in not long before closing. Sticks a gun in Fancy's face and tells her he's going to blow her fucking head off unless she puts all the money in the sack. Everyone is frozen in shock. I don't think anyone has ever uttered those words to Fancy Lucette before. Imagine doing that to a woman who's in her seventies?" Saul shook his head. "He said if anyone hit the silent alarm, he'd shoot the lot of us." Saul pressed his fist to his chin. "Might have been funny if we hadn't been pissing ourselves in fright." He swallowed. "I didn't even pull my weapon. I stood there like some little kid crapping his pants."

The coffeepot hissed, and Saul jumped then looked embarrassed.

His friend looked like he had a bad dose of PTSD.

Grady felt a little guilty that he hadn't kept in touch with Saul over the years. They'd been a threesome along with Darrell, but Grady had genuinely liked this guy. Darrell was a selfish sonofabitch, but then again, so was Grady.

There had come a point when Grady had desperately needed to escape this town or suffocate on other people's lack of expectations. He'd never given much thought to the people he'd left behind.

"Did you recognize him?" asked Grady.

Saul shook his head, a frown marring his brow. "No, but at the same time I feel like I should have, you know. His voice was familiar but... not familiar enough."

"You didn't see the getaway car?"

Saul shook his head. "Too busy writhing on the floor trying not to bleed out."

"Shit. Sorry, man."

"Yeah. Definitely shit. Wish I hadn't found any last-minute courage. Not like the bank pays me enough for it to be worth it."

He turned awkwardly and poured two cups of coffee. Grady even recognized the faded mug.

Grady took it from Saul. Blew on the hot liquid before taking a sip. "I heard Brandy left you."

His friend's expression turned bitter. "Bitch cleaned me out. Emptied the bank accounts. Opened store credit in my name. Cheated on me. Dumped me. And still demanded half the house." He looked around despondently. "I can't believe I'm back living with my mother at age thirty-four. And she's more cantankerous than ever." Saul's gaze shot to Grady's. "I should have gotten out like you did."

"I'm sorry you were shot, and I'm sorry about Brandy, too, but at least you're alive and have a roof over your head." He'd learned to count his blessings over the years—knowing they could be stripped from him in an instant.

"I guess." Saul shrugged. His gaze turned assessing. "Word is you ran over someone and left them to die at the side of the road."

Grady gritted his teeth together and stared out of the salt-stained window at the clouds that had begun to boil in the iron-gray sky. "It's bullshit."

Saul stared at him suspiciously. "Then you arrive home and the first thing you do is drag my dead boss out of the harbor. The gossips are sitting around having orgasms."

"There's a vision I did not need to have in my head." Grady rolled his shoulder. "Despite claims otherwise, I wasn't responsible for the hit and run and expect to be cleared as soon as the evidence techs finish analyzing my truck. And if I was planning to shoot Milton Bodurek, I wouldn't have shown my face around town beforehand." He grinned. "I'd have waited a couple of days first."

Saul's eyes popped.

"I'd forgotten he was your boss though." He hadn't forgotten a damn thing. "I'm sorry. Were you close to him?"

"Yeah, he was my boss. Good old Milt." Saul's expression was guarded. "We weren't close. How come you were at the harbor anyway?"

"I argued with Crystal as soon as I got here last night. She was pissed I put a stop to her covertly making rental money off my property as I needed somewhere to stay." Grady stuffed his hands in his pockets. "I went for a walk afterward."

"You didn't know about Crys renting the house out?" Saul asked curiously.

Grady shook his head.

"She told everyone she bought the place from you after your grandma died. I was surprised, but then when you didn't come back…"

Grady expected to feel anger, instead pity welled up inside him. "Do me a favor. Don't tell anyone that it's my place not hers. Crys would die rather than lose face."

"More likely she'd kill rather than lose face," Saul muttered into his mug.

Grady grimaced. "True. And I don't want to be a target any more than I have to be."

"So, you went for a walk and just happened to see Milton floating around the harbor?"

Grady shook his head. He ran his finger along the edge of the veneer on the table that was so smooth with age he could see the worn-down layers at the edges. "When I was reacquainting myself with the sea air, I heard someone calling for help."

"Brynn Webster?"

Grady nodded. "You know her?"

Saul shrugged. "Not well, unfortunately. Pretty thing, but a bit standoffish. Darrell dated her a couple of times before she went off to Yale to study art or something. She moved to Boston afterward and got married. She only came home recently because of this business with her mother."

Grady didn't know why he was so surprised that she'd dated Darrell, but he was. It was obvious Darrell wanted to rekindle that relationship, but she didn't seem so keen. Or maybe that was wishful thinking on Grady's part.

"This was back when you worked as a state trooper before joining the FBI," Saul continued, angling his head. "Darrell seemed smitten with Brynn, but then he started dating Lorraine. The rest is history."

"What happened to the guy Brynn married? Crystal said he left her."

"Yeah. Dumped her for another woman apparently. Sent her some photos from Vegas or somewhere and told her they were done."

Grady winced. "Harsh."

"I felt for her," Saul's mouth pinched. "Then Brandy basically did the same to me. I think she got the idea from Brynn's husband. Fuckers."

"It sucks, man."

Saul's eyes grew curious. "You never met anyone?"

Grady forced a grim smile. "No one that would put up with me for any length of time." Not that he ever let things get serious. He was too busy for a real relationship. And maybe too much like his father to risk it.

"I heard that when you reached the harbor, Brynn was already in the water?"

Saul had obviously heard a lot more than he'd originally let on.

"Yeah. It was fucking freezing. I had to jump in after her. I couldn't stand on the sidelines like a useless prick."

"Like Caleb Quayle, you mean?"

Grady snorted out a quiet laugh. "You said it."

"Caleb is a loudmouth little shit like the rest of his family." Saul rubbed his chin.

"Not so little anymore." The guy had height and weight on Grady.

Saul frowned.

"What is it?" asked Grady.

Saul blinked. "Nothing." He blew on his coffee to cool it.

Was Saul being evasive? Or was Grady's suspicion tainting every interaction? "Can you think of any reason someone might murder your boss?"

"Aside from me?"

That startled Grady. "You didn't like him?"

Saul shook his head. "Everyone thought Milton Bodurek was the cat's meow, but he threatened to fire me when I was in the hospital with a gunshot wound. Said I didn't do my job properly and then threatened to take the bank's losses out of my wages—as if he paid me that much." Anger burned along Saul's cheekbones. "Worst thing was, he was right."

"What do you mean?"

"I didn't even draw my gun to start with."

"Were you expected to start a shootout in a bank full of people?"

"No, but according to Milton Bodurek, I was supposed to finish one." Saul blinked away what might have been tears.

Not everyone trained with live ammo until it was muscle memory. Not everyone understood the effects of elevated stress levels on accuracy, making even a good marksman's aim waver under duress. "You did the right thing keeping it holstered."

"Well, then I fucked it up in the end." He stroked his palm over his face. "Not sure what will happen to my job now he's dead." Saul looked thoroughly miserable.

"Any chance you're entitled to compensation?" Grady asked.

"Maybe. Spoke to a lawyer but I don't even know what will happen to the bank now Bodurek's dead. I mean it's still officially open, and the cops are investigating, but I'm not sure who'll be in charge. Or whether they'll want me back."

It was entirely possible Milton's death had something to do

with greed and personal gain rather than anything to do with Eli Kane—but it was a hell of a coincidence.

Grady didn't believe in coincidence.

Saul's eyes turned assessing. "Don't suppose you can put in a good word for me with the cops? The local deputies questioned me as if they thought I was in on it."

"I'm not sure me vouching for you would do you much good right now, not until the FBI officially clears my name." He rubbed the back of his neck. A prickle of guilt crossed his mind at lying to his old friend, but this community was too small to risk telling him the truth—his job was too important. "As long as you weren't in on the robbery, I wouldn't worry about it."

Saul's expression turned bitter. "I wish I was in on it. A few grand would be pretty useful right about now. Hey, maybe if you leave the FBI, we could go into business together like we used to talk about when we were kids."

Grady smiled. "Running whale watching tours for the tourists?"

"Beats getting shot in the leg." Saul rubbed his thigh as if the muscles ached.

"Anything beats getting shot in the leg." Grady rose to his feet. "Better get going. I'll see you around?"

"I'm not going anywhere."

The words were filled with a bitterness Grady recognized from his own feelings of frustration as a youth.

Grady headed out the back door to avoid Saul's mother, who'd probably come up with a list of cutting insults in the time he'd been here. He'd rather die than admit he was scared of one old lady. He opened the door and caught another flash of the gray mutt. "Hey, you seen a stray dog running around?"

"Gray thing?"

"Yeah. Big shaggy dog."

"Belongs to the Quayle family." Saul's eyes hardened. "They don't take care of it. Poor thing is half starved. It almost got hit on the street the other day, but no one can catch it."

Anger rose inside Grady.

Saul's eyes narrowed with a glint of humor. "Thinking of getting yourself a dog, Grade?"

"I don't have time for a dog." But it didn't mean he couldn't do something to help this stray.

He looked back at his old friend's house as he walked away.

Saul was hiding something.

It made his heart hurt to know it, but it was Grady's job to figure out if that something had anything to do with Eli Kane, a murder, or a bank robbery.

18

B rynn's feet ached as she finished loading the dishwasher.
Thankfully, the café closed early on Sundays, and they were shut on Mondays. Not only did she have a full day off to look forward to, but Linda's niece, Pru, had called and could come in for a few hours on Tuesday.

Brynn hoped to recruit another waitress in addition to Pru, who could do odd hours here and there, to cover some of her own current schedule. She'd placed an ad in the local paper without clearing it with her mother first.

If her parents wanted her to manage the place for six months, then they'd have to trust her to make decisions. Perhaps she could create a sustainable system that allowed her mom to work a couple of hours a week when she felt like it. Perhaps that would be enough to satisfy her.

Brynn had a stack of freelance work to catch up on tomorrow. She didn't want to lose the client base she'd already built, and hiring more staff for the café would give her some breathing space.

It would also allow her to spend more time with her mom.

As if sensing her thoughts, Brynn's phone rang. She glanced at it in surprise and wondered what had taken her mother so long.

"Hey, how are you feeling?" Brynn asked brightly.

"I'm fine. I slept most of the day after going to the hospital which is why I missed the big news in town."

"Oh?"

"*Oh*, indeed. What's this I hear about you jumping in the harbor last night?"

Brynn heard fatigue and pain in her mother's voice and so forced an upbeat note into her own. "It's not like I decided it might be fun to go skinny dipping, Mom. Someone was in the water. Would you rather I'd left them to drown?"

"Of course not, but wasn't he…" Her mom trailed off.

Dead.

Funny how hyperaware of the word they'd all become since her mother's diagnosis.

"Yeah, he was. But I didn't know that until we pulled him out. How was chemo?"

"Don't change the subject."

"That's all I have on the subject."

"Do they know how he died?"

"Shot between the eyes."

Her mother's indrawn breath reminded Brynn of the shock she'd felt last night. "Poor Milton. I don't know what this town is coming to. First the robbery, now a murder? Does anyone know what happened?"

"The police aren't saying anything." Brynn started the dishwasher and moved away from the noise of the machine. "But the gossips think that maybe the bank heist was an inside job and Milton was involved."

"That's ridiculous. Poor Edith."

"Yeah, according to Sheriff York she had to be sedated when she heard the news."

"I can imagine. How is *Darrell*?" Her mother's tone contained suppressed derision.

"Annoying."

Gwendolyn Webster snorted. "He used to come into the café

and ask how you were getting on in the months after you left. Then Lorraine became pregnant—"

"She didn't get pregnant on her own," Brynn reminded her.

"I'm aware." Her mom huffed. "Still, I used to enjoy telling him how much fun you were having in college."

Brynn didn't want to talk about Darrell. "How was treatment today?"

Her mom sighed. "Honestly? It was brutal."

Brynn's heart squeezed, and she closed her eyes. "I'm sorry, Mom."

"I'm starting to wonder if it's worth it—"

"Don't say that." Brynn closed her eyes tight against the words.

"You sound like your father. I'm fine, really. Just tired, and I enjoy complaining. What's the point in getting old and having cancer if you can't complain about it?"

"You're not old."

"Ha. I feel old. Your dad has been fantastic as always, but he's feeling the strain, too. How's business?"

"Are you kidding? Lineup was out of the door in the hopes I'd tell them some juicy tidbit about finding poor Milton."

"Ghouls."

"Paying customers."

Her mother huffed. "They pay for good food and ambience, not my daughter's blood." Her voice grew hoarse.

Fear bloomed at the thought of losing this woman from her life. "I'm gonna come see you tomorrow after lunch." She'd tell her about the new waitress then.

"That will be lovely. Here, I'm going to pass you to your dad. He has a shopping list if you're coming over."

"Let me grab a pen."

"Oh, he's changed his mind and says he'll text you the list and see you tomorrow. No jumping into the harbor on the way home."

"And here's me already in my bathing suit."

"Smartass."

"Where do I get that from?"

Her mom snort-laughed, but even that sounded weak. "I bet it was cold."

"It was *so* cold."

"Crazy kid. Get some rest. You've earned it."

"You too, Mom. Love you."

"Love you, too."

They hung up. Brynn caught her reflection in the glass of the picture window as she looked out toward the harbor.

She was twenty-eight years old, but the reflection looked older. Dark circles under her eyes made her look tired. What was worse, she felt old and dreary. Not quite frumpy, but not exactly young and sexy either.

Aiden had done this to her. Not her parents. Not working in a job she didn't want. Aiden and his casual discarding of their life together. It had battered her optimism. Wrecked her self-confidence. Destroyed her ability to trust and robbed her of her joy.

Tears burned in her eyes, but she blinked them away. She'd cried a million tears over the man who'd vowed to love her and then had left without a word. At first, she'd worried he might be dead and had reported him missing to the Boston police.

Humiliation crawled up her cheeks with familiar heat as she remembered their pity when he'd finally contacted her.

She refused to waste another moment on that cheating jerk. The only thing that mattered was her mom beating cancer.

Gwendolyn Webster was Brynn's rock, her inspiration. Running the café might be less than ideal, but she would do it if she had to. Hopefully, with extra staff she'd have more time for her parents, herself, and her clients, and feel less smothered and overwhelmed by all the things she couldn't control.

She turned off the rest of the lights and checked the kitchen one last time. Wrapping herself up in her coat and hat, she stepped outside the back door and turned to lock it. A shadow detached itself from the wall and her hand flew to her chest as she let out a shriek.

19

"Whoa. Sorry." Grady Steel stood with his hands raised in front of him, palms out. "I didn't mean to startle you. I should have thought."

"Ya think?" Brynn's eyes bugged out of her skull, and her heartbeat felt like a drumroll before the rope dropped.

"I was walking past to go grab a drink and saw you turning off the lights, thought I'd wait and see if you wanted to join me."

Her eyebrows climbed her forehead. "Like on a *date*?"

"Considering how horrified you sound, definitely not a date." He laughed with self-deprecation and that damned smile of his got to her again. "I was thinking more of a neighborly drink and polite conversation after a long day."

She blew out a breath, tempted. Her habitual after-work walk around the harbor was out until the cops figured out what happened to Milton Bodurek. "I shouldn't…"

"Because…?"

Because she'd invented a fake boyfriend to avoid the attentions of Sheriff Darrell York and wasn't in the mood for complications.

The wind blasted across the deck, and she shivered. The fact she was changing how she lived her life due to a man, a *married* man, pissed her off. The fact that everyone else seemed to have a life except for her made her resolve start to crumble…

"You have plans?"

"I don't have plans." Bitterness leaked out, aimed at herself. "I figured I'd go home and crash. I was up late last night."

"Me, too." He took a step back. "No worries. Thought I'd ask before I braved the lion's den on my own, but I didn't mean to pressure you."

They'd chew him up and spit him out, but he knew that. He'd grown up here.

"One drink." She conceded, feeling strangely protective of the guy, which was ridiculous. He was an FBI agent, for goodness' sake.

"Great."

She followed him up the alley on to Main Street. Except for the breadth of his shoulders, he'd barely changed over the years, but there was a lot to be said for broad shoulders and narrow hips, and she wished she hadn't noticed either.

He waited on the sidewalk, hands in pockets, looking suddenly ridiculously handsome for a man she'd known and ignored virtually her whole life.

"The Thirsty Pig or the Wine Bar?" he asked.

She thought about it. What did she want? In the past she'd always let Aiden choose. Gone were those days. "I'm in the mood for a beer."

"The Thirsty Pig it is then."

He wore a leather jacket and faded jeans and a blue plaid shirt that brought out the color of his eyes.

"Busy day?" he asked as he matched his step to hers.

"Very."

"What's the consensus then?" The humor in his voice surprised her.

"There are two competing theories, and both seem to have equal support. First that you're no good and the fact you turned up on the same night Milton died can't be a coincidence and, therefore, you must have killed him. Alternately, Milton was involved in the bank robbery and his accomplice shot him. You're simply a bad penny or harbinger of misfortune, depending on your spiritual beliefs."

He laughed. "Jesus. Wait five minutes until they decide I'm the one who robbed the bank and then shot Milton."

Brynn smiled reluctantly. "I was surprised no one went with that option. I'm sure it's only a matter of time."

"Better figure out what I was doing on the date of the robbery. When was it?"

"January fifteenth—a week ago last Friday."

"Ah. That day I was involved in a suspect takedown in Charlotte, so I'm finally in the clear for something."

He said it so casually she blinked. "Sounds dangerous."

"On this occasion, it was a lot of waiting around for nothing, but at least it puts me far away from here when someone pulled a gun on poor Miss Fancy." His voice was even but Brynn wasn't fooled.

"Like you observed last night, it's always easier to think an outsider did this."

He flinched.

"I don't mean to imply you're an outsider—"

His voice cracked into a harsh laugh. "Oh, I am though. I haven't even been back here in eight years and before that I was in Bangor."

"Yeah, but unlike me, you have family roots here that go back generations. You belong whether you, or they, like it or not."

His brows rose. "Your family isn't from here?"

She shook her head. "Vermont. We moved here when I was two."

"I was seven when me and Crystal came back to live here." Grady drew his shoulders up as if against the cold. "I hate coming back but figured while I had a little unexpected time on my hands, I should finally decide what to do about Gran's house."

Brynn smiled and ignored the embarrassment that wanted to

clutch at her heart. "Since my ex dumped me, I hate coming back, too. Everyone looks at me with such pity, as if my character is somehow reduced by his being a dick."

"You came back anyway."

"I don't have any choice. I love my parents." The wind cut through her layers, and she buttoned her coat even though they didn't have far to walk. "But I miss my apartment in Boston. I miss my anonymity. I miss everyone I meet not knowing all the details of my life and judging me for it."

Grady's gaze held real understanding. "In the eyes of this town, I'm still a teenager causing trouble—they seem to have forgotten the dozen or so years I've spent in law enforcement." He shrugged like it didn't bother him, but it clearly did.

She shot him a look. "What will you do if the FBI doesn't clear you?"

"They will."

"But what if they don't?" she asked, needing to know. "Would you stay?"

Grady looked uncomfortable. "Probably sell the house and my condo in Quantico and find a job somewhere warm. Maybe run whale watching tours—in Hawaii?"

"That sounds amazing."

They both shuddered as the winter wind gusted and blasted them with ice. Another blizzard was forecast for later this week. She couldn't believe that last night she'd jumped into the sea. It was too damn frigid to even contemplate now. And someone had murdered Milton Bodurek only yards away—that didn't exactly make her feel warm and cozy.

"What do you do when you're not running the café? Saul mentioned you're an artist."

He'd discussed her with Saul Jones? She wasn't sure how to feel about that. The two of them had been tight with Darrell York in high school but obviously weren't friendly now.

"I'm a graphic designer. I have my own company. I do a lot of work for corporate clients based in Boston." She tucked her chin down and hunched her shoulders against the onslaught of January.

"That's impressive."

She shrugged. "Not really. I'm small beans."

But she paid her own way, and there was something to be said for that.

They arrived at The Thirsty Pig, which took up the bottom floor of a huge Victorian hotel on the corner of Main and Oak. Grady held the door for her. The guest rooms were upstairs, and the place had been renovated and modernized many times over the years, but the bar area probably looked the same as it had a hundred years ago—with dark corners and a fire in the hearth.

They walked inside and were met by a wall of warmth and the scent of woodsmoke and beer. People smiled until they saw Grady behind her. Then brows rose and scowls formed.

Unfazed, Grady asked. "Want to grab a table while I order?"

She shook her head. "Let's both sit. Harry will be over lickety-split."

Grady's intense blue eyes assessed her before he nodded.

She led the way to an empty table near the fire. Caleb Quayle sat on a stool at the bar. His glassy expression hardened as they walked past.

She knew most of the locals, but there were a few tourists even at this time of year. A tall man in a cowboy hat stood at the bar, a pretty woman with long, loose brown hair on a stool beside him. Definitely not from around here. He was telling tall stories to the locals and people were laughing loudly. The woman was taking selfies on her cell phone.

The couple who'd eaten in the café who had thick Eastern European accents were occupying a table in a far corner of the bar, finishing a meal.

People kept shooting glances at her and Grady.

Brynn huffed out a deep breath resignedly. "This is what I've always hated about this place."

"Being stared at. Being judged."

She caught his gaze as something passed between them. A deeper understanding of how it felt to be an outsider in the town where you grew up. "Makes me think of the Salem Witch Trials and how those times aren't so very far behind us."

A smile cut into his right cheek. "If it's any consolation, I'm pretty sure I'm the one they want to burn."

Brynn shuddered again. "That doesn't make me feel any happier. I used to think people were more civilized, but I don't think we are anymore. We hide it better, but there would still be crowds at public executions and people would still cheer for more."

"That's a scary thought."

"It's reality." Brynn pulled a face. Her patience for self-delusion had reduced to ashes nowadays. Maybe she was the one with the problem. Maybe everyone else was fine. Bitter and cynical felt comfortable and familiar. It also felt smart.

The bar owner, Harry Butler, came over to take their order. "Nice to see you out, Brynn. How's your mom and dad?" His face held pity rather than sympathy. He wanted the gory details of her mother's cancer battle, and of her family's emotional fallout.

"Fine, thanks, Harry. They're both doing well, considering."

Obviously disappointed with the lack of insider juice, Harry slid his gaze to Grady, who was measuring the other man with a smile that didn't reach his eyes.

"Grady Steel." Harry nodded. "Been a long time."

"It has indeed." Grady stretched back in the booth. "Not a lot has changed around here though. How have you been?"

"Can't complain."

Brynn barely refrained from snorting out loud. The guy did nothing but complain when he came into the café. Her mom figured he only came in to check out the competition. Thankfully, the coffee at The Thirsty Pig sucked, and Harry couldn't keep a decent cook because he was too tight with his money and too demanding with his requirements. His current chef wasn't even close to Angus in caliber.

Grady ordered a pint of Maine Beer Dinner and she asked for a Stoneface Double Clip. Grady also ordered food, but she'd eaten a bowl of Angus's delicious seafood chowder earlier and wasn't hungry.

"Did you manage to pick up groceries?" she asked after Harry left. She was curious about this man who seemed as much a misfit as she was.

"I did. Although, I'm not much into cooking, so I might be first in line in the mornings for breakfast."

"We're closed tomorrow, so I'm afraid you'll have to starve." She wiggled her toes in her ugly but comfortable shoes, refusing to feel bad. Grady Steel was a grown man who was more than capable of looking after himself.

"Do you have big plans for your day off?"

She gave a rueful laugh. "Gosh, yes. It'll be all relaxation and glamor after I catch up on my design contracts and go visit my mom. The excitement never ends."

A young woman Brynn didn't recognize delivered the drinks. The woman's interested gaze travelled slowly over Grady and warmed as it hooked onto that unexpectedly handsome face. Heat flickered in the woman's eyes and Grady gave her a wide smile. "Thanks."

A dart of annoyance shot through Brynn which made her feel small and cantankerous. They weren't on a date.

She had Bowie to think about.

She took a drink of beer.

The man in the cowboy hat held his arms wide as he spun some tale. Harry laughed loudly at something the tourist said while the pretty brunette preened in front of the camera.

Brynn felt Grady's eyes on her and flicked her gaze to his.

There was interest there, lurking in the clear depths. She ignored the delicious shiver that slid along her nerves.

"Do you mind if I ask exactly what happened with your ex?"

Shock sucker-punched her in the face. She placed her drink on the table but held onto the glass. "He left me."

"I'm sorry."

"I was, too, but I'm not now." She pulled her lips to one side. "We'd only been married for eighteen months but we'd been having a few issues. One of which was he wanted me to give up the idea of running my own business and get a nine-to-five job that paid better." And destroyed her soul. "I didn't think it was anything that serious. Growing pains of a marriage, you know?"

Grady nodded.

"One day he goes off to a conference and simply never comes home. I guess I should have guessed something was up when he packed his large suitcase and passport, but I was at a conference in Boston and didn't notice until after he didn't return. I freaked out and filed a missing person report with the Boston police. Then he sent me a couple of photos of himself in bed with some bimbo and asked for a divorce. A few weeks later he sent me a postcard from Belize. After that I never heard from him again."

Emotion clutched around her throat. The sense of betrayal had cut her off at the knees and it still hurt two years later.

"Bastard."

"Yeah. Bastard." Her fingers strangled her beer glass before taking another sip. "What about you? Ever been gutted by someone you loved?"

20

"Well, I've been dumped plenty, but I'm not sure I've ever been in love."

She licked foam from around her top lip, and Grady found his eyes drawn to her shiny mouth.

"If you weren't eviscerated when they left you, then you weren't in love."

He looked down to make a show of checking his gut. "I guess not."

Grady didn't quite know what to make of this woman with her burnished copper hair and gray-green eyes that were full of pain and betrayal. He wasn't planning on ever leaving himself open to being that hurt or used, the way his father had hurt and used his mother, or Brynn's ex had hurt her. He liked being alone. He was used to it. He took risks in his job, not with his heart. He was driven and devoted to his work. Put his teammates above anyone else.

Women didn't like that. They didn't like plans being dropped at a moment's notice. He wouldn't like it either in their position. If that left him with an overall sense of dissatisfaction with his personal life, it was nothing he wasn't used to.

"Was it worth it?" he asked. "Falling in love. Getting married?"

Her eyes were massive when they met his. "Not even close."

He'd invited Brynn out for a drink because he wanted to get to know her better and gain her trust. Now she looked thoroughly miserable.

He reached out and touched the hand that rested on the seat between them where no one could see and gave it a squeeze. He wasn't expecting the frisson of electricity that snapped along his skin like a lightning strike. They'd touched each other yesterday, but they'd both been almost hypothermic from cold. This time was different.

Her eyes shot to his.

She withdrew her fingers, but not before Grady spotted a flush of awareness fill her cheeks. She'd felt it too, that weird and untimely sizzle. At least it had snapped her out of her heartbreak.

He pressed his lips together ruefully. "I didn't mean to pry or depress you. I was curious and figured I'd ask you directly rather than listen to rumors."

"The rumors at the time were I either killed Aiden and buried the body or that I'm so terrible at sex the guy had no choice but to find what he needed somewhere else." A grim smile curved her lips and lifted her cheeks into tight little apples, but then she laughed and it seemed to catch her unaware. "I appreciate the directness. It's usually difficult to talk about, but fuck him."

Grady raised his glass. "I'll drink to that. Fuck that loser."

They chinked glasses.

Damn, she was pretty. The firelight danced on her fiery hair and warmed that pale skin to cream, and she looked like some fairy princess.

Fairy princess?

What the fuck?

He couldn't afford to be distracted. She was his passport to inserting himself into this community again and quickly figuring out this town's secrets and maybe catching one of the evilest men ever to carry a badge. The FBI agent who'd murdered his wife and two young boys in cold blood. Left them in shallow graves in the woods where he'd believed they'd never be found.

Could Brynn's father be Eli Kane?

He couldn't see any physical resemblance with the fugitive, but that didn't mean much. Until she was cleared by DNA, he had to remember this wasn't real. Dammit, even if she wasn't Kane's daughter he couldn't afford to be distracted by a pretty face and intelligent mind.

Grady took a sip of his beer and forced his brain back to the moment and the goal. Eli Kane.

"One thing Harry does know how to do is keep his beer." Brynn licked her lips again and took another big swallow.

"It always tastes better closer to home." He licked his own lips. "It's probably the only thing I miss about Maine."

She laughed. "The beer? Not the wild ocean, or rugged coastline and beautiful countryside?"

"Now that you mention it." His gaze slid to the bar. "Seems to still be drawing in the tourists."

"Hard to beat the romantic image of a lighthouse and lobster pots."

Grady gave a mock shudder. "In the Antilles maybe."

Brynn snorted.

Grady watched as Cowboy wrapped an arm around Donnelly's shoulders and met his eyes in the mirror behind the bar. He gave the guy a slanted look. Ryan Sullivan was living dangerously.

Donnelly hitched herself back onto the stool beside him, breaking the connection. Then she ran her hand over Ryan's butt, pinching him hard enough to make him visibly flinch.

Grady hid his smile in his beer. Donnelly could stand up for herself, but she had teammates who would do it for her if necessary. Cowboy was a serial womanizer, but if he messed with Donnelly there'd be trouble.

He glanced around the bar and recognized a couple of the old fellas sitting at the table opposite. He nodded, and they nodded back but without a friendly smile.

Thank you, Agent Ropero.

He didn't recognize everyone, but it had been a while.

Brynn checked her watch. "I'm going to the restroom. Watch my drink for me, would you?"

She headed off, and Grady was surprised she trusted him—although as everyone in the bar was openly staring at him maybe it wasn't so surprising.

As soon as she disappeared a screech of legs across the old floorboards alerted him that Caleb Quayle had finally found his gumption at the bottom of his glass.

Caleb sauntered over with two of his skinny friends shadowing him. They were all tall lads. White, young, stupid. Grady had been exactly like them before he'd decided to clean up his act and live a life that would make his grandmother proud.

"Hey, asshole. Brynn doesn't need the likes of you sniffing around her."

Grady caught Cowboy's amused gaze as he swiveled to watch the show. Grady took another sip of beer. "Don't you think it's up to Brynn as to who she spends time with?"

Caleb's reddened eyes narrowed. He didn't like that idea, and he didn't like being talked back to. He leaned closer. "Why don't you go back where you came from? No one wants you around here. You don't belong here anymore."

Grady slowly finished his beer and then stood. The three younger men started to relax as if they thought they were scaring him off.

Big mistake.

"You need to step away and mind your own business. I don't want any trouble, but I will give it back to you if you start something," he said slowly.

Caleb stuck his face close to Grady's. His breath was as potent as lighter fuel. "Get out before we kick your ass, old man."

It was the "old man" that hit the mark.

Grady had Caleb turned around and his arm pinned behind his back before the other man could blink. He used the big lummox as a shield against the attempts the other idiots made to punch him.

Cowboy sat on the stool openly grinning while Donnelly looked on impatiently.

Harry Butler came out of the kitchen. "I don't want any trouble here. Grady, you need to leave—"

"Oh, I don't think so, Harry." The voice was high and clear, but Grady didn't glance away from one shaven-headed goon who looked as if he might be especially brainless. "Caleb and his friends are obviously drunk and harassing Special Agent Steel who has the right to defend himself." Brynn stood at the end of the bar with her chin up and her arms crossed. "You should punish the perpetrators, not the victim."

Grady's eyebrows rose at being classed as a victim and also the fact Brynn Webster, who'd been so shy she'd hidden in her mother's skirts when she was a little girl, was sticking up for him. *Him.*

When was the last time anyone in this town had taken his side?

Most likely it was his grandmother. Who'd supported him even when he hadn't deserved it. A woman he'd loved so much it had levelled him with grief when she died. He still missed her every single day.

Caleb was trying to squirm free of his hold and managed a vicious kick into Grady's shin. Grady bit back a curse and shoved the young man's arm high enough that if Caleb moved again, he'd pop it out of the shoulder joint. Grady was tempted to arrest the guy—or kick his ass. The former would break his cover, and he wasn't willing to sacrifice a chance at Eli Kane for this little shit. Kicking his ass might give him temporary satisfaction but would be unfair considering Grady's training and Caleb's current state of inebriation. Even with three-on-one it would only take seconds to put them all down. He had no desire to inflict pain, but he would protect himself and others if he had to.

"They were defending your honor, little lady." Cowboy laid on the Montana drawl thick as honey and hopped off his stool before tipping his cowboy hat to Brynn.

Brynn stared at Ryan with wide eyes. "What does my honor have to do with anything? What even *is* that?"

"These men suggested the gentlemen you're sitting with should leave you alone." Cowboy's drawl was so exaggerated Grady could barely understand what he was saying. But he recognized Ryan was stirring the pot, something he excelled at. "They suggested he wasn't good enough for you."

The muscles in Brynn's jaw flexed, and she tapped her foot impatiently. "No one tells me who I spend time with, Caleb Quayle. At least Agent Steel helped me pull Milton out of the water last night—unlike some people who just watched."

"Probably killed him first," one of the others muttered.

"I could have shot Milton for all you know." Brynn pointed at Caleb. "He's as likely to have murdered Milton before running around to the other side of the harbor and standing there like a spare part on the pier to watch me and Grady take a swim in arctic conditions."

"I didn't kill no-one."

"Well, you certainly didn't dive in to help me when I was half drowned and on the verge of freezing to death either. You and your idiot friends can keep your thoughts about who I spend time with to yourselves. It's none of your damn business."

Brynn took a breath.

She was glorious when she was mad, and Grady would be lying if he said he didn't fall for her just a little in that moment. Grady shoved the younger man away.

"Out. The three of you. Out before I call the cops who've better things to do." Harry had finally come to the decision to oust the troublemakers.

A little late, but Grady had never really trusted the guy. He eyed him again contemplatively. Harry Butler fit the age and size of Eli Kane. He didn't have a safe deposit box in his own name, but there was one for the business.

Brynn walked over and grabbed her coat. "We're leaving, too." She wrapped her scarf around her neck as she eyed Caleb and his friends, who were all standing there uncertain as to what to do. "Consider yourselves banned from the café until you've apologized to both me and Agent Steel."

All three of them looked horrified by the announcement, but Caleb's pride was still ruling his mouth. He sneered. "We'll wait until the café has new owners. Won't be long from what I've heard."

Brynn's expression went flat and emotionless as the barb struck home. "Then you're banned for as long as anyone named Webster owns the place, and I might even make it a condition of sale that you're banned after that, too." She whirled and walked away.

Grady wanted to punch the guy, but that wasn't exactly taking the high road.

He narrowed his eyes at all of them. "Assaulting a federal agent is a felony offence." Caleb's friends went sheet white at that. "I'm going to keep it to a verbal warning this one time because I don't want to drive to Bangor to have you all processed. Next time, I won't be so understanding." He picked up his own coat, exchanged a glance with Cowboy and Donnelly before hurrying after Brynn, who'd already left the bar.

He ran to catch up with her. The night was dark. The clouds playing hide-and-go-seek with the moon. "Hey, let me walk you home. I'm going the same way."

He meant it as a joke to break the tension, but she shot him a look he couldn't read. She'd been magnificent. He wanted to hug her. Worse, he wanted to plant a kiss on her lips and see if they tasted as good as they looked.

She looked as if she might throw up.

"I'm sorry that happened, Brynn." He spoke carefully, struggling to navigate her mood, knowing she was justifiably upset.

Her hand clutched her coat together near her throat, and her eyes flashed in the glow of a streetlight. "It wasn't your fault. None of that was your fault." Her voice vibrated with emotion. Gone was the flat gaze. It was replaced by burning anger.

It had his own feelings sticking in his throat. "Yeah, but I'm sorry anyway."

They walked in silence for a few moments. The snow had almost melted off the sidewalks, but it was still icy. The temperatures were slated to drop even further until that blizzard arrived later in the week. He hoped they found Kane before it hit.

"Did you get your gun back yet?" she asked.

"Not yet," he said in surprise. He wore the concealed weapon Novak had given him on his ankle but wasn't about to advertise the fact.

"You should go talk to the Sheriff about getting it back ASAP." She blew out a breath of frosted air. "Caleb Quayle is a thug. Worse, he comes from an entire family of thugs. The fact you're suspended from duty means he'll think he has an opportunity to hurt you without any serious consequences." She shot him a glance. "He's hotheaded, but he's also cunning."

He hadn't expected her to give a damn. "I can take care of myself."

She threw up her hands. "Now you're a superhero."

"I never said that."

"What if he pulls a gun on you when he finds you alone somewhere?"

"He won't."

"What if he does?" she pushed.

He scratched his forehead. Was she really worried about him, or was something else bothering her? "I'm sorry about what he said about new owners. It was a dick move, and it hurt you."

Her eyes looked glassy with tears. "He knew exactly what he was saying. The worst thing is that's what I've been trying to persuade my parents to do with the café. Sell and enjoy their retirement while they can."

"Why don't they?"

Brynn stopped walking for a moment and forcibly swallowed. "My mom built that place from a struggling dive into a thriving business. I think she sees the café as a reflection of herself. If she's not strong enough to run it, then…she's not strong enough to survive." Her words trailed away as she hurried ahead.

Hell.

Brynn's pain was a reminder of why it was so much easier to be alone.

The wind sliced through him with the precision of a scalpel blade. Damn, it was cold.

"Why do you think someone killed Milton Bodurek?" she asked suddenly.

"I don't know." He thought about what Saul had told him— that Milton hadn't been such a nice guy after all. People like that made quiet enemies. "But, like we've established, I've been gone for a long time."

A frown worried her brows.

"Why?"

She shook herself. Glanced at him sideways. "I keep thinking that he must have been shot either when I was cleaning up in the café or as I was walking down to the harbor."

"I thought you said you didn't hear a shot."

"I didn't." Her teeth pulled distractedly at her lower lip.

"But…" What wasn't she telling him?

"Nothing."

Was there something in Milton's life that had gotten him killed? Or was his murder somehow related to Grady's investigation?

"What's bothering you?"

"Sounds silly now."

"What?" he pushed.

"I thought I heard someone behind me when I cut down the

alley last night. But when I turned around it was just a tomcat. Scared the crap out of me."

Could someone have been following her? Watching her? "Ever experienced something like that before?"

Her laughter came out as another puff of frost. "Only weekly in Boston."

The gift of fear. "You listen to your intuition. That's good."

"Yeah, that's what my father always says."

"He's a smart man."

"He is."

"And he loves you."

Her smile was soft. "He does." Her eyes got that far away look again. "I'm not sure what he's going to do if we lose Mom…"

Grady reached out and squeezed her hand through her gloves. "Treatments are getting better all the time."

She nodded. "Yeah. They are."

He wanted to ask more about her dad, but he couldn't think of a way to do it without raising suspicion.

"Are there any security cameras at the back of the café?" he asked.

"No, there aren't." She tucked her chin into her scarf out of the bitter wind. "You sound like a law enforcement officer now."

"I *am* a law enforcement officer."

"Yeah," she sighed softly. "I keep forgetting."

21

"Aren't we going to follow him?" Donnelly asked, her mouth way too close to his ear.

Ryan watched the three drunken young men file bullishly out of the bar after Grady and the fiery redhead.

"Might look a bit suspicious if we all leave. Grady's a big boy. He can handle those yahoos."

Ryan glanced at the two Russian tourists who were also climbing to their feet and preparing to leave. They'd shared a brief exchange at the bar earlier, comparing notes on the best places to visit. "Did you get photos of everybody in here?"

It had been the main reason for coming to the bar, plus the fact he was avoiding being alone with Donnelly for as long as humanly possible.

"Yeah. Already sent them to Novak."

Hopefully, biometrics would eliminate some of the people here, but it was possible Kane had undergone enough plastic surgery on his boney facial structures, like his forehead and nose bone, or had had jaw and chin implants, which could make the algorithms useless. Even makeup could mess up the software on occasion if you knew what you were doing.

The photos they had of Kane were few and of a much younger

man, so the algorithms were already based on projections made from limited sources. Kane had taken or destroyed all the personal photographs of himself and his family, presumably to impede the hunt.

It had worked.

Eli Kane had been a master of disguise. He could have gone anywhere in the world. Why come here to Deception Cove? Maybe a better question would be, why not?

It was close to both the sea and the Canadian border which meant he had options. Did he have a bolt hole with the Canucks? Another identity with a Maple Leaf passport?

Kane had worked in the Counterintelligence Division for a stint in the eighties. Had he known the traitors Ames, Hanssen, or Clarkson? Ryan eyed the Russians as they headed to the door.

Were they simple tourists? Or something more sinister?

"Let's head back to the room and see if there were any hits." Donnelly yawned widely, seemingly unaffected by the situation the two of them found themselves in. "We should get some sleep."

Sleep?

Goddamn it. He didn't even know what the problem was. He'd dated prettier women. Had a yen for redheads like the woman Grady was targeting.

The way she'd stuck up for Grady was admirable, but he was reserving judgment because he recognized the glint in Grady's gaze when he looked at Brynn Webster.

Ryan, for once, planned to be the objective observer when it came to women.

Right.

He finished his beer and stepped off the stool, nodded to the barkeep as he followed Donnelly out the door and up the wooden staircase and through a maze of corridors until they reached their room in a gothic tower on the top floor. Their cover was that he owned a ranch out in Montana, and he and his girl were taking a short vacation during what was generally a quiet time. It was close enough to the truth that if anyone asked him a question about ranch life, he could bore them to death with the details. Donnelly was a former soldier who now lived with him, and they'd met on vacation in Hawaii a couple of years ago.

She unlocked the door, and he steeled himself as he walked inside.

In daylight, they had a sea view apparently. He kept his eyes on the light from the lighthouse as Donnelly stretched and yawned. According to the desk clerk, you could see Nova Scotia from the window on a good day. So far all they'd seen was fog.

"Want to use the shower?" Donnelly seemed to have forgotten that she'd propositioned him less than a week ago, but he was having trouble putting it out of his mind. She'd been upset following news of her father's death and looking for anything to distract her. He understood the mindset better than most.

Fortunately, he only had one unbreakable rule when it came to who he had sex with—absolutely no work colleagues, not even civilian contractors for the FBI.

"Later. You go ahead. I'll call Novak."

She sent him a grateful smile as she picked up the things she needed and headed into the bathroom.

Ryan avoided complications the way mice avoided cats. He didn't date. He was open and honest about the fact that anything that happened would be a purely physical encounter that would hopefully be mutually pleasing. There were women he'd had sex with more than once but only the ones that didn't have that soft vulnerability in their eyes.

Despite being the first woman to get into the Hostage Rescue Team, Meghan Donnelly had vulnerability in spades. And she was his teammate.

You didn't fuck a teammate.

Ever.

The bed was king-size and had those wooden posts that made his mind go blank to everything but the possibilities. He tossed his cowboy hat on the dresser and toed off his boots. He eyed the two-seater sofa and decided instead on the recliner that faced the ocean.

He heard the shower turn on, and his mouth went dry. He dug out his cell to call Novak and was punched in the throat by the background image.

He sat, heavily, his knees giving way. His wife Becky, riding a quiet, gray mare back at the ranch. She'd been his twin sister's best friend in high school, and he'd stolen her away for himself as soon as he'd gotten the chance.

The love of his damn life.

She'd died shortly after giving birth to their daughter, and he'd died as well, for the longest time. Emotion had tears welling in his eyes and his throat begging for the numbing effect of a whisky or ten.

He closed his eyes as an old familiar misery crashed over him, but it was different this time, and he knew why. He knew exactly why. He breathed in. Counted to ten.

Then he called Novak.

22

When they reached the house, Grady waved Brynn to go ahead of him up the dark path. Out of the corner of his eye, something gray and shaggy moved in the shadows.

He swore quietly, then ran around Brynn and up the stairs to the main house. He let himself inside, grabbed a bowl and fork and tin of dog food he'd picked up at the store earlier. He ran back outside as Brynn stood there staring at him as if he'd lost his mind. His eyes scanned the area.

He peeled open the can and set the bowl on the ground. He whistled and tapped the fork against the side of the tin.

Brynn watched him silently.

He felt like an idiot.

He was about to give up when the dog peered around the corner of the building next door.

"Here, boy." Grady scooped the canned food into the bowl and stood back.

They watched together as the dog slunk toward them. He sniffed cautiously, then licked at the gravy before crouching warily away. When the meat hit his tastebuds, the dog levered forward again and started eating hungrily, gulping down the food.

"Don't move," Grady murmured under his breath. He took Brynn's hand when she looked as if she was about to approach the animal. She'd removed her glove, and her skin was cold. That flash of electricity flared between them again as he rubbed her fingers.

The dog's fur was dirty and knotted. His hips were visible despite the thick coat and he seemed to be favoring one front paw.

Grady drew Brynn down so they were both at eye level with the dog, who ate like a starved wolf but kept a wary eye on them both.

"Poor thing," Brynn said sympathetically.

"Yeah, poor thing."

Grady let go of her hand and scraped the fork around the remainder of the food in the tin. He held it out as the dog licked the bowl so clean it gleamed.

After a brief hesitation the dog stretched out his nose toward the fork, but a door banged nearby, and the dog shot off down the street.

Brynn released a breath. "Any idea who it belongs to?"

"Saul said it belonged to Caleb Quayle." His voice firmed. He wished he'd punched the guy now.

"What are you planning to do?" Brynn eyed him like she knew him already.

"Feed him. See if I can gain his trust and get him in from the cold before this blizzard hits. Get him cleaned up and take him to the vet."

"I'm not sure Caleb's going to be too pleased with that."

"I don't give a…" He cleared his throat. "Caleb will be too busy dealing with Animal Control to complain."

He realized suddenly that they were both kneeling on the frozen front lawn in the shifting moonlight. They stared at one another for a long moment.

Grady would have kissed her if it wasn't for the fact he was supposed to be working and it wouldn't be fair to pile more hurt on this woman. She deserved better.

Her lips twitched. "Careful. People will start seeing beneath that tough-guy exterior and realize you're actually a big softy."

Soft was the last thing he was feeling right now.

He helped her to her feet, felt the weird urge to keep holding onto her. Instead, he let go. "I wouldn't want to deprive them of their long-cherished prejudices."

He picked up the bowl. He'd clean it, fill it with warm water, and leave it at the base of his steps. It would freeze overnight, but he'd replace it in the morning.

"I'm sorry I've never noticed the poor thing running around before." Guilt dragged at Brynn's expression.

Grady wanted to slide his hand around the back of her head and draw her closer for a kiss. "You've had a lot going on."

She looked at him. "Maybe. Maybe not. I should have noticed he was suffering." She stepped back abruptly. "Good night, Grady."

"Good night, Brynn."

She flashed a look over her shoulder. Dragged her lips to one side before saying. "You're not the villain this town wants to paint you, are you?"

His gaze locked onto hers. "Maybe I like being seen as the town bad boy."

"Because you get all the girls?"

He realized with sudden clarity he didn't want all the girls. He wanted one. This one. "You should probably go inside."

Instead, she came toward him and planted a hand against his chest. He held himself perfectly still. She rose onto tiptoe and kissed his cheek, just glancing over the side of his mouth. He closed his eyes and concentrated on the feel of her soft lips, the scent of her, pretty and floral like the freesias his grandmother used to grow right here in this garden.

She was gone before he opened his eyes. Maybe he'd dreamed the whole episode.

No, he hadn't dreamed it.

A grin broke out over his face.

Then his mood fell. His plan was working, but he had no desire to hurt Brynn any more than she'd already been hurt. He was lying to her—not about what he might or might not be feeling, which was a dose of horny and a mix of something else, something that felt a lot like friendship—but about why he was here.

He was using her, and he was pretty sure that if she found out, she'd never forgive him.

It was too late to change things. Too late to reject that innocent, soul-consuming kiss. Not that he would have. Could have.

He trudged up the stairs to the house, feeling like the world's biggest asshole. He needed to back away from intimacy with Brynn, no matter how much he enjoyed it.

Keep it friendly but platonic.

Don't lose focus.

He had a job to do. Catching Eli Kane was all that mattered, along with the person who'd callously murdered Milton Bodurek last night. Maybe prove to this town he really wasn't the bad guy.

Sure.

23

B rynn sat on the side of the bed staring at her last images of Aiden. He was propped against the dark wooden headboard of a bed with a goofy smile on his face, chest naked, blankets bunched around his waist.

The reason for the goofy expression was probably the woman sitting beside him, pressed close enough that her face was largely hidden by her sweep of shiny blonde hair.

Aiden had always wanted Brynn to dye her hair blonde—just for fun.

The blonde woman had her hand under the covers, and there was no doubt what she was doing.

If blondes were his type why the hell had he married her?

The second photo was a sideview selfie of the two of them laying down in the same bed, kissing.

It was the more innocent of the two, but the fact he looked so consumed with passion for the other woman…

Brynn remembered the cops had asked about her sex life when the bastard had first disappeared, as if they thought she might have harmed Aiden in some way. She had wanted to die.

She could probably have forgiven Aiden for leaving her if he'd done it in such a way that she hadn't been quite so blindsided and humiliated. What he'd done had been cruel, though she doubted he'd seen it that way.

He hadn't thought of her at all. Not with the blonde taking care of his needs.

Were they still together?

Who cared?

He'd stolen everything from their joint bank accounts. They'd been saving for the down payment on a house where they'd planned to raise a family together.

He'd been estranged from his own family. She should have seen that as a warning sign and not assumed that they were the assholes.

Her finger hovered over the delete button, but still she hesitated. She closed her eyes.

She wasn't ready to delete the images and not because she still loved her cheating ex.

It was a reminder.

That, despite all the flowery promises, Aiden hadn't loved her enough to stay. At the first sign of trouble, he'd dumped her without a word of remorse.

She turned off her phone and tossed it on the bedside table.

She needed that reminder right now more than ever.

Men were jerks.

And yet…

She smiled.

The good news was that kissing Grady Steel earlier hadn't felt like cheating. Of course, it had only been a restrained, polite peck. But inside, feelings and desires had started to uncoil and escape the tight braids where she'd constrained them.

Suddenly, there was a growing ache inside her, an ache she wanted filled. She wasn't looking for a man in her life, but maybe a little fooling around wouldn't kill her.

Might even be fun.

She suspected the man upstairs would be excellent in bed. She wasn't looking for anything complicated. She didn't have room in her life for a relationship.

But sex…

Damn.

Now she couldn't stop thinking about it.

No one had to know. He wasn't staying around.

She liked sex. She didn't want to spend her life without occasionally having wild, hot, monkey sex with someone who caught her eye.

No one had caught her eye since Aiden. Only Grady Steel.

Her heart raced a little.

What was wrong with right now?

Slowly, she threw back the covers and tiptoed across the apartment floor and up the stairs to the main house.

She quietly slipped both bolts back and flipped the lock. She turned the knob slowly and pushed the door wide. Ironic that she was entering uninvited when she'd been so fearful the night before.

She'd been upstairs when she'd first moved in. Crystal had shown her around, hoping to tempt her into renting the larger space.

"Grady?"

The house was quiet, only the sound of the heating and the wind against the windows breaking the silence.

She snuck along the hallway and climbed the stairs, quickly, before she lost her nerve.

"Grady? Are you awake?" She crept to the door of the primary bedroom and knocked before pushing it open. "Grady?"

The room stood empty. She closed her eyes and laughed as she leaned her forehead against the cool wood of the doorjamb.

He wasn't here. Or he was staying quiet and pretending not to be here…

A feeling of foolishness swept over her. She looked down at her old, comfy pajamas. What the hell was she thinking?

She backed quickly away and then ran down the moonlit stairs not wanting to be caught now.

What did she actually *know* about the guy? That he was suspended from the FBI for being accused of a terrible crime. So what if he was kind to a dog? He could still be a villain.

She locked and bolted the basement door and slipped silently back down to the basement suite. Crawled into bed and huddled beneath the comforter.

Men were overrated. Sex was overrated.

She closed her eyes and tried to forget both existed.

Her phone buzzed, and she quickly picked it up, scared something had happened with her mother.

> STAY AWAY FROM GRADY STEEL IF YOU
> KNOW WHATS GOOD 4U.

She squinted at the text that came from an unknown source. "You have got to be kidding me."

> Is this you, Caleb?

She stared at her messages, but the phone remained stubbornly unresponsive.

24

G rady had taken the time to change into all black before he'd headed back out into the snowy night. He'd stuck to the shadows as he'd silently worked his way to the alley that bordered the Sea Spray Café.

Had Brynn sensed something last night? Something beside a feral cat?

Milton Bodurek's killer perhaps?

Grady stood for a few minutes listening for anyone else who might be out here in the darkness.

The smell of frozen, stale garbage from a nearby trashcan filtered through the ever-present scents of a Down East winter—brine, seaweed, dirty snow.

The gulls were silent for once, but the boats rang out their perpetual percussion to the restless motion of the ocean.

The air felt taut, as if waiting for something to happen.

He inched up the alley until he reached the café and shone his red flashlight over the ground. The slicing wind scoured away any trace of footprints. Even his own had disappeared behind him.

A quiet hiss almost made him jump out of his skin, but he

thrust aside the surprise and pushed open the wooden gate that led into the yard of the building next door to the café.

He shone the flashlight quickly around the shadows, but there was no one there except for a ferocious-looking orange tabby who eyed Grady as if he was considering him for dinner.

He ignored the cat and turned his attention to the ground. Paw prints crisscrossed the frozen mud, along with a few bird tracks and a scatter of bloody feathers.

Several shoe and boot prints were clearly visible on the ground along with a smattering of cigarette butts.

Margery Tomey, who ran the high-end gift shop, was a tiny woman in her early sixties. He didn't think she was the boot-wearing, cigarette-smoking type.

She wasn't married or living with anyone. Maybe she had someone who worked for her, but it didn't seem to fit his idea of the woman or her shop. Deliveries went in the front door from his recollection.

He placed a quarter beside the prints and took a few shots with his cell, including some close-ups.

He pulled out an evidence envelope from a vest pocket and collected the cigarette butts. Stuffed them in his pocket.

It was probably nothing. People having a quick smoke. Maybe the cook from the café…

Grady's FBI colleagues were doing a deep dive into Angus Hubner, but getting a sample of his DNA might speed up the process.

The cat hissed again and Grady wondered if he could find a way to trap it and take it to the vet, find it a nice home in a warm barn somewhere.

The animal seemed to read his mind and turned and jumped up and over the neighboring fence.

He smiled.

Instinct was a beautiful thing.

A moment later something crashed into his skull and Grady was driven to his knees.

He swore.

Another blow had his brain ringing as he lay for a split-second face down in the snow, bleeding like a stuck pig from his scalp.

He quickly rolled, breathing hard. Spotted his assailant, also wearing dark clothing complete with a ski mask, darting out the gate. Grady got to his knees and braced one leg to stand. Nausea hit him in a wave that had him swaying.

Fuck.

He threw up, then staggered to his feet. Followed his attacker down the alleyway. He spotted the asshole jumping into a white van before accelerating away.

Grady braced himself against a lamppost feeling like a goddamn fool. He'd let himself get distracted by a *cat*. Blood continued to drip down his face and neck, and his vision wasn't as sharp as he'd like. He spit out the sour taste in his mouth.

The blows could have killed him. If he didn't have such a thick head, they probably would have. The cold started to penetrate his layers, and he wondered if his attackers' plan had been to leave him unconscious in the snow, slowly bleeding out and freezing to death.

Grady took photographs of the tire tracks and footprints and watched the crime scene tape flutter at the marina. Then he called his boss.

25

Brynn carried the shopping bags through the door of her parents' house and placed them on the kitchen counter. "Hey there."

Her dad turned from the stove where he was tasting from a large saucepan. "You're early."

She pulled him down to kiss his bearded cheek. She wasn't about to tell him she couldn't sleep because whenever she'd closed her eyes, she dreamed of Milton Bodurek's pale corpse waking up and smiling at her. Or that someone had used an anonymous text as a cowardly way of warning her away from a man she'd almost thrown herself at last night.

She peered into the pot. "What're you making?"

The corners of her father's blue eyes crinkled attractively as he smiled. "Chicken noodle soup. Good for the soul, apparently. Not as good as Angus's, but pretty damn tasty if I do say so myself."

"No one is as good as Angus. Let's hope he never figures it out, or he'll want a raise."

"We should probably give him one anyway."

"I'll speak to the manager." She took a spoon and tasted. "Wow, Dad, that's delicious. I know who to call if we get stuck in the café."

He chuckled the way she'd hoped.

"I'll go fetch the rest of the shopping before—"

"I'll do it. You go in to see your mother. She's sick of my face. I'll bring you some brunch through in a little while. In the conservatory."

"Okay. Thanks." Brynn slipped off her shoes then unwound her scarf and draped it over the back of a bench that sat under the kitchen table. She slipped off her coat and did the same, then braced herself before walking through the formal living room to the bright sunny conservatory that her dad had put on the house years ago. Even though it was January, the room was full of lush, blooming plants and two matching recliners. Her mom sat in one, her eyes closed, her skin almost translucent. Today she wore a soft T-shirt and stretchy pants. Her mom had gained a few pounds, either from the treatment itself or the fact she wasn't as active as she used to be. Her formerly thick red hair was shaved off, and she wore a silk scarf on her head that was deep crimson.

Brynn knew her mother's changed appearance bothered her, but hair grew back, and people could regain their fitness—as long as they were alive.

Brynn held her breath, unwilling to disturb her mother's rest but Gwendolyn Webster must have sensed her presence and opened her eyes. She scanned Brynn up and down as if to reassure herself that she was okay.

Brynn came fully inside the room, leaned over, and kissed her papery cheek. "How are you feeling?"

"Better than I did yesterday. I thought you weren't coming by until this afternoon. It's not even eleven."

"I woke at the crack of dawn and knocked out the projects I needed to get done in record time. Figured I'd come over early and scrounge some food."

"Ha. Hardly scrounging. We owe you so much for coming back to run the café." Her mother's smile was slightly bashful. "I guess your father and I both secretly hope you might decide to stay." She squeezed Brynn's hand. "But we also realize that's self-ish. I miss you when you aren't around, though."

A wave of guilt rushed over Brynn.

"And I want you to be happy." Her mom might be sick, but she didn't miss much. "Ever since that idiot left, I've been worried about you."

"I don't want to talk about Aiden."

Brynn sat in what was usually her dad's recliner. From here, they could look outside and see the birds on the feeders that her dad had hung on high branches out of the reach of deer.

In summer, the hummingbirds returned, and those feeders were maintained religiously.

Her parents had five acres surrounded by a mixed forest of evergreens and deciduous trees. A small stream ran behind the property. They had a large vegetable plot and a flower garden that was full of daisies, salvia, lavender bushes, and hydrangeas when it bloomed. A climbing rose sprawled over the brick wall of the original part of the house. The addition sat at a right angle.

Her mother was the architect of what went where in the house and the garden, but Brynn's father was the brawn. A former military man, he enjoyed the work. He might grumble when he had to move a shrub for the third time, but Brynn had a feeling he secretly loved it. As long as her mother was happy, he was happy.

"I hear we have a new server?" Her mom thankfully changed the subject.

"You spoke to Linda?"

"I did indeed. I could hear Kent grumbling in the background about wanting his wife back." Gwendolyn rolled her eyes. She wasn't a fan of her friend's husband.

"Kent wants her to retire. You both should think about retiring."

"And do what? Sit here day after day driving your father batty?"

"That's generally what happens." Brynn reached out a hand and took her mom's. "Travel maybe? Get a hobby?"

Her mother snorted. "Maybe I'll take up horseback riding."

"Why not?" asked Brynn. "You have fields for a couple of horses and room in the barn for dad to make a stable. And just so you know, I put an ad in the paper for another server."

Her mother's eyes widened. "Can we afford two new hires?"

Brynn leaned back in the chair and flicked the mechanism so it went back. "Yes, you can afford two new hires, and I can't afford to neglect my own business, which I have been doing the past few weeks. Jackie isn't reliable, and Linda wants to cut her hours or retire. Hiring two new people would give us all some breathing room."

Brynn watched her mother through her lashes. She didn't look happy, but she also didn't look like she was going to fight her on this either.

A welcome change.

She heard the rattle of the trolley, and a moment later, her father rolled in two bowls of soup, freshly made bread still steaming from the oven, and a plate of cheese, crackers, and fruit.

"You're not having any?" asked Brynn.

"I'm going to nip out to the hardware store and pick up a few things. I want to make a chicken coop and start producing our own eggs."

Her mother's expression was not impressed, nor was her tone. "Chickens."

"What's wrong with chickens?" her dad asked patiently.

Her mother's lips quirked. "Who's going to look after them when we retire and travel the world?"

Her dad grinned. "Maybe Brynn will house-sit."

"She's not going to meet a man sitting out here looking after chickens."

"I don't want to meet a man," Brynn muttered in annoyance. Nor did she particularly want to look after chickens.

"I heard that Grady Steel has matured into quite a hotty." There was a gleam in her mother's eyes. "I always liked that young man despite what some people said about him."

Brynn's brows stretched high.

She thought about the kiss she'd pressed to his cheek last night. It had been chaste, and it was almost sweet that he hadn't grabbed her and tried for more—*possibly disappointing*. But she was quietly relieved that he hadn't been home when she'd gone upstairs, although she did wonder where he'd disappeared to. She realized now she wasn't quite ready to make the leap into a physical relationship. She wasn't sure she'd ever be truly ready to make that leap again.

"You and Linda apparently had a lot to discuss," Brynn said wryly.

Her mom cackled then started coughing. Her dad quickly raised the back of her chair. Her mom waved him away as she recovered. "I'm fine. I'm fine. Go buy your bits and pieces you need for your chicken coop. Although, why you don't already have everything in that enormous workshop of yours…"

He hovered beside the chair. "You're sure you're okay, love?"

"Yes." She smiled patiently. "I'm fine. Now go so I can eat before it gets cold."

"I'll be here, Dad. Take all the time you need." Brynn knew looking after her mom had taken a toll on him, not just the daily care, but taking her to treatment, worrying about her constantly. Maybe Brynn *should* move back home and help out more. She'd wanted to maintain some independence, and her mother didn't like being fussed over at the best of times but…

Her dad hesitated. "If you're sure."

"Get out of here. I want to pump Brynn for information about hot guys, and you need a break. Go relax for a few hours."

He rested his hands on his hips. "I'm going to buy wood, not hit the spa."

"Do you *want* to hit the spa?" her mom asked.

"I'd rather stick pins in my eyes, but I'll go if it makes you happy."

Her mom's eyes grew shiny. "What did I ever do to deserve you?"

Her dad leaned down and kissed her. "I'm the lucky one. You concentrate on getting better." Her father's voice wasn't quite steady as he squeezed his wife's thin shoulders and strode quickly out the door.

Her mom watched him go, and they both listened as the car started and he drove away.

"The man is a damn saint to put up with me all these years."

Brynn rolled her eyes. "I think he likes it well enough."

"I guess. Promise me you'll look after him if anything happens to me, Brynn."

"Don't think that way."

"I have cancer. I have to think that way." Her mom arched the bare skin where her eyebrows used to be. She meticulously drew them back on when she went out and wore a stylish wig, but she didn't bother when at home. "Promise."

Brynn huffed out a breath and picked up her soup bowl. "Eat your lunch, and I'll think about it."

"Stubborn minx."

She sipped her soup. "Who do I take after, I wonder?"

Her mother's smile grew sad as she carefully picked up a hunk of bread and slowly started chewing.

"So is Grady Steel hot, or is Linda exaggerating?" her mom asked after a few bites. "I mean, she married Kent." She chuckled at her own joke.

"I suppose." Brynn shook her head in exasperation. "Well, he looks like he works out."

"Ha!" Her mother was delighted with the observation. "Did he say why he was in town beside the obvious that we've all seen on the Internet?"

"Only that he was deciding what to do with his grandmother's house while the FBI cleared his name." Brynn took a hunk of bread to go with the soup and thought about that text warning her off the guy. "I can tell you one thing you are not allowed to share, not even with Linda."

"Okay."

"Promise?"

"Pinky swear."

"He didn't know Crystal was using the place as an online B&B."

"What?"

"From what I can gather it's his house, but she was supposed to be looking after it for him."

"But she told us it was both of theirs and that she bought him out."

"Apparently not." Brynn spoke around the bread she chewed.

"That's hateful. She's spent years ripping into him when he's not here to defend himself, and the whole time she was fleecing him. What a miserable human being Crystal Grogan is." She ate another swallow of soup. "Why aren't I allowed to share? Might make the people around here a little less liable to think badly of him. Ban her from the café."

"I'm not going to ban her from the café. Grady doesn't want to give her a reason to hate him more." She cleared her throat. "And it's possible I already banned Caleb Quayle and two of his asinine friends from the café for attacking Grady in the bar last night. Probably shouldn't ban everyone in town if we want to survive."

"Caleb Quayle is like his father and uncles. A drunk and a bully. I take it Grady dealt with them?"

"Yeah. He wasn't hurt. Caleb was drunk and said some things that upset me. I banned him for life."

"You were in the bar?" Her mother wore an innocent smile.

"I went for a quick drink after I closed up—"

"With Grady?"

"Don't read anything into it," she warned.

"I wouldn't dream of it." The smile on her mother's face suggested otherwise.

"I'm not interested in relationships. Not after…"

"Who is talking about a relationship? A fling would be fine."

"Mom!"

"You're twenty-eight years old, Brynn, not seventy-eight. Just because you married a loser doesn't mean you have to stop living."

Brynn froze. "I haven't stopped living."

Her mother picked at her bread like a little bird. "You're scared, love. I understand that." She finished her soup and put the spoon on the tray. "But life is short, and it's a crime to waste it."

"Dammit, Mom." She held out her hand and gripped her mother's. "How am I supposed to argue with you right now?"

"Don't argue. I'm always right anyway. Live a little. Enjoy yourself while you can."

"Ironic, given all those years you spent telling me not to have sex…"

"When you were a kid, sure. That's my job."

"Remember when I went on a date with Darrell York those few times? You practically frog marched me to the doctor's office for birth control."

Her mom gave an exaggerated shudder. "You were going off to college. The idea of you getting pregnant when the world was on the verge of opening up for you horrified me."

Brynn didn't disagree. "You needn't have worried."

She'd had some old-fashioned notion of saving herself for someone special. Unfortunately, that someone special had destroyed her. But she smiled remembering that awful first date with Darrell. "The best contraception in the world was spending a little one-on-one time with the good deputy."

They both started laughing, giggling until tears rolled down their faces.

Finally, her mom lay back as if exhausted and grew serious. "I need to know you're happy." Her mother swallowed with difficulty. "In case I'm not around to fight all those battles with you that you'll no doubt have to face."

Worry lanced her. Brynn squeezed her mom's hand so hard they both winced, but neither let go.

"I am happy, Mom. I don't need a partner. I like being alone.

But maybe I'll think about hooking up with hot strangers for sex every once in a while."

"Fiend. That's not what I meant, and you know it."

Brynn had certainly thought about it last night. More than thought about it. And she was beginning to regret Grady hadn't been there when she'd turned up in his bedroom, ready and willing.

26

Grady's head still throbbed from last night's encounter. Figured he'd been hit with the butt end of a pistol, which beat a hollow-point from the other end but still sucked.

He'd met up with Ryan on the edge of town and, as ordered by his boss, visited the nearest emergency room in Blue Hill. Scans had shown the only thing seriously damaged had been his pride.

Hurt like hell though.

Ryan had dropped him back at home around 4 a.m., and Grady had taken some pain meds and slept for a few hours.

Now he headed down the street on foot, drawing his leather jacket closer together as the wind bit into his flesh like fangs. He wore a woolen cap to hide the two-inch gash that had needed four Steri-Strips to close.

Brynn had driven away in her car an hour ago. He didn't know where she'd gone.

He'd spent a couple of hours changing the locks and setting up his own top-of-the-line security cameras, front and back, aimed at the street. Feeds went straight to the task force. Ropero and Dobson would run any passing faces through facial rec programs looking for Kane.

Then Grady had gone through the list of males in the area that they could definitively rule out of being Kane based on his personal knowledge and their morphology. Kane was a white male, sixty-three years old. Six-foot-even. Anyone non-white or who'd lived in the town their whole lives could be eliminated. It cut the list dramatically, but not enough.

With a growing retirement population thanks to the beauty and isolation of the area, several hundred names remained. But when those names were crosschecked against people who rented safe deposit boxes in the only bank in town, the list shrank to twenty-eight.

An itch had started between Grady's shoulder blades as he'd stared at those names. They were getting closer to catching this guy. He knew it.

Gulls squawked on the tops of chimneys, and he realized how much he'd missed that sound, as irritating as it had been growing up. He hadn't seen the stray dog this morning, but he'd left a bowl of food and another of water at the bottom of the front steps before he'd headed out.

He walked north for two blocks then turned toward the impressive red brick building that housed the Hearst Savings & Loan. The bank sat in a large lot surrounded by neatly cut grass that appeared devoid of any fallen leaves. The building had an ornate gable above a central arched window with the date embossed in gold. 1876. All the ground floor windows were capped in delicate arches. The main double doors were protected by an elegant, curved stone porch held upright by four white columns.

He didn't know all the correct terminology for the architecture, but it was a magnificent building. Grady had never really appreciated that until now.

Funny how time seemed to have mellowed his feelings regarding the town itself. Maybe it was the knowledge he wasn't stuck here any longer. He was free to come and go as he pleased—

assuming he wasn't arrested for murder by a cop who apparently hated his guts.

Could his assailant last night have been Darrell?

It was possible. But what would the guy have been doing skulking around in the darkness?

Following him?

He didn't know.

Grady climbed the bank's steps and headed through the huge front door. There was a short queue of customers, so he took the opportunity to look around. A security guard, whose face he didn't recognize, stood looking bored to one side of the door. The floor was the same black-and-white checkered tile he remembered, but the rest of the space had been fully modernized. The old, tall, solid-oak counters had been ripped out and replaced by snazzy eye-level desks, with the tellers sitting in comfortable-looking chairs with modern computer screens in front of them.

The main vault was still housed in the same large space, off to the left. It was old-fashioned but probably impenetrable from everyone except the most skilled safe-cracker. The safe deposit boxes were in the first vaulted room. The safe with all the money in it was set within another structure built inside the first.

Grady glanced at the tellers, surprised to see Miss Fancy Lucette at her post despite her recent ordeal.

The mood was somber, many eyes reddened from crying. Everyone wore black.

What would happen to the bank now Milton was dead? People must presumably be worried about their jobs.

Luck was with him, and Fancy had an opening just as he was next in line to be served.

She glanced up, and her eyes widened in warm surprise. "Why Grady Steel. It's been a long time."

She'd been a good friend of his grandma's, but she'd rarely visited the house. His grandmother and Miss Lucette had tended to go have tea and cake out somewhere on Fancy's days off.

"Miss Lucette. How are you?"

She had a hooked nose and deep-set brown eyes that missed nothing. Her hair was iron-gray, cut pixie-short these days. "I've been better."

Grady pressed his lips together in a sympathetic twist. "I heard about the robbery."

A visible shudder ran over her narrow shoulders. "I was thinking more of the terrible murder of Mr. Bodurek, but I take your point."

"I'm sorry for your loss."

"Thank you. He was a good man—most of the time. It's despicable, what one man will do to another."

She wasn't wrong.

"I spoke to Saul yesterday."

Her eyes flashed at that, but she didn't speak.

"He told me someone pointed a gun directly at you and threatened you. That must have been terrifying."

"No respect." She shook her head. "Not like in the old days." She blinked away the sudden sheen of tears.

Crime had been going on since man had crawled out of the swamp, but Grady regretted pushing her. "Have they arrested anyone yet?"

Her expression turned rueful. "I would have thought you'd hear before me. Have the FBI sorted out that issue of mistaken identity yet?"

He stood there staring at her stupidly.

"What? Any fool who knew you as a little boy would know you'd never abandon someone on the side of the road, let alone a senior." Her gaze was compassionate, clearly waiting for him to catch up. "I watched you with your grandparents. You'd have cut your arm off before hurting them or anyone else—unless they were your own age and they threatened you first."

"Perhaps I could get you to contact my superiors and tell the lab techs to get a move on clearing my name?"

"I would be happy to do so, young man, just give me their

details." She laughed, a sweet delicate sound. "But maybe it was time for you to come home, if only for a short visit."

"Fancy." A new voice joined the conversation. "We have other customers waiting."

Grady looked up. A woman stood there wearing a simple black business suit, skirt resting at the knee, a single strand of pearls at her white throat. Her eyes were reddened, her expression severe.

Fancy turned slowly to face the other woman and raised her chin. "I've been doing this job for more than fifty years, Edith, and you've been doing it for a few hours. Trust me, I know my job."

The woman, Edith Bodurek—Grady recognized her now—bristled, clearly shocked that Fancy spoke back to her in such a way.

"I realize this is a difficult time for you, but one thing I've learned is that what sets us apart from any other bank is the personal connection we have with our clients." Fancy drew herself up to her full height even though she was barely five-foot and currently sitting down. "If that has changed, I'll hand in my notice today."

Edith looked around the silent room, and her cheeks flushed with embarrassment. She clasped her hands together and turned on her heel to walk quickly back to the office her husband had occupied for the past twenty-five years.

Fancy pursed her lips. "Sorry you had to see that. I like Edith well enough, and I'm more than sorry for her loss. But I'm too old to be told how to do my job by a new manager trying to stamp their authority over me. I didn't take it from Milton, nor his grandfather before him, and I won't take it from someone who hasn't a clue how to run this business."

"She's taken over Milton's job? Why not hire a manager?"

"Oh, I suspect she'll hire a manager as soon as she can find one willing to move here for what she'll pay them, but she's terrified people will lose confidence in the meantime, what with the robbery and the murder. If people jump ship, this place will fold."

"It's not like people around here have many options." Grady leaned closer and whispered, "It's the only bank in town."

"For now. Those soulless corporations you see up and down the coast are always sending people here to try to buy the family out. They'll come in droves now. Wouldn't surprise me one bit if Edith sells out."

"What about her son?"

Fancy snorted. "Never worked a day in his life. I'd place money he wants to sell so he can get his inheritance without waiting for his mother to pass."

Could Milton Bodurek's murder be due to simple greed or corporate machinations? The FBI couldn't afford to rule it out.

"Now, young man, what can I do for you?"

He held up the key to the safe deposit box. "Figured it was time I checked Gran's box."

Delight lit her features, and she pushed away from her desk. "I still miss that woman every day. She'd be happy that you're back."

The emotional hit had him catching his breath. He swallowed hard to hide the effect her words had on him.

She took a keycard over to the vault and then used it on the keypad before entering a six-digit code.

He walked slowly after her, scanning the room. "This door was open the day of the robbery?"

"Yes, Jim Fehrman, the mailman had gone inside to check his box. Carol Tinto was waiting outside the open door when the robber came in. He probably thought he'd be able to get into the main vault, but that is on a fixed timer, and all the threats in the world won't open it." Fancy nodded toward another teller who was serving a customer.

Carol Tinto.

The woman shot him a curious smile. She was dark-haired and pretty. His type usually, but he couldn't quite shake the image of a certain prickly redhead from his mind. He frowned. Despite the moment they'd shared in the moonlight, he couldn't afford to think of Brynn Webster as anything except a potential source. Even if DNA proved she wasn't related to Eli Kane, getting involved with anyone when he was hunting one of the country's most notorious fugitives was unwise. Last night had proven he couldn't afford to drop his guard.

The queue had grown, but Fancy seemed in no hurry.

"Did you recognize him?" Grady asked.

"You don't think I'd have told the police if I had?" she asked sharply.

"Of course, but sometimes things come to us later. The guy didn't seem familiar in some way?"

She frowned and looked suddenly unsure. "The scene keeps replaying in my head. But it changes a little each time and with each person who also recounts it." She touched her lips. "Now I'm not a hundred percent certain about anything."

"Eyewitness reports are notoriously unreliable because we're all susceptible to suggestion whether we know it or not. That's why statements are taken immediately after the event, when possible, while everything is still in our short-term memory banks. It can shift by the time it is added to long-term memory."

Prosecutors and defense attorneys used changes in a person's story as evidence of a lack of veracity, but psychology was more complicated than that.

"It all happened so fast, and I thought I was about to die." Her hand gripped her throat and she laughed self-consciously. "All those years of training and when the time came, I forgot everything. Gave him all the cash without a thought for the dye pack. I'm sure the cops think I was in on it."

He raised his brows. If they were any good, they would check everyone who worked here to look for evidence of an inside job. He was hoping Ropero could find a way to access the sheriff's department files on the bank robbery and Bodurek's murder. He'd like to read those witness statements.

He took Fancy's hand, noting the paper-thin skin. "Then they obviously don't know you. You could have retired years ago. You care about the people of this town too much to hurt them or steal their money."

She gave him a watery smile and squeezed his fingers before letting go and smoothing her hair. "Most people think I still work here because I need the money."

"Unless you've developed a gambling habit over the past eight years, I doubt that."

She lived in a neat little cottage walking distance from the branch. She'd bought and paid for the place before he'd arrived in town as a grief-stricken brat.

"Gambling is a fool's game unless you're the one in control of the odds." She rubbed her hands together and shivered. It was cool inside the vault.

"Ain't that the truth." The only time he bet for money was with his teammates about some antic or other, always pushing one another to be better than they were the day before.

Grief unexpectedly flooded his mind as he thought of the two colleagues he'd lost this month. No one could prepare against explosives or improve their odds of surviving a plane crash. He forced the thoughts out of his mind so he could do his job. He loved them but they'd have wanted him to catch Kane rather than wallow in grief over their deaths.

He grieved in his own way.

"I know the police are doing their jobs but having Darrell York question *my* integrity…" Fancy Lucette snorted indelicately.

Grady grinned.

He knew this woman was clean. His grandmother had been an excellent judge of character and didn't tolerate fools.

"I take it Darrell hasn't changed much even though he's the sheriff now." Grady wanted to know more about his childhood friend and apparent rival.

"Still a selfish and self-absorbed asshat."

"That's probably why we got along so well." Grady grinned. "When did his daddy retire?"

"Two years ago now." She sniffed. "Temple was a good sheriff and often held out a helping hand to raise people out of their bad decisions."

"He did indeed." Grady tipped his head in reference to his own checkered history. "I'm grateful he gave me a chance." Even if Grady had needed to force his hand when the guy had reneged on a promise.

Fancy nodded. "Darrell has forgotten that part of the job. He's all about how things look statistically and therefore reflect upon himself. This crime wave will have what's left of his hair falling out."

The Bureau was big on their stats, too, but math only told part of the story. "If he cracks both cases, he'll be the town hero," Grady pointed out.

"As long as he arrests the *right* culprits. That's all I ask." Her tone was clipped.

Grady hoped to hell the idiot didn't arrest him and thereby threaten the FBI's own investigation.

"Do the town gossips have a favorite theory about who the robber or the murderer is?"

"Apart from you?"

He winced. "Dammit. I knew it was only a matter of time."

"I've been defending you the way your grandma would have expected me to." Fancy smiled at him.

He felt strangely numb at her words. Maybe it was the head injury. "Thank you."

"Most people blame strangers passing through on both counts. It helps them sleep at night. You going to open that box today, young man?"

So much for stalling.

Grady turned to the wall of small rectangular metal boxes. He inserted his key and opened the tiny door, pulled out the box, expecting to find a roll of papers that would likely be the deeds to the house and maybe some other boring documents.

He was hit instead by old photographs. His mother as a child. His grandparents on their wedding day. Himself as a sturdy little boy in bathing trunks laughing as a handful of wet sand streamed out of his hand.

Fancy watched him with a knowing smile. "I was here the day she put them in there. She was worried about you even though you'd gone and become a State Trooper. I guess she thought Crystal might not share these with you, especially after she decided to leave you the house."

"You knew about that? Why didn't you say anything when Crys lied to everyone?"

She put her hand on her bony hip. "First, it wasn't my place. Second,"—she paused for a long moment—"I was waiting for you to care enough to do something about it."

The words hurt more than the hit on the head last night.

"Apparently, I'm still a self-absorbed asshat." He reached out and touched the smile on his beloved grandmother's face. He swallowed, forced out the words. "It wasn't that I didn't care…"

She nodded and took a step back. "It was that you cared too much. I see that now. I'll wait outside."

"Do you know why she left everything to me when she died?" he asked quickly.

Her eyes grew soft. "You know why."

Because she'd loved him. Because she'd worried. The lump in his throat almost strangled him.

Christ.

He pulled out everything and spread it on the table behind him. His sole intention for coming here had been to talk to Fancy Lucette, and it shamed him that he hadn't gotten his thumb out of his ass to check this box after his grandmother had died.

The lawyer had had a copy of the will, and the deeds were kept here in the safety deposit box. Grady had been on his way to the FBI Academy, and he'd never looked back.

He'd spent all these years running from the pain of loss. And here he was, finally confronting it, and it brought him to his knees.

So much for being a tough guy.

He spread out the images, saw the faces of his long dead family staring back at him.

They looked happy, he realized in surprise.

He'd forgotten a lot of the joy of his childhood amongst the memories of pain and loss and bitterness. Despite everything his father had tried to do, to destroy them with his fists and his violence. Baxter Steel had failed.

Crys looked happy, too.

And then their mother had died and everything had crumpled. His grandmother had saved him, but he had a feeling she hadn't been able to save Crys in the same way.

At least his sister had someone she loved in her life now. Hopefully, he didn't have to arrest her father-in-law for triple homicide.

Bob Grogan's stepfather was on the shortlist of suspects for being Eli Kane. His sister would never forgive him if he did anything to ruin her family, even if it was to catch one of the country's most callous killers. Not that it made much of a difference. He doubted she'd forgive him anyway, and there was no way he would let Eli Kane get away if he could help it.

How would that look in his personnel file? He and Grogan's stepdad had both been at the wedding, so probably not good.

Grady placed the photographs carefully in his inside pocket. He'd scan them and give Crys copies even though she must have a bunch that had been in their grandparents' house, on the walls and in cupboards, that she hadn't shared with him after their grandma had died.

Why had his grandmother saved these particular images for him?

And then with a jolt he realized. It was to remind him there had been joy as well as hardship in his past. He may have been a poor, pathetic little shit who had struggled to fit in, but he'd also been loved and had loved back.

He put the documents away and slid the box back into its slot. Locked it. He glanced around for the boxes that had been robbed, but they'd been processed and repaired. He couldn't tell which they were. He stared around the room that was separated by a high, narrow wooden table.

It seemed to him that there would be no reason to touch the opposite wall of boxes if yours was on this side of the room or vice versa.

If they knew which side the fingerprint had been found, they could probably safely eliminate, or at least de-prioritize, boxes on the other side of the room, which should significantly reduce the suspect list.

They were getting there. Slowly. The noose was tightening around Eli Kane's neck—assuming he hadn't already fled. But time was running out.

"Mr. Steel?"

Grady jolted out of his contemplation. "Mrs. Bodurek. I'm very sorry for your loss."

Edith Bodurek's brown eyes swam with tears that she refused to let fall. She cleared her throat noisily. "I was wondering if you had a few minutes to spare?"

27

B rynn let herself quietly out of the house. Her mother had fallen asleep. Brynn had stayed with her for a little while then cleaned up from their early lunch. After a last check showed her mother was still napping, she decided to go home and get a head start on two projects that were due next week.

Her dad was back and working in his workshop. Their property had an enormous barn that housed their vehicles in winter and a tractor that her father used to plow the road if the snow was heavy like it was forecast to be in a couple of days. He didn't only plow their driveway. He'd been known to go around to all the neighbors and dig them out, too.

Brynn wasn't sure if it was altruism or if he simply liked an excuse to play with his toys.

Another building housed a large generator that her parents had installed in case they lost power, which was regularly. Once, when she was a kid and not long after they'd moved here, they'd been without power for three weeks. That had sucked, although they had a wood burning stove which meant the house had been warm enough.

There was a loft space above the generator that could have been converted into a living space, except, should the generator be running, it would stink of diesel fumes. Plus, her parents didn't need the extra space. It was just the two of them now.

They used the space to store Christmas decorations or anything seasonal from the café, like the outside tables and their umbrellas.

She headed over to the workshop to say goodbye to her dad.

"You headed back into town?" Paul Webster looked up from his tinkering when she opened the door. "Mind dropping off a chainsaw at Angus's? I fixed it for him, and it'll save me going out again. I put it in the trunk of your car. Leave it in the woodshed if he's not home."

Angus's home was between here and town. "Sure. How's Project Chicken Coop going?"

He grinned and put down his saw. "You two are mocking me now but won't be when we start producing enough eggs to supply the café."

She raised her brow. "That's a lot of chicks."

"I like chickens. They keep vermin down." He shrugged, looking older suddenly, his shoulders hunching forward. "It's difficult to fill the days with mindless inane stuff when I can see your mother getting sicker and sicker every day and can do nothing to stop it."

She touched his arm. "The doctors warned you it would get worse before it got better."

He shuddered and nodded. "I know. I know." He looked away, but she spotted red eyes that battled tears. "I'm not sure what I'd do without her, Brynn."

She wrapped her arms around his waist and laid her head on his chest. "She'll be okay. You know how strong she is."

He squeezed her back so tightly it almost hurt. "Yeah. Yeah. I know." He let her go and took a step away. "I'm sorry for dragging you away from your life."

Her mouth trembled. "It's not like I had a lot to leave behind, if I'm honest. A few friends, but they are all starting to move away from the city now and have babies."

"No special someone you haven't told us about?"

She smiled tearfully. "Not since Aiden."

Her father wrapped his arms around her again. "That prick wasn't worth your tears."

She laughed and pushed away. "I guess not, but it's hard to find someone who checks all the boxes, you know? Not only because of Aiden, but also because of my role models. You and mom have the best marriage of anyone I've ever seen. I'm not willing to settle for less, although I doubt there will be a next time."

"Me and your mother aren't perfect, sweetheart, but…" He smiled sadly. "I knew the moment I saw her that *she* was perfect." His eyes turned distant as if remembering. "She definitely checked all my boxes." He winked at her and his voice turned wistful. "It'll happen when you least expect it. Be patient and don't rush into anything. You'll know when it's the real deal."

She shook her head and headed for the door. "Today has been bizarre. Both my parents giving me advice on my love life. I can't tell you how that upsets the balance of the universe."

She paused at the doorway and turned to watch her father fight a smile.

He followed her out. "Watch the roads. They're icy."

"Yes, Dad." She shook her head as she climbed into her Honda Civic and waved before heading down the long driveway, through the woods, and out onto the main road and turning right.

At least she'd given her parents some amusement discussing her non-existent love life.

A vision of Grady Steel standing statue still with his eyes closed in his front yard as she'd gone on tiptoes to kiss him flashed through her mind. He'd been so sweet with the stray dog. And sexy. Very sexy.

She highly doubted someone like Grady was looking for true love. He seemed much too independent and career-oriented to be the type to settle down. But a fling? She didn't think he'd have a problem with that at all.

172

A shiver ran over her senses at the thought of seducing him, but she still wasn't sure she could go through with it.

Would she ever be sure?

Probably not.

And then there was that text message telling her to stay away. Had to have been Caleb Quayle in retaliation for her banning him from the café. Ass.

She thrust it out of her mind. She didn't have to figure this all out on her one day off.

Almost at Angus's property, she spotted a car on the side of the road, the two tourists with the Eastern European accents struggling with a jack and a spare tire.

She pulled abreast of them and, as it was quiet on the road, rolled down her window. "Are you okay?"

"*Da.* Our tire break, so we change but only find this in the trunk." The man held up the donut.

"It'll get you to the nearest rental place or repair garage, but I wouldn't go any farther on that."

The man looked perplexed. Obviously, this was not how they did things wherever he came from.

"Are you sure you're okay? I can change it for you if you need help."

The man brushed away her offer as his wife stood on the edge of the road looking impatient.

The man frowned. "Aren't you the one who found the dead man? You jumped into the harbor?"

A shiver rolled over her shoulders. She didn't want to talk about it.

"Did you see the killer?" The man looked around. "Should we be concerned for our safety?" He gave her a wide-eyed look and took a step back as if suddenly worried she was going to hurt him.

She pinched her lips together. "I didn't see anything, and this is a very safe community—although bad things can happen anywhere. I'm sure it's the same where you're from."

Another car approached in the rearview. It was a sheriff's department cruiser. It signaled to pull over.

"I'm going to leave you in this deputy's capable hands. He can assist you if you need it."

Brynn drove away as the sheriff himself climbed out of his vehicle. She didn't miss the fact he looked pissed that she'd left. Whatever. She hadn't broken any laws.

Ten minutes later, after dropping the chainsaw inside Angus's woodshed as instructed, she pulled up behind her rental place and stared at the house as the engine cooled.

Should she go for it?

If anything, the text message warning her off made her even more intrigued. Maybe Grady had sent it himself, knowing that deep down she was perverse and cantankerous.

She laughed and shook her head at herself. Not likely.

Where'd he gone last night?

Perhaps he had an old girlfriend he'd reconnected with after they'd said goodnight, or maybe he'd headed back to the bar and walked the pretty waitress home...

She pushed those ideas aside. They didn't seem to fit the man she'd started to get to know. He probably had a partner down in Virginia which made her innocent kiss a lot less innocent. Someone who could keep up with that honed body and make him sweat.

The image of Grady sweating made her heart flutter. She was very good at visualization. *She* was an *artist*.

She was also out of milk and had forgotten to buy any when she'd been at the shops earlier. With a strangled sound she started the engine again and headed toward the grocery store on the edge of town. Seduction would have to wait until she'd restocked her fridge.

28

Grady followed Edith Bodurek through the main banking area, past Milton's personal secretary, who kept her face averted, and into a room with tall windows, high ceilings, and old-fashioned, heavy furniture, including dark oak bookcases that lined the walls.

Milton Bodurek's office hadn't been renovated to the same degree as the rest of the bank and retained the feeling of old money and institutional power.

Edith was a beautiful woman, if a little brittle around the edges. Perhaps it was grief that drew the harsh lines on her face. Perhaps it was character.

Grady hadn't had many personal interactions with the Bodureks in the past. They ran in vastly different social circles, and their one son was even younger than Brynn.

Edith ran her fingers over the shiny wood of the uncluttered desk. A framed photograph, presumably of the family, sat on the desk, next to an old-fashioned blotter. A computer sat off at a slight angle so that there was nothing between the manager and any clients or staff he was speaking with.

She didn't sit but indicated the chair to him. "Please have a seat."

He did, more out of curiosity than anything else. He fought the instinct to doff his hat. The two-inch gash on the back of his skull might put this woman off anything she wanted to say.

Appearances were everything to some.

"I wanted to thank you for finding my husband and therefore making sure his body was returned to us for burial."

Grady frowned. "Brynn Webster is the person you should thank. If she hadn't dived in when she did…" And made a lot of noise about it. "Well, we wouldn't have found him."

Edith's reddened eyes widened and her nostrils flared. "Oh. I knew, of course, that you were both there, but the sheriff has been scant with the details. I assumed… Thank you for telling me that. I'll speak to Brynn and make sure she knows how very grateful —" Her voice caught and tripped.

Grady nodded, although he didn't think Brynn wanted thanks any more than he did. The more he thought about how close Brynn had been to a killer two nights ago, the less he liked it.

"Do you have any idea who might have wanted to murder your husband?"

She sank heavily into the uncomfortable-looking wooden chair behind Milton Bodurek's desk. "I don't. I wish I did."

"Who stood to gain financially from his death?"

Her lips trembled. "That's what the sheriff kept asking me. As if Milt was somehow worth more dead than alive."

"Unfortunately, money is a common motivator."

"I'm the wife of a banker. I realize how important money is," she snapped. Then she covered her mouth and stifled a sob. "Or, at least, I used to be."

She wiped a tear that had escaped the leash. "Sorry, I shouldn't have spoken to you like that. It's just…I can't believe he's gone and Sheriff York, junior, is more interested in the fact that Milt carried a large life insurance policy than in answering my questions."

"How large?"

"Five million."

"That's a lot of reasons."

"Only if you care about money more than happiness." Her sigh was close to a hiss. "I loved my husband. I expected to grow old with him. He was thinking about retiring."

Grady held her gaze, looking for honesty. Wasn't sure he found it. "Why the large insurance policy?"

She looked away. Played with the edge of the blotter. "Milt was worried about what would happen to me if he died. The bank is doing fine right now, but he was aware that could quickly change in today's market. He would never have taken out the policy if he'd thought it would make me a suspect when he died."

"Milton didn't die. He was murdered."

Her chin snapped up. "So I've been told." There was pride there, beneath the grief. This woman was not used to having her integrity questioned.

He understood that. It did something to you. Twisted something that either snapped or became stronger.

"What about your son?"

"Andrew? Andrew loved his father."

"Rumor has it he needed money."

She laughed bitterly. "I would have thought you'd be the last person to spout rumor at me."

"You're right." He didn't want to scare her away with pressing questions and cop talk, but there were a million reasons to investigate her and her son—make that five million. Grady was impressed Darrell was considering the widow a suspect as she was friends with his parents. "Presumably Andrew stands to inherit a great deal of money on his father's death?"

Her fingers tore the edge of the purple paper, and she smoothed it back down into place. "Andrew has a trust fund that he comes into when he's twenty-five. He's twenty-four now so I think he could probably wait a year rather than cold-bloodedly murder his beloved father."

Grady wouldn't rule it out. "If it wasn't money, is there another reason someone might have hurt Milton?"

"Not that I know of." She shook her head.

"Your marriage was happy?"

Anger shone through the tears. "Milt was not having an affair."

And wives were always the last to know.

"Did he often go down to the harbor at night?"

She looked a little confused by the change of subject. "At least once a week. More if he planned to go out for a sail."

"Was he planning to go sailing this weekend?"

She shook her head. "I don't think so. The wind was expected to kick up again with this cold front moving in. He…he didn't like taking risks, especially if he was sailing alone."

"Did you ever go with him? Or Andrew?"

She looked wistful suddenly. "Andrew used to go as a boy but lost interest after he left for college. I only go out in summer when it's warm and calm. I'm not a big fan of the water, but Milt loves it…"

She seemed to realize her slip in tense and pressed the back of her hand hard against her lips.

"Any idea what he was doing there on Saturday night?"

"No." She shook her head. "We'd spent the day hiking around Jordan Pond in Acadia National Park."

Mount Desert Island was about a forty-minute drive this time of year.

"We love it there, but it's always so busy in the summer we tend to save our trips for later in the year." She raised her tearstained face. "When we arrived home, I was too bushed to cook, so we ordered takeout and watched a movie. I was tired after all that fresh air so I went to bed early, around nine. That's the last time I saw him alive." She gave a heartbroken little sob. "I often go to bed early. I get up around five every day," she explained as if she needed to justify her life to him. "Milt was the opposite in so many ways. He stayed up late and rose at eight every day." She blinked a little. "He was in the office by nine sharp every morning, but he was not a morning person."

"Did you hear him leave the house that night?"

She shook her head.

"Did he often leave without telling you where he was going?"

"If I was asleep, he wouldn't disturb me." That seemed slightly evasive.

"Why do you think he went to the boat?"

"The only reason I can think of was either there was a problem with the vessel and the marina called. Or someone called him about the robbery."

"The robbery?"

"It was eating him up—being held up at gunpoint. That's why I made him come for a hike that day. Get him out of himself." She drew in a breath. "He saw it as a personal failure. He believed he'd let everyone down, and he wanted the criminals punished to the full extent of the law."

"I spoke to Saul Jones." He watched her eyes widen and then shame bloom in her cheeks.

"Milt wasn't usually a bad person, but he was so angry. He took it out on Saul, and I need to apologize to the man." She looked suddenly drained of energy.

"Did Milton have any idea who robbed the bank?"

"I don't think so."

"You don't seem sure."

A frown marred her smooth brow. "Initially, he was content to let the police investigate, but after a few days he seemed to lose faith in the sheriff's department and started asking questions of his own. Ironic that they are now in charge of finding out who killed him." Her hands fisted on top of the massive desk.

"Who did Milton question?"

She shook her head. "He wouldn't tell me, but I'm afraid it was those questions that may have gotten him killed."

"Did you tell this to the sheriff?"

She huffed. "I did but he didn't seem to care." She flicked a glance at Grady that was laden with dark emotion. "The sheriff's main suspects for Milt's murder are in this room, which is why I thought you might be in a position to help me—and yourself."

"In what way?" He didn't want to seem too eager but inside he was fist-pumping.

"You are a trained FBI agent, aren't you? Currently with time on your hands?" When he remained silent, she added, "If you are not available perhaps you could ask your FBI friends to look into it?"

"That's not how the FBI works."

"I can pay you." Her eyes hardened.

"That's not how I work." Despite what she might think, he couldn't be bought. "Like you say, I'm an FBI agent, not a private investigator."

The silence was suddenly heavy with despair.

"I don't have access to the crime scene information. Makes investigating difficult." At her crestfallen expression he added, "But maybe I could ask around a little as long as you give me everything you find out."

"I can tell you what I know. Pass on anything that the sheriff or the insurance investigator tells me."

This could give him an excuse to poke around a little. "If I agreed to make a few inquiries, no one can know." He hated to see the hope dance in her eyes. "Not the sheriff when he says something to piss you off, not your son when he screams at you because the cops think he killed his daddy"—her eyes widened at that—"not your friends at the country club."

Her knuckles were white with strain. "I need to know who stole my husband from me. Who destroyed the life I thought I was going to live. And somehow, I doubt Sheriff York is going to provide that."

She seemed genuine, but Grady didn't trust quite so easily. He'd been in law enforcement too long. "Do the cops have his cell phone and laptop?"

"They found his phone on the boat." She covered her mouth. "I think that's where they think he was killed. I haven't been allowed back onboard yet. They also have Milt's Lexus. They came and took his laptop from our home office…"

Grady tried to hide his disappointment.

"But."

Grady lifted his head.

"I have his old one. Laptop, that is. We did that through the years. I'd inherit his older machine, which was never that old, as he liked to keep everything as up-to-date as possible."

Grady remained quiet, knowing silence was generally voluntarily filled with information.

"The thing is, he only bought his new laptop before Christmas, and I haven't switched over to the new one yet." She reached down into a messenger bag that sat on the floor and withdrew a computer. Laid it on the desk.

"You have what is basically a copy of all your husband's emails and messages?"

"All that I know about." She swallowed. "I realize from watching movies and TV shows that maybe he had some sort of secret life, but I find it difficult to believe Milton concealed anything of note from me."

Could Milton Bodurek be Eli Kane? Was this conversation some sort of play to help reinforce Edith's innocence or ignorance should the cops figure that out? Could Edith be a suspect in her husband's murder?

"Write the passcode down. Can I take the bag, too?"

Her eyes widened in surprise. "That's mine, not Milt's."

"People might not notice if I walk out of here with a bag, but they sure as hell will notice if I have a laptop in my hand that I wasn't carrying on the way in."

"Yes, of course." She reached down and put the bag on the desk. It was thin and plain black. She slipped the laptop back inside. "Do you want my cell number?"

He thought about it. Shook his head. "If you and I start texting each other the sheriff will have us conspiring to commit murder before you even have time to get your husband buried."

She looked horrified by the realization.

"If you need to reach me, call me from here, and we can keep it more official. If you discover any information that might be useful to me or that seems out of the ordinary, let me know. If it's urgent, come by the house or call 911."

It was possible she was also in danger. Depending on where the threat came from.

He slipped his business card across the desk. The embossed seal glinted mockingly in the sunlight streaming in from the window. His personal number was written on the back. "You can at least pretend we spoke about my account if you call from here."

Grady picked up the messenger bag and slipped his family photographs into the side pocket before slinging it over his shoulder.

"If there's anything else, anything you're not telling me, it would be better to say now."

Her expression remained grief-stricken and slightly confused. "I want my husband's killer brought to justice, Mr. Steel." Her eyes became hard. "I actually want them to burn in hell for shooting a man who was kind and considerate, and for stealing the future I'd been looking forward to my entire married life. But I'll settle for what we call justice if that's all I can get. As long as they pay for what they've done."

Her eyes burned into his back as he walked away.

29

Brynn grabbed the groceries from the trunk and locked the car where she'd parked it in her designated spot at the back of the house before she headed down the side of the building toward her door. She frowned at an unfamiliar sound and kept going until she reached the front garden.

The fluffy gray dog was eating noisily out of the bowl Grady must have left for him.

She held her breath, but the dog sensed her and swung his hind legs away from her, eyeing her warily while still eating.

The fear in his eyes struck her like a blow.

"It's okay, boy." Her heart ached that she hadn't noticed his ghostly form haunting the town. Not until Grady had shown her.

She squatted to be less threatening, not wanting him to fear her as well as the rest of the world.

He was favoring his front left paw. She frowned. He really needed to see a veterinarian, and Grady wasn't wrong about the blizzard that the forecasters were warning about. The windchills were expected to drop into the minus thirties with at least a foot of snow falling, probably more.

The dog finished the food and dipped his head into the water bowl, drops splashing everywhere.

She wanted to grab him but didn't think she'd be able to catch him, and she didn't want to scare him or get bitten. She needed to earn his trust, which was obviously what Grady was trying to do with the food.

She dug into the shopping bag and pulled out a packet of oatmeal cookies she really didn't need and ripped it open. She tossed one into the grass beside the dog, and he sniffed it cautiously before eating it almost delicately.

Sugar probably wasn't great for dogs, but she didn't have anything else handy. "It's okay, boy. I won't hurt you."

She tossed the next one closer, and he eased forward another foot to snatch it up before retreating again.

She broke the next one in half and tossed it closer still, crooning softly the whole time. "You poor thing. Are you cold? I think you need a bath and somewhere cozy to curl up."

And a vet to look at that front paw.

It took time and patience but finally, when she held a cookie out to him, he leaned forward and, with infinite caution, took the morsel gently from her fingers.

Her heart gave a little jolt.

"Good boy. What a good boy."

He crunched the cookie and stood there looking quizzically from the packet of cookies to her face. But she needed to get him somewhere she could contain him, and she had nothing resembling a leash. He wasn't wearing a collar.

She stared at her door and climbed slowly to her feet.

The dog darted back a few feet and stopped, watching her.

She held up another smaller piece of cookie because she didn't want to run out before she got him inside. *If* she could get him inside.

According to her rental agreement there was a no pets policy, but she didn't think the current owner would object.

Small black eyes peered nervously through overgrown bangs.

What if he ran away again? What if he realized she meant to trap him?

He backed up a step.

She feared she was losing his trust and forced herself to calm down. *Relax.* Dogs sensed fear.

She shuffled her bags and inched slowly backward, offering another piece of treat goodness. The dog followed. Belatedly, she remembered the ham she'd bought. She ripped into the packaging. The dog looked expectantly at her.

"You poor thing." She unlocked her door and pushed it open.

She held out a piece of ham, and the dog ate it. He licked his lips. Gave her a look as if he thought she'd been holding out on him.

She went inside and set her bags on the side table by the door. She hung on to the ham and cookies.

She gave him another slice and walked over to the small kitchenette, pulled a large metal mixing bowl from the cupboard. The dog watched her from the threshold as she filled the bowl with water and placed it on the floor.

The dog looked unimpressed, and she laughed.

"Expected one of Grady's tins of dog food, huh?" She needed to call the guy. She was doing this for him because there was no way she could look after a dog and run the café.

Technically, it was Caleb Quayle's dog, although he obviously didn't want it or care for it. The idea of that man reclaiming the poor animal did not sit well with her.

She moved closer and crouched down with another piece of ham. The dog eased closer, keeping his belly low to the ground, nervous by the change in surroundings.

Sadness filled her as he licked her fingers.

She tossed a piece of meat onto the kitchen floor. He waited for a hand delivery but when she didn't move, the dog edged closer to the food while she moved closer to the door.

It took most of the ham and all the remaining cookies before she finally reached the door and gently closed it, locking them both inside.

The dog started to pace back and forth now, clearly realizing he was stuck here. The fact he was so clearly distressed broke Brynn's heart.

"It's okay. I won't hurt you. I promise."

The dog looked afraid.

Had someone beaten him?

The idea filled her with rage, but she let it go. She sat on the floor and leaned against the kitchen counter. She needed to track down Grady's number somehow and call to let him know she had his dog. But first, she had to repeat what she'd done outside and gain this poor creature's trust.

"I'm not gonna hurt you, baby. I'm gonna make sure you're taken care of and that front paw of yours is all fixed up."

He stopped and cocked his head. Listening.

When she pulled the last strip of ham out of the packet he came to her again and the small wag of his tail made tears well up. And when he finally laid beside her and rested his head on her thigh, she let them fall.

30

Grady met Ropero a few miles outside Bangor in the parking lot of a small industrial complex.

She climbed into his car. "I don't have much time. We can't be seen together. What do you have for me?"

Not even an "how's the head?"

He refrained from rolling his eyes as he passed her the laptop. "Milton Bodurek's widow, Edith, gave me this about an hour ago. Seems he'd bought himself a new computer for Christmas, which is in the hands of the Montrose County Sheriff's Department. He gave her the old one, but she hasn't switched it out yet with her own email and shit."

Ropero frowned as she took it. "Think she wanted to keep tabs on him because she thought he was having an affair?"

"I think if he was having an affair, he would have wiped it first. Passwords are written on sticky notes inside."

"Did you turn it on?" she asked suspiciously.

"No," he said with more patience than she deserved. "I know how to do my job, Agent Ropero."

She swore. Dragged her hand through a hunk of her hair. "Sorry. I'm being a bitch."

"I didn't realize you had any other setting."

The agent surprised him with a grin. "I also apologize for steamrolling you into this case. Dobson told me I should approach you as a fellow agent, but I didn't listen to him."

"Why not?"

Her eyes flashed. "Because once upon a time Eli Kane was a fellow agent, too. Having a badge is not a guarantee of good character—plus, there is the issue of your daddy…"

"I am not my father." He let the insult slide. He was in no mood to discuss the parent he'd disowned. One thing had always bothered him. "How'd Kane pass the polygraphs back in the eighties? I mean, I crap myself every time I have to take one, and I haven't done anything wrong. It's like confession but with electrodes helping the great God Almighty."

Ropero grunted. "Good old Catholic guilt. That's one thing you never outgrow." She shifted in her seat. "The system is more robust nowadays. Back then the agents were all chums with the polygraph techs. Or they fooled it by taking a Xanax and having a good laugh with their pals beforehand."

Grady thought about the polygrapher who'd been murdered for his part in the Stone case a year ago last Christmas. Grady had been assigned to help guard Senator LeMay and his wife's brownstone in DC while the Bureau had searched for their kidnapped daughter.

Polygraphs were a tool to get a confession or leverage information. Not truth serum. Not even strictly admissible in court.

"The tests aren't infallible, as you know. And my theory is, Kane was and is a psychopath who knows how to fake positive emotion rather than being someone who needs to hide stress."

Any man who could execute his wife and kids the way Kane had done had to have something defective with their brain.

"Family annihilators usually have some sort of trigger. Did we ever figure out what Kane's was?"

"Not really." She stared out the front window. "According to the wife's best friend, Kane asked for a divorce a few months before the murders, but Lisa begged for him to try to make it work. Things appeared to settle down again, and the wife told everyone they were okay now and going on a family vacation to Florida."

"She had no clue?"

"According to this friend of hers, she and the boys were giddy with excitement."

"Instead, he killed them." Grady watched the wind clip the tops of the nearby trees.

"His cover story of the trip gave him three full weeks to disappear without anyone realizing he wasn't where he was supposed to be. Then he called in sick—we now know from a pay phone in New Mexico—so it was another week before his colleagues grew truly concerned and started looking for him. But it wasn't until some hikers tripped over the family car packed up for a vacation hidden in the bushes in Cumberland Gap National Historical Park that the Feds realized something bad had happened. Search dogs found the bodies, and the rest is history."

"Why kill them? Why not just move on?" At least his own father had spared them that. "People get rejected all the time."

"Control? Hate?"

They both stared silently at the bare winter landscape.

"We should pull in someone from BAU to work with us on his profile. We know they've been studying him for years."

"I don't want to risk—"

"Yeah, yeah, yeah. I get what you do and don't want, but no one from the BAU is going to tip our hand, and they might give us the insight we need."

Her jaw worked as she stared at him. Finally, she conceded, "I'll talk to Dobson. See what he thinks of the idea."

Grady suspected the two agents were more than colleagues, but he wasn't about to ask questions.

An image of Brynn popped into his head, and his pulse raced a little as he remembered the damn kiss. So innocent and so hot.

She was pretty and fun to spend time with, but something tugged at him beyond that.

Was it her sense of humor? The intelligence in her pretty eyes or the hurt he saw lurking in the shadows? He didn't want to be the asshole to deepen that hurt. Their futures didn't meld. Their paths diverged.

But he liked her.

More than he should.

"Why'd the widow give you the laptop?" Ropero asked after a minute of silence.

"She wants me to help find her husband's killer. Believes the sheriff's main suspects are the two of us, which would give me a reason to want to investigate further." Grady rolled his window down and let the fresh air blow inside.

"What did you tell her?"

"I said I'd help her provided she didn't tell anyone, not even her son, who's still at college doing a master's degree in business, despite the news of his father's murder. Maybe she plans to set me up to take the fall, but I guess we know something she doesn't."

They exchanged an amused look.

"Figured she might have some information that could prove useful at some point so decided to keep her on my side. There's a five-million-dollar life insurance policy on the dead guy. People have killed for less."

Ropero cradled her forehead. "If that idiot sheriff arrests you and fucks up this operation, I'm going to shoot him myself."

He turned in his seat and frowned. "This thing with Kane seems personal for you. I mean, I get wanting to nail this bastard, but…"

She looked at him with annoyance then relented. "I guess it is, although I have no personal connection to the case. My family lived in the same Maryland town as Kane when I was growing up. His kids were similar in age to me and my sister. It made an impression—that an entire family could disappear that way. I remember how shocked everyone was. The disappearance, then the discovery of the bodies. Usually, it was the stranger danger that was being pushed on us kids back then, so that's the first time I realized the threat could come from inside a family."

She flicked a glance at Grady, but he didn't say anything. He'd been born into a household that had been dangerous from the get-go.

"It's all the adults talked about for weeks. People started to lose faith in the FBI and police. That bothered me even though I was young. That one man could destroy so much. It's one of my first memories."

She wiped condensation from her side window. "I joined the Bureau in some ways to try to redress the balance, I guess. I never imagined getting a place on the squad tasked with hunting him. I was doing a rotation at HQ when the Australia tipoff came in. Dobson was on the team. I asked to be put on it, too." She shook her head and looked at him. "I would love to take this asshole down."

"You're an idealist."

"I'm a goddamn pragmatist," she snapped and hugged herself.

"Aren't we all?" The air was frigid but Grady liked the breeze. "Did you manage to get hold of Bodurek's autopsy report?"

"Yeah. One shot to the head from a 9-mm at point blank range."

"Execution style."

"Bullet is worthless for ballistics. Too fragmented. Lab's testing the constituents in case we get a hit, but I doubt it. Bullets aren't exactly uncommon in the US."

"You ran Bodurek's DNA?"

She nodded tiredly. "He's not Kane. Neither is Brynn Webster's daddy, by the way. That would have been too easy," she muttered despondently.

The news made him very happy, but he squashed it. Brynn was off-limits. He was working.

He dug in his pocket and pulled out the evidence bag with the cigarette butts he'd picked up last night. "Almost forgot. I found this near those boot prints I sent you before having my brains bashed in."

"Why were you there, anyway?"

He shrugged. "Brynn thought she heard someone in the alley behind her the night Bodurek bought it. Blamed it on a stray cat. I got to wondering if someone deliberately flushed out the animal when she paused and looked behind her."

Ropero took the bag of cigarette butts with a grimace of distaste. "I'll get them analyzed ASAP, but I don't know what it will tell us."

Grady shrugged. "Someone hanging around."

"Could have been someone who's homeless."

"The person who attacked me was someone with training."

"That could be your ego." She smirked.

"My ego died the day you dragged me out of a HRT meeting in handcuffs."

"I said I was sorry."

"The guy could have killed me." His head still throbbed. "It's not my ego saying he knew what he was doing to put me down as quickly and effectively as he did."

"We scoured security cameras, but the plates of the van were obscured. White vans aren't exactly rare in that part of the world."

Grady swore. "Went to see my old friend Saul Jones. He told me Bodurek was an asshole to him after he was shot. Edith admitted it and claimed it was out of character, but we should keep digging into Bodurek's background."

"He could have been having a bad day." Ropero grinned. "It happens."

"Don't tell me you have a sense of humor, Ropero. Not now after I've already pegged you as a heartless bitch."

She shook her head. "I'm exactly who you think I am." At least she admitted it. "I'll keep digging into Bodurek's background in case something pops. Who do you think killed him?"

"His death so soon after the robbery can't be a coincidence." Grady stared into the distance. "Maybe it's financial and one of the family did the robbery and the murder—or a competitor. Edith was very convincing as the grieving widow. I'd dig into the son." He pulled a stick of gum from a packet in the Jeep's dash. Offered one to Ropero which she took. "Part of me wants to believe Kane killed him but I can't help thinking he'd avoid trouble rather than create more. Unless Milton had something Kane needed in order to escape again…in which case he's already gone. The other thing that crossed my mind is a little more disturbing."

Ropero twisted around to face him.

"What if someone else is looking for Kane?"

"Like who?"

He shrugged.

"How would they know to look here? They'd have had to know we found the fingerprint." She scowled.

"Your paranoia is probably rubbing off on me." Grady shrugged.

Ropero's expression became fierce. "Donnelly and Sullivan sent some images to be analyzed. Sullivan was particularly interested—"

"In the two Russian tourists in the bar last night?"

She nodded.

"Kane worked counterintelligence, right?"

"He did, but there was nothing in his file to suggest he was spying for Russia and no hits in the database regarding the tourists. One Muscovite is on a three-month tourist visa. She flew into Boston and met her friend who arrived from Prague. The two have spent the past week working their way up the coast."

Grady rolled his shoulder. "Like I said. Paranoia."

A crinkle pinched her dark brows. "I'll talk to Kane's old boss again."

"Any luck tracing the call that lured Milton Bodurek to the harbor?"

She shook her head. "Came from a burner that is probably at the bottom of the harbor."

"The divers find anything?"

She shook her head. "Nothing useful according to what we could access."

Grady gritted his teeth. The lack of clues was becoming frustrating. "I set up a couple of cameras around my house. Did surveillance pick up any hits for the person Brynn Webster saw walking away from the harbor?"

"Nothing. The only camera in town is above the ATM on Main Street. We brought in a consultant name of Alex Parker to go through the footage as far back as he is able, in case we get lucky with Kane using it or walking by." She rubbed her eye. "I didn't want to, but the tech on the team told me it would take up most of his time for weeks to analyze the footage. This guy Parker can run it in a couple of days. How is that even possible?" She looked pissed. "I'm assured this guy is discreet, and he hasn't been told who he's looking for, just to look for any hits in the database."

"We've worked with Parker before." Grady forced the grit out of his voice as memories surged from the last time. "He's good."

And his friend had still died.

Emotions threatened but he forced them away. He hoped Grace and the kids were doing okay, although, really, how could she be? He hoped he could be around to help when the new baby arrived. Losing Montana on top of that was still a devastating blow.

They were still trying to find enough of him to bury.

Ropero grunted. "Fine."

That shook him out of his funk. Even he knew "fine" was anything but.

"I plan to go visit the former sheriff this afternoon," Grady said. "Thank him for helping me out as a teenager and all that bullshit."

"He'll think you're trying to get off the suspect list."

"They can't pin it on me without a lot of poor police work."

Ropero snorted. "Like that's never happened. You get your weapon back yet?"

"No. I guess Quantico isn't the only lab that's backed up." He pulled his lips to one side. "If you don't hear from me in the next twelve hours start looking for a shallow grave."

"Not funny. That's exactly what Eli Kane did to his family."

"Gallows humor. You find anything in the former sheriff's financials?"

She angled her chin. "Yes and no."

He raised a brow and waited.

"They live simply and within their means, but they paid rock bottom prices for the land and the new build."

"Huh. You figure out who sold it to them?"

"Company called 'Serenity Construction,' which sounds like an oxymoron. We're digging into who owned it. The business shut down not long after the Yorks house was completed. Traced it to a shell company based in the Caribbean."

Definitely suspicious.

"We're probing deeper, but we have a lot to deal with and I'm not convinced this is tied to Kane."

His phone rang and he checked it. An unknown number. "I better take it."

"Go ahead."

"Steel," he answered his phone on speaker.

"Grady. It's Brynn, Brynn Webster?"

"You're the only Brynn I know." He smiled and ignored the kick to his pulse.

"Do you have a leash and a collar?"

He laughed. "Er, do you have some sort of fetish I need to know about?"

Ropero placed a hand over her mouth as if to stop from laughing.

"No," Brynn said impatiently. "I have your dog."

"My dog? I don't have a dog." He frowned in confusion, then straightened. "The stray?"

"Yeah."

"You caught him?"

"I guess."

He could hear whimpering in the background. And scratching.

"I lured him into my apartment with an offer he couldn't refuse. Now I'm afraid to open the door, as I suspect he'll slip out and no amount of cookies or baked ham will get him to trust me again."

He checked his watch. "I'm going to be about forty minutes, more actually as I need to stop to buy a leash on the way. Think you can survive that long?"

The scratching sound grew louder. "It's your house."

"Sit on the floor and watch TV or something. He'll settle down."

"Okay. It's not like I have a life or anything."

"Thank you. I'll call the veterinarian on the way, book him in to check him over. Be there shortly." He hung up.

Ropero paused with the door open. "Do not get distracted from the reason you're really in Deception Cove."

"Just when I was starting to like you." Grady shook his head wryly.

She stood, grunted, and leaned back inside. "I meant to say that the redhead's background check came in clean, but there's something odd about the ex."

"Odd how?" Grady had the vehicle in reverse and was impatiently waiting for the other agent to close the door.

"We haven't been able to locate him."

"Keep trying."

"We are." She slammed the door, and he reversed quickly and sped away.

31

TWENTY-SEVEN YEARS AGO

Spring

E li sat outside a small, exclusive boutique hotel in Maryland. Far enough away not to be spotted and close enough to watch the front door. It was spring and the cherry blossoms were blooming. His favorite time of year in this part of the world.

He watched his dutiful wife hurry inside. She was wearing a navy sheath dress and scarlet high heels. That morning she'd kissed him then told him she had a dental appointment and planned to do a little shopping afterward while a sitter watched the boys.

They were not his boys.

A few months ago, he'd taken samples of their DNA and submitted them to a private lab for analysis along with his own.

Not his boys, but full siblings, with rich brown eyes the color of dark chocolate.

That discovery had gutted him.

Lisa had indeed visited the dentist earlier, where she'd had a clean and polish scheduled.

She had great teeth.

Probably a job requirement.

She hadn't done any shopping though, not yet anyway. He suspected he knew what was happening but was helpless to stop the jaws of this intricately laid trap from snapping shut and devouring him whole.

But he wasn't ready to roll over and die just yet.

He glanced up at the elegant stone façade and listened without surprise as his wife greeted her lover. He wanted to know who he was, to see his face.

He listened as they fucked. He listened as they lay in bed, plotting his downfall.

He mulled over his options. Even if he went to his superiors right now with everything he knew, he'd be thrown out of the Bureau, a laughingstock.

His pride wouldn't allow that.

He could take his own life. It was tempting. The Russians would probably be irritated they'd wasted so much time on him. His wife justifiably angry she'd had to be with him for so long with nothing to show for it.

He could disappear…

And then what?

Would they look for him? Would his colleagues even care? Probably not as much as the fucking Russians, he thought bitterly. They'd be mad their long-term *kompromat* scheme hadn't paid off.

But then Lisa, the grieving widow, would likely seduce one of his colleagues who'd happily raise "Eli's" orphans as their own.

The DNA results wouldn't be quite so shocking to them, he thought with dark humor.

He listened to the two of them grunt and groan and pound without a hint of jealousy.

She wasn't his. She never had been.

He was the mark, the dupe. And she'd played him like a pro —still was.

How long would Lisa live this charade? Until the Russians

were pumping him for information the way her lover was pumping her right now? Or until the two of them retired and they'd wasted their entire lives on a lie?

Yeah, the latter. They'd let him raise those brats as his own, feed them, clothe them, educate them, love them, but they were cuckoos in the nest. Parasites.

Eli smiled.

No, he'd think of a different plan. In the meantime, he'd nail his lovely wife every chance he could. He'd save as much money as he could while cutting that bitch off from their accounts. His fingers drummed the steering wheel. He'd give her an allowance. A small one with bonuses only he understood for various sex acts. That's what she basically was, a prostitute.

A whore.

A lying, fucking whore.

He waited for them to finish. His wife's lover had stamina, that was for damn sure.

He watched her leave her nooner looking as fresh and put together as when she'd arrived. She climbed into the little sedan he'd taken out a loan to buy for her.

That would go back tomorrow.

She hadn't showered. Would he still smell the prick on her when he came home tonight?

He thought of their small dining table as his hands squeezed the steering wheel. As soon as the boys were down for the night, he was going to fuck her right there, with the drapes wide open so that anyone walking by the house would see.

He smiled grimly.

He was going to enjoy this game for the next few months. Make her feel unsure and uncertain the way he had before he'd finally figured it out.

Angry. Humiliated. Stupid. Used.

When the lover exited the hotel, his identity wasn't a shock. It wasn't even a surprise. It confirmed everything Eli had already suspected. The rush of humiliation and revulsion slid all the way down his spine to the base of his coccyx.

But he was the one in control now.

He was the one calling the shots.

32

PRESENT DAY

Brynn watched Grady run his hand gently over the dog's bony skull and along the sagittal crest as they sat in the veterinarian's waiting room.

It had taken time and an infinite amount of patience on Grady's behalf for the dog to accept the collar and leash. The massive bag of dog treats he'd picked up had helped. Coaxing the dog into the car had proven near impossible until Grady had tossed her the keys and climbed into the cargo area of the Jeep with the large, filthy dog in his lap.

They'd been here for ten minutes now, and the dog had finally calmed down, thanks mainly to the comfort of Grady's touch. She couldn't help wondering what it would feel like being stroked that way…

A perky assistant came out of an exam room and jerked Brynn out of her salacious thoughts. She'd spent more time thinking about sex in the past twenty-four hours than she had in the entire two years previous.

The assistant ushered them inside. Brynn didn't miss the disapproving glances sent their way when the woman noticed the dog's matted coat and pronounced limp.

"He's a stray. We found him this way," Brynn explained quickly.

The assistant's expression cleared. "Oh, well we'll take him from here. See if he's chipped or tattooed. Make sure he's reunited—"

"His owner has obviously abandoned him. He can't go back to him," Grady said sharply.

The assistant pursed her lips. "It's possible he ran away and they were unable to catch him. I suspect his family is going to be thrilled to have him back."

Grady sat with his arms crossed, looking deceptively relaxed. "Someone told me he belonged to Caleb Quayle. Why don't you call him to confirm? See if he wants to come down here and claim his dog. First, I'd like the vet to examine him and look for any old injuries and check the infection in the front left paw. I'll pay for the work if the owner is…reluctant."

The woman's expression went carefully blank. "Okay, let's get this pupper examined as a priority, and then we'll figure out what to do next."

The assistant took the lead of the skittish dog from Grady's tight grip. The dog wasn't keen and sent Brynn and Grady a woeful look of betrayal. Brynn wanted to reassure him that everything would be okay, but his future was uncertain. Brynn couldn't make false promises, not even to a dog.

"What's going to happen to him now?" she asked when the assistant left the room.

"I don't know, but it has to be better than being on the streets."

"Unless he is forced to go back to his original owner."

"Not going to happen." Grady looked at her. "You want me to drive you home? I suspect they're going to be awhile."

The blue eyes that held hers were deceptively calm. But she was aware of emotions sizzling just beneath the surface.

"I don't mind waiting for a little while." She smiled in an attempt to soothe the tension that seemed to crackle off him. "I don't have anything urgent at home waiting for my attention, and my social calendar is empty for this evening."

His expression softened, and he unexpectedly reached out to cup her cheek, his thumb brushing over her bottom lip.

Wildfire stripped her nerves bare and made her catch her breath.

"Why is that?" Three lines formed between his brows. "A beautiful, smart, outgoing woman like you?"

The touch continued to send shockwaves of sensation over her. She covered her reaction with humor as he removed his hand.

"Outgoing isn't the usual descriptor people use for me." She'd never really considered herself to be beautiful, but she wasn't about to argue.

His lips quirked. "What would they use then?"

She inhaled shakily. "Boring, grumpy, demanding."

"Hardworking, serious, someone who knows what she wants? That I can see."

She grimaced. "I guess that's my ex still in my head. I hadn't realized how deeply his rejection and poor opinion of me hurt."

"That's what he actually called you?" Grady sounded outraged.

"No." She exhaled. "Damn, I can't even blame him for that." It had been two years and she finally felt able to talk about it. Or maybe that was simply because of who was asking. "I guess that's what I internalized after he left me. It was so quick I never had the chance to defend myself. I have all these words and arguments stored up inside my head, but I never had the opportunity to unload them. I guess he did me a favor, really. Why waste the energy arguing if he was that desperate to leave?"

"And why put in the effort for someone who doesn't want you?" he agreed, and she knew he really got it.

He understood the power of rejection.

"Was I really so awful to live with that I didn't warrant a simple goodbye or explanation?" She'd known there was something on Aiden's mind, something he wouldn't talk to her about.

When she'd asked, he'd denied it, claimed it was nothing, until the wedge that had been inserted between them split them wide apart like an axe through a piece of wood.

"There hasn't been anyone since?"

The question felt heavy with import, but she didn't want that heaviness. Aiden's legacy had been an anchor around her neck for long enough. She didn't want the weight of her past reflecting on her future. Not anymore.

"Only Bowie."

"Bowie?"

She enjoyed seeing his eyes widen in surprise. "The fake boyfriend I invented in an effort to deflect Darrell's unwanted attentions yesterday."

"He hit on you?"

"When I was making my official statement in his office."

Grady stretched out his legs and crossed them at the ankles. "Sleaze."

"Yeah, I know. He has a wife and three kids who I serve in the café on a weekly basis. I think he thinks that because we went on a couple of dates a decade ago, I still have a thing for him."

Grady looked surprised. "You had a thing for him?"

She rolled her eyes. "In *high school*. That lasted for about one hour into our first date until he jabbed his tongue into my mouth like he was performing oral surgery."

Grady tilted his head to one side. "But you went on more than one date with him?"

She grimaced, pretending to be intent on a poster detailing the life cycles of parasites in dogs and cats. "He was one of the *popular* guys around here, and it was the first time anyone had asked me out on a date. I wasn't quite sure if my expectations were skewed. By the third date, he was insistent we have sex in his car."

Grady tensed.

"I said no. It made me realize why my dad always told me to drive myself on dates rather than get picked up. Easier to extricate yourself from unwanted situations when you have your own transportation and—"

"And they don't know where you live," Grady finished. "Except in Deception Cove everyone knows where everyone else lives."

"Which I think is why my parents settled in Pike's Turning. Close enough to town, but not where the neighbors can look through your drapes on the way home from work."

Grady grinned. "How did young Darrell take the rejection?"

"He was pissed for about a week, but he kept calling me up in the hopes I'd change my mind. But I was off to college that fall so it made it easy to say no."

"He was a cop then, too. And you were, what, eighteen?" Grady's lips twisted. "What a fucking asshole."

She wanted to run her palm over the sexy stubble on his cheek. "I'm surprised you guys were ever friends."

Grady made a disgusted sound. "Pretty sure he figured me and Saul would follow him around doing whatever he suggested like some idiot sidekicks. But that wasn't how we rolled."

"Why'd he stick with you?"

"Because Darrell enjoyed breaking the rules, and having a couple of friends to use as scapegoats to blame suited him just fine." Grady sent her a hooded look that made her mouth go dry with want.

She'd obviously lusted after the wrong boy in high school.

"For our part, we enjoyed having a friend whose daddy didn't immediately throw us all in jail the moment one of our schemes went haywire. Although, there was a price to pay."

And Grady had been the one to pay it, obviously.

"You all became cops."

"We did." He shifted as if uncomfortable with the topic of conversation. "Saul didn't stick, but I found my calling, which some people think displayed a degree of irony. What about you?"

"Me?"

"Yeah, I'm baring my soul here." He rolled his shoulders. "What did you get up to in high school?"

"Absolutely nothing." That was depressing.

"No drunken parties?"

She shook her head. "I read."

He snorted. "While drunk I hope?"

She grinned. "Sometimes. I told you. I was boring. I lived out in the sticks. My parents warned if I ever climbed behind the wheel of a car over the limit, they'd take it away. Not that I ever even considered it. Boring, remember?"

"Reading. What a rebel."

"It feels like a rebellion sometimes. Not going with the flow and chasing all those expectations people have of each other. I did what I wanted, and what I wanted was peace and quiet and the opportunity to hang out with a good book."

"College changed that?"

She pressed her lips together. Unfortunately, her college memories were inextricably bound to her ex. "I bloomed away from home, and I guess I did the party scene there. Aiden was on the varsity water polo team. But I was always pretty nerdy." She shrugged. "I still like peace and quiet over clubbing."

"Fuck, I haven't been to a club since before I joined the FBI. I hang out with my teammates at this bar we like to go to, or at each other's houses—" His voice caught.

She put her hand on his arm at his look of distress. "What?"

He cleared his throat. "We, er, lost a couple of people this month. An explosion and a plane crash."

"Oh my god, you were in Houston?"

He flinched and she wished she hadn't said anything. "I saw on the news that the FBI lost a man."

He gave a slight nod.

"I'm so sorry for your loss."

"Yeah." He cleared his throat. "Scotty's wife has two little kids and is pregnant with number three. It's his Jeep I'm driving. I borrowed it off Grace to use while the lab processes my truck."

"You were obviously close. I'm so sorry."

He nodded and looked as if he didn't want to talk about it. She totally understood. They sat in companionable silence for a few minutes.

"You heard anything from the FBI yet?" she asked.

His head snapped around, but his expression was blank.

"About the hit-and-run and your truck?" She kept her voice down, feeling the need to whisper even though they were alone in the room.

He grunted. "Lab is backed up. My boss told me to hang tight and enjoy my vacation."

"Perhaps that's exactly what you should do."

Those pale cerulean eyes were intent on her face. "You have something in mind?"

The look he sent her made her breath catch and her cheeks heat. "I—"

The door opened, and the spell was broken.

A woman came inside wearing a white coat holding out her hand. "I'm Dr. Vilamitjana. I understand you brought in the bearded collie for treatment?"

Grady stood. "That's right, Doc. FBI Operator Grady Steel. This is Ms. Brynn Webster. She actually caught the dog."

"With cookies and ham," Brynn put in helpfully.

"Did you notice his paw?" Grady asked the vet. "Looked infected."

The veterinarian was young and pretty, with deep, almost black eyes and warm brown skin. "I removed a shard of broken glass I found embedded there, cleaned, stitched, and bandaged the wound. He needs a bath, grooming, some nutritious food, vaccinations, and deworming."

"He's generally healthy?"

Brynn tried hard not to feel superfluous as the two spoke quickly about the dog's condition.

"I'll need to run more tests, take x-rays." Dr. Vilamitjana raised an unimpressed brow. "He's not even a year old but is severely malnourished and appears he's been on the streets for months. I need to test for heartworm and Lyme disease. I'll keep him overnight to give him some intravenous antibiotics to knock out the foot infection." Her voice firmed. "You said you know who his legal owner is?"

Shouting started outside.

"Yep. I think that's him now." Grady's smile was broad but didn't reach his eyes.

Dr. Vilamitjana straightened her shoulders and opened the door into the main waiting area.

Brynn followed them out, surprised to see Jackie, her server, standing next to an angry-looking Caleb Quayle.

Caleb turned to Grady and stabbed his finger into his chest. "What the fuck are you doing with my dog?"

Grady widened his stance. "What you should have been doing all along."

"You own the bearded collie that has been a stray in town for the last few months?" Dr. Vilamitjana valiantly attempted to take control of the situation even as the receptionist picked up the phone, presumably to call the cops.

Grady looked completely relaxed, but Brynn was not fooled.

"Yeah. He's mine." Caleb tucked in his lantern jaw, and his eyes darted over them, assessing the opposition. "He ran off. Couldn't catch the little fucker." He raised his chin and narrowed his eyes. "Where is he? Little bastard won't be getting out again."

Brynn shied away at the threat in his tone.

"I'm afraid it isn't as simple as that," Dr. Vilamitjana stated firmly.

Jackie stepped forward. "Give him his dog back. You can't keep him. Or are you running a bunch of tests to rack up a bill Caleb never agreed to pay?"

"I'm not paying for anything I haven't sanctioned." Caleb raised his voice in case the receptionist got any ideas in the billing department.

"Is that so?" Dr. Vilamitjana stuffed her hands deep in the pockets of her white coat. "Mr. Quayle, isn't it?"

Caleb nodded. Then shot Brynn a look of loathing. She smiled at him sweetly.

"I'm afraid that your dog was brought to me in a sorry state and needed emergency treatment for a cut and an infection. He also has fleas and possibly mange."

Brynn hid her reaction. She hated parasites, but she hated bullies more.

"He ran away," Caleb growled. "How am I supposed to—"

"These two people found him and in a few short hours managed to get him to me for treatment."

Caleb sniffed. "I tried calling him. He wouldn't come, even when I brought food."

Too aware of the price, Brynn thought, narrowing her eyes.

"Before he ran away did you license him? Did he have his full quota of vaccinations?"

Caleb sneered. "Don't believe in 'em."

The vet smiled like he was an idiot. "Be that as it may, licenses are mandatory, and it is required by state law to vaccinate your dog against rabies. Do you believe in rabies, Mr. Quayle, because I can assure you it is a truly horrific disease."

Caleb said nothing but his eyes glittered.

"X-rays also suggest this dog has been the victim of repeated abuse." The doctor was bluffing because she hadn't taken X-rays yet.

"I never touched him." Caleb craned his head closer to the doctor but she stood her ground. Brynn was impressed. Grady took a half-step forward. "If you found something then he was probably hit by a car."

"These wounds are older, likely occurring when he was a young puppy—as if he was kicked repeatedly."

Jackie frowned at Caleb.

"I let him know who was boss. Maybe someone else kicked him."

Brynn flinched.

"Regardless, I'm going to have to report you to Animal Services—"

"You fucking dare." Caleb shoved the doctor back a step.

Grady held out his hand to block Caleb. "That's assault, pal."

Jackie screeched and grabbed his arm. "Caleb, stop!"

"You can't steal my dog. I'd rather put a bullet in it than let you assholes take him."

Well, Caleb was clearly no Solomon.

"You can't attack people because they're saying something you don't like," said Brynn.

Caleb's head swung toward her, struck her without warning.

Pain lanced through her in a flash of white, overwhelming her, as her nose gushed warm blood down the front of her shirt.

"Oh my god. Caleb, what the hell? Brynn. Brynn. Are you all right?" Jackie's voice was shocked.

Brynn felt hands maneuvering her into a seat. "I'm fine. It's your asshole boyfriend who has the problem."

Brynn pried her eyes open to see Caleb on the floor with Grady kneeling on his back. He pulled a zip tie out of his back pocket as he gazed at her. "You okay?"

His voice was soft and intent, cutting through all the noise as a Sheriff's Department cruiser drew up out front.

She nodded. She couldn't believe she'd been punched in the face by that jerk.

Someone stuffed a tissue into her hand and she held it to her nose, then leaned forward over a bowl, pinching her nostrils closed and spitting out blood as instructed by the veterinarian.

Great.

Dr. Vilamitjana asked her to look up and then shone a light into her eyes, before standing back. "I don't think you have a concussion but, as you're not furry, you probably want to get checked out at a health center. Keep your head over the bowl, and breathe through your mouth."

Darrell York swaggered through the doors and his eyes took in the situation quickly before landing on her. "You okay, Brynn? Somebody hit you?"

Brynn did not like the way he was looking at Grady. "Caleb hit me because he's a bully. Grady apprehended him. Caleb also shoved Grady and the doctor."

Darrell grunted.

"This young woman was standing up for me," Dr. Vilamitjana pointed to Brynn. "I want that man charged with assault, animal abuse, and anything else you can think of."

Caleb began shouting that they'd stolen his dog. Jackie huddled in a corner, talking to another deputy. She kept sending worried glances at Brynn. Brynn eyed her balefully and wondered if the young woman would turn up for work tomorrow. Or if she even wanted her to.

Her pulse pounded, and her head was sore.

The sheriff came over, touching her shoulder as he examined her swollen nose.

"You'll be lucky not to have a black eye tomorrow." He smiled, and she saw a flash of the young man she'd been so taken with half a lifetime ago. "We'll need statements if you want to press charges."

"Will he get his dog back when it's obvious he doesn't take care of the poor animal?" she asked.

"I don't know all the facts yet." Darrell placed his hands on his hips.

"Seems like a pretty easy decision to me." She didn't bother to hide the bitterness in her tone.

Grady moved toward her as another deputy helped Caleb to his feet and out the door.

Darrell shifted his body between her and Grady. "Want me to drive you home so you can put some ice on that face? Or take you to the ER?" His fingers curved over her shoulder.

She shrugged him away. "I'm more worried about the dog. About getting assurances he won't go back to the Quayle household and will be properly cared for."

"I never figured you for a dog lover, Brynn."

"You really don't know me that well, do you, Darrell?"

"I wanted to," he said under his breath.

"And I said no." The pounding in her head intensified.

He stood back. "Why are you so interested in this stray anyway? Is it something to do with Caleb being the owner?" Darrell rested his hands on his equipment belt. "I heard you had words with him at the bar last night."

"Where he and two of his idiot friends physically *attacked* Grady."

Darrell's lip curled. "Grady's a highly trained FBI agent. Pretty sure he didn't need you interfering or defending him."

She glared through the haze of pain. "Are you suggesting I don't have a right to say something in defense of another human being, or a dog for that matter?"

"That's not what I meant—"

"Sure it isn't." She felt her lip curl. "Seen and not heard. Pregnant and barefoot in the kitchen. Is that where you think women should be, Sheriff York?"

"I didn't say—" Darrell took a breath. "What was the argument about last night?"

She crossed her arms over her chest. "Why is *that* relevant to him punching me in the face? Why am I the one who's being interrogated about this?"

Darrell adjusted his hat. He still stood way too close. "I am trying to figure out what's going on around here. The three of you keep turning up together in troubling incidents. Is there something going on I don't know about?"

"Like what?" Brynn had no clue what he was getting at. "He and two of his friends attacked Grady in the bar. Accused him of killing Milton. I called him on it, pointing out he was as likely a suspect in the murder, and Caleb said something hurtful to me regarding my mother when I banned him from the café for life."

"What did he say?"

Brynn's mouth went dry, furious he was making her repeat it.

"That a ban for life wouldn't last long, as my mother would be dead soon anyway."

Darrell's lips tightened.

Grady stepped around the sheriff and handed her an icepack wrapped in a paper towel. The differences between the two men as they stood side-by-side was stark. Both were good-looking in their own way, but Grady was lean and honed whereas Darrell was bullish and fleshy, like his father.

More, one showed genuine concern. The other wanted to use the situation to get into her good graces and ultimately her pants.

She pressed the icepack to the spot between her eyes and felt the cold begin to numb the throbbing pain.

"What happens to Quayle now?" asked Grady.

Darrell answered reluctantly. "We will charge him with assault. The veterinarian wants to press additional charges of animal abuse, but I don't know if we have enough to make that stick."

"You have to be kidding me." Brynn wanted to scream with frustration. "So, he'll be allowed to own animals even though he obviously can't be bothered to care for them?"

"Unless there's clear evidence of abuse, there's not a lot I can do," said Darrell impatiently.

Grady's expression narrowed. "What happens to this particular dog now?"

"Why are you two so caught up with that damn dog? You planning to adopt it?"

She waited for Grady to say something, but, though muscles flexed in his jaw, he remained silent.

The sheriff scoffed. "A little too much commitment for you, Grady?"

Brynn met Grady's gaze but the man still said nothing.

"There have to be a hundred better homes than him living on the street," Grady said finally.

Darrell sighed. "Tell that to all the dogs stuck in the pound or put to sleep because no one wants them."

TONI ANDERSON

"Then, yes, I'll take him," Grady growled as Brynn was about to say the same.

No way would she let that dog be euthanized.

Darrell rolled a meaty shoulder. "We'll see. He will stay here until the veterinarian releases him. Then we'll talk to Caleb, see if he'll voluntarily relinquish ownership. Otherwise, the dog might have to stay in the pound until the courts sort it all out."

"That's barbaric," Brynn stated quietly. "You're basically putting the dog in jail for his owner's abuse."

"Alleged abuse," Darrell stated firmly.

Brynn put a hand to her head and frowned at the absurdity of the situation.

"Are you really okay?" asked Grady.

"I'm fine. I'm angry. But I'm fine." She put aside the bowl and tossed the bloody tissue in a wastepaper bin before standing shakily. "Do you need another official statement or will Dr. Vilamitjana's suffice?"

"To have any hope of charges sticking we need official statements from everyone involved."

She gritted her teeth. "As I have to work tomorrow, I'd like to get it over with now, as quickly as possible."

"We can go down to the sheriff's department right now." Darrell took her arm, but she broke the contact. "Then I'll give you a ride home."

"I'll ride with Grady. If you don't mind?" she asked the man in question.

"It would be my pleasure," Grady said solemnly.

She didn't miss the spark of anger in the look Darrell shot Grady, but she wasn't some trophy or toy to be fought over.

"Fine," Darrell said. "I'll meet you there in fifteen minutes after I speak to the receptionist here."

"You really okay?" Grady asked again when they were outside in the cold winter air.

"Yeah." She took a deep breath and felt her face throb. "At least we got the dog a temporary reprieve."

"Caleb isn't getting his hands on that dog ever again. Not if I can help it."

"Don't make promises you can't keep."

Those intense blue eyes with their dark lashes stared down at her. "I never do, Brynn. I never do."

33

Grady stood outside the Montrose County Sheriff's Department where he'd once worked in what seemed a different lifetime. He was waiting for Brynn to finish filing her statement. It didn't escape his notice that Darrell was dealing with Brynn personally, while he and the other witnesses were all handled by a young deputy who was so shiny new Grady had needed to quietly remind him about proper procedure.

On the outside, the department had changed little in the intervening years, but most of the old-timers who'd been here when he'd first started his career were now retired. A few of the faces he did recognize sent him uneasy smiles. Most avoided meeting his gaze altogether.

So much for a hero's homecoming.

For some reason, his reputation in this town had taken a nose-dive over the past eight years, and he hadn't even been here.

Was his sister to blame—or Darrell? Or both?

He'd been accepted by one of the preeminent law enforcement agencies in the world, not only as a case agent, but as a Hostage Rescue Team operator. The most elite tactical enforcement unit in the US. Apparently, local gossips still somehow managed to tarnish his good name and reduce his hard work to nothing more than good luck and bad judgment—on the FBI's part.

Had Darrell and Crystal fed off one another with their petty jealousy and resentment until the town believed he was some kind of villain? HRT did not tolerate operatives who didn't play by the book or work as a team—or who weren't genuinely decent people.

Of course, the hit-and-run fabrication didn't help. Nor the fact his father had served time for murder. The general situation made digging for inside information on who might be, or know, Eli Kane, particularly difficult, but HRT operators thrived on challenge.

Kane was smart as hell. IQ off the charts and balls of steel.

Grady had balls of steel, too. His eyes narrowed and his lips curved into a flat smile. He'd been born with them.

Like Ropero had said earlier, criminals like Kane cast a stain of evil and mistrust over the organization he loved—which made catching him so damn important. And Grady wanted to be part of the team to bring him down. It was personal now. He wanted Kane in a cage, and he wanted to be one of the ones who put him there.

Pride.

Not a particularly useful trait, but one he'd been dealt right along with his steel balls.

He watched Jackie Somers leave the Sheriff's Department with her mother's arm wrapped around her shoulders.

The mother, Julie, sent him a look that morphed into a smile of recognition. Maybe not everyone here hated him. They'd been friendly in high school. She'd gotten pregnant before graduation, he recalled, but couldn't remember who the father had been. He intended to find out and check that line of inquiry, looking for Kane.

He smiled back but didn't try to start a conversation. He was too on edge by what had happened earlier.

The fact Brynn was in physical pain because someone had

assaulted her in his presence, infuriated him and made him feel guilty as hell.

Grady had expected Caleb to go for the veterinarian, partly because she was the one spelling out the rules and partly because of her brown skin. Grady knew a racist and misogynist when he saw one.

Caleb's family lived in a small group of cabins tucked into a little clearing in the woods about five miles out of town. They were hard-drinking, tough guys. Loggers, construction workers, railroaders. A rougher flavor of blue collar than Grady's own family, unless you counted his asshole father, which Grady didn't.

Grady had placed himself where he could easily intercept an attack on Dr. Vilamitjana. He hadn't been able to risk laying hands on Caleb until the other guy had escalated things to criminal levels in front of witnesses. Grady didn't want to be arrested by an over-zealous sheriff looking for an excuse.

He'd wanted Caleb to be clearly in the wrong so that the poor cowering beast he'd brought to the vet today would never have to suffer at his owner's hands again.

When Caleb had instead struck Brynn, Grady had been caught completely unprepared. And he'd been shocked by the rage that had ripped through him. He'd wanted to pound Caleb into the ground, but training had prevailed. Grady had restrained Caleb without so much as a much-desired punch to the face.

But no matter how self-congratulatory he felt at keeping control, Brynn had still been physically assaulted, and that made him sick to his stomach.

Grady knew, ultimately, he'd get more satisfaction knowing the guy was going to have to pay real consequences for his actions, but a small part of Grady still wanted to beat the asshole to a pulp.

Brynn had been stoic as hell. His admiration for her kept growing.

His phone rang. Cowboy. "S'up?"

"Wondering how come you're hovering outside the sheriff's department like a bad smell. Trouble?"

Grady glanced around and spotted his teammate in the upper turret window of the hotel then looked away again. "Nothing I couldn't handle."

"How's the head?"

"Ugly as ever. Find out anything today?"

"The pizzeria serves a decent meat lover's pizza, and Donnelly snores like a freight train."

Grady heard a vehement protest from a female voice in the background. "Any hits on the images?"

"Everything we've taken so far has come back with zero hits."

"Even those two Russians?"

"Nothing popped in our system yet." Ryan Sullivan lowered his voice to a quiet murmur. "Something about them makes me suspicious as hell though, and it's not the accent."

"Maybe one of us should take a look inside their room when we know it's empty," Grady suggested.

"Maybe one of us should," Cowboy agreed. "What are your plans for the evening?"

"Probably not that. Planned to check out the fine dining at the local golf club and see if I can spot anyone matching Kane's description or jog my own memory."

"You have something suitable to wear? I don't think I've ever seen you in anything except a T-shirt."

Grady let a smile tug his lip. "Don't worry, Mom. I'll figure it out. They serve great steaks there—or at least they did ten years ago."

"I'll see if I can make a reservation for me and my gal."

"See you later."

"I'll be the loud obnoxious one in the cowboy hat in case you don't recognize me."

"As opposed to what exactly?" Grady watched Brynn step through the door. She glanced up, and her expression softened with relief when she spotted him standing there. He felt a subtle shift in his chest when she smiled. Some weird part of him locking into place.

"Go easy with the redhead," said Ryan.

Cowboy ended the call before Grady could snap at him to do the same with Donnelly.

Go easy with the damn redhead, indeed.

"You okay?" Grady shoved his cell in his pocket and walked toward Brynn, surreptitiously flashing Ryan the finger behind his back.

"I'm fine." The wind ruffled her fiery hair and blew it into her eyes. She was pale but the redness and swelling of her nose had gone down some. "It's the first time I've ever been physically attacked. I was knocked off balance—"

"I should have stopped him."

She laid a hand on his arm and gripped his wrist. Her strength surprised him. "You did. You couldn't have predicted he'd hit me. Even though I don't recommend taking a blow to the face, at least he's locked up now. I spoke to my dad. He says he's going to punch Caleb when he gets out and that the entire family is banned from the café for life and that if Jackie doesn't dump his ass, she's fired."

"He's obviously pissed."

"He is. So am I."

And they had a right to be.

Guilt ate at him. "How about I take you out for dinner as a thank you for not only luring a flea-ridden stray into your home, but also as an apology for being assaulted by the owner?"

Her eyes were huge in her face. "Like on a date?"

He hesitated. The idea made something vulnerable swell up inside him, even as his conscience began to rebel.

He couldn't tell her the truth.

He was undercover.

He wasn't playacting or being duplicitous because he was a jerk. He was hunting one of the FBI Ten Most Wanted Fugitives who'd evaded the law for the past twenty-seven years. Going out to dinner with Brynn was good cover—as long as he didn't forget his mission.

Most people would understand the need for deception, but Brynn had been hurt before…

When Kane was caught or they determined he was no longer in the area, he could probably tell Brynn the truth—or some of it. She'd get it.

And, maybe he didn't need to make this anything more complicated than dinner.

"Yeah, but a no-pressure, 'thanks for being awesome' sort of date, rather than 'you worrying I'm trying to get into your pants' date." He felt heat bloom in his cheeks.

Why the hell had he mentioned sex?

Maybe she didn't want to go on anything approaching a *date* with a guy like him. She'd said there had been no one since her asshole ex had left her. Why would he be the man to break her dry spell?

Fuck.

And now he was thinking about getting into her pants.

"We'll run by the house and throw on clothes that aren't covered in blood and go find something decent to eat before I personally starve to death."

She blinked at him, and he was pretty sure that she was going to beg off and say she was tired or sore or simply not interested.

She smiled. "I'd like that."

34

B rynn changed into a green dress that flattered her figure and made her hair look a vivid russet. She pulled on stockings and tall black boots that made her feel like a badass. She quickly cleaned her face and put on some foundation to cover the bruising. Then added lipstick, eyeshadow, and mascara to stop feeling like such a washed-out hag.

Jackie's mom had called to apologize for her daughter and express how terrible the young woman felt about what had happened.

Brynn's mom and dad were furious and talking about a civil suit. But if being fired-up on her behalf gave them something to think about besides cancer, then she was all for it. They'd wanted her to come home tonight and sleep there, but she didn't want to.

She had other plans.

Her nose was sore but not broken. Pain meds had gotten rid of the headache. Makeup disguised the rest.

The knock on the door from the upstairs apartment to the basement echoed around her ribcage. Her hand went to her chest and she swallowed.

"Give me one minute!" She felt nervous to be going on a date.

A date with Grady Steel, who was hot as hell and so much sweeter than anyone wanted to give him credit for.

She wasn't going to let herself get tangled up with him emotionally. She knew this was nothing more than a short-term interlude. He'd go back to his life as soon as the FBI finished investigating, and she'd return to her life in Boston when…

Yeah.

She didn't want to think about that either. She wanted the chance to enjoy a man's company with no pressure and no expectations.

Aiden had been shacked up with some bimbo since he'd left her, but Brynn still hadn't been able to think about dating until the divorce had been finalized. Not that she'd met anyone she'd been even vaguely interested in.

But now, finally, that little frisson of possibility had sprung to life, and, to her surprise, it didn't scare her half to death. It was simply on the table. Something to be explored or not, not something to run screaming from, for the comfort of her couch and a good book.

She rubbed her lips together one final time before tossing the lipstick into a small purse and grabbing her thick winter coat and heading up the stairs to unlock the door.

She stepped into the kitchen. The appreciation in Grady's eyes when he saw her made her glow inside. He held her coat as she slipped into it, the touch of his fingers against the bare skin of her arms making her shiver.

"You look amazing." His warm breath brushed her neck.

"Thank you." Considering she'd taken fifteen minutes to get ready, she felt pretty damn amazing. She turned to face him. "So do you."

He wore a pressed pale blue shirt that brought out the blue of his eyes, a navy tie, beige pants, and shoes polished to a high sheen.

Her breath caught at the interest she saw in his gaze. Then her stomach growled, breaking the sudden tension. She pressed her hand there. "I haven't had anything to eat since before noon. I fed the dog all my cookies."

"I am sure that dog appreciated them as much, if not more, than you would have."

"True. Have you decided what you're going to call him yet?"

His expression darkened. "Not yet."

"That animal is so ready for a good home."

"He'd love anyone who fed him cookies." Grady indicated she walk ahead of him through the house and down the front steps to the Jeep. His touch burned her through all the layers of clothing when he helped her climb inside.

He got in, started the engine. Hesitated. "It's not that I don't want him…" There was a subtle note of yearning in his voice.

"Then take him. Be his person."

His eyes were worried. "I'm away a lot."

"Surely there must be someone amongst your friends who can watch him when you are away?"

He frowned at her, then his expression cleared. "There's someone who might. I'll have to ask her."

The *her* made Brynn trip. Did Grady have someone waiting for him back in Quantico?

She didn't know. So, she made herself ask. She wasn't getting involved with anyone she couldn't trust, not even on a casual level. "A girlfriend?"

His eyes widened in surprise then grew both amused and pained. "No. The widow of a teammate."

The woman he'd told her about earlier. "I'm really sorry for your loss." The words felt hollow but what else could she say?

"Me, too." He adjusted the temperature, and a little heat finally came through the vents.

It was still cold though, and she was touched when Grady reached into the back seat, grabbed a blanket, and handed it to her.

"Thanks." She spread it over her lap and legs.

"Grace has spoken about getting a dog in the past, but I know she has her hands full with her kids right now. But if the dog can be trusted with the children and is well behaved, I'm sure she'd be cool with a part-time arrangement. I can hire a dog-walker to exercise him when I am away on assignment."

"I'm sure he'll be a great family dog." A lump formed at the fact she wouldn't be taking the dog home with her, but she was at the café six days a week until late into the evening, and in her "spare" time she was running her own business. Her dad might take him during the day, but he'd have his chickens to worry about.

It might do her dad good to have a dog, especially if—

Her mind screeched to a halt. She didn't want to think about that future in any shape or form.

She'd talk to her dad. A shared puppy might bring them all some joy.

They drove out of town. The roads were icy but the four-wheel drive handled the conditions well, and Grady obviously knew how to drive. The blizzard was forecast to start tomorrow, which was not a fun prospect, especially when her mom had to travel almost daily for treatment. Maybe they'd stay in Bangor a few nights.

Brynn put it all out of her mind. There were only so many things she could worry about at one time, and she was about at her limit.

"Where are we going?"

"Clubbing."

"*Wut*?"

"Golf clubbing."

"Ha. Funny." To capture the tourist market, the local golf club allowed non-members to dine there, especially during the low season. Maine in January was as low as it got. The flags were out of the holes and the greens covered in protective sheets beneath a thick layer of snow.

They arrived at the club house, which had a grand-looking stone façade. She folded the blanket and was surprised when

Grady came around to her door and opened it for her. When he took her fingers, her nerves jumped.

The gleam in his eyes suggested he felt it, too, although neither of them commented. They walked through the doors and left their coats at the coat check. Inside, the lighting was muted and the tables topped in white linen and candlelight.

It was very romantic.

It hit her suddenly that the last time she'd been here she'd been having dinner with her parents and Aiden.

She stopped moving.

Grady rested his hand warmly on her back. "Is this okay?"

She swallowed. "Yes. Sorry. A few unanticipated memories."

His eyes grew concerned. "We can leave."

She shook her head. "No. No. I'd like to vanquish some of these ghosts. Today seems like as good a time as any."

The pretty greeter waited at their table with a patient smile. Brynn forced her feet to move forward.

Grady held out her chair and then took the seat with his back to the wall and a view of the room. The greeter went away to find their waiter.

The town's former sheriff, Temple York, was sitting across the other side of the room with his wife, daughter-in-law, and a small group of friends. Brynn could feel the speculation in their gazes as they took turns glancing over.

"You come here often with your parents?" Grady asked.

"Yeah, well, I did. They both like their golf, and this place is closer to their house than town so it was a regular stop. But Mom isn't up to socializing since her diagnosis."

Grady nodded. "You're close?"

"Yeah. Very." Brynn blinked. "My parents are great. We've always managed to have fun together as a family. I'm not sure what we're going to do if anything happens to her."

He reached out and squeezed her hand. "I remember her well, and she's a fighter. If anyone can beat it, she can."

Brynn remembered he'd lost his own mother at a young age and felt selfish for not being considerate of his feelings.

"Do you remember your mom at all?"

He withdrew his hand to pick up the menu. "Barely."

"That must hurt."

He looked surprised she'd thought about it.

"What happened to her?"

She watched his Adam's apple move up and down before he spoke. "Brain aneurysm. It was quick. She didn't suffer. Thankfully, we were with a sitter at the time, so I didn't see her…" His mouth firmed. Then he smiled, but it didn't reach his eyes. "Sorry. I don't talk about it much. It was tough. My mom made a happy home for us once my father was out of the picture. Losing her at such a young age shattered my world." He pressed his lips together. "As a kid, it hurt to see everyone else have loving parents, and I was a little shit about it sometimes. I don't think of her much nowadays."

"It must have been awful."

"It wasn't easy." His expression changed. "Don't get me wrong, Gran was great. Better than great. In her safe deposit box at the bank today, I found a bunch of family photographs that reminded me of some of the good times. She'd left the photos for me, and I was such a dick I hadn't even thought to look."

She could tell that the find had moved him. "Thank goodness the robber didn't steal those."

"They're worth more to me than the deeds to the house. Don't tell Crystal." His lips tipped up at one side. "Did you have anything taken during the robbery?"

"No. My parents keep their will and property deeds there. All the legal stuff. No gold bars or family heirlooms—more's the pity."

The server came over and they ordered.

Steak for Grady. Pasta with lobster sauce for Brynn. She saw the tall cowboy and his girlfriend walk in and loudly ask for a table. Then she noticed Darrell York arrive behind them, still in uniform. It took him a moment to spot them, but when he did, he headed straight for their table.

She swore.

He removed his sheriff's hat. "Brynn. You look good. You feeling better?"

"I'm feeling better now that animal is locked up, and I don't mean the dog."

A frown marred Darrell's forehead. "Quayle made bail."

"You let him go?" A shiver of alarm ran down her spine, and she slumped back in her chair. "Well, that's great."

"Judge granted bail. Not a lot I can do about it." He gave her a sly smile. "Maybe you should get your boyfriend to move up here to protect you."

Was he trying to call her out on her lie? Out her fake relationship with Bowie to Grady? Or was he insulting her ability to look out for herself as a woman? He seemed to have covered all three.

"I was hoping that law enforcement might do their jobs and deal with it. More fool me."

Darrell flushed angrily. "The law doesn't always work the way civilians expect."

"How about fellow professionals? The guy punched her in the face and would have seriously hurt everyone in that office if he'd had the opportunity." Grady let the words rest for a moment.

"Well, luckily you were there to save the day." There was no missing the snideness in Darrell's tone now.

"When do I get my gun back?" Grady asked.

"Why the hurry?" asked Darrell.

"Because you confiscating it is bullshit, and I know my rights."

"As soon as we get the results back from the lab you can pick it up—assuming the ballistics don't match."

"Match what?" Grady picked up his water and took a drink. "I heard the bullet was too fragmented for comparison."

"Who did you hear that from?" Darrell's eyes narrowed.

Grady said nothing but a small smile caught the outer edge of his lips.

"You'll get it back when you get it back." Darrell rolled his shoulders and raised a hand to his family's table. "I'm sure a highly trained professional like yourself doesn't even need a gun."

"Depends who I'm dealing with." The derision in Grady's tone was clearly aimed at the sheriff.

Darrell's smile grew spiteful. "Well, unfortunately your alibi doesn't clear you for Milton Bodurek's murder, so I'll wait on the official ballistics report. The ME says the body was likely only in the water for a few minutes and was still warm when he examined him. You had time to shoot him if you wanted to."

Brynn felt nauseous. How close had she been to seeing the murder?

Grady looked unconcerned. "Then I guess I'll have to get my lawyer involved unless you confiscated every handgun in town?"

The cowboy laughed loudly with his server, drawing Brynn's attention. The pretty, dark-eyed woman he was with caught her gaze. The direct stare made Brynn shift uncomfortably in her seat.

"You know I can't comment on an active investigation." Darrell hitched his pants. "I'll let you two get back to your meal."

Grady gave him another lazy smile. "Tell your wife I said 'Hi.'"

Darrell froze then nodded curtly before walking away with a scowl.

Brynn watched Darrell lean down to kiss Lorraine on the cheek in a rare display of public affection. Lorraine looked surprised, then blushed prettily.

Brynn turned to Grady and asked suspiciously, "Did you date Lorraine before she married Darrell?"

Grady grinned. "Way back. In high school. But his interest in you is not why I asked you out tonight," he assured her quickly.

"I'm sure it played a part," she said wryly. "Nothing like competition to whet someone's appetite, if my memory serves me."

He snorted. "I guess. But I don't poach someone's girl."

"I'm nobody's girl," she said sharply. "I don't belong to any man and don't want to. Especially not a married man."

"And I like independent women." Grady smiled at her with those wicked eyes fully engaged, and Brynn felt the jolt all the way to her toes.

Her skin felt hot just from one look.

She resisted fanning herself. Their food arrived, and she suddenly realized how ravenous she was. For food. For excitement. For life.

35

Grady hadn't discovered much at dinner except he liked Brynn Webster. A lot.

She was smart, independent, and spoke her mind. She struck him as straightforward and honest. He admired that about her, too.

But his conscience was seriously starting to trouble him. He wanted to get in deeper with her on a personal level. He wanted her. He *really* wanted her, but he was living a lie that would hurt her when she learned the truth.

They had almost finished with their main course when the two Russian tourists walked in.

He exchanged a quick look with Ryan, who reached out and grabbed Donnelly's hand and kissed it, eyeing her like he wanted to drag her across the table and eat her for dessert.

Son of a bitch.

But Grady knew what the other man was doing and, when a few minutes later Ryan and Donnelly asked for their food to be boxed up to go, it looked more like they were ready for a hot and heavy hook-up than an opportunity to do a little covert B&E.

Brynn excused herself to use the restroom.

Grady decided it was time to go say hello to Temple York and his cronies. See if any of them looked like they could be the fugitive he was searching for, or if talking to them shook lose any memories.

He sauntered over, knowing the former sheriff clocked him immediately. The guy had always been a good tactical lawman, even if his ethics had been questionable.

Grady held out his hand and shook that of his former boss. "Temple. Good to see you. Rose." He nodded to Temple's wife who smiled at him with narrowed eyes. He scanned the table. He recognized some of the players. Brian Gesbriecht, the mayor, and his wife. Constance Fenneck, a local author, and her husband, who was about the right age and height for Kane.

There were way too many middle-aged white dudes in this damn town.

All three couples had safe deposit boxes at the bank.

"Lorraine." Grady nodded.

The girl he'd dated in high school had been replaced by a woman with soft cheeks and tired eyes. He knew she had three kids now and seriously doubted Darrell spent much time doing hands-on parenting, too busy chatting up other women around town.

She smiled. "Grady Steel. As I live and breathe. I heard you were in town."

Grady nodded. "I had a little time on my hands."

"I heard." Temple guffawed.

Rose snorted nastily. "We all heard."

Grady ignored the digs while mentally consigning Agent Ropero to the depths of hell and simultaneously hoping she found some dirt on the couple. "Figured it would take the lab a couple of weeks to process the vehicle to clear my name, so I decided to drive up and talk to Crys about what to do with Gran's house. I hear the real estate market is hot around here."

He held Rose's gaze and watched her expression flicker.

Interesting.

"Market prices are still going up. Don't let Crys undercut you when she buys you out, although I thought she already had." Temple leaned forward and picked up his wine glass.

"I'm a silent partner."

"No one ever accused your sister of being silent."

The laughter grated across Grady's nerves. They might not get along, but Crystal was the only blood he had left that counted. He moved his lips into an easy smile that made his face ache.

"Maybe I'll hold onto the place and move out to your neck of the woods in a few years when I retire. Do what you guys did. Buy a plot of land and build a dream house. You have a builder you can recommend?" He noted the glance Temple and Rose sent one another.

Definitely something hinky going on there.

Did it have something to do with Kane, or was it some tax dodge or insider deal?

Grady only cared about Kane, but he'd be lying if he said he wouldn't be happy to dish out a little humility to this crowd. People who'd lied and been willing to sacrifice him in favor of one of their own. And then failed to live up to their promises until he'd forced them to.

Pride.

He was full of it.

He glanced over his shoulder, and Brynn was back at their table looking like a million dollars in her figure-hugging green dress.

"Excuse me. I better get back to my date." He held Darrell's gaze, deliberately wanting to get a rise out of the guy.

"Have a good night, Grady. Keep your eyes on the road on the drive home." Darrell's beady eyes gleamed with malice. "Don't want to hit anything."

"You'd know all about that now, wouldn't you, D?" He sent Darrell and Temple a pointed look.

Grady walked back to Brynn. Her eyes sparkled with amusement.

"Were you causing trouble?" she asked on a murmured laugh.

"Perhaps."

"What did you do to the back of your head?"

He'd forgotten about the injury. He touched a tentative hand to the wound not quite hidden by his short hair. It was healing well. "I went for a walk last night to see if I could figure out where the dog was hiding. Slipped on the ice and whacked the back of my head. Ended up driving to the nearest ER to make sure I wasn't concussed."

Her eyes were wide as saucers. "You should have woken me."

He pulled a face. "You have enough going on, and I felt like a fool." He hated lying but he was all in for this mission. No point blowing it now. "Probably wasn't smart driving, but the docs patched me up and said I was fine."

The Russian couple were still eating and, as much as he wanted to get out of here, he needed to make sure they stayed put for a little while longer.

"I don't know about you, but after the things we've been through the past few days, I think we've earned some dessert." He raised his hand to their server and asked for the menu again. "Are you a whoopie pie or a wild-blueberry type of girl?"

Brynn snorted. "I'm more of a death-by-chocolate person willing to sell my soul for a piece of three-layer chocolate ganache cake." She bit her lip. "But I am willing to share."

Grady dragged his eyes away from Brynn's lush bottom lip. Cleared the lust from his throat. "You heard the lady," he told the server. "And better bring a couple of spoons—in case I get lucky."

36

"Want to get out of that dress, first?" Ryan didn't know where Donnelly had come up with the little black number she was wearing at such short notice, but the sooner she climbed into tactical pants and a shirt the better.

"Yeah, but we need to be fast. We might not have that much time."

He gripped her hand as she pushed through the door into the hotel. He carried their bag of food in the other. Waste not, want not. After all, steak was steak.

They hurried up the stairs like two people on a mission to bang as fast and hard as possible.

Heat poured off him even though he knew this was theater. Playacting for the public.

They reached their room, and he quickly opened the door. Once inside and hidden from view, he released her hand and placed the food on the side.

She shut the door as he reached into his pocket, grabbed the electronic surveillance detector that TacOps had recently come up with, and turned it on.

It identified even those energetically inert devices that only transmitted intermittently. Novak wanted to be certain no one was spying on their operation.

"Anything?" Donnelly had kicked off the dainty heels and stood with her hands on her hips, which unfortunately drew his attention to her figure.

"Nothing." He went into the bathroom as much to get away from her as to check for more bugs. "All clear. What about our stuff. Anyone mess with it?"

They'd unpacked some casual clothes and toiletries into the wardrobe and bathroom to look like real tourists. They'd also placed some of their gear—couple of burner phones, their fake passports, in the hotel safe that a three-year-old could crack. Their government issue tactical gear, electronics, and weaponry, they left inside specially designed suitcases.

He watched Donnelly run a wand over the hotel safe panel and then over the lock on the cases. It scanned for fingerprints and would alert the user if the pattern differed from the last time it had been checked.

"All good."

His eyes almost bugged out of his head when she put the wand down and turned away from him, whipping off her dress and pulling on a black, long-sleeved shirt and then black pants.

His mouth went so dry it fused into one solid block. She had long lines and sleek muscles, and a tattoo peeked out from a pair of black sheer panties that were barely bigger than a handkerchief.

He ignored his little brain, threw off his hat and shirt, and tossed them on the nearest chair. He opened the drawer and dragged out a plain black shirt like the one Donnelly wore. His and hers. They were on a mission and not a vacation, so that was okay.

He turned around quickly and caught Donnelly staring.

He raised a brow. "What?"

"Nothing."

"Ready?"

She placed her weapon in a pancake holster at the small of her back. "Ready."

He tossed her a ski mask. "In case they set up a camera inside their room."

They pulled on nitrile gloves before heading out. When he was sure it was clear, he opened the door for Donnelly, and she stepped out. They moved in unison down the corridor. The Russians were down a floor and on the other side of the hotel.

It was early in the evening, and the hotel was quiet with a lot of people leaving early ahead of this storm and others cancelling, presumably for the same reason.

The hotelier was not happy about the fact, bemoaning the economy and the weather with equal ferocity. Ryan had regaled him with tales of ranching cattle when it was minus thirty outside and the price of beef kept dropping. The guy had finally stopped complaining, but Ryan figured not for long. Harry Butler was a whiner by nature, but would be easy to bribe if the need arose. Always good to know.

They reached the room, and Donnelly blocked the view from one side as he made short work of the lock.

"Misspent youth?" she asked.

He raised his eyes to her dark brown ones. "Misspent life."

They both pulled the ski masks over their faces before they slipped inside.

He held up his hand to signal a halt. He wanted to get a feel for the room first. There were clothes strewn over the back of a chair. A laptop and a few paperback guidebooks on the side.

He pulled out his bug detector as his cell buzzed. Checked it. "They just left the golf club."

Donnelly's brows knitted.

Did the Russians know they were in their room, or was it a coincidence they'd left the restaurant the exact same moment he and Donnelly stepped inside?

The gadget didn't show any surveillance devices in play.

Donnelly began to carefully go through the drawers. Ryan stopped her before she opened the bottom drawer. Pointed to the hair draped over one of the knobs. He picked it up and held it while she carefully looked through the contents, a couple of T-shirts. She felt beneath. Nothing.

She replaced the drawers, and he gently draped the hair back over the knob. Rudimentary and old-fashioned, but definite tradecraft.

These weren't a couple of tourists on a sightseeing vacation, but that didn't explain who they were or what they were really doing here.

He and Donnelly searched for another five minutes but found nothing out of the ordinary.

Donnelly tugged his shirt. "We need to go."

"We're missing something." He stared around the room and then spotted something under the window frame and crossed the floor.

He peered outside.

The occupants had hung a plastic bag out of the window. He hooked the bag with a gloved finger and lifted the sash.

He and Donnelly peered inside at a small perfume bottle. Donnelly frowned and went to pick it up. Ryan caught her hand.

"Remember what happened to Sergei Skripel and his daughter."

"You think that's *Novichok*?" Donnelly looked shocked.

Ryan shrugged. "Who the hell hangs perfume out the window?"

Her brown eyes assessed his. "What do we do?"

As much as he wanted to take it. Neutralize it. He couldn't. Not yet. Not without running it by his boss first.

"Photograph it. Quickly."

Donnelly took shots from as many angles as she was safely able with her cell.

Then, with extreme care, Ryan hung the bag back outside the

window while Donnelly drew the sash down. "Let's get out of here."

His heart hammered as they strode back to their room. Sweat slicked down his spine.

Once inside, he called Novak. "You need to get the team together. We have a situation."

37

Brynn was stuffed and having more fun than she could remember in a long time. Grady was amusing, attentive, seductive. And he'd been out looking for a stray dog last night, not getting into some other woman's panties.

She sighed contentedly.

The chocolate cake she'd consumed was the closest she'd come to sex in the past couple of years, and that was a very sad state of affairs indeed.

She'd missed this, she realized.

She'd missed the excitement and thrill of a growing attraction. The slip and slide of anticipation. The anxious rollercoaster of emotions.

She thought she'd lost the capacity to enjoy it.

She thought she'd lost it for good.

He held her coat as she slipped her arms inside, and she felt a quiver of arousal licking at her senses.

She wasn't sure what would happen next—and that was okay.

For once it was okay not to have her life planned out minute by minute, second by boring second.

He opened the car door for her, and then they stood there staring at each other with what felt a lot like wonder. The noise of more customers leaving the restaurant broke the spell, and he moved away and climbed into the driver's seat.

Once inside, he cleared his throat. "Thanks for tonight, it was—"

She grabbed his shirt and pulled him to her for a kiss that was anything but polite.

And this time he kissed her back. Dragged her against his chest and let his tongue tangle with hers.

He tasted like chocolate-flavored sin.

She was draped across the console, his one hand under her coat, gripping her ass, and his other hand sinking into her hair and tugging her head back so he had better access to her mouth.

He devoured her.

She groaned, and he growled right back.

It was ferocious.

It was ravenous.

It was *divine*.

He kissed her with the confidence of a man who knew exactly what he was doing. No sloppiness. No amateur groping. Just pure lustful sensation. She was desperate for more. Desperate to lose herself in the now rather than worry about the future or the past.

Her lips cruised his mouth, his neck. She felt him, hard and ready against her.

He swore and pulled away. "Not here."

She drew back and blew out a shuddering breath.

"Not here," she agreed.

He put the Jeep into gear as she drew her seatbelt around her.

She didn't feel cold now. Not even close. Desire coiled inside her. Insistent. Demanding. Greedy.

Tension stretched taut.

Grady's jaw clenched. His knuckles shone white as they held the steering wheel in a death grip. She half expected him to pull over in the woods somewhere so they could fuck like monkeys.

As if reading her mind he said, "I want you in a bed."

She shivered at his words. She wanted him anywhere.

They passed a vehicle as they hit the town limits. Grady pumped the brakes. He looked pissed at the need to slow down.

She knew exactly how he felt. A shiver ran down her spine. Her skin felt like brushed velvet. Her nerves like live wires.

They passed the veterinarian clinic, and Brynn briefly glanced toward the building and wondered if the dog was okay with his enforced confinement.

A flicker of orange had her sitting up. "Stop."

"What?" Grady turned to her in surprise with not a little disappointment in his voice.

"Stop. Go back. Go back to the animal clinic."

He braked hard. "It's closed."

"I thought I saw something." Dread wound through her, obliterating lust.

Grady didn't argue, which she appreciated. He did a smooth U-turn and headed back to the clinic. "What did you see?"

"I don't know." Her mouth went dry. "I thought I saw a flicker of something inside."

"A flicker?" he asked sharply.

She met his gaze. "A flame."

He pressed his foot harder on the accelerator and floored it. They were at the clinic in seconds. Grady drove around the building and pulled up at the back. They both jumped out.

At first, she thought she'd made a stupid error. Maybe her subconscious was giving her an excuse to put a halt to the passion that had leapt between them. Then the scent of smoke had her taking a step forward.

"Call 911." Grady was already jogging around the corner.

She grabbed her cell and stabbed in the numbers.

The operator answered as Grady reappeared, and she gave the woman the address and nature of the emergency. She watched Grady remove a weapon from an ankle holster and use the butt to smash the glass, before reaching through and unlocking the back door. She blinked in surprise at the fact he was armed, although she should have expected it.

Smoke billowed out of the doorway as he wedged the entryway open with a large planter.

He took off his coat, then ripped his shirt over his head and wrapped it around his lower face before pulling the leather jacket back on.

"Stay outside," he warned. "I don't want to have to go searching for you, too."

Brynn stood there watching in horror as he disappeared into the burning building.

38

Flames licked the floor and walls of the reception area, the stench of gasoline prevalent even over the noxious fumes that filled the room. A smoke alarm started its high-pitched wail which, in turn, triggered the animals to cry out in distress.

Son of a fucking bitch.

The cacophony was ear numbing.

Coughing, he grabbed the fire extinguisher off the wall and opened it up to tackle the blaze. The blinds had ignited and the chairs, even the reception desk and papers that lined it and the walls.

The extinguisher quickly ran out but the flames kept leaping higher, into the roof tiles.

Shit.

He looked outside for signs of a fire truck but there was nothing.

"Fuck."

He threw down the empty extinguisher and dashed back along the corridor, opening doors as he went. Kicking in those that were locked.

Most were empty. He finally reached the area where the

animals were locked in cages. Some were obviously recovering from operations or procedures. Many were scratching at the metal bars of their cages in agitation.

Grady felt someone beside him.

"There are some carriers and leashes over here." Brynn ran to the corner and tossed a small carrier at him.

Dammit. He didn't want her in here.

"Let's deal with the smaller animals first." She'd found some gloves and was already reaching for a Siamese cat that meowed pitifully.

Grady pulled on a pair of full-length leather gloves that were resting on top of the cage. He reached inside and grabbed a hostile cat, placed it in the carrier, and slammed the door closed. They worked side-by-side, one animal at a time, trying not to traumatize them further but unable to wait for them to calm down as the smoke grew thicker. Both he and Brynn were coughing now.

"Take the cats outside." He shouted. "I'll start on the dogs. Stay outside."

Most people were killed by smoke inhalation and not the fire itself. He didn't want to put Brynn in more danger than necessary.

He couldn't see the gray dog—his dog—anywhere but tried to ignore the panic.

Panic killed.

Brynn nodded and started lifting as many carriers as she was able to grip and headed outside the burning building.

Grady grabbed a leash and eyed a large German shepherd who was eyeing him back distrustfully. He spied a jar of what looked like cooked, cubed liver, and picked it up. Scooping out a handful of treats, he opened the cage and wrapped the leash around the dog's neck to form a loop. None of the animals were wearing collars.

"I'll take him." Brynn was back and ready to help.

He pressed his lips together. No time to argue.

He handed her the leash. She coaxed the dog through the door and into the fresh air. She was back twenty seconds later with the leash.

He didn't have time to ask questions. They quickly got all the dogs out of the one room, and he opened another door. In this area, many of the dogs looked to be sedated.

And there, in the corner, was his friend, sporting a brand-new haircut and anxious eyes.

"Grab our friend there. I'll lift the others."

The first was an old chocolate lab who was sleeping so heavily Grady at first worried she was dead until he touched her warm flank.

As he gently shifted his hands under her, she opened liquid brown eyes to stare at him.

He hurried into the cold, fresh air and laid the lab on the blanket Brynn had pulled out of his Jeep.

He looked around for the dogs and realized they were all inside the Jeep, sitting in seats and staring out like they were going on an adventure.

His lips quirked.

"Stay here with them," he said. "I'll fetch the others out."

But she tied the gray dog to the rear bumper of the Jeep and followed him anyway.

The distant sound of a siren finally pierced the night, but the firefighters were too far away to help. The flames were spearing out of the roof now.

The heat was intense as they went back inside.

They ran into the last room again, crouching low to keep out of the smoke. Brynn wet a towel in the sink and wrapped it around her lower face as he lifted a three-legged dog that had a fresh incision on its rear end.

He was gentle, but it snarled at him and snapped. Grady ignored the teeth and the trembling fear and cradled it gently in his arms. Brynn held another. A puppy.

They hurried outside and laid the dogs down on the blanket.

"Stay with them." He rested a heavy arm on her shoulder and squeezed. "There's only one left. I can handle him."

"He's big." Brynn wanted to fight him.

"Stay here, or neither of us is going in." He gentled his touch as the fire roared behind them. "These guys are going to need you when the fire truck pulls up and scares the shit out of them."

"Hurry," she said reluctantly.

He didn't wait for more. He sprinted back into the building, felt the heat sear his flesh. Saw a beam fall in the reception area.

He skidded into the room and eyed the biggest dog he had ever seen in his life.

He opened the cage door and wrangled a leash around the mastiff's neck, but the dog refused to budge.

Grady spied another jar of treats and fed the dog one. The dog ate it up, then another. Grady poured a small pile on the ground just outside the confines of the cage. The dog stood shakily.

"Come on, boy." Grady didn't know what the hell sex the mastiff was, but it didn't matter. "Come on. I've got you."

A squawk grabbed his attention. A parakeet flew around its cage. "Fuck." This was the last run. The flames were too intense to come back after this. He saw a towel on the side. Opened the cage and used the towel to catch the bird. Grady wrapped it up and trapped the wriggling pecking scrapper under his arm.

The big dog turned as if to go back into his cage and Grady couldn't wait any longer. He nudged the dog from behind, forcing it toward the flames and noise even though it was terrified.

He pushed the massive furry creature along the linoleum and out the back door and then they both stood panting in the fresh air with the flames behind them.

The fire truck was there now, and firefighters were rolling out their hoses.

Grady dragged the big lumbering mastiff to the blanket where Brynn knelt as she attempted to calm the animals there. The dogs in the Jeep were barking with excitement.

He handed Brynn the mastiff's leash, but the dog lay down at her feet without urging. She had the three-legged dog on her lap and was stroking the chocolate lab who lay at her side.

The bird bit him, and he flinched.

"You're bleeding." Brynn's gaze was worried.

"Yeah." He removed the wrapped-up parakeet from under his arm, avoiding the sharp beak that had broken through the cloth.

"Can you hold this guy for a minute?" His voice was hoarse as he handed Brynn the bird and pulled his shirt back on. The evil little fuck had pecked him a few times, and there were several small, angry patches of skin where sparks had landed on him. Sore, but nothing life threatening. He'd get cleaned up later at home.

He pulled on his jacket again before the fire department ran over it in their muddy boots.

He wiggled his brows as he stared down at Brynn who looked sooty and disheveled on the blanket. "Hell of a first date, huh?"

She laughed even though it sounded a little teary. "Certainly an exciting one." Her fingers rested on the soft fur of the lab. "Do you want your bird back?"

He took it even though he was not a fan. He eyed the gray dog who was pulling on the leash tied to his bumper. He went over and ran his hand over the shorn fur on his head. "You're not going anywhere, pal, not without me." He undid the leash and held tight as one of the firefighters came over.

"Any more animals inside?" one man shouted.

"I fucking hope not."

They both watched as part of the roof collapsed. Hoses were raining water down on the building now, but there was no saving it.

"How come you took so long to get here?" Grady tried to keep the censure out of his tone. They might have been at another fire.

"The automated alarm must have failed. First we heard of it was the call from Brynn. Soon as we received the message we hit the road."

"It felt like forever," Grady admitted. But it had probably been only a few minutes.

The firefighter rested his hand on Grady's arm. "If you hadn't been here, these guys would all have perished. Who knows how long it would have taken for someone else to report it."

The veterinary practice wasn't in town, but a ways back, isolated.

If not for Brynn, all the animals would have died.

He'd been too busy thinking about sex and unable to look at anything except her.

Eli Kane could have stood in the middle of the road and waved a red flag, and Grady would have simply driven around him and aimed for home.

He looked up at the black sky as self-disgust rushed through him. He'd known being distracted by a personal relationship with Brynn would be a mistake, and he'd done it anyway.

He'd fucked up.

So much for training. So much for self-control. So much for his goddamned mission.

The dog whined. And Grady hugged him against his leg with one hand. He held the bird out of reach, just in case.

"You're going to need a name, pal." He looked at the Jeep that was full of anxious pups and Brynn soothing the ones who were too sick or drugged to move.

"Where's Dr. Vilamitjana?"

"Dispatch called her. This is gonna break her heart."

Grady nodded and then saw a SUV speeding down the road and swerving around the corner.

"That looks like her now." The firefighter went to step away.

"You better call the sheriff. I smelled gasoline when I first went in."

The firefighter's eyes went hard. "Someone deliberately set fire to the building, knowing there were animals inside?"

Grady nodded. The smoke in his throat made him parched.

"Who the hell would do something like that?" the guy asked.

Grady said nothing as he watched the veterinarian pull up and then rush over to Brynn to start checking each of the dogs. But he knew exactly who would do something like that.

He hoped the fucker was ready to pay.

39

G rady's phone rang. He eased the parakeet into his inside coat pocket and ignored the pinch of the strong beak even through the thick material. He didn't know what else to do to keep the bird protected. He answered even as anger roared in his ears much the way the fire had.

"We have a situation," Novak said without preamble.

Grady ran the back of his hand over his forehead. "Me, too. What's yours? Did you find him?"

"Not yet. Cowboy and Donnelly's excursion means we have to immediately ramp up our response in another area."

"Tell me." Grady was out of earshot. He wasn't about to risk being overheard.

"They found some indications that we *might* be dealing with a couple of SVR or GRU agents. But the main point of concern was as to why anyone might hang a bottle of perfume outside the hotel window in a plastic bag."

Dread drenched Grady. "Nerve agent?"

"We don't know for sure."

"Why the hell fuck else would they—"

"I don't know," Novak said testily. "Maybe so that we'd think that and throw on the brakes?" Novak sounded tired.

Grady wound in his anger and frustration and need for answers. His boss would be working on it. "What's the plan?" He sounded like he'd been garroted, and his throat felt the same way.

"We're going to detain them both on suspicion."

"Kane's going to find out—"

"Not necessarily. We plan to meet up with Cowboy and Donnelly at the hotel. We have biohazard gear with us here. Apparently, the hotel doesn't have many guests. Cowboy booked a couple more rooms on that floor for his 'friends' and picked up keys because we'll be arriving after midnight. There's a rear entrance we can use to avoid the bar area. Hopefully, everyone else should be tucked in, asleep, by the time we get there and make the arrests. We sweep them up, quickly and quietly, before they know we're onto them. Get the bottle analyzed and swab every motherfucking doorknob in the building with test kits."

"If someone notices a team of FBI agents in biohazard suits?" asked Grady.

"I'll deal with that, if and when. We'll transport the suspects to Bangor and then to DC. Counterintelligence wants a crack at them. If they're innocent, we'll deal with the fallout later."

Yeah, sorry to ruin your vacation, but about that perfume…

"One more thing. Thanks to that laptop you recovered, we figured out the last thing Milton Bodurek accessed from his computer before he died was a copy of the insurance report. It contains a list of owners of safe deposit boxes at the bank."

"Are the Russians here looking for Kane?" Grady rubbed the back of his neck. "Why? And how the fuck did they know he was here if the only reason we know was a flagged fingerprint? Is there a leak in the FBI?"

"That's what Dobson and Ropero are trying to figure out."

Grady glanced over at Brynn and the destroyed building that was still burning behind him. The dog at his side whined. The parakeet pecked.

He needed to be with his teammates, but, strangely, he also wanted to finish getting these animals to safety.

His job came first. It had to. "Want me to gear up?"

"No. We've got this. Stay undercover and keep out of the hotel bar tonight. We can handle a couple of suspected Russian agents."

Grady looked around as a Montrose County Sheriff's Department cruiser pulled into the parking lot. "As much as I'd appreciate a beer right now, I don't think avoiding the bar is going to be a problem tonight."

He told Novak about the fire.

"Could it be related to Kane?"

"I doubt it. I figure the asshole who punched Brynn in the face today decided to get some revenge for getting arrested. If he can't have the dog, no one can." Grady gritted his teeth as the dog he held on the leash rubbed his head against his thigh. Grady scratched the dog behind its ears. It had been a close call.

"I don't like it," his boss said quietly.

"I don't like it either. Let me know when you have the other suspects in detention."

"Roger that. Grady…" His boss hesitated. "Be careful."

———

Brynn was shaken and cold as she sat on the coarse woolen blanket and tried to soothe not only the animals, but also herself. Her feet were cold as she was only wearing stockings in her boots, but the enormous, furry, black beast leaning against them was quickly warming them up.

Dr. Vilamitjana was checking each patient and trying to arrange space for them in the clinic of a neighboring town. The firefighters were getting the animals water, cutting lengths of rope to form makeshift leashes. The cats were meowing loudly, but she couldn't do much to soothe them without risking them running away.

Brynn looked up, and there was Grady striding toward her, looking soot-stained and grim.

"Is that a parakeet in your pocket, or are you just glad to see me?" Her voice was croaky as she cracked her terrible joke.

He swore and then gently eased the bird that had to be terrified out of his inside pocket and handed it over to the vet.

"I'm sorry. I didn't know where else to put it," he apologized.

He looked shocked when the vet threw herself around him and started sobbing. "You got them all out. Thank you. Thank you so much."

Grady patted her shoulder with his free hand. "It was Brynn who spotted the fire. She's the real hero."

Brynn hunched her shoulders and felt a tremble work through the old chocolate lab who lay beside her. "Grady's the one who rushed inside. I would probably have waited for the fire department." She didn't like that realization.

Dr. Vilamitjana wiped her face and pulled away. "I'm grateful to both of you. So incredibly grateful." She turned to face the devastated building. "I wouldn't have been able to bear it if one of the animals in my care died that way. I can't believe we had faulty electrics in a building that's only a couple of years old. Or that the alarm didn't go straight to the fire department the way it was supposed to."

Grady cleared his throat. "I don't think it was an electrical fire."

Dr. Vilamitjana frowned. "I don't understand…"

"I think someone doused the place with gasoline and lit it up."

"What?" Dr. Vilamitjana's mouth dropped open.

"And they may have cut the alarm. You might get the sheriff's department to check that." He scratched the head of the bearded collie at his side.

"Someone wanted these animals to die?" Dr. Vilamitjana drew her coat closer together over what looked like pink PJs. "Who would do such a heinous thing?"

Brynn exchanged a glance with Grady.

"You think it was that Quayle man." Dr. Vilamitjana shuddered before straightening her shoulders. "That man is dangerous, and the cops let him walk free."

Grady shrugged. "Seems a hell of a coincidence otherwise. Unless you can think of anyone else who'd want to do this?"

She shook her head, and they all turned to watch Sheriff Darrell York stride toward them.

"Want me to call the pound and see if they have any space available for tonight?" Darrell asked.

The vet looked surprised. "Actually, yes. If they can assure me they can keep my patients separate from the dogs who need rehoming. I don't want to upset my customers further than they already will be." She rubbed her furrowed brow. "I need to call them all before they find out via other methods. Some patients can go home. Some can hopefully go to the Veterinary Hospital in Sedgwick, but having secure kennels for those who don't need serious veterinary care might be very useful. Thank you, Sheriff."

Darrell nodded and turned away to make a call.

"I can help you make calls if you give me some numbers," Brynn offered, seeing the stress of the evening's events taking a toll on the other woman. It must be hard enough thinking about the business aspects of this, much less the animals themselves.

"Really?" The woman's deep brown eyes glistened with emotion.

Brynn nodded.

"We can both help make sure everyone gets somewhere safe for the night," Grady offered. "I'll take this guy home until someone tells me different, if that's okay?"

The dog sat obediently by his side and made Brynn smile.

Dr. Vilamitjana looked down at the dog. "I'll release him into your care. Most of his tests were sent off and vaccinations administered. I'll get results tomorrow." She covered her mouth, "I guess on my laptop. Dammit."

"I hope you're insured," Brynn said quietly.

"I am, but they are always so awful to deal with. It's like being traumatized over and over again until you crawl away bleeding."

"Have you experienced something like this before?" Brynn asked in surprise.

"No," the doctor shook her head. "Someone once stole my camera while on vacation." Her soft smile made them all grin and dissolve into laughter.

When they finally quieted, Grady suggested, "Let's deal with this one step at a time. We'll get the animals sorted while the cops deal with the crime scene."

"Crime scene?" Darrell York had walked back over to them. "What makes you think it's a crime scene and not an accident?"

"I smelled gasoline when I went inside."

Darrell's lip curled.

"And I want you to check to see if the alarm was tampered with," Dr. Vilamitjana added firmly. "It should have notified my cell and the fire department automatically. It did neither. I will talk to the company, but if this was arson there needs to be an investigation. You need to question the young man who threatened me today."

"I know how to do my job." Darrell nodded. "Once again, I'll need you all to come in to make a statement."

Brynn gave a rough laugh. "We know the drill."

"Tomorrow. After we've settled all my patients, Sheriff. I'm sure neither of us wants a lawsuit from an upset owner."

His expression changed then, and he wiped his forehead. "Absolutely. Let me know what I can do to help."

"How about you go arrest the most obvious suspect—"

Darrell's gaze flicked to Brynn. "Let's not jump to conclusions. I'll question everyone involved and find the culprit if it turns out it is arson. We don't need rumor and speculation escalating the situation."

"Rumor and speculation are only allowed if Grady is the focus, huh, Darrell? Seems hypocritical for you to hold others to different standards."

Darrell's eyes went hard and flat. "I'm dealing with a series of major crimes, *Ms. Webster*. And last I heard, you served coffee as opposed to being a law enforcement professional, so how about you stick to what you know best?"

Brynn flinched.

He strode away, barking orders and looking important.

"Well, that told you, Ms. Coffeepants." Dr. Vilamitjana stared after the sheriff with a shake of her head. "And to think I used to have such faith in the system."

Grady's eyes glittered with reflected flames. "We'll figure out who did this, Dr. Vilamitjana. I promise you that on behalf of myself and the FBI. This motherfucker will not get away with this."

The woman's eyes shone as she swallowed and pressed her hand to her chest. "Call me Kalpa." She glanced down at Brynn. "And apologies in advance but I'm about to kiss your boyfriend."

Brynn's eyes widened as she caught Grady's startled expression when the woman kissed him on the lips.

Brynn opened her mouth to deny he was her boyfriend, more out of habit than the desire to correct the record, but something in his fierce but vulnerable expression made her stop.

The man would run into a burning building but looked terrified right now.

The idea of being in a relationship was scary, but only because of what Aiden had done to her heart. It was frightening because, for once, she wanted to see where it led. She wanted to explore the two of them together and find all the pieces that made the whole of Grady Steel.

"As long as I get to kiss him next." She smiled at the look he threw her when Kalpa pulled back.

"Anytime, *Ms. Webster*." Lines cut into his cheeks as he held her gaze. "Any time."

40

TWENTY-SEVEN YEARS AGO

Summer

I t was late June, and the sun was hot enough to burn. The party was being held at a mansion in the country this time. A canopy had been erected over the pool area and the back of the house to screen from prying eyes.

It gave the illusion of privacy that lulled everyone into a false sense of security.

Everything was set up now. He knew exactly what he was going to do about his wife. He veered away from thoughts about the boys. He had detached himself from them over the past few months. Busy with work and plans. He'd loved them once but not anymore.

It turned his stomach even to look at them now and see her handler, her lover, in their eyes.

Eli spent a little fun time with a redhead in one of the rooms the organizers had made available to them. He made sure to toss a cushion in such a way he knocked out the bedside lamp. He giggled as if drunk.

Afterward, the redhead left with a slap on the ass and a smile on her face while he cleaned up.

Aware of the other camera in the room, he'd carefully set up his own, below, and out of range of the first. It was inside a small fluffy pussycat he pulled out of his suit jacket pocket and placed on top of the chair in the corner.

This room had been his first stop, so it didn't look strange he was still carrying his clothes. Pretty much everyone got naked fast and stashed their belongings in a corner somewhere. He put the bedside table to rights and made sure their camera still covered most of the bed. He didn't want them coming in here and seeing the stuffed toy.

Satisfied, he made sure he had all his belongings, acting drunk but not too drunk as he exited the room.

He wore nothing except a black bow tie that looked ridiculous but also contained a tiny camera. The battery wouldn't last long but he didn't need much, a glimpse of certain people in action would be enough.

He was careful to only pick a blue pill from the bowl on the living room coffee table, although he did indulge in a glass of champagne that he poured from a new bottle.

He raised his glass to the judge who was being sucked off by a barely pubescent young woman.

Eli wasn't falling for that one again. Being a pedo wasn't high on his to-do list. The organizers may claim everyone here was a consenting adult, but given those same organizers were collecting compromising information on high-level targets, he didn't trust a word of it.

He made sure to watch for long enough to catch the girl's face and budding breasts. He stroked himself because the only thing that stood out in a room like this was not being turned on by the activities of those around them.

He searched for the senator next and found the guy tied cross-wise over the dining table wearing a ball-gag and a cock-ring while a dominatrix strode around him in a leather outfit and high-heeled black boots. She lashed the senator's upper thighs and sent Eli a look before licking the leather on the end of her crop.

"Let me know if you want to play." Her smile was pleasant, like she was a croupier asking if he wanted to be dealt into a game of Blackjack.

"Pain's not my gig."

She bit her lip. "You can always be the one with the whip."

She grinned at him and sent another lash so close to the senator's straining cock Eli winced. He shook his head, knocked back the champagne, and went to find a refill.

Where was Lisa?

He found her in the old-fashioned library where she was riding her lover, a KGB operative by the name of Sergei Lushko, as he lay back on an ebony table that was low enough that she had both feet planted on the floor. No wonder she loved these parties.

Sergei was in the US supposedly as some embassy drone, but Eli knew the truth.

Eli watched his wife and saw the exact moment the two became aware he'd entered the room. They cloaked their expressions to less of adoration and more of plain old lust.

Eli was an idiot for not seeing it before.

He'd always wondered how they'd gotten an invite to such an exclusive event, but it was obvious now. It wasn't because Lisa was incredibly beautiful and everyone wanted her. It was because he was a mark, a dupe.

Anger rose inside him as he drank his champagne and wandered over to the two lovers on the table. There were others around. An older, white woman was getting banged from behind so hard her sagging breasts wobbled. The guy doing the deed looked about ninety, and they both seemed to be enjoying themselves, so Eli had no issue with them finding their pleasure in each other. As long as it was honest. As long as it was legal. As long as it was consensual.

Eli was a big believer in consent, and he'd remembered a few more details from the last party. Flashes still, but flashes that made sense now. Flashes that made the rage inside him climb.

He picked up a bottle of lube off the side and poured copious amounts into his cupped hand. He placed the bottle back on the bookshelves, walked over to his wife, and gave her a sloppy kiss on the ear.

"I want to join you."

She sent him a look that was slightly annoyed at the edges before her lips curved into a smile.

"Of course, darling." She went to stand but he pressed her back down with a hand on her shoulder.

"Like this. While you're fucking your other lover."

She tensed under his hand. He let nothing show on his face except a stupid grin.

He pushed her down. "Kiss him. I want you to feel both of us inside you."

He found a condom. They were everywhere. Slipped it on one handed, still cupping the lube.

He moved until he stood behind her. He dripped lube over her ass and watched it dribble over them both. Noticed how Sergei's grip on Eli's wife's thighs tightened.

The guy was possessive of her, but was forced to share, to pretend. Eli understood perfectly.

It was sad, really. To be forced to live these false lives.

The real pity was they'd picked him to snare in their little trap. Eli had always had a problem with people screwing him over.

He slathered lube all over his cock and then took his sweet wife from behind. He was gentle and slow. Considerate. He felt her gripping his cock so tight it was a good thing he'd already come with the redhead.

It took a minute to seat himself fully inside her and then he used her steadily until she came hard. He could feel the other man there, too. Competing for space.

Eli pulled all the way out and then adjusted himself before pressing into the man lying prone on the table.

He hadn't received an invitation, but fair was fair in love and war.

Eli used his position and weight to squash Lisa between them as he forced himself inside Sergei.

Sergei froze with a look of horror, then shock.

Muscles gripped Eli like a vise.

"Is this all right?" he asked quickly, but far too late. "I thought you enjoyed it last time…" He let his voice trail away in confusion as he held himself still.

The other man's rich, dark-chocolate brown eyes widened. Sergei hadn't expected him to remember because Eli had been so wasted.

"Of course."

Eli forced himself to laugh drunkenly even though he felt nothing except rage as he drove into the man, over and over. Eli watched Sergei's eyes go flat, his hand reach out to wrap around Lisa in a protective gesture that made Eli hate them both even more.

This was their fault. They'd done this ⁹to him. They'd destroyed him, and he intended to destroy them both right back.

He felt his own climax building as he held the stare of the other man. They were each trying to outlast the other but Sergei was still inside Lisa's tight little cunt, and Eli knew exactly how incredible that felt.

Eli drove hard enough to move the table.

Lisa started to come or at least pretended to. They had a show to perform after all.

Eli drove over and over and finally watched Sergei crash over that edge with a yell. He took Eli with him, but Eli didn't care.

Not anymore.

He had no pride left. No honor. No scruples.

He was a husk of the man he'd been, and it was their fault.

He pulled himself free and kissed the spot between his wife's shoulder blades as she shuddered on top of the other man.

"Thank you. That was amazing." He looked around and picked up his glass. "Everyone should try that at least once."

He raised his glass to a wealthy businessman who'd been

watching with his cock down a woman's throat. The old lech pushed the woman aside and headed toward where Lisa and Sergei lay as if asleep on the coffee table.

Eli felt a little sick but didn't care. He didn't wait to see what happened next. Instead, he wandered into the bathroom and flushed the condom. He was very careful with his DNA nowadays.

It was almost over.

He'd disappear, and these people would help him. Lisa and Sergei could live happily ever after for all he cared. He headed to the pool deck to see what more scandalous debauchery he could find.

41

PRESENT DAY

R yan let his teammates in through the side door of the hotel. Nash, Keeme, Griffin, and Novak piled quickly inside. One assault team should be enough. Novak was a former Green Beret and a card-carrying member of Mensa. Between the rest of them they had decades of HRT experience. Even the newbies were no slouches. Griffin had been part of the enhanced SWAT team in Atlanta and Donnelly in the 82nd Airborne.

He didn't need to worry about her.

She'd be fine.

No one spoke as he led the way through the empty hallways to a room three down from the Russians.

He rapped quietly on the solid wood. Donnelly opened it, weapon in hand. They hurried inside.

Nash, Keeme, and Griffin tossed the heavy gear bags on the bed, and everyone silently began climbing into black Nomex flight suits. They pulled on a biohazard suit over the top and thin protective gloves. Instead of tactical helmets they wore biohazard helmets with comms.

It looked like an alien invasion, and the chilling effect of these suits never failed to send a quiver of fear straight to his heart.

Ryan couldn't help himself as he checked Donnelly over and

made sure she'd properly fitted the respirator. He did the same to Griffin and told himself he was a good teammate and leader.

Sure.

They all readied their weapons as quietly as possible.

Then they huddled close even though they wore earpieces that meant they could hear a whisper perfectly clearly across town.

"Donnelly and Griffin, take either end of the corridor. Watch for civilians and block the Russians' escape if one of them gets past us," Novak stated.

Ryan ignored the rush of relief that washed over him at the knowledge that Donnelly wouldn't be going back into that room.

It was chauvinistic and wrong. Donnelly would skewer him for it.

"We want them alive if possible, but if they go for a weapon—including anything that could spray or be thrown at us—we put them down. Be mindful the walls are thin and the bullets will travel. We don't want any civilian casualties, and we don't want the release of any nerve agent by a foreign actor on US soil."

It would be an act of war.

Ryan folded his arms. "No one is checked into the adjacent rooms."

Nash pulled out the handheld radar. "Let's double-check, and then see where they are and figure out how we do this."

Ryan paced the carpet, waiting for the unit to power up.

Nash pointed the device at the Russians' room. Frowned. "Not seeing anyone."

The tension in the room deflated as if someone had stuck a pin in it.

"Shit." Ryan ground out between clenched teeth.

"Are you sure they came back here from the golf club?"

Ryan nodded. "We sat in the bar after we booked more rooms and saw them pull into the parking lot and enter the hotel around ten. The female came into the bar and ordered a couple of whiskies to go and was busy chatting to a couple of the locals, so we lost eyes on the male for maybe ten minutes. After the woman left, we came up here separately maybe five minutes later and took turns watching the peephole to make sure they didn't leave their room. Fuck." Ryan wanted to hit something. "We gave them a little space because we didn't want them to get spooked."

Donnelly shot him a glance. "Their car is still in the parking lot."

"They couldn't know we searched their rooms or were onto them. We didn't move anything, even draped the hair back across a handle on the chest of drawers."

"Old school." Nash's tone held a degree of appreciation.

"We blocked electronic transmissions so they didn't see us even if they'd planted a bug."

"Maybe they noted the lack of signal?" Nash pointed the hand-held radar at the nearby rooms.

"Car's here so they might have simply gone for a midnight stroll," Griffin put in.

"Whatever the reason they aren't in their room right now, we need to search it and retrieve that perfume bottle," Ryan insisted. "We cannot afford for them to start poisoning people with nerve gas even if that tips off Kane."

"He's right," Donnelly agreed to his surprise. "We need to secure the chemical weapon and then worry about apprehending them all afterward. The Russians can't have gone far if they're on foot. Get the locals to put out an APB."

"We'll hold off on the all-points bulletin until we take it up the line." Novak nodded. "Keeme. Watch their vehicle." Novak tossed Malik Keeme the keys to their rental SUV. "Touch nothing with your bare skin until we can verify it's safe, including our own vehicle. Nash and Griffin will check all the rooms on this floor for heat signatures and make sure no one slips out of another room while we're busy. The three of us will retrieve the suspected poison."

Novak sent them all a look readable despite his mask. "We don't need any heroes here today. Let's take our time and be careful but try to avoid being seen."

Ryan ground his teeth that Donnelly was coming into the hot zone, but he let it go. They were equipped. They were prepared.

He led the way and Donnelly stacked behind him with a hand on his back. Novak stood opposite. Ryan breathed slowly to calm his heart rate. Thought about the ranch on a summer's day. Thought about his daughter's smile.

Novak gave him the nod, and Ryan didn't bother picking the lock this time. He stood back and kicked the door open. Novak swept inside. Ryan right on his tail. Donnelly took the rear.

The room looked as if a cyclone had hit it. All the drawers were tossed, and the clothes were all gone. So was the laptop and guidebooks.

Ryan strode to the window, all the time scanning his surroundings, looking for boobytraps. He peered through the glass, disappointment and dread settling into his stomach as dense and uncomfortable as an anvil.

The plastic bag was missing. He opened the sash anyway. Leaned out to check. Nothing.

He left it open. Just in case.

He turned to Novak who was coming out of the bathroom. "It's gone."

Novak nodded. "We need forensic techs in here but first…" He pushed his weapon aside and pulled a small, capped tube out of his pocket. Shook it. Out of another pocket he pulled a plastic bag full of swabs. "DoD recently designed these for the battlefield. We dip the swabs into this liquid and then test whatever surface we decide most likely to be contaminated. The swabs turn purple in the presence of a nerve agent. If that happens, we get the hell out and evacuate the building."

"Chemical and biological weapons make me want to hurt someone," said Ryan.

"Doorknobs or light switches make most sense to check, although, unless they left the hotel looking like us, I doubt there will be any trace."

"I'm fine with that," Donnelly muttered.

"Me, too," Ryan agreed.

They each took swabs and tested various parts of the room, including the doorknob from the hallway. The windowsill.

"Nothing." Ryan's relief was massive, and he could feel the sweat drenching his back. He wished to hell he'd grabbed that perfume bottle when he'd had the chance. He thought they'd had it covered. He'd been wrong.

"Let's get out of here and let Ropero organize the rest of the examination using whatever subterfuge she decides."

"We need to figure out how they seem to know everything we do before we do," Ryan murmured, aware the walls could have ears and they needed to sweep the room for electronic surveillance again before speaking freely. "What do you want us to do? Dump the undercover roles?"

The idea of spending more time alone in Donnelly's company was torture and, if he betrayed that fact, Novak would torment him endlessly—or toss him off the team.

"Stay in your roles for now, but check your doorknob before you enter because I don't trust these fuckers one inch—although, presumably killing FBI agents isn't the end goal here. See what the locals think of events tomorrow. See if our actions tonight were noticed or caused any speculation we can use."

Ryan hid his disappointment, but Donnelly nudged his arm. "I think I'm growing on you, Cowboy."

"Like a pimple," he replied dryly.

42

By the time they got back to the house, it was after six in the morning, and Brynn was punchy with fatigue.

Grady had delivered the pets in need of constant medical care to a clinic run by a friend of hers. Dr. Vilamitjana—Kalpa—had allowed most pets to go home with their owners with a promise to check up on them in the morning. Brynn and Kalpa had dropped off three of the dogs, including the enormous fluffy Tibetan Mastiff to animal services, as their owners couldn't be reached immediately. They'd be safe there in the meantime. The staff obviously adored animals and were happy to help.

Amid violence and destruction, Brynn had found a friend today. She hoped Kalpa was able to rebuild and show whatever bastard had destroyed her clinic that she wasn't going to be intimidated. That she wasn't going anywhere.

Brynn found it hard to believe someone would deliberately set fire to the clinic knowing there were animals inside. Caleb Quayle was the obvious culprit. The timing was too coincidental otherwise.

What did Jackie see in him? Were they still an item?

Brynn shook off the thoughts whirling inside her head. Let the sheriff figure it all out if he was capable.

Grady followed her inside leading the gray dog, who went and lay on the rug near the couch. He clearly wasn't ready to leave her alone yet and she didn't want him to.

There was a bowl of water on the kitchen floor from the previous day, although they'd given all the animals a drink and treats earlier.

"Did you think of a name for him yet?" She nodded to the animal as she poured two tall glasses of water. Her throat was sore from the smoke, although the medics had released her after some oxygen treatment. Grady had gotten the worst of it.

Grady looked at the dog, who appeared to be asleep already, probably even more exhausted than they were. "I was thinking about Murphy."

"I love Murphy. Suits him." She held a glass out to him. "Are you staying?"

Grady closed the door, met her gaze as he flipped the lock. "Do you want me to?"

Brynn's pulse punched up a notch as he walked toward her with an expression that made her toes curl. She put down the glasses before she dropped them. "Yes."

He took her mouth in a smoky kiss that had her plastering herself against him. His hand smoothed down her back and drew her even closer.

She reached up and gripped his shirt. "I have an hour before I need to go to work. Come to bed with me."

He touched his forehead to hers. "What I have planned will take much longer than an hour."

Her blood sizzled.

He went to pull away, but she tightened her grip. "Then go faster."

He stared at her for a moment, pupils flaring. He seemed to read the hunger in her eyes, the demand.

He grinned. "Yes, ma'am."

He picked her up in his arms, and she wrapped her arm around his neck, rearing up to capture his lips with hers.

He nudged open her bedroom door but didn't stop at the bed. He walked into the bathroom and let her slide to her feet, never stopping the kiss or releasing his hold. He reached into the shower stall and turned on the water, checking the temperature with his hand as she undid the buttons of his filthy shirt and pushed it off his shoulders.

He flinched under her fingers, and she drew back, stared at the nasty scratches and welts that marred his otherwise perfect torso.

She opened her mouth to say something, but he spun her around. "Where the hell is the zipper on this thing?"

She lifted her arm, and he found it, tugging the pull carefully down and helping her drag the dress over her head. She stood there in her best underwear and stay-up stockings which were filthy and full of snags.

His eyes widened appreciatively as he traced the tip of his finger over the top of her plain black bra. "You're beautiful."

She fought not to fold her arms. "I don't feel beautiful."

And it wasn't the smoke and dirt and sleepless night. It was inside, where the demons lived.

His eyes flicked back to hers, sharp with attention. "We'll have to do something about that."

"Therapy or hypnosis?" She joked as she peeled off her ruined stockings and kicked them aside. Then she unclipped her bra and shimmied out of her panties.

Those sky-blue eyes of his glowed neon as he took her in. "How about a little positive reinforcement?"

He picked her up, strong fingers spanning her waist and placed her in the shower. She gasped, but the warm water was the perfect temperature as it plastered her hair against her skull. Hot but not scalding.

She absorbed the pummeling spray with a sigh. She'd been so cold. For hours and hours, her feet had felt like icicles. She hadn't dressed for the weather. She'd dressed for seduction.

And she was finally getting around to it.

She leaned against the cold tile and opened her eyes just in time to see him kick off his pants and underwear. He turned but not before she spotted more burns and blisters on his neck. With the gash just visible in his hair, the guy looked like he'd been in a war zone.

"You're hurt."

Those bright eyes held hers. "Nothing serious. I'll deal with it later. First," he picked up her soap from a shelf, "I want to deal with you."

His confidence was sexy as hell, and she wanted that. Wanted a man who knew what he wanted. For now, anyway.

For this moment.

Temporarily.

He lathered the soap as she leaned back and watched him. Water sluiced over his body, causing the soot and smoke to streak his skin. He'd been so incredibly brave and competent this evening. He hadn't hesitated to enter a burning building to rescue those animals and get them to safety.

A hero.

A real-life hero.

She wasn't sure she'd met one before.

He washed her like she was precious, deft touches of clever fingers igniting her nerves in a wildfire of their own. He poured shampoo into her hair, which he then used to tip back her head, and kiss her mouth as he lathered the wet strands.

She could dive into those kisses and never surface. They were like a drug she didn't want to quit, creating a craving that kept growing. A storm brewing in her blood.

For more.

For everything.

She took the soap and began her own exploration. His short hair, the strong bones of his handsome face. Soft bottom lip. His neck and broad shoulders. Wide chest with all those bumps and ridges that had her fingers dancing.

She placed a kiss beside each burn and scratch, in a vain attempt to ease some of the pain. She had a blister on her wrist that smarted like hell, so she knew he must be hurting despite his stoic denial.

Her hands ranged down to his lean waist to the jut of his hip bones. She wrapped a soapy hand around the hard length of him and watched his pupils flare.

"I don't have a condom." His voice was rough with smoke and regret.

She was on birth control because her periods were irregular and painful, but she wasn't ready to have sex without protection. She wasn't a risk taker with her health—only with her heart apparently.

"I have some in my bedside drawer."

He walked away, uncaring of the water dripping off his naked body, and came back with the entire unopened box.

He ripped it open and grabbed a foil package. Climbed back into the shower and kissed her again. Then he worked his way down her body, finally centering on all the areas that were desperate for his touch and that he'd assiduously avoided until now. He took her nipple into his mouth, sucking hard enough to have her quake before he shifted to the other side. He palmed her breast and rolled one puckered areole between his thumb and forefinger and pressed, just firmly enough for sensation to shoot through her body to her sex, which clenched and throbbed with want.

Could a woman have an orgasm from having her nipples touched?

He sank to his knees before she could find out.

He looked up.

Rivulets of water ran down her front and dripped off her body onto his.

He ran his tongue firmly across her clit. Sensation hit her like a bullet. He looked up at her with hunger shining in his feral gaze. "I like you wet."

Her knees shook as he went back for more.

Holy.

He moved her legs wider apart, and she watched as he lapped at her, the rough stubble on his cheeks scraping her soft skin in a way that was unbelievably arousing. She wanted to press against him. His tongue was magic, and his fingers joined in until she felt herself tipping over the edge, and a cry was wrung out of her, along with a shudder.

His satisfied grin was cocky, but he'd earned it.

She pulled away, and he stood. She pushed him back until he was against the tiled wall, and she copied what he'd done to her. Exactly. Slow deliberate torture until his knees were quivering as she took him inside her mouth. His grip on her hair tightened as her hands roamed. It didn't take long for him to groan and swear. He gently pulled away and drew her to her feet.

The water was starting to cool. He shut it off.

His eyes gleamed as they held hers.

"You're playing with fire, Ms. Webster."

She tilted her head to one side. "I'm not sure what you mean, Agent Steel. I'm just an innocent bystander." She stroked her hand up and down his throbbing cock. "Minding my own business."

She gasped in surprise as he spun her around, and she found herself face to the wall. His warm breath tickled her neck as his teeth sank gently into the spot where it met her shoulder. He dragged her hands high over her head and pressed them there.

A bolt of excitement shot through her as she felt him hard against her.

"Interfering with an FBI Special Agent is a federal offense."

She gulped. "I—"

"Don't move." His voice roughened. "I need to search you."

"Oh…" She shook with anticipation.

His hands paused and his grip tightened. "Assuming I'm not violating any of your civil rights?" There was enough hesitation to make it a really sweet request for permission.

"Hmm." She cleared her throat. "I guess if you have to search me, you have to search me." Her voice trembled but she didn't care.

She could feel his laughter as he nuzzled her neck before he gently scraped his teeth over the skin beneath her ear. A shiver of lust whispered down her spine in response.

His hands stroked seductively down her arms, and the flat of his hand brushed the side of her breasts before his flattened palm skimmed the tips of her pebbled nipples. Then he planted one foot between hers and tapped her ankles.

"Spread 'em."

She melted with lust.

43

Grady couldn't remember the last time he'd been this turned on. And he'd never played games. Life was always too damn serious for games.

But after everything that had happened tonight and the way Brynn reacted to him, he figured he'd keep going.

He'd heard sex was supposed to be fun.

He was usually too aware of the minefield of potential fuckups waiting for him in the aftermath. Right now, all he could think about was Brynn and making her feel good.

Her body was soft and lush. He ran his lips over the curve of her neck which was his favorite spot right now. She smelled like herbal shampoo and tasted sweet as a promise.

He cupped one perfect breast in his hand and tweaked the nipple until it formed a tight, dark pink bud. His other hand slipped between her legs and found her swollen clit. His cock throbbed against her ass but he put his own needs out of his mind. He didn't want this to be over before it began. They didn't have as much time as he wanted, but he was damn well going to make it good for her before it was over.

"You have the right to remain silent."

She moaned as he found the right pressure to touch her and

laid her head back against his shoulder. The view down her front was the most erotic thing he'd ever seen.

"Oh, god." Her expression was lost in pleasure.

He smiled against her wet hair as he kissed her there.

"Anything you do say can and may be used against you in a court of law."

"I want you inside me." Her voice was ragged.

"Attempting to bribe a federal agent. That's prison time, lady. You have the right to an attorney present before and during questioning."

"I don't think they'd fit in the stall." She laughed and then tumbled over that edge again with a shocked gasp, shaking so violently he thought she was going to slip through his arms.

He wasn't about to let that happen.

His grip tightened, and then he turned her around and lifted her over his shoulder, snagging a towel and the condom off the side as he went back into the bedroom.

He eased her gently to her feet and stood back to wrap the towel around her.

She took the condom from his hand and dragged him down to lay beside her on the comforter.

She grinned at him, and he didn't think he'd ever seen anyone more beautiful. She ripped the packet open and slid the condom over his throbbing cock as he stared deep into those smokey gray-green eyes. He'd never felt quite like this before. On some level he knew it was a mistake to do this now, without all the facts being laid out. But he didn't think those facts affected what was going on here between the two of them. How either of them felt about the other. There was nothing he wanted more, right now, than Brynn Webster.

She rose to her knees and he rolled over onto his back, knowing what she needed. Control. She needed to be in charge because others had taken that away from her and destroyed her self-confidence.

She straddled him, and her hot flesh took him inside her. The brilliance of the sensation threatened to destroy him, but he gritted his teeth and watched her move her spectacular body over his, weaving her magical spell.

She rode him like a sensual goddess. Like a woman who knew exactly what she wanted.

He reached up to touch her breast. Seeing how that pleased her, he kept doing it. Watching her expression as her teeth caught her bottom lip, and then she gasped as she tumbled into the void again.

"You're so beautiful." His voice came out in a broken rumble, his throat raw.

And suddenly his control snapped, and he was moving her over him and going deeper, harder, his fingers gripping her thighs and knowing he should let go but couldn't.

He couldn't.

Brynn's mouth opened and her eyes closed, and he could feel her clenching around him in one long wave of an orgasm that didn't stop. His own release rushed through him now, and he couldn't see. The climax hit him like a concussion wave and knocked him out of his body, as white light crashed through his brain.

She collapsed on top of him, and he wrapped his arms around her, cradling her to him.

Slowly she eased back and blinked at him as if she was coming out of a deep dream.

She moved away and found the towel and drew it around herself. This was the part he usually sucked at.

"Wow," she said.

"Yeah." His heart pounded. "Wow."

Uncertainty formed lines between her brows.

He took her hand and kissed her knuckles. He might not be being one hundred percent truthful, but he wasn't lying about what he felt about her, even though these feelings were bigger than he'd expected or experienced in the past.

She pushed her hair behind her ear and for the first time he noticed a burn on the inside of her wrist.

He sat up. "You're hurt."

She angled the injury for a better look. "It's small but it's sore."

"Do you have any first aid supplies?" He rolled to his feet and went into the bathroom. Got rid of the condom.

"I have a travel pack. Under the sink."

He found it and pulled it out. Checked inside. "This'll do."

He went back and sat on the bed, naked.

She stood near the bedside table where she kept a nice little Springfield Hellcat RDP. Hopefully she wasn't planning to use it on him.

"Sit."

"I don't have much time—"

"Sit," he ordered. He was trained in first aid and knew what he was doing.

She sat with a *humph*. Held out her wrist obediently but with a pout on her lips.

The skin wasn't broken, which was a plus.

"We'll put a little steroid cream on it and wrap it in a clean bandage." She was stiff with tension. He was gentle with the cream and the bandage, knowing it wasn't the pain that bothered her. It was letting someone else take care of her when she was used to doing it herself. It took her a minute to relax, but he felt a warmth spread through him when she did.

"See." He raised her fingers to his lips again and held her gaze. "All done."

It was 7:45 a.m. and if she hurried, she wouldn't be late to work.

"What about you?" she asked.

"I'm fine. I'll take care of the burns in a little while. You need to get to the café."

A frown dented her forehead. "Stand up and turn around."

He was unsure why she was asking him to do that, but he climbed to his feet, stood there, naked, tense.

She picked up the pot of antiseptic cream, and he blinked in surprise.

Her fingers were gentle and the ointment cool on his hot skin. Her breath skimmed his flesh with the sensuality of a delicately drawn feather. "Some of these must really hurt."

"Right now, nothing hurts," he muttered. It was an allusion to the sex they'd just shared. The endorphins flowing through his bloodstream were better than any manufactured narcotics.

Her fingers hesitated and then gently stroked over another wound.

Maybe she wasn't feeling the same way. Maybe she hadn't wanted any after sex interaction. Maybe she'd wanted a quick bang and then to be left alone. Suddenly, it felt awkward and presumptuous of him to be here still, standing naked in her bedroom.

She came around to his front and after a moment met his gaze. But she still didn't say anything, and doubts swirled inside him.

She silently treated each welt and blister and he felt his muscles tense for the rejection he knew was surely coming.

Then she rose on tiptoes and kissed his mouth.

"You're right." She broke away and searched his eyes. "Right now, nothing hurts."

Her words echoed his, but the pain that shadowed her gaze was all Brynn Webster and her idiot ex. She popped the top back on the ointment.

"I have to go."

He cleared the gravel out of his throat. "You want any help at the café this morning?"

Her smile broke out like sunshine. "You'd do that for me after being up all night?"

He grinned slowly but ignored the response that wanted to leap onto his lips. He'd do anything for her, any time she wanted.

Sex had turned him into a sap.

"Sure. I have a couple of hours." He was pretty sure there

would be a team briefing at some point today, but he may as well make himself useful in the meantime.

Murphy whined and scratched at the door.

"*After* I've taken my dog for a quick walk." It felt good to say it. He had a dog. At least, until Caleb Quayle lodged some kind of formal complaint, which he was bound to do. Although Caleb must be the main suspect in last night's arson attack, so he should be busy getting arrested and too occupied to fight for doggy custody. Assuming Darrell was capable of putting a case together.

Grady had considered tracking Quayle down last night and repaying him for his actions. He'd reminded himself he had a job to do, and animals to take care of.

Not to mention, Brynn…

And maybe he'd needed the reminder for himself, that he wasn't that young hothead anymore. He wasn't his father. He was part of an elite tactical team of law enforcement professionals who knew how to follow orders and enforce the rules equitably.

He went over and picked up his filthy shirt off the bathroom floor. It stank of smoke. The last thing he wanted to do was put it back on but neither did he want to walk outside in nothing but his skin and give the gossips something else to chew on.

Brynn eyed him with amusement. "I have a T-shirt that might fit you."

Then he remembered the fact he hadn't locked the connecting door after they'd gone out last night. He gathered his clothes, shoes, wallet, gun, and keys. "I'll meet you at the café in about thirty minutes."

He ran up the stairs naked as the day he was born, jiggling his keys. Murphy followed him and Grady knew he needed to get the dog outside fast if he wanted to avoid an accident.

He opened the door and pushed inside only to come face-to-face with Sheriff Darrell York standing in his kitchen. The sheriff whirled around and drew his weapon.

44

"Whoa. Easy there, Sheriff." Grady held his pile of belongings in front of him. "I'm going to slowly put this down on the floor so you don't make a mistake we both regret."

Grady eased the smoke-saturated pile onto the floor, his gun hidden but still within reach should Darrell be a bad guy in league with Kane or the Russians.

Could Darrell have killed Milton? Maybe that's why he was so keen to pin it on Grady.

Grady held his hands high and spread his fingers wide. Murphy sniffed around the kitchen.

"What's going on?" Grady eyed Darrell's twitchy finger and sweaty expression. "I'm definitely unarmed here." Not to mention, dangling in the wind.

"Get on the floor. Get on the floor!" Darrell screamed, getting into a firing stance.

Another deputy came to the door, and Grady relaxed a little. Something was going on, but unless the whole department was dirty, he wasn't about to be shot first and questioned later.

The advantage of being born white.

He knelt and then lay on the cold tile. Darrell jerked his head in Grady's direction to indicate the deputy cuff him. Darrell kept his gun aimed fixedly between Grady's eyes.

"You are making a serious mistake here." The cuffs were tight and pressed painfully into his wrist bones.

"Is that a threat?" Darrell took two tries to slip his gun back into his holster.

"More like an observation," Grady said dryly. "You need to know I have a handgun in that pile of clothes. Please note that, whatever this is about, I didn't shoot your sorry ass even though you were standing armed and uninvited in my kitchen."

The deputy kicked the gun away as if Grady were about to go for it.

He gave the guy a look. Gritted his teeth and hoped to hell the sheriff and his deputies hadn't searched the place. He calculated what they'd find. Some ammo. Another weapon. His kitbag, which he could justify if he had to. Surveillance units. He could say he was installing them on his property. Plus, his laptop. All the electronics were government issue that the locals couldn't access. Nothing too revealing on the surface.

"You better have a warrant to be in here. What the hell is going on?"

Ropero was going to kill either him or Darrell. He voted for Darrell. "Can I get a pair of sweatpants or something? It's fucking freezing with the door open."

The weather was getting worse. This cold snap they'd been predicting finally kicking in ahead of the Arctic low headed their way.

Darrell crouched beside him. "I always figured you for an evil sonofabitch but last night was twisted, even for you."

Last night?

"If you're trying to blame me for that fire you are barking up the wrong tree." Grady scowled. "Hey, someone put a damn leash on that dog before he escapes again."

Darrell huffed out an unamused laugh and rose to his feet.

"You care more about that animal than I've ever seen you care about anything."

That wasn't true.

Grady had people he loved and cared about in his life. Just not his old high school buddy who used bullying in the guise of friendship to manipulate and control him and whose father had tried to fuck him over. Darrell and Temple hadn't exactly stood on the side of justice that day. Grady wouldn't forget that.

He heard a noise behind him and closed his eyes as humiliation engulfed him. Fuck.

He turned his head. Watched Brynn climb the stairs with Murphy's new leash. She stepped across Grady's naked ass and handed the leash to the deputy. "Take the dog outside for a bathroom break, would you, Lee?"

The deputy nodded politely.

Brynn turned to face Darrell. She was dressed in dark jeans now and a cherry-red sweater that brought out the fire in her hair. Matching socks and black ankle boots.

"What's going on, Sheriff?"

"Grady Steel, you are under arrest for the murders of Caleb, Colin, Dick, Hap, and Tom Quayle. And the unlawful detention of Hetty and Susannah Quayle."

"What the fuck…" Acid churned in Grady's stomach. "What the hell are you talking about?"

Brynn covered her mouth. "Someone killed them? All of them?"

"Yeah, your boyfriend here." Darrell jeered, his eyes full of bitter resentment. He knew exactly what Brynn and Grady had been doing downstairs and was jealous as hell. "Know anyone else with an axe to grind with any of those folks?"

"You think…" Brynn's mouth opened in shock, and she shook her head. "That's impossible. We were busy all last night." Embarrassment suddenly stained her cheeks.

Grady turned away. Fuck. He hadn't wanted to embarrass her.

"How were they murdered?" Grady gritted out.

The sheriff's lip curled. "Like you don't know."

Grady didn't even bother rolling his eyes. What did it mean? Who'd killed them? Why?

Darrell dragged Grady awkwardly to his feet, and shame rained down on him even though he knew it was all bullshit.

To be arrested naked in his grandmother's kitchen by one of his childhood best friends was the ultimate disgrace.

He heard his sister's voice, screeching something outside and closed his eyes. Ah, well, now *that* was truly the icing on the shit cake.

"Grady was with me, all last night and all this morning," Brynn declared loudly. So loudly everyone outside would have heard her, too. "He wasn't out of my sight long enough to have murdered a fly, let alone an entire family."

Grady glanced at her in surprise.

When Darrell pulled out his handcuffs, Grady felt a rage explode through him he hadn't experienced since he'd been a wild teen. He tried to get between the sheriff and Brynn.

"Don't touch her. Don't you fucking touch her. She has nothing to do with whatever happened." Grady suddenly found himself once more pinned to the ground by two large, overly zealous deputies. He could attempt to escape their grip, but he didn't trust the sheriff not to put a bullet in him and call it justifiable homicide.

Plus, Brynn was in the line of fire. It wasn't worth the risk.

"By her own admission, she said she was with you all last night." Darrell secured the cuffs to Brynn's wrist, and Grady watched her wince as they ratcheted tight against her bandaged burn.

Grady lost his shit. "I'm going to bring you down to your knees for this, you motherfucker. You have a vendetta against me? You deal with me. You do not bring her into this."

Darrell took a step back. "Someone get some goddamn pants on this loser. We're taking him in."

"Don't talk to these guys without a lawyer, Brynn. They are

not your friends right now. The sheriff is nothing but a desperate man with his eyes on the polling numbers and a crime spree he can't handle." Grady shouted to the back of Brynn's head as they paraded her out of the house.

The kick in the gut took him by surprise. It shouldn't have. The second one knocked the wind out of him. Darrell and the other deputies dragged him to his feet.

Grady sneered at the guy. "That all you got, Darrell? You used to hit harder than that in high school."

The punch to the mouth made his ears ring.

Grady laughed. "You deputies need to prepare yourselves to be questioned under oath about police brutality and assault of a federal agent." He bared his teeth in a savage grin. "I'm actually excited at the prospect."

The two men exchanged nervous glances.

"He's nothing. He's a has-been. Even the FBI don't want him." Darrell hit him again.

"Oh, you're gonna pay for that, asshole." Grady spat blood onto the white tile. "You are going to pay for all of it, especially for putting handcuffs on Brynn just because she wouldn't sleep with you when you pressured her. Now, how about rather than getting a hard-on from beating a man who can't fight back, you engage that tiny brain of yours and do your job."

Darrell suddenly looked uncertain as Grady continued giving orders.

"Somebody take the dog to the vet, Dr. Kalpa Vilamitjana. She owes me one for last night." Plus, she actually seemed to like him. "While you're at it, why don't you get her to verify my alibi. Although, I did have about three spare minutes last night. I'm sure I could wipe out an entire family. Hell, you solved the crime, Sheriff York. Give yourself a commendation." Grady shook his head. "Fucking asshole. And get me that goddamned phone call. Right now."

45

Brynn had never been arrested before. Never seen the inside of a police cell except on TV. It was a remarkably inefficient and uncomfortable experience with the slight scent of vomit wafting on the cold air to fully round it out.

It had taken more than an hour to have her photo and finger-prints processed.

Linda could have booked her in fifteen minutes flat. These guys needed better organization and a kick up the ass.

Afterwards, she'd been left to sit on this cold, concrete bench with nothing to do except think.

For three hours.

Three long hours she'd sat here, uselessly, when she had things to do.

How did people cope with it for a lifetime?

Her butt ached. Her throat was still sore from the smoke she'd inhaled last night. To think she'd basked in the glow of being one of the heroes of the hour. Well, that hadn't lasted long.

She'd used her phone call on Linda. Asked her to open the café and told her to call Kalpa to get the woman to verify their alibis. Brynn should probably have asked for a lawyer, although she knew Linda would see to that, too.

Brynn had also made Linda swear on her life not to tell her parents until she was out of here. She didn't want them to worry.

Where was Grady? Was he okay?

Part of her wanted to regret this morning, but she couldn't. It had been incredible. Stupendous. Not only physically but mentally. It had exorcised ghosts and made her think she might have another chance at love.

Not that she was in love with Grady Steel.

No.

Love took time and effort to grow and nurture, and he wasn't the sort to be looking to settle down. He'd be going back to his exciting life in Virginia, and she'd be left behind to run her parents' café.

She was fine with that.

She sniffed.

Absolutely fine.

She preferred to be alone anyway. But damn, she'd take the sex for as long and as often as she was able before he left.

And there was no way he'd killed someone in his truck and then tried to hide the fact. She knew it with certainty even after only a few days of acquaintance.

He was a hero.

Couldn't even help himself.

She smiled to herself.

He did seem to be suffering a lot of bad luck recently. Darrell definitely had it in for him, which seemed to say more about Darrell than it did about Grady.

The fact everyone in town would know they'd slept together didn't bother her the way she'd thought it might. It wasn't anyone else's business, and she'd be lying if she wasn't even relishing, just a little, the prospect of not being an object of pity for a change.

Poor Brynn. Husband dumped her for another woman. *Probably isn't very good in bed. Probably doesn't know how to look after a man. Wink, wink.*

Yeah.

Whatever.

She felt more alive than she had in years. It hadn't been like this with Aiden. It hadn't been this *incendiary*. The feelings she had for Grady felt magnified in comparison. Magnified and accelerated.

She should probably rein it all in, but she didn't want to. Life was short.

Which reminded her of why she was locked up behind bars.

She couldn't believe five members of the Quayle family were dead. That had to be some mistake. At least the woman with the little girl who'd come regularly into the café during the winter months had survived. Surely Hetty Quayle could help the cops identify the killer?

Brynn had never really spoken to the other men in Caleb's family. They didn't tend to hang around in coffeeshops when there were bars nearby.

Grady couldn't have killed anyone last night. He'd been out of her sight for less than an hour and had to drive to Sedgwick and hand over the animals who needed medical observation and then drive back. There was no way he had time for a murder spree. More importantly, she did not believe him capable of such a thing. Despite what the town liked to think, he was a good man. She felt it in her bones.

She twisted her fingers together. Her bones had been wrong before…

Could she trust her own judgment?

She'd married Aiden, for goodness sake.

He'd deceived her, and she'd been oblivious. She untangled her fingers and squeezed them into fists. Pressed them together. She didn't intend to make the same mistake again, but this thing with Grady was different. They weren't getting married. They were simply having fun while they got to know one another better.

And if the 'fun' felt like a gigantic rush of anticipation…?

She'd deal with it. Curb her emotions before they took off in a direction she couldn't control.

She stood impatiently and paced. When was she gonna get out of here?

She eyed the bathroom facilities in the corner of the cell. A steel toilet with no seat. The thought of being here so long that she needed to use it made her stomach roll.

If she had to pee in here, she was refusing to serve a single member of the Montrose County Sheriff Department at the café until…*ever*.

She sat back down. Tears wanted to form, but she fought them back. They were angry tears, not upset ones. She was furious. Especially at the way Grady had been treated. Riding the testosterone wave helped keep the anxiety at bay.

She satisfied her immediate need for vengeance by plotting her payback on all the officers involved with her and Grady's arrest. Never upset someone responsible for the food you put in your mouth.

Sure, they were only doing their jobs.

But Darrell York had made it personal. Very personal. The fact she wanted to hurt him physically probably wasn't the healthiest way of dealing with her anger, but she figured she'd learn to live with herself. He was another example of her poor judgment. She'd mooned over him as a girl, and he'd only ever wanted her for sex. She wasn't a person to him. She was a gap on his scorecard. A challenge.

Last night, he'd derided her abilities because she ran the café, as if that was a measure of her intelligence. She'd see how smart he thought her next time he tried to buy anything from her. And maybe she'd permanently blacklist only him from the café so he knew it was personal right back.

A door clanged and footsteps approached.

And there was the man himself. Sheriff Darrell York. Jerk.

He approached with the man who'd locked her up. Stan Noble. They unlocked the door and stood off to the side.

She came silently to her feet. Refused to be the first to speak.

"You're free to go," Darrell said without a lick of apology.

"What about Grady?"

Darrell's smile was feral. "Still being questioned. We have your statement. You can leave now. Go call your other boyfriend, Bowie."

It felt as if steam was rising inside and blowing out of her ears like some cartoon character. Part of her wanted to scream at them, but that would achieve nothing, except personal satisfaction.

Head high she went to walk past Darrell but he grabbed her arm, squeezing painfully. "I'm investigating the murder of five people, Brynn, not counting Milton Bodurek. A little girl and her mother were tied up and left in a room with duct tape over their mouths. When deputies arrived, they thought the killer was coming to finish them off. They were terrified." He sucked in a mouthful of air. "I can't afford to play favorites."

"Favorites?" She snarled at him. "The fact you considered for a moment that either myself or Grady Steel would have anything to do with their deaths—"

"What the hell do you think Grady does in HRT?" Darrell spat in her face. "He trains to kill people. Every. Single. Day."

She moved closer until they were almost nose to nose to prove he didn't scare her. Not anymore. "And you are so jealous of him you can't see past your own goddamn inadequacies to realize he'd never hurt anyone who didn't deserve it."

"Maybe he considers someone who'd burn down an animal clinic as deserving it."

"Yeah, maybe he would. But he wouldn't extend that to an entire family or *terrorize a little girl*." She was shouting now, and her words ricocheted off the walls.

She spotted the raw patches on Darrell's knuckles, and her mouth dropped open. She jerked her arm away from his grip. "You hit him."

Darrell clenched his hand into a fist and opened it again. "He ran into it while attempting to resist arrest."

"You are a despicable excuse for a human being, Darrell York."
Damn him. "I'm going to make sure everyone I speak to between
now and re-election knows exactly the sort of man you are." Her
eyes must have told him she meant everything, all of it.

He took a step back. "Maybe you should remember which of
us can afford the good lawyers for a defamation case and which of
us can't?"

"Oh. Ha." She shook her head and headed to the exit. "You
should remember where everyone lines up at the front door every
morning for coffee. And I don't think your daddy is going to be
too happy using *his* money to defend your shitty reputation." She
turned and looked at him. "Not when everyone knows it's true.
I'm sure I'm not the only woman you've made uncomfortable
with your sexual overtures during the past ten years."

Darrell leaned forward. "Getting laid makes most people
mellow, Brynn. Fucking Grady turned you into a complete bitch."

Stan sniggered.

He was banned for life, too.

"Sex with Grady Steel was the best experience of my entire
life. And it made me realize I don't have to pretend anymore.
Pretend you aren't a sleaze trying to worm your way into my bed.
Pretend I'm not scared that you might use your badge to punish
me for not capitulating. Pretend the way you cheat on your wife is
anything except disgusting."

"I don't cheat on my wife." Darrell angrily waved his finger
at her.

Stan looked away. They all knew which of them was telling the
truth.

"You start spouting your nonsense, but no one's going to take
you seriously. I have crimes to solve. Real crimes. You're vindic-
tive because I'm doing my job. Shows how shallow you really
are."

Sexual harassment was a real crime. But he was also right
about having other serious incidents to investigate. She hated the
idea a murderer was on the loose in a town of people she loved.

She paused before she reached the door. "We've had six murders in the past few days…"

"Yeah, six murders since Grady Steel came home."

"That's right." She nodded slowly and didn't like the coincidence at all.

46

Grady had used his one call to contact Ropero. After she'd finished swearing, she'd told him to keep his mouth shut, and she'd send someone to spring him ASAP.

That had been several hours ago, and he was getting fed up with being treated like a common criminal when he was simply doing his job. Something that appeared beyond the scope of the local cops.

Darrell strutted into the interview room even though Grady had told him he was invoking his right to remain silent while waiting on the lawyer.

But there were some questions he needed answered. "Where's Brynn? You release her yet?"

"Ms. Webster is singing like a canary, telling us everything the two of you did last night."

"I seriously doubt that." Grady's steady smile made Darrell's lips tighten. Damn, but he shouldn't enjoy baiting the guy so much. Still, Darrell was using such an obvious ploy, Grady couldn't help himself. Suddenly impatient, he drummed his fingers on the tabletop. "If she was, you'd have released me already. You speak to Dr. Vilamitjana?"

"She said you went on your own to Sedgwick between two and three a.m."

Grady shook his head. "I spent the whole time driving, then dropping the dogs and cats off with the other vet who met me there. I drove straight back to Deception Cove."

He leaned forward because he wanted out of here.

Were these murders related to the Russians who'd done a runner last night according to a quick call he'd had with Cowboy during that same drive? What about Milton Bodurek's murder or the bank robbery? Or all three?

Was Eli Kane to blame? Or the Russians? Or was someone else the FBI didn't know about in play?

Grady wanted to help his team figure it out, but he was stuck here because he was dealing with Darrell fucking York who'd always wanted to best him and had always failed.

It was exasperating.

Fuck.

"You really think I snuck over to the Quayles' place to murder Caleb and his idiot family?"

"You were pretty angry with Caleb yesterday."

Grady did shut up. There was no reasoning with this guy.

"We found another gun at your house. And knives. We're testing them all."

Grady lifted his chin and frowned. "The Quayles were knifed?"

Darrell's eyes flickered away.

"You saw the clothes I was carrying this morning. Same as I was wearing at the fire last night. The only blood on them was mine, and if I'd knifed that many people to death, I'd have been soaked in it." Grady stared unseeing at the desk.

Was someone trying to set him up?

He eyed his old high school buddy thoughtfully.

Could Darrell be responsible for these murders and therefore eager to make an arrest? The thought of Darrell getting the drop on five men who, from Grady's recollection, were all suspicious types, didn't seem likely.

Grady needed to see if Ropero had checked into Darrell's movements after he'd finished eating at the golf club last night, and on Saturday night when someone had killed Milton Bodurek, execution style.

At the golf club, Grady had asked about the land and building contractor Darrell's parents had used to build their house. Could the Yorks have plotted to get rid of him? Had Milton also suspected something? Had it gotten him a bullet in the skull for his troubles?

Perhaps all the hullabaloo around Grady was nothing more than a desperate man trying to cover his or his parents' asses. And Grady had foiled their plans by having a solid alibi when they'd probably assumed he'd have been alone.

A knock on the door was followed by someone walking inside without waiting for permission. The woman was about fifty, dark-haired and stunningly attractive. She wore a red, wool suit that probably cost more than Grady's monthly mortgage payment, and she carried a leather briefcase that looked like real alligator. It matched her shoes. And her attitude.

"I'm Estelle Koba. Operator Steel's attorney. What happened to your face?" she demanded, giving him a hard stare.

"Same thing that happened to my ribs. The sheriff assaulted me."

"Your client resisted arrest." Darrell shrugged, and the smile he shot him made Grady want to kick the shit out of him. Grady drew in a deep breath.

Darrell was deliberately baiting him for a reaction.

"My client will be lodging a formal complaint." The wonderful Estelle spoke for him with a slight Mexican accent.

"Knock yourself out, sweetheart."

"Sweetheart?" Her tone was as cold as a scalpel blade sliding across a corpse's skin. "I will be adding an official complaint of my own, *Sheriff*. You may address me as Ms. Koba, *Esquire*. Now, I suggest you release my client as you have zero grounds to hold him. He has an alibi for the time in question and, despite a recent misunderstanding, an impeccable service record."

Darrell sat back in his chair. "If you say so."

She widened her eyes, then drew a sheaf of papers from her briefcase. Slapped them down on the table.

"It's not me that says so. This is why I was a little late, Operator Steel. Apologies." Her black eyes shone with humor. "I was obtaining copies of your commendations, as well as written support from your supervising agents throughout your career. Now…" She stood with her hand on her hip, and Grady wondered how he didn't fall in love with her on the spot. But another face rose in his mind and his mouth went dry with realization. "I suggest unless you have actual legal grounds to hold Operator Steel then you release him immediately. Release him or charge him, Sheriff, but don't try to bluff or stonewall me."

Darrell slumped. Grady grinned, proving he was not the bigger man.

"What about Brynn?" he asked.

Darrell rubbed his eye sockets, clearly exhausted. "I released her an hour ago. I may have more questions for you, so don't leave town."

Ms. Koba, *Esquire,* huffed. "My client is free to travel as much as he wishes or needs to. He agrees to answer any questions that arise, and we can use a video link if necessary." Estelle gathered her briefcase and waited for Grady to join her.

Grady stood. "Where's the dog?"

Darrell looked away. "Why don't you ask your friend, Dr. Vilamitjana?"

Darrell seemed completely defeated. This close to the start of a mass murder investigation that didn't bode well for catching the killer.

Grady paused. "You know, if you'd let go of your pride for five minutes, I would be happy to help you—"

"Fuck you, Steel. Get out while you still can."

47

Grady shook his head and followed Estelle out of the room to sign the release paperwork. He needed to talk to Novak and Ropero. He needed to find his dog. Above all of that he needed to see Brynn, to make sure she was okay.

He didn't question it. He effusively thanked and then said goodbye to his amazing attorney, and before he even tried to call his boss about the most important case of his career, he sprinted along Main Street to the Sea Spray Café.

He stood outside the window for a few seconds and watched Brynn serve a customer but without her customary spark. Watched an older woman nudge Brynn's arm and point to him standing on the street. He held his breath as she looked over, wondering if he'd see anger in her eyes—anger that he'd played a part in getting her arrested. Or reluctance, if she regretted what had happened between them this morning.

Instead, a smile lit up her face and ignited something in his chest. He pushed inside, ignoring the avid gazes of the customers.

The waitress, Linda Callow, nee-Pritchard he remembered now, walked past him with a wide smile and said out of the side of her mouth, "Hurt her, and I'll kill you."

He grimaced.

Considering there was a murderer on the loose he didn't want to take any chances, but then again, he wasn't planning to hurt Brynn. He'd tell her the truth about his job eventually. When he was cleared to.

She'd understand.

He took her hand and pulled her behind the counter, then down the corridor and into what seemed to be a broom closet.

He turned on the light and shut the door behind them.

He pushed her hair away from her face with shaking hands. He could take down an armed criminal without a quiver, but this scared the shit out of him. What if he got it wrong? What if he fucked up?

She gripped his forearm and stared into his eyes, a million questions lurking on her pensive features.

Then he fused his mouth to hers and kissed her. He ignored the sting of his split lip. The ache of his ribs.

The taste of her was fresh as lime, the smell of her soap from their shower that morning reminded him of the two of them together, naked, and it had been so good. The feel of her, soft but supple, hot and inviting, made him want to sink inside her and take everything she might offer while he still had the chance.

She kissed him back, greedily, gripping his shirt hard enough to hurt but he wanted more. Much more.

He forced himself to pull away. Leaned his brow against hers. "You okay?"

She nodded. "Kalpa made a sworn statement regarding the timing of our movements, as did the veterinarian in Sedgwick. There's not a lot of time left for you to do what they said you'd done. In fact, everyone calculated you were going way over the posted limit to get there in the time you did."

"Only on the way back after I'd dropped off the patients." He grinned. "Don't tell the sheriff. I don't want to get arrested for a traffic offense." He slid his hands to her waist.

"Darrell York is a complete dick," she said.

"Such a complete dick, but there is a killer out there, Brynn, and I'm worried. I'm going to talk to my contacts and see what I can find out, but I need you to promise not to go anywhere alone."

"Me?" Her eyes looked stricken. "You don't seriously think I'm in danger. Why would I be?"

Grady noticed she had a scattering of pale freckles around her eyes, but also strain from her sleepless night and what she'd endured earlier. He released a breath. "I don't have reason to think you're in any more danger than anyone else, but the body count this town is racking up is making me nervous."

So was the fact they had possible Russian agents running around with nerve agent and one of the FBI's Most Wanted criminals potentially in the area. Not to mention all the other creeps who inhabited quiet corners and crevasses of any state.

"What time do you finish?" he asked.

"Probably not until close to ten."

She already looked exhausted.

"I think you should call your boss and ask her to close up early."

She chuckled. Bit her lip. "I guess I could get out of here by seven. Not like people won't understand, and business booms every time I speak to the cops. We might not have any food left by seven. And with this storm coming in sooner than anticipated, it's a smart thing to do. I was too tired to think of it."

He smoothed a hand over her hair. "Call me when you're done for the day. I'll pick you up and make sure you get home safely. Maybe we can order pizza or something…"

She drew in a shuddering breath then smiled. "Okay, I'd like that, but I'll bring home some food." She frowned. "Forecasters are calling for twenty inches of snow in places by morning. Maybe we'll get snowed in."

"That sounds awesome." Grady would like nothing better than to spend a week snowed in with Brynn, but he wanted these Russian agents contained first. Plus, he had a feeling Kane knew the FBI were here now. If he hadn't already disappeared, the window for catching him was closing fast. This storm might help them corner the bastard. Reduce the escape routes to only the main roads that they could watch…

Unless the guy had a Ski-Doo, or was already in Canada, or on a boat god knows where.

But right now, Brynn was looking at him with questions in her eyes. Had she figured out he wasn't telling her the truth about why he was in town? She was smart. He wouldn't put it past her.

He wanted to kiss her again, unable to resist the temptation of her lips. But he stopped himself and pulled fully away so he wasn't touching her. Making out in a broom closet with her customers so close was not what he wanted, no matter how drawn he was to her.

He didn't want her embarrassed by whatever this was between them. He wanted to show her the respect she deserved.

"Did you get Murphy back yet?" she asked, sliding a hand down his sternum and resting it against the beat of his heart.

"Not yet. I came straight here from the sheriff's department."

Her eyes lit up a little at that.

"I'm going to drive over to Kalpa's and pick him up shortly." He checked his watch. "I have a few errands to run first."

She nodded. "Gotta get ready for this storm."

"Yeah." The lie left a bad taste in his mouth. He'd pick up a few more supplies to negate the deceit and increase his preparedness—a handgun would be pretty damn useful now Darrell had taken all three of his and probably Brynn's.

Blizzards were nothing to take lightly. Where the hell had the Russians holed up? Had to be somewhere warm. Somewhere sheltered. He went to open the door.

"Grady?" Brynn stopped him.

"Yeah?"

"Be careful."

A lump formed in his throat. When was the last time someone outside of HRT had given a damn if he was careful or not? He nodded, unable to speak for a moment.

"Brynn—"

"Shhh." She pressed a finger to his lips and rose on tiptoe to press a small kiss to the edge of his mouth. "Don't say anything. Let's not jinx it."

"But—"

"I know." Her eyes swirled like smoke. "I *know*."

The emotions gripping him were the scariest he'd ever felt, and he saw them reflected in Brynn's bright gaze. Part of him wanted to grab the feelings and mold them into something solid, something tangible. Because he was not used to being sideswiped this way and he didn't like it at all. At the same time, he was filled with a strange joy.

He wasn't used to contemplating taking a chance that might result in his heart getting ripped out of his chest.

But he wanted promises even though he wasn't ready to make any of his own. Not with his heart on the line. Not when he couldn't tell her the truth about why he was here.

Not yet.

He nodded slowly and stepped away, creating a gap. A gap he didn't want but which was necessary so he could do his job and she could do hers. He opened the door to find the cook standing there glaring at him.

"Angus. Do you need something?" Brynn brushed past Grady into the corridor.

"Wanted to make sure you're okay." Angus's voice was a rough growl. "What with all these murders happening."

Grady held his stare.

"Grady isn't responsible for the murders any more than you are."

An expression of shock crossed the cook's craggy face. "I don't want you getting hurt again, Brynn."

Brynn patted his grizzled cheek. "Leave Grady alone. I like him."

She walked away and left the big guy blushing even as he continued to glare at Grady.

"She liked the last one, too," Angus mumbled. "He was an asshole." He shook his finger at Grady.

Grady didn't bother to defend himself, just held Angus's stare.

Could Angus be Eli Kane? Did he know Grady was working undercover, or was he genuinely concerned about Brynn's wellbeing?

The big man headed back to the kitchen with a final glare. Grady stepped into the corridor and watched him go.

As he glanced around, he noticed Jackie Somers wasn't here. Had the sheriff questioned her? What did she know about her boyfriend's death?

His cell started buzzing. He checked the time as he read the message. 11:57 a.m. It felt more like five p.m. He went out the back door. The harbor was empty today, but the crime scene tape still fluttered across the slip to Milton's sailboat. Snowflakes danced daintily in the air, precursors on the edge of the storm that the forecasters warned they'd be busy digging their way out of by this time tomorrow.

Being held back by the weather was frustrating but maybe the storm would give them the breathing room they needed.

The cops here were way out of their depth with a third major crime scene to process in a few short weeks, but damned if the FBI had a firm handle on events either.

Grady jogged back to his house, jumped into his Jeep. He called Kalpa, but she didn't answer so he sent her a voicemail asking her to call him.

He wanted his dog back, but first he had a job to do.

48

Her dad came in not long after Grady left.

"Linda called me." He gripped her upper arms as he stared intently down into her face, examining her bruises, which she'd covered with makeup after leaving the sheriff's department earlier. "Are you okay?"

They'd been going flat out all day. Notoriety was better advertising than a paid ad had ever been.

Brynn grinned, feeling weirdly happy despite all the awful things going on in her life and in Deception Cove. "First time in a burning building, and first time as a murder suspect locked up in a jail cell, but I'm fine."

Worry ate into the lines around her father's mouth and the corner of his eyes. "I don't like it. Trouble is following young Grady Steel around like a bad smell."

"You make him sound like he's twelve-years-old." She laughed and pulled away. She glanced over at the customers but, except for the couple Linda was giving the bill to, no one required immediate assistance. Brynn needed a moment to catch her breath, and speaking to the people she loved had become a priority.

Her dad scratched his head. "Last time I saw him, Grady was

about sixteen. I yelled at him for riding his dirt bike up and down Main Street like some hoodlum."

"Get off my lawn." Brynn dropped her voice and shook her fist.

"Yeah, yeah. I'm an old fart. I know it."

"Well, that hoodlum is now an FBI agent, so you don't need to worry."

"I heard he's been suspended."

"He didn't do what he's been accused of, Dad. He's a good guy."

"You're sure of that?" Her dad held her gaze in that unsettlingly direct way he had sometimes.

Because she'd defended Aiden to her parents, too, and he'd turned out to be a jerk.

She stacked the dishwasher so she didn't reveal the jumble of emotions churning inside her about the person in question. She wasn't sure what she felt, just that it was *big*. Bigger than she was comfortable with. Bigger than she wanted anyone to know about, but especially Grady and her father. She wasn't ready to examine it just yet. She wanted to enjoy it for a little while first.

"A man who would break into a burning veterinary clinic to save a bunch of animals is not the type of person who runs someone over and leaves them for dead at the side of the road. Nor is he someone who murders five men because one of them punched me in the face and probably set fire to the clinic."

Paul Webster looked unconvinced. "Maybe he's looking for redemption."

She planted her fisted hand on her hip. "Wow. You sound just like the sheriff."

"Ouch. You don't have to insult me. I'm your father, for God's sake." He guffawed and held up his hands in surrender. "Fine, I'll shut up."

She swatted him with the tea towel, and then asked the question she'd been avoiding. "Does Mom know about me being questioned for murder?"

Her father shook his head and started placing stacks of dishes on the higher shelves. "I've lied more to that woman in the past six months than I have in the entire rest of our married life."

"You're protecting her. It's natural. Acceptable even."

"Maybe, but she always finds out eventually, and then I have to pay." He gave a mock shudder.

"The Internet has a lot to answer for."

He snorted. "Linda's worse than freaking Flitter or whatever the hell it is nowadays. But I unplugged the router so your mother won't come across anything about last night's incidents on one of her many online sites. Don't worry, she can still call out on her cell,"—her dad correctly interpreted Brynn's concerned look— "but you know how much she hates using data." He pressed his lips together as he wiped a cloth over the counter. "Figure it'll get us through until tomorrow before she checks the unit and by then this storm will have hopefully knocked the signal out for another few days. Maybe by the time the storm dies down and is cleaned up, everything will have blown over."

"Five people were murdered and the animal clinic set on fire. I don't think that will be out of the local news cycle for the foreseeable future."

"Maybe not," he eyed her shrewdly, "but your involvement could be."

"Let's hope so," she agreed vehemently.

"What are you two plotting, thick as thieves?" Linda came around the corner and pressed a quick kiss on her father's cheek. "How's our girl today?"

"Not great, frankly. Very tired, weak." Her dad's Adam's apple bobbed up and down his throat. "I'm determined to spare her any unnecessary stress, so I'm trying to keep her away from the news and internet."

Linda didn't miss the pointed look they both shot her.

"Okay, okay. I surrender. I won't call and tell her everything, but once she knows and she starts asking questions, I'm not gonna lie to her."

"Give her a few peaceful days first. She needs to concentrate on her recovery," Paul Webster's voice stumbled. "I'm scared she's going to quit chemo because it's so damn hard on her." His jaw firmed and then his voice rose. "I don't want her to quit. I don't want her to worry. I want her to rest and beat this goddamned thing." Her father winced. "Sorry."

"How about you make yourself useful for half an hour and help serve some customers," Brynn suggested lightly.

"I need to get home to your mother—"

"And Linda needs a break. Jackie didn't turn up again."

Her father's brows beetled. "How'd the new girl work out?"

"Pru. She's great, actually—very like Linda. But she could only work a few hours today. I caught her briefly after I got out of jail."

Her father scowled. "The sheriff is an idiot. Next time you talk to him make sure you have a lawyer with you. I mean it."

Brynn grinned. Her father was overprotective, but this time he was probably right. "Pru said she can do a couple more hours tomorrow afternoon, assuming we bother to open with this blizzard coming in. She starts full-time next week."

Her father smiled broadly. "That's fantastic. But you're right. It might not be worth opening tomorrow," her father agreed. "In fact, what the hell. Put a sign on the door and social media. Tell everyone we're closed because of the weather. That's the responsible thing to do."

Brynn smiled. "I also plan to close early tonight."

"Good. Want to come out to the house and ride this thing out with the olds?"

Brynn shook her head.

Her dad looked disappointed.

Linda nudged her father's arm on the way past. "Your girl's got a hot date with Grady Steel and some *pizza*."

Brynn's mouth dropped open. "You were eavesdropping!"

"No wonder you were defending the guy." Her dad gave her a rueful look.

"Young love." Linda grabbed her jacket and her cigarettes and walked out the back door while she had the chance.

Her father's brows rose as if he was expecting her to expand on Linda's announcement.

Instead, Brynn slapped an apron into her father's hand. "Table three wants their bill, and two new customers just walked in. Look lively," she said when he hesitated.

"Fine. I'll give you half an hour of my valuable time." He grumbled good-naturedly and put the apron on with the ease of having been roped in many times to help. Then he paused for a moment and looked deep into her eyes. "I love you, Brynn. One day you're gonna meet someone who's worthy of you. Aiden was nothing but a two-bit grifter."

She flinched at the mention of her ex, but it was more reflex than stinging pain. "I want what you and mom have."

He smiled softly and swallowed. "I want that for you, too. You'll find someone to love all the things that make you so uniquely you, Brynn Webster. All the quirks and idiosyncrasies."

"Gee, you make me sound like such a catch."

"You are a catch. You're worth a thousand of most people."

Emotion caught her unexpectedly in the throat. Her dad wasn't usually quite so vocal with his affection. Her mom's illness was changing them all. Maybe for the better. Maybe because they knew they might not have the time they'd counted on.

"Go deal with the customers, and I'll cut you a piece of apple pie and make you some tea."

He left her with a smile, and she wondered how he would survive without her mom. How either of them would survive.

49

_____

G rady entered the hotel via the back door that one of the team had surreptitiously left ajar. He hurried upstairs to Room 33 and rapped on the door in the code they generally used with one another. He was pleased that when Donnelly opened up, she had a gun in her hand.

She stood back, and he slipped inside.

Five of his teammates were crowded into the room. He'd spotted Griffin hunkered down in the front seat of their rented SUV on the way past. Nash and Keeme both stretched out on the bed side-by-side.

"You guys make a cute couple," said Grady.

Nash threw a candy bar at him so forcefully it smacked him in center chest like a bullet. Grady caught it, unwrapped the candy, and took a bite.

"Could say the same about you and the sexy redhead, Steel," Nash said dryly. "We heard all sorts of interesting things over the police scanner this morning."

"What happened to your face?" asked Novak with an edge Grady recognized as angry Papa Bear.

"Local sheriff would tell you I resisted arrest." He lifted his shirt and revealed the dark patches of bruising along with the small burns and abrasions from last night.

Novak's jaw flexed. "The FBI will be dealing with the local sheriff when this operation is concluded. Witnesses?"

"A couple of green deputies who received a thorough demonstration in poor policing methods."

"I'll be dealing with them also. I want a full report by end of day along with a photographic catalogue of your injuries. I want the ones that the sheriff caused recorded. Get one of these guys to photograph your back."

"Not so easy to get rid of an elected official," Nash noted.

"Once Daniel Ackers finds out what happened, it'll be a matter of him taking it up the food chain, until someone in DC contacts the county commissioners with an official complaint. They will take it to the Governor. This prick will pay for his actions. Now, I want to know *everything* that happened last night." Novak eyed him archly.

Grady felt heat creep into his cheeks. *Like hell.* "Sure, boss."

"Hey, Grady, I think you have the record for the number of times getting arrested as a serving member of the Hostage Rescue Team." Cowboy was looking out the window at the iron-gray sky, which hung heavily over a pewter ocean. A scattering of snowflakes swirled outside the window, dancing with the sea gulls. "Probably even amongst serving Special Agents as a whole. Hanssen was only arrested once."

"Don't compare me to that traitor." Grady tucked his shirt back in, grateful for the distraction Ryan had purposely created to get Novak off his case.

"Well, he certainly wasn't naked at the time," Donnelly put in with a smirk.

"Don't get excited. Cops caught me coming out of the shower."

"Yeah, but whose shower?" Keeme teased good naturedly.

"And coming how?" Cowboy said out of the side of his mouth.

Grady whacked him around the back of the head.

"Seriously, I'm worried about you, Grade." Cowboy rubbed his scalp as he turned around to face him. "What do you really know about this woman?"

"More than you know about most of the women you roll," Grady snapped.

Shit.

Ryan pressed his lips into a thin line, but he didn't react in any other way. If you didn't know better, you'd think he didn't care.

Grady knew better. "Sorry."

"Her ex-husband hasn't been heard from since he left her. That isn't raising any red flags for you?"

"He sent her a postcard from Belize."

"So she says."

Grady frowned. "He's living off the grid somewhere, probably with the woman he left Brynn for. He's not the first to want to disappear."

"Seems highly suspect."

"What are you suggesting? She offed him?" Her words came back to him along with the pain and shadows he'd seen in her eyes and the mortification and shame at having been dumped that way.

Cowboy raised a brow in question. "It's been known to happen."

"Brynn isn't like that."

"What is she like?" Cowboy asked.

"She's funny and kind. Brave enough to dive into the harbor at night in January to pull out a dead body."

He didn't miss the weighty look that Nash and Keeme exchanged.

"She has a sharp wit and a wicked sense of humor."

Cowboy crossed his arms. "Not the old 'good sense of humor' bullshit."

Grady shouldered his teammate out of his face. "It's not bullshit." He moved away, paced. He wasn't about to say he thought she was the prettiest woman on the entire East Coast, and had the most fascinating eyes he'd ever seen, the color of tornadoes and magic. Or that her body was soft and lush and had felt like coming home when he'd been inside her.

Hell no.

"We ran her DNA, remember? She's not related to Kane." Grady ran his hand over his face. "Look, I know I shouldn't have been distracted from the case, but I haven't neglected my duties."

His teammates were all looking at him with varying degrees of disquiet.

What was he supposed to say?

Nothing right now.

"I haven't told her anything about why I'm here, so don't get your panties in a twist." He turned and held Novak's gaze. "She doesn't know anything about the case."

And she was going to be furious when she found out he'd lied to her, but this was his job. He couldn't discuss most of the cases he worked on.

He'd deal with the fallout with Brynn when he had to. "Can we double-down looking for the jerk ex-husband if only so Ryan can get off my ass?" Grady shot the guy a glare.

Novak shifted from where he leaned against the bureau. "I'll request Ropero get an analyst from HQ to dig deeper—as much to avoid any issues for you should the two of you become an item after this is over."

The idea was both shocking and tantalizing.

"Grady's got a girlfriend. Grady's got a girlfriend," Donnelly teased in a sing-song voice. But it wasn't mean-spirited and, as she gently patted his back, he realized his teammates were concerned about him. It moved him enough to put his irritation aside.

"Any sign of the Russians?" Grady didn't want the team to be thinking about him when they had more important things to worry about.

"Fucking Russians," Nash muttered.

Novak shook his head. "Nothing. And no trace of any nerve agent either, thank God."

"We have to figure they're after Kane the same as we are," said Grady.

Nothing else made sense.

Another rap on the door had everyone tensing. Donnelly did the honors again. Checking the peephole before letting Ropero and Dobson inside.

Ropero looked pale and tense. She waited for Donnelly to close the door before she spoke. "We figured out how the Russians know Kane was in Deception Cove and possibly why they want him."

Keeme sat up and moved his feet as Ropero sat on the foot of the bed. She held her face in her hands. "It was my fault."

"It wasn't your fault," Dobson interrupted. "Someone, presumably Moscow, planted a listening device in Ropero's apartment."

Ropero swore and visibly ground her teeth. "I'll understand if you all want me off this case. I busted everyone else's balls about leaks, and all the time I was the one feeding them information. I was sloppy. I made a mistake."

"Did you make a mistake?" Novak asked quietly. "Or did Moscow cross a line by actively surveilling an FBI case agent?"

Ropero's lips pressed together into a thin line. "I should have had it swept. I should have suspected—"

"Why?" Novak asked. "Did you even know that the Russians were interested in Kane? I'm assuming Kane's why you were targeted, not some other case."

"It was related to Kane." She shook her head again, her expression sour. "I finally got Kane's old boss to talk to me. Lionel Perkins is a real old-school Hoover-era dude. Turns out during the investigation into the murders of Eli Kane's wife and kids, the Bureau discovered the Kanes belonged to a sex club in DC. Real swinger stuff."

"The sort of place where we know the Soviets loved to collect *Kompromat*," Novak said with disgust.

"I spoke to Ridley Branson, chief of the Counterespionage Section in the Counterintelligence Division after I spoke to Perkins. He finally admitted everything and thinks it ran deeper than just a swingers' club."

Grady helped himself to a coffee from the pot on the side. Like everyone else he'd been awake all night and needed a caffeine hit even if it tasted like garbage.

Dobson pulled a photograph out of his briefcase. "Sergei Lushko was a suspected Russian KGB agent implanted at the embassy in DC a few years before Kane went AWOL. Lushko is also believed to have attended these parties, although, of course, none of the participants used their real names. According to statements made at the time, by people reluctant to go on record, Kane's wife and Lushko were seen having sex at these parties on multiple occasions while Kane was with other women. One person intimated that on one memorable occasion the Kanes were involved in a threesome with Lushko on a library coffee table."

"Eli Kane belonged to the USSR." Grady took another sip of his drink and tried not to compare it to the coffee at Brynn's café.

"Whether he wanted to or not," Dobson agreed.

"The wife was, what? Seduced by a Russian spy? A pawn? Or was she an agent for Moscow?"

Ropero licked her lips. "The Washington Field Office suspected the latter, but when she turned up dead, murdered by one of their own, they decided it was prudent not to draw attention to the fact. They didn't think it would reflect well on the FBI to paint the victim of a familicide as a Russian spy."

"Are we thinking that at some point Kane rebelled about the idea of being used by Moscow? He knew if he hung around DC, the Ruskies would betray him to the DOJ. He'd go to prison for life for treason—assuming he'd given them anything."

"He did give them information. Minor stuff from what we can

tell, but enough to stall them, presumably while he made his plans to escape."

Bile rose in Grady's throat. "While he planned the cold-blooded murder of his wife and kids."

"How could a man murder his own children?" Cowboy asked in disgust.

"Some people don't give a shit about others even if they are related by blood," Grady kept his voice level. He had no doubt his father would have killed him and his sister as easily as not. He simply hadn't had a reason to before he'd been incarcerated.

"One thing we discovered, long after the initial investigation into the murders was over, that might shed some light on that." Ropero looked around the room, and her gaze landed on Grady. "Kane cleaned up after himself so thoroughly the Bureau had to exhume Kane's parents to get his DNA lineage. It was controversial at the time. When the labs finally ran the DNA samples of the dead wife and kids for reference a few years back, they discovered the kids didn't match what we had for Kane. They weren't his biological children."

"And they were definitely his biological parents in the graves?" asked Grady.

Ropero nodded. "We're as certain as we can be without a verified sample."

Grady frowned. "Hey, give me that photo you have of our Russian tourists from the bar and compare it to that old photo of Lushko."

Donnelly pulled out her phone and sent the image to a large iPad which they crowded around. Dobson placed the printout of Lushko's face beside it.

"Look at the ears and shape of the nostrils. It could be the same guy," Grady said.

"Why didn't he pop in the system?"

"Presumably, he had some kind of facial surgery that threw off the algorithm," Ropero said. "And also, because Sergei Lushko supposedly died around the same time Lisa Kane did."

Grady frowned. "Eli Kane cleaning house?"

Ropero shook her head. "According to Ridley, the KGB or SVR or whoever ran Lushko in those days was pissed that an op they'd taken considerable effort to set up had failed so dramatically and risked bringing down some of their other deep-cover operations."

"The Cold War never really ended, did it?" Nash commented dryly.

"They had people go so deep undercover they'd marry and raise families with a mark?" Grady reared back in disgust. It turned his stomach but he wondered how different that was from his lying to Brynn about his real reason for being in town. Still, that was a few days, not a lifetime. But he wasn't sure she'd see it that way, not after they'd had sex. And not after being deceived by her ex.

"If this Russian is Lushko, but Lushko is supposed to be dead, why is he risking being found by chasing after Kane?" Nash asked.

"Maybe the Russians faked his death so he could go back undercover at some point," Dobson said. "We know how the Kremlin can hold a grudge."

"Or maybe this was personal..." Grady looked up. "Were the Kane boys full siblings?"

Ropero nodded and walked over to stare down at the two images.

"Could Lushko be after Eli Kane because he had feelings for Lisa Kane, feelings he wasn't supposed to have?"

"If he was in love with Lisa and the kids were his..." Cowboy nodded. "Makes sense the guy would come out of hiding for a chance to avenge their deaths. I would. I'd burn it all down to get to him."

"So perhaps Lushko isn't acting on orders from Moscow," Grady said. "Maybe he's gone rogue." He looked at Ropero. "It would have been easy enough for him to identify the FBI agents on the Kane case after the Australia debacle. He decides to surveil one of them." He shot Dobson a look. "Heard about the fingerprint being found at the scene of a bank robbery in Deception Cove when you mention it at home, maybe on the phone. Maybe when plotting to bring me into this thing."

Ropero shook her head. "I haven't been back to my apartment since I learned there was a serving FBI agent with a connection to the area."

Grady nodded. "Good. At least they don't directly know about my existence, even if they've guessed that the FBI is onto them." He paced. He did his best thinking while in motion. "Maybe Moscow didn't kill Lushko. Maybe they just claimed he was dead. Maybe he ran. Maybe he ran with all that juicy *kompromat* and has been bleeding some of the other members of the swingers' club dry ever since. Hell, maybe Kane collected intelligence of his own, and that's how he funded his presumed face change and new life."

"The FBI team hunting Kane gets this red flag of a fingerprint and, because of the electronic surveillance on Ropero, that brings Lushko to town. Is Lushko the person killing locals?" Cowboy asked.

"Why bring the perfume bottle, which may or may not contain poison?" Novak went back to leaning on the bureau.

There wasn't enough space for this many large adults in one hotel room.

"What do we know about the other Russian?" Grady asked.

"I have an analyst looking, but we've been stretched thin." Ropero cupped her forehead. "We need to bring in more people."

"Using a Novichok agent in the US would plunge Russia into deep shit," Dobson added. "Either the Russians want to send a message to anyone who betrays them, or this Lushko character is using what he hopes is Kane's painful death as a way of getting back at his former bosses."

"For making the woman you love spend her life with another man and raise your kids without them ever knowing you exist," suggested Grady.

"From the laptop you gave us," Ropero said, clearly deep in

thought, "we know that the last thing Bodurek did was print a copy of the report he'd sent to the insurance company on his boat. The report included a list of all the types of evidence collected at the scene, the surveillance footage of the incident, an inventory of what was taken, and a list of all the owners of the safe deposit boxes at Hearst Savings and Loan Bank…"

Grady slowly turned to face Ropero. "If we assume Lushko and his associate killed Milton Bodurek to get hold of that list, then that suggests they don't have access to our files."

"Which is good news," Nash put in.

"Presumably they've been spending the past few days getting eyes on as many suspects as possible." Grady tried to think like an old KGB henchman, but it was tricky without the bone-deep megalomania. "They've been narrowing down the list in much the same way we have."

"We could start approaching the remaining suspects directly, and see how they react." Dobson chewed his lip.

"We can't risk it until we have enough people in place to surveil them all afterwards," argued Ropero. "Which we don't have unless we pull in local police."

"In which case you may as well take out an ad." Grady tried to hide his impatience. "Get HRT up here in force, and we'll lock this place down so the fuckers can't go anywhere."

"Why'd the Russians disappear?" Donnelly asked. "Did they find Kane already, or did they figure out we were onto them?"

The idea of losing Kane to the Russians stuck in Grady's craw.

"Perhaps they somehow knew someone had entered their room. Or it could be pure instinct," Grady said. "Presumably Lushko's survived on the run for almost as long as Kane has. He wouldn't ignore that itch between his shoulder blades that told him he was being watched, even if it meant losing Kane."

"I wouldn't bet on that." Cowboy shook his head. "The only thing this guy cares about at this point is making the sonofabitch who killed his family pay. Those two have either gotten to Kane already and are feeding him *Novichok*-laced sandwiches as we speak or they're hunkered down somewhere, waiting."

"That Quayle family last night?" Ropero asked the room in general. "Did the Russians kill them? Could one of those men be Eli Kane?"

Grady shrugged. Jesus, he was tired, and his brain hurt. "Quayles didn't have a safe deposit box at the bank. More likely to bury stuff in the woods than put it in a bank. Can't see a reason for any of them being in the bank vault."

Dobson pressed his lips together. "I ran Caleb Quayle and his family after he was one of the people at the scene of Bodurek's body recovery. We have DNA in CODIS from two of the dead uncles, Colin and Dick. Not a particularly pleasant family, but those two didn't match Kane's likely DNA profile. Caleb was too young."

They pulled up the information for the other two victims. One guy, Hap Quayle, was mixed race. The other, Tom, was a possible for Kane in terms of age and size.

Grady didn't remember much about Tom Quayle. "It doesn't play for me. Why would the Quayles let Kane stay with them?"

"For money?" Nash suggested.

"Can you get Tom's DNA from the ME?"

Dobson nodded. "Already requested in the guise of an IRS investigation. I had an agent pick it up this morning."

"Doesn't fit for it being the Russian who killed the Quayles thinking one of them was Eli Kane," Cowboy argued. "Whoever killed the Quayle men didn't kill the woman or the little girl. If it was Lushko extracting his revenge, then he'd have killed them first."

Ropero muttered, "Unless he simply couldn't bring himself to kill innocents. Who do you think did it, Steel?"

"Fuck," he scrubbed his hand over his face. "The way the sheriff is determined to pin it on me and Brynn despite us both having solid alibis made me wonder if he wasn't responsible."

"Sheriff York?" Dobson asked.

At Grady's nod, Dobson frowned. "There are a few large cash deposits to his father's bank accounts we can't trace. Could be unrelated to illegal activity, of course."

Or not. The more Grady thought about it, the more convinced he was the former sheriff was dirty. Was Darrell also on the take or simply trying to protect his old man?

"We have a warrant to covertly access any investigation reports kept online, see what sort of case he's building. Our consultant, Alex Parker, is still running all available images from the surveillance cameras in town. So far nothing."

"But if it wasn't the Russians looking for Eli Kane, then who'd want to kill the Quayles?" Nash asked. "Why?"

Grady stared around the room as his thoughts finally clicked into place. "To set me up? Get me out of the picture?"

Novak crossed his arms over his chest. "You think someone knows you're FBI and not as suspended as we wanted them to believe?"

Grady shrugged. "I had an altercation with a guy the day before he was murdered, so the cops are bound to look at me." He narrowed his eyes. "Something Darrell York said made me think they were knifed rather than shot to death. Bastard took my gun away again."

Novak let out a long sigh and went over to a big black bag. He pulled out a Glock 17 and another 1911.

He passed them both to him along with ammo. "If he tries to take these off you, shoot him."

Grady grunted. "Don't even joke about it."

"Who said I was joking?" Novak looked pissed. "I'm ready to shoot him myself."

Ropero stared out of the window at the icy ocean. "I'd like a look at this latest crime scene before the storm starts laying down snow." She looked at Dobson. "Fancy a trip out there? We can flash our badges. Doubtful whoever's guarding the scene will keep us out."

"Then you'll definitely tip our hand that the FBI is in town, and Kane *will* be in the wind," said Novak.

"It's a pity we don't have the full team here. We could have put the drones up in the air and taken a closer look from the comfort of our hotel room." Cowboy had all the subtlety of a rutting stag but he certainly knew how to drive home a point.

Ropero blew out a deep breath. "That was the wrong call, and it's on me. I admit it. How long would it take for them to arrive?"

Novak shook his head. "With this storm being forecast to be a doozy? Late tomorrow afternoon at the earliest, and that's only if the pilots will fly."

"We waiting it out in town or in Bangor?" Nash asked, examining his boots.

"Bangor," said Ropero.

"Here," said Novak.

She opened her mouth to argue.

"I'm not leaving members of my team cut off from what limited support they have."

"If Kane runs—"

"Maybe we're thinking about this all wrong. Maybe it's time to put out an alert or media statement. Let's force this sonofabitch to make his move," Grady suggested.

Ropero pressed her lips together thoughtfully. "If he hasn't already bolted, he might try to use the storm as cover."

"And if all law enforcement in the state and across the border know to be on the lookout for him, we might get lucky. There will be a lot less people on the road."

Dobson nodded. "Might be time to make that call."

Ropero put her hands on her waist. "I'll draft a press release and send it to HQ for verification and to request permission."

Cowboy rolled his eyes. "I'm sure it'll be ready in time for Christmas."

She shot his buddy a death glare. "That's the way it works, I'm afraid. All decisions regarding this issue and the public must be approved by the new director."

"Give me her number in case we're in a shootout and I need permission to return fire."

To stop the two stubborn agents going at it further, Grady interrupted. "I should pay a visit to Caleb Quayle's girlfriend. She didn't turn up for work at the café today." He checked his watch. "Maybe she knows something she isn't saying to the cops."

"You think she'll talk to you?" Novak asked intently.

"Yeah," Grady nodded. "I think she will. I went to school with her mother."

"First let's get photographs of your chest." Novak insisted and tossed Cowboy his cell phone.

"Fine, I'll sacrifice myself to seeing Grady naked," said Cowboy.

Donnelly snatched the phone out of his hand. "He's my partner. Come on, Steel."

Grady swore under his breath. And pulled off his shirt. "Let's do it here so Cowboy can see what a real man looks like."

Donnelly pulled a face when she got a good look at him. "Jesus."

Cowboy smirked.

"I mean, I know you're built," Donnelly's gaze turned sympathetic, "but you must have twenty small burns and that bruising… Are you sure you didn't bust a rib?"

Suddenly, all his teammates were surrounding him and examining him.

"Nothing's broken," he insisted. "You probably did worse crashing into that canyon wall last week."

Donnelly grinned. "Nice deflection, Steel." She shot Cowboy a look. "I'm *not* showing you my bruises."

"Spoilsport."

Donnelly began taking photos, while Grady stood there as self-conscious as a naked virgin in a strip joint.

"Drop your pants," she ordered, trying to get a shot of a bruise that had bled down his hip.

He gripped the button of his trousers and stared down his teammate. "Over your dead body."

Donnelly smirked and gave up.

Then, as soon as she backed away, he found himself being smeared with cream along with some colorful suggestions. Someone poked his ribcage, and he was about to snarl when he realized it was Novak.

His boss eyed him critically. "Tape it. Bandage it. Do not get it wet."

"No more showers for you." Donnelly clicked her tongue at him.

Cowboy grinned, but Grady saw the worry still there in his buddy's gaze. "Watch your back. Someone killed five men without blinking last night. I don't want to have to bury another teammate."

They all sobered fast. Grady nodded. The stakes had never been higher.

50

TWENTY-SEVEN YEARS AGO

Fall

Eli drove the Volvo wagon he'd bought a few weeks ago specifically for this trip.

"Why are we going this way?" Lisa asked irritably.

She didn't like the car. It was brown and ugly, apparently. She didn't like the way he'd taken her Dodge Colt Turbo back to the dealer saying they couldn't afford it right now. He'd cut off her credit card and access to the accounts. She'd already bled him dry, so maybe it was a petty move. But he wanted her isolated. He wanted her miserable.

"I told you. I have a surprise."

Her mouth thinned. He didn't know if he was getting harder to endure, or if she was tired of the pretense.

He'd done his best to make her leave him, even asked her for a divorce, but Lisa had told him they could fix the problems in their marriage. She was dedicated, he'd say that for her.

He wished it had never come to this. The bitch had stolen everything from him. He was taking it back.

It was almost full dark now. He'd timed it just so.

He turned off the highway on to the Wilderness Road. "I

rented us a cabin for the night. Figured we'd break up the journey."

Her fingers clenched in her lap, and she picked up her heavy purse from the footwell.

"Thought we'd check out the Gap Cave tomorrow morning before we drive south. The boys will like that." His voice almost broke then.

Not his fault. Not his game. Not his boys.

"They'd rather be at a theme park," Lisa sniped. "Riding rollercoasters."

He forced them out of his mind.

He took another turn, and the tires rumbled over the increasingly rough terrain. He jerked the wheel to one side and deliberately stalled the engine.

"Shit. I think we've gotten a flat."

"Don't curse in front of the boys."

It set his teeth on edge that this woman who had enticed him into her life, seduced him into her debauchery, with the sole aim of destroying him, admonished him for something as mundane as profanity.

"They're asleep." He shoved open the door, angrily, and lifted the trunk. His fingers curled around the suppressed pistol he'd stowed there. Stuffed it in the back of his jeans.

She got out of the car to join him, still carrying her purse. "I don't want them hearing foul language."

"Maybe I don't give a shit what you want anymore."

Her head came up like a raptor scenting prey—or a mongoose scenting danger.

"Your KGB buddies shook me down a couple of months ago."

Her mouth opened, and her brow furrowed prettily. "I don't have any 'KGB buddies.' Is something going on at work? Are you in trouble?"

"You don't have to pretend anymore, Lisa. I know."

"I have no idea what you're talking about."

"For God's sake, give it up. *Give it up.*"

"Give what up? Are you sick?"

They were speaking in hushed whispers.

She didn't want to wake the kids.

He didn't want to draw attention.

He stuck his neck out. "I *know*. I've been following you and that sick bastard Sergei since the spring. I know. I know *everything*. I knew at the last party. Did you really think I was that drunk?"

He saw her swallow. The taillights outlined her perfect features.

"I'm ashamed to say how much I enjoyed that threesome. Bet I fucked you both up pretty good for a while."

Her jaw firmed.

"But not half as much as you fucked me up, huh."

Her eyes darted to the children, but they were out of it. He'd drugged their orange juice.

"What I don't understand is why you chose me." His fingers curled around the weapon's grip as he drew it out but he kept it hidden behind his back. He might be many things, but he wasn't a traitor. "Of everyone in the FBI, why choose me?"

Her eyes flashed then, the first real honesty he'd seen.

"Because you were arrogant. So arrogant you never believed you could be fooled. And when you found out the truth, you'd have too much pride to admit you'd made a mistake. You'd lie and cheat in order to keep face with your colleagues. And that's exactly what you've been doing, isn't it?"

It was humbling that they'd pegged him so accurately, although not quite accurately enough.

"What's the plan now? The Iron Curtain is crumbling. It's a relic of another age. The Cold War is over."

"The Cold War will never be over." Her eyes gleamed as she dipped her hand into her purse and pulled out a revolver. Cocked the gun.

He felt his lips form a cold smile as she pulled the trigger. Once. Twice. He stepped forward and removed the pistol from her delicate fingers.

It was good to know she'd have killed him without blinking.

Made everything to come that much easier.

"I forgot to mention I also *listened* in on your meetings with good old Sergei. Heard all the action. You guys could have made a fortune in porn films. Heard you say how much you wished I was dead so you didn't have to—what was the term you used, Mrs. Pottymouth? Oh, yes, 'screw that disgusting piece of shit every night.'"

He tossed the revolver into the trunk. He'd removed the bullets before they'd started driving. She'd gotten sloppy.

"I'm going to give you one chance to get out. Run, Lisa. Run with the boys. You and good old Sergei. Escape. Live a good life, and raise your family. I'm sure with both of your skills, you know how to disappear."

Her laugh was ugly. "You think we were forced to play our parts for Mother Russia?"

"I know how the Kremlin presents its choices. I know first-hand, thanks to you."

For a moment her expression was stricken.

Could she not see he was giving her a chance? To save herself. "You love him. I know you love him. You have two children by the man."

She closed her eyes and raised her face to the night sky. "He would never agree. He'd never betray his country. The way you betrayed yours." Her tone turned derisive.

Hate began to boil along his veins. "The information I gave them was useless."

"But you gave it to them, didn't you?" Her smile was sharp. "You gave it to them, and they will have recorded every step. You want to know the other reasons we chose you? And, yes, I had a say in the decision, as I was the one who'd have to screw you regularly."

Rage pressed along the inside of his brain. That she despised him so much when she'd been the one to make him fall.

She clutched her bag to her like a shield, but it wouldn't work.

She expected the transponder inside to lead her rescuer to her, but Eli had placed the bug on an eighteen-wheeler at the first gas station they stopped at. They were out of range of any kind of listening or tracking device here anyway. She was completely on her own, but also completely free, possibly for the first time in her life, to speak her mind.

"Because you're weak and vain and pathetic. What are you going to do, Eli?" The way she spoke his name was full of loathing. "Run? They'll find you. You can't kill me without killing the boys and you wouldn't have the balls—"

She jolted with the quiet hiss of four bullets fired into the back seats.

"They didn't feel anything. I put sleeping pills into their juice earlier."

Her face contorted with grief and rage as she threw herself at him. He shot her in the chest, and she dropped to the ground.

He squatted beside her.

"You killed my babies." The heartbreak was there in her eyes, finally. The destruction.

"How does it feel to know it was all for nothing? All the theatrics with me. All the sex parties, fucking people for the good old USSR, which is about to collapse—any idiot can see it's all about to come tumbling down. Doing them because that's what Sergei ordered."

"Not Sergei."

"Who then?"

Tears ran down the side of her face. "You think if you find out and bring them down, they'll let you back in the FBI fold?" She laughed as she clutched at the wound, blood spilling out. "You really are a fool."

"Maybe if I hadn't shot your spawn, I could have made it work. But you had to push me one last time, didn't you?"

"You are a monster." Tears filled her eyes… Rage. Despair.

It was the despair he was waiting for. The knowledge he'd

broken and destroyed her the way she'd broken and planned to destroy him.

But he had other ideas.

He stood and aimed down at her head. Time to end this wretched chapter of his life.

51

PRESENT DAY

G rady went to pick up Murphy from Kalpa, who was working out of her home until she could find a more suitable temporary clinic. A pack of dogs started barking as he walked in the front door. All shapes and sizes. A couple of cats were also in the mix, and he noticed the devil parakeet in a large cage in the corner of the living room.

It was chaos.

Murphy lay on top of another woman on the couch but jumped down when Grady walked in. He shook his newly shorn butt and licked Grady's hand.

Emotion punched him in the throat with the realization that this dog and so many others would have died last night if not for Brynn and him.

Fuck.

"What happened to your face?" Kalpa asked with a frown.

He must look worse than he realized. He glanced at his reflection in a mirror near the door. Winced. "According to Sheriff York, I resisted arrest."

The vet locked her jaw and shook her head. "This is my partner, Muriel."

Kalpa eyed him warily like he might have a negative opinion on her living arrangements or sexuality. Like it was his business.

He held out his hand. "Nice to meet you, Muriel. Thanks for looking after this guy while I was under arrest for multiple homicides." He scratched Murphy's head.

"Sheriff York is a moron," Kalpa muttered. "At least the insurance company sent out their own investigator for the fire. The chances of the sheriff catching a killer seem remote at best, which leaves us all scared spitless."

"I can see why he might question me. After yesterday." Grady shrugged. "The cops will find the killer." He didn't say which cops.

Muriel stood and brushed off her T-shirt. "Well, that dog is adorable. If you decide not to keep him—"

"I'm keeping him," he said firmly.

"You better," Kalpa whispered as Muriel headed into the kitchen with the pack following her. "We are not getting another dog. We already have three. And a cat." She indicated vaguely at the retreating animals.

"You contact all the owners yet?"

"Just about." Her expression fell. "Not sure if I'll be able to weather the financial hit, frankly." Strain made her features tighten. "I'm probably going to need a bridging loan and I'm not sure how the new bank manager will view the recently arrived brown, lesbian, veterinarian in town."

As someone who knew exactly how judgmental people in town could be even when you were a cishet, white male, he sympathized. "Let me call her. Put in a good word," Grady suggested.

"You'd do that for me?"

"Of course." He frowned. "I'm not sure it'll do you much good, but I'll mention your situation to Edith and hope it makes a difference."

Kalpa's dark eyes sparkled. "Thank you." Her lips curved and eyebrows bobbed. "You walked into my life less than twenty-four hours ago and nothing has been the same since. If we weren't both already in love with other people…"

He jolted.

She covered her mouth. "Oh, I'm sorry. I spoke out of turn."

He rubbed the back of his neck. Frowned. "What makes you think I'm in love with Brynn?"

"Could it be the way you can't take your eyes off her when she's nearby? The way you pay attention to her needs before your own. Or the way her happiness is more important than anyone else's?"

He grunted.

Kalpa laughed. "Hey, if it helps, from what I could see yesterday, she feels the same about you."

Was that even possible?

"She's been hurt in the past."

Kalpa's eyes held a depth of wisdom. "Everyone's been hurt at some point, Grady. Even Caleb Quayle started life as an innocent who was at some point taught to be a loud, bullying, cruel, and obnoxious young man. God rest his soul."

"My early role models weren't so different from his."

"Then maybe you're the example of nature over nurture. I don't know." Her lips curved into a sweet half smile. "I just know when I found my second chance at love, I didn't waste it, even though it came from a direction I never expected."

Muriel walked back into the room and handed him a bag of dog food. "To keep you going through this blizzard they're forecasting."

Kalpa rolled her eyes. "It'll probably be three inches that all melts by tomorrow morning after the fuss they've made."

Grady laughed as he hefted the bag with the same arm that held the leash Muriel had handed him. "Whatever the weather I'd prepare to batten down the hatches for the next twenty-four hours. Keep the doors locked."

Brynn was so tired she thought she was hallucinating when Jackie walked in the back door and pulled on an apron.

Brynn squinted but the girl was still there.

"Hey, I thought your mother said you couldn't come in."

Jackie sniffed. Her eyes were reddened, and so was her nose. "I slept some and feel a lot better."

Angus walked over to stand beside her. Linda came around the corner with a narrow-eyed expression on her thin, foxy face.

"Then I got to thinking how you and that Grady guy were up all night helping with the animals and everyone is saying how Caleb must have done it—the fire, that is. And Mom said how Grady Steel wasn't the kind to have murdered anyone no matter what that idiot Darrell York said—they all went to school together." She sniffed and more tears formed. "It's all such a mess, and I feel like it's all my fault, so I figured the least I could do was come in and help out."

Brynn wasn't sure how much help the girl would be, but her heart softened at the obvious effort Jackie was making. Brynn touched her arm gently. "Jackie, your boyfriend was murdered last night. You don't have to come in to work."

The girl grabbed a tissue and blew her nose. "We broke up— after he hit you." Her eyes were huge and full of shame. "I couldn't believe he did that, Brynn, honestly. I was horrified."

"He'd never shown any violent tendencies in front of you before?"

Jackie shook her head.

Thank goodness for small mercies.

"We'd been dating just a couple of weeks. I only went out to his place once, a few days ago." She grimaced. "Knew Hetty and little Susie from them coming into the café so figured it would be okay, you know? But his dad and uncles totally gave me the creeps." She shivered.

Angus's expression darkened behind Jackie's back.

"They didn't want me wandering around the place. Told Caleb to keep an eye on me like I was some sort of thief. Anyway, after mom found out that I went there, she said I wasn't to go again. If I really wanted to see Caleb then he could come to the house." She wiped her nose again. "She never lets anyone come to the house, so that was a big deal."

Jackie looked over her shoulder as Angus went back to stir the fresh pot of clam chowder he had on the stove. It was Brynn's mother's favorite, and she'd set aside two bowls from the last batch for her dad to take home.

A sudden wave of longing welled up inside her. To see her mom. To kiss her cheek. To tell her she loved her.

Jackie lowered her voice. "Mom made me go on birth control. And gave me a bunch of condoms." Crimson stained the young woman's cheeks. "I told her we hadn't, *I* hadn't, but she made me swear…"

Brynn knew Jackie's mother had gotten pregnant in high school. She obviously wanted something else for her daughter. "Your mother is smart to look out for your health and welfare."

Jackie nodded. "I know. She can be hard, but she loves me. She didn't mention it to my stepdad. Ed would go ballistic if he thought Caleb touched me that way…"

Brynn's eyes bugged and Jackie laughed. "I don't mean he would actually *kill* him."

"Someone did, darling." Linda exchanged a look with Brynn. "You talk to the sheriff?"

Jackie's expression soured. "He came to the house and questioned me this morning. Tried to get me to say how you had some sort of ongoing vendetta against Caleb, but it wasn't true. Mom was there. She told him you and Grady were the least likely murder suspects in this entire town. Although, then Darrell pointed out how your asshole ex—his emphasis on the word, not mine—'disappeared.' Mom told him that if he couldn't come up with any better ideas than you two, she was going to run for sheriff come re-election, and she'd win."

"I'd certainly vote for her." Ice washed over Brynn at the thought Darrell was resurrecting what had happened with Aiden.

As if she hadn't lived through enough humiliation where her ex was concerned.

Jackie blew her nose. "Anyway, Mom's better than any lawyer. Thankfully, Dad was out checking pots before this storm hits. He's home now."

Jackie's dad, Ed, would be Brynn's number one suspect if she was a cop. He was a scary sonofabitch. But not Darrell York. Darrell arrested the manager of the local café and an FBI agent he'd once called friend. And it sounded like he was trying to dredge up old dirt to support his asinine theories.

The growing noise on the other side of the counter suggested someone was about to leave and someone else had just arrived. Brynn took a long look at the girl's tear-blotched face. "Are you sure you want to stay?"

Jackie nodded.

"Okay. You work the counter. Linda and I will do tables."

"As soon as I have a quick break." Linda gave them both a hug and hurried off to pull on her jacket.

Jackie wiped her eyes. "I'm really sorry, Brynn."

Brynn gave the girl a shoulder bump. "Come on. I don't want people to think I make the staff cry."

Jackie laughed. "I'm so sorry about what happened yesterday."

Brynn nodded. "Forget it." Her nose was a little sore, but no real lasting harm had been done, except to her sense of personal safety. "And I'm sorry about the Quayles. As much as I disagreed with Caleb these past few days, he didn't deserve what happened."

Jackie's expression drooped again, and Brynn knew she'd said the wrong thing.

"Let's get these people seated and served," she said briskly. "You divide up anything that needs eating in the next couple of days, and we can all take some home." She looked out at the thin veil of snow. The atmosphere felt like it was on a precipice suddenly, the storm about to break. But it could as easily fizzle out into nothing.

Maybe the warnings wouldn't live up to the hype, but she wouldn't mind the excuse for a snow day.

"We'll make these new people the last full menu table. Anyone who comes in after can get a drink and baked goods but no meals unless it's bread and soup. Then we'll all leave early and be safe home before this blizzard hits."

52

Ryan Sullivan yawned widely as he took a seat in the Sea Spray Café. Donnelly had snagged the prime position facing the door, and he was left looking out the window like a rookie.

All because he'd held the door like a gentleman.

"I can't believe you're still thinking about your gut with everything going on." Donnelly shrugged out of her jacket, pulled off her cute wooly hat, and left them both on the seat beside her.

She was armed to the teeth, but you'd never know. That face looked more like a college student than a member of an elite tactical unit.

"What?" she asked quickly, wiping her mouth as if worried she had something on it.

"Nothing." He looked toward the harbor where he could make out the tops of the boat masts. He leaned closer to her, determined to ignore the weird effect she had on him. "I'm not thinking about my gut, as you so eloquently put it, although I could eat."

"You can always eat."

He flicked a glance sideways and understanding dawned in Donnelly's eyes as Brynn Webster approached their table with a notepad.

"Hi there. You caught us just in time. We're closing early today because of the storm. What can I get you both?"

Ryan ordered chowder and a salad with extra bread. Donnelly ordered a chicken burger and fries.

Before Brynn could walk away, he asked, "You really think this blizzard is going to be something to worry about?"

She was attractive. Very attractive. But she also had a reserve and distance he didn't completely trust.

She pulled her mouth to one side. "Honestly, it could go either way, but up here it's wise to pay attention to the forecast. We could have six inches or six feet by morning, and if you get caught out in it unprepared it can be very dangerous."

He smiled. "Like back home in Montana."

Brynn folded her arms, obviously eager to get their order to the chef but also being a good hostess. "Then you know exactly how it is—deceptive." Her brows gave a little wiggle. "Like the town." She pasted a bright smile on her lips. "When are you guys planning on leaving?"

"Day after tomorrow."

"Roads should be fine by then, but I'd avoid going for any wilderness hikes in the next twenty-four hours."

Ryan smiled at Donnelly. "Planning to stay in and hunker down with my honey."

Donnelly kicked him under the table. Brynn surprised him by leaning closer and whispering, "Me, too. Now let me get that order in before the chef closes the kitchen."

"Call me 'honey' again," Donnelly warned after Brynn Webster left, "and I'll slit your throat next time you fall asleep."

"Considering the recliner I'm using is about forty years old, that'll be never, darling."

She narrowed her eyes. "Sleep in the bed then. I won't bite. I'll even sleep in the damn recliner if it stops you whining about it, *sweetheart*."

He opened his mouth to say no way would he let her sleep in the recliner, but she spoke right over him.

"I don't know what the big deal is. Are you scared you're gonna get confused in your sleep that I'm one of your conquests?" Her dark brows fused. "Trust me, it wouldn't take me long to remind you that I'm not."

He gritted his teeth. "That's not it."

"Then what? What's your issue? Shit, it's not me coming on to you last week like an idiot?"

"It's not that either." He looked away from her intense gaze, unable to hold it. Maybe that was a lie, but it wasn't the only reason. Outside the wind blew the snow and the gulls rode the gusts of wind. Inside the café was warm and quiet—a haven that felt about as safe as a gin trap. He cleared his throat. "If you must know, I haven't slept with a woman since my wife died."

Donnelly gaped at him. Her shocked expression was almost worth the price of that confession. Almost.

"But you have sex *all the time*." She dropped her voice so low he could barely hear it.

"A slight exaggeration," he said evenly, "and I'm usually not asleep during the act."

"So, what, you just get up and leave? Wham, bam, thank you, ma'am?"

He shrugged and picked up the glass of beer another waitress dropped off. "Assuming myself and the lady in question make it to a bed, which is honestly rarer than you'd think. But sure. I get up, get dressed, and kiss them goodbye."

"That's cold."

"Like hell it is."

"Most women at least like the pretense they are more than a vessel for your pleasure."

A vessel for your pleasure?

"Are you kidding me?" He smiled grimly at Brynn as she delivered his steaming soup and salad and Donnelly's enormous mound of fries.

He stole one.

When they were alone again, he hissed, "Women I have sex

with know exactly what the deal is, and I make damn sure they get off before I do. Damn. And I can't believe we're having this conversation."

"These women you hit on." Donnelly's brow crinkled as she munched her food. "Do you announce the no-strings, no-sleeping-over deets before or after the first kiss?"

He raised his shoulders. "I generally let women come on to me. Then when they're suggesting we go have some fun somewhere, I tell them it'll be a one-time thing and I don't have much time for an after-party."

She looked so confused. "All these conquests, all these assignations the guys are always talking about. The women come on to you?"

Ryan gave her his most winning smile. "I'm not saying I don't send out signals that I'm interested or attracted to someone, but, yeah, I generally let them make the moves."

"*Why*?"

The question made him swallow. He delayed answering by eating another delicious spoonful of chowder. When it was clear she was still waiting on an answer he said quietly, "It feels less like cheating then."

Donnelly's eyes went wide and her head reared back. "You still feel married to her, don't you? To your dead wife."

He flinched. Nodded. "I did. For a long time."

"And now?"

Why the hell was she asking all these questions?

"And now?" He ripped off a hunk of bread. Chewed slowly. "I guess it's another of my bad habits."

"You are taking the bed tonight even if I have to tranq you."

He caught her hand as Brynn started walking toward them again. "I was raised to be a gentleman. I can't simply turn it off. You have the bed."

Her eyes flashed at him. "Think of me as a teammate, not as a woman."

"I do." He thought of her as both. It didn't change his fundamental personality.

"Everything okay?" Brynn asked. Then her attention was caught by something down at the harbor. She shook it off and turned back to them.

"Yes. Thanks," Donnelly said. "Delicious."

Brynn smiled as she gathered their dishes. "Tea? Coffee?"

"Coffee." He needed to stay awake and wanted to avoid going back to the hotel for as long as possible even though the others were there now, too. Everyone else was staying in their own rooms to avoid notice. "Can I see the dessert menu?"

Brynn nodded. "And yourself?" she asked Donnelly.

Donnelly patted her stomach. "Just an Americano for me, thanks. That was delicious."

"I'll pass on your compliments to the chef."

Ryan watched Brynn walk away.

"Why don't you like her?" Donnelly asked. "She seems nice."

"It's not that I don't like her. I just…"

"You're overprotective of your friends."

He shot her a glare. "I'm not overprotective. Grady's a big boy. *Built* even."

She snorted.

"I think it's hinky what she says happened to her husband." He mouthed the last as Brynn was approaching to clear the rest of their dishes and deliver the dessert menu.

She picked up everything and then frowned again as she looked down at the harbor. She turned around and went back into the kitchen.

Ryan stood and followed Brynn's gaze and tried to see what had caught her attention. The harbor was full of boats. Trawlers and sailboats hunkered down to ride out the bad weather.

Yellow crime scene tape was strung across the side of the dead banker's boat. Then Ryan saw it. A stream of steam coming from one of the vents on the cordoned-off sailboat. A heater was on.

Someone was onboard that boat.

53

No one answered the door at Jackie Somers' home so Grady took Murphy for a quick run down on the beach. The snow was starting to thicken, but he needed this energy release, and so did the dog, especially if they were going to be cooped up for the next little while.

Perversely, Grady was looking forward to it. Hopefully, all the bad guys stayed holed up while the FBI analysts figured out who and where Eli Kane was. HRT could be waiting for the guy the minute the snow stopped.

And until it did, Grady would be hanging out with Brynn…

He hit the beach and wished he could let Murphy off the leash, but not yet. It would take time until they learned to trust one another.

Somehow that made him think of Brynn again.

Could he really be in love with her?

How did anyone know for certain?

It would explain the jittery, mixed-up feeling in his chest that he'd never experienced before. The almost-overwhelming fear of screwing up.

That she might feel the same way about a guy like him… And maybe that was wishful thinking on his and Kalpa's part.

As he turned a corner, the wind slammed into him like a wall.

What did a guy like him know about love? His parents' marriage had been a warzone that had reinforced the idea that love was a dangerous weakness. His father had dominated them all with anger and fear. The very last thing Grady wanted was to hurt a woman who'd already gone through hell with her ex.

He grimaced. Would she forgive him for deceiving her? He wasn't sure.

How long until he could risk telling her the truth about why he was in town?

He wanted to do it today.

Wouldn't. Couldn't. But he wanted to.

His cell rang. He slowed to check it, was surprised when Edith Bodurek spoke.

"Mr. Steel, I know you said not to call, but I heard the police released you, and I wanted to know, *needed* to know if you told the sheriff about the laptop I lent you, or if it was found when they searched your home?"

The icy wind stole his breath as he stood on the shore watching the Atlantic roar. "No."

"You're certain?"

"It didn't come up, Mrs. Bodurek, and I didn't raise it. As Sheriff York is trying to pin five new murders on me, I wasn't exactly feeling like sharing any information that might link me to the sixth."

"Oh, that's good, I suppose. I was worried he might decide I had something to do with my husband's murder, and I don't think I can deal with that on top of losing Milt." She sounded like she was hanging on by a thread. "Although, now I wonder if Sheriff York, junior, is even vaguely capable of finding who killed my poor Milt."

"Are you okay?"

"No. Not really. Did you find out anything that might help find his killer?"

It was easy to forget sometimes that cases weren't simply puzzles to solve. Real people were impacted. Lives ruined.

He thought of the Russians and Kane. Lied. "Not yet."

"Is it possible the same person who killed Milt also murdered the Quayles and robbed the bank?"

Grady stared at the crashing waves as thoughts started to coalesce. They had to be connected. But how?

"I don't know, Mrs. Bodurek, but I promise you I will find out."

"Do you think I'm in any danger?"

"I honestly don't know, but lock the doors and stay inside."

"I hear you're seeing the Webster girl. Brynn," she interrupted quickly.

Grady didn't answer.

"It's okay. None of my business I realize, but it's all over town that she vigorously came to your defense this morning."

"You should know better than to listen to gossip."

She sighed. "You're right, but it was nice to hear about romance rather than death."

Grady shivered as his body cooled. He was dressed for running not standing around talking on the phone.

"I saw her with her father at the bank a couple of weeks ago. I was visiting Milt for lunch and she was being added as a signatory to the business account. Such a lovely young woman. I'm truly sorry for what that family is going through. I'm glad she has you."

Grady didn't know what the hell to say to that.

"Please let me know if you discover anything. My brain is spinning in endless circles, sitting here waiting for news, watching the world carry on while mine is in ruins." Her breath caught. "I can't even bury him yet. My poor Milt."

"I'm sorry, Mrs. Bodurek—"

"Edith. Call me Edith."

"I'm sorry, Edith." Maybe there was a way he could distract

the woman from her own misery. "Look, there is one thing, the new veterinarian—"

"I saw her practice had burned down. Dreadful. Simply dreadful."

"It was arson," Grady stated. "Someone wanted to drive her out of town." Or maybe to give Grady an apparent motive to kill Caleb Quayle. That made more sense than anything else… He wondered if Ropero had a time of death for the Quayles yet.

"That's terrible. Just terrible." She sucked in a breath. "I heard you and Brynn saved all the animals."

"We were lucky to be passing by when we were." He stared down at the black eyes of his running companion and the idea of this dog dying was like a physical blow. "But the veterinarian is going to need local support to get through this."

"Is there anything I can do to help?"

"Perhaps organize some sort of fundraiser. Help her find temporary accommodation for her clinic. Have the bank offer her a bridging loan until the insurance company comes through."

"I can do all of those things. I'm disappointed I didn't think of that myself. I should have reached out…"

"You've had a lot on your mind."

Edith sniffed and Grady was pretty sure she was crying. "I have but it's no excuse."

He gave her Kalpa's cell number. "Keep warm and out of this storm, Edith. I promise I'll do everything I can to find Milton's killer." He hated making promises he might not be able to keep, but he was confident in this. Everything was coming to a head. "I have to go."

He hung up, then clicked his tongue to get Murphy's attention away from a piece of driftwood, and they set off at a fast run back toward town.

As he neared Saul Jones's house, he slowed.

He suspected his old friend hadn't told him everything. Now might be a good time to squeeze him. Grady knocked on the front door and decided, what the hell, he'd try the handle. The fact it was locked bought him up short.

He frowned and decided to go around the back. Perhaps the Joneses were concerned about these murders.

People should be.

Or perhaps Saul had something to hide.

Grady debated knocking versus walking in and decided on the former. He waited a full ten seconds and, after no reply, tried the handle.

This time the door swung open. Something didn't feel right. Grady held Murphy in one hand while he rested the other on his borrowed Glock. He stepped inside and was brought up short by the barrel of a gun pointed at his head.

54

"Come on." Ryan stood, pulling out his wallet and putting enough money on the table to cover the bill along with a generous tip.

"What about the—"

"Now, Donnelly. *Move*." He pulled on his jacket and placed his wide brimmed hat on his head.

Her eyes widened before she recognized the words for what they were. An order.

She stood up, dragged on her bobble hat and coat. He took her hand, pulling her out the rear entrance onto the back deck even though there was a big sign saying that customers were to go out the front.

"Sorry," Donnelly shouted to the scowling staff.

He headed down the alley and reluctantly let go of her hand.

"What's going on?" she asked.

"There's someone on the dead guy's boat." He rested his hand on his SIG under his jacket, eyes scanning the harbor for threats.

"Could be family or someone cleaning it or something."

"Cops still have crime scene tape up."

"Could be cops."

"It could be, which is why I can't go charging in there without taking a closer look."

"Let's call it in to Novak. See what he says."

"You call Novak. I'm going to take a wander down the end of the marina. You wait here and watch my six."

He heard her sputter a complaint, but there was no time to lose. He strolled along the harbor, shoulders hunched against the bitter cold, head down to protect his face from the now stinging flakes. The metal security gate of the marina was open, so he walked straight through. He strolled along, examining all the yachts. Acid yellow tape fluttered across the fourth boat slip along. The banker's yacht was one of the larger crafts, the sort that could sail around the world if that was what floated your boat.

He smiled at his own little joke.

No obvious sign of life inside except the steam coming from that vent. Perhaps the heating was on a thermostat? Any footprints would have been obliterated by the fierce wind and the thin, fresh layer of snow. Fishing boats lined up on a separate pier off to the left. Ryan wandered to the end of the walkway and stared into the ink-black water. It looked about as appealing as getting castrated. The fact Brynn Webster had gone in there alone late last Friday night suddenly put her up a notch in his estimation.

Grady wasn't an idiot, but Ryan knew he was vulnerable the way they were all vulnerable. In matters of the heart.

He didn't want his buddy to get hurt.

He turned around and stared up at the café. Spotted Donnelly leaning against the wall of a nearby building, sheltered from the wind, texting on her phone as if she were bored.

Ryan knew with sudden certainty that either the Russians or Eli Kane were hidden on that boat and they probably planned to set sail as soon as it got dark or the storm calmed down a bit.

He needed to call in the troops.

Grady brought up his arm and knocked the gun out of Saul's hand. The weapon went off, the bullet exiting straight through the kitchen wall. Murphy panicked on the end of the leash, but Grady didn't let go. He ignored the frightened dog as he forced Saul down to the ground and knelt on his back.

The guy bucked. "Get the fuck off me, Grady! Get off me!"

Grady shoved the door so that it slammed shut. Then he let go of Murphy's leash and scooped up Saul's dad's old 1911 off the faded linoleum.

It was locked and loaded.

"What's going on, Saul?"

"I was worried about the murders is all. Thought you were one of the killers."

"Why would the killers be coming after you?" Grady spotted the crutches propped against the kitchen counter and a bag on the table. Suitcase on the floor next to the door. "Where are you going in such a rush? Don't you know there's a blizzard coming?"

"Pah," Saul spat. "It's nothing."

"Your leg seems a lot better." Had the guy been pretending to be more hurt than he was?

"I'm healing well, but not with a great lummox sitting on top of me. Get *off*."

Grady eased off him and stepped over to look inside the bag on the table. Cash.

"Now don't get the wrong idea, Grade. When Brandy left me, I maybe fudged some of the details about how much she took out of the bank accounts."

Grady shook his head. "Do you think I'm just off the boat? Where's your mother? Did you kill her the way you killed the Quayles and Milton Bodurek?"

"What? No." Sweat beaded on Saul's forehead despite the coolness of the kitchen. He held his hands up. Fingers spread wide. "I haven't killed anyone. I swear it."

"Turn around. Hands against the wall."

"Grady, I swear—"

"Turn around, goddammit." Emotion was strangling him. "I don't want to hurt you, but I will if you fight me on this."

He opened the kitchen drawer that had been a catch-all when they'd been growing up, found a zip tie.

Saul did as he was told. "I'm begging you, Grady. Let me go. Say you never saw me. I'll split the cash with you—"

"Are you seriously attempting to bribe a federal agent right now?"

"I didn't do anything! I swear. Hear me out."

Grady zip-tied his childhood friend's wrists together behind his back. "Sit." He kicked a chair out for him. Saul sat.

Murphy whined at the door, and Grady stopped long enough to stroke the dog and calm him down.

Then Grady went cautiously through to the living room. He held his breath when he saw Mrs. Jones sitting unmoving in her chair in the corner of the room. A blanket was tucked over her lap and chest.

He checked her pulse. It thrummed strong and steady.

"I love the old bitch. I haven't hurt her. I put one of the tranquilizers the docs gave to help me sleep in her coffee," Saul spoke from the doorway. "I needed a couple of hours to leave town, and I needed to do it without her calling the cops on me or…"

"Or what?"

Saul's eyes flashed. "Or her being interrogated by whoever the hell killed Milton and the Quayles."

"Why do you think they might come here for information, Saul?" Grady asked with forced patience. "Were you in on the bank robbery?"

Saul shook his head. Tried to scratch his nose on his shoulder. "I wasn't, no."

Grady went to walk past him, unwilling to listen to bullshit.

"Look, I figured it out after I spoke with you. Realized who the robber was. I drove out to the compound on Catfish Crossing. Told Colin Quayle that he owed me for shooting me in the leg, otherwise I was going to the cops. I made him give me a cut of the stolen money." Saul looked down at the faded old linoleum. "Ten grand. Enough to get me started somewhere else. Told him if anything happened to me there was a dead man's switch and all the details would go to the sheriff. Colin just laughed and said Darrell York couldn't catch a duck in a barrel. Then I told him I'd copied you, and he took me a bit more seriously."

"Not sure using my name to commit a crime will get you any brownie points from me. When did you speak to him?" Grady snapped.

"A couple of hours after I spoke with you."

"Was Milton in on the bank robbery?" Was Edith keeping tabs on any information that might incriminate her and her dead husband?

"Not that I know of. Asshole was too strait-laced to rob his own bank." Saul's features twisted bitterly. "After what he said to me when I was in the hospital, I figured that I didn't owe the bank anything. Not when I was shot in the leg for a lousy forty grand a year. The insurance will cover his money. The only person who lost anything that day was me."

"Did you shoot Milton?"

Saul's mouth dropped open. "Shit, Grady. No. No. I didn't shoot anyone."

"Did the Quayles kill Milton?"

Saul shook his head. "They said they didn't, and I believed them. They had enough cash to see them through a year or more. They didn't have no reason to kill someone and turn up the heat on themselves."

"You had cause. You told me yourself."

Sweat started to bead on Saul's brow.

"I'm not a killer. Took all my balls to approach the Quayles. I didn't like Bodurek, but I wouldn't have killed him." His gaze held Grady's. "I wouldn't kill anyone. You know that."

"Then who did?"

Saul's lip curled. "According to Darrell York, you did it."

Grady's smile felt lethal as a blade. "Well, under the circumstances, you better hope that's not the case."

Saul sighed. "I know you didn't do it. Always did have a clear sense of right and wrong, even as a kid. Me and Darrell were always happy to do whatever came into our heads, but you would never cross certain lines."

That wasn't how Grady remembered his childhood. "Did you see anything suspicious at the Quayle place when you were there?"

Saul sniffed. "They didn't let me into the main house. But two tourists came tramping through while I was there. Claimed to be lost while hiking."

"Tourists?"

"Foreigners."

"Foreigners? French? German? Canadian?"

Saul shook his head. "Eastern European. Colin told them to get off his land and fired a shotgun into the air to scare them away." Saul's lips pinched. "I about shit my pants thinking he was going to shoot me next."

"What did the tourists do?"

"The man stared real hard at each of the Quayles, and I thought there might be trouble, but then he raised his hand and apologized. Backed away. Hap shadowed them back to their vehicle."

"What were they driving?"

Saul shook his head. "I don't know. Hap didn't say. Colin went inside the barn and came back with this bag of cash. Told me if I splashed it around or ratted on them, I'd be dead and so would my mother."

He looked aghast at the notion. "I told them to leave her out of it, but they said I'd brought her into it by shaking them down. I came back home and spent a sleepless night staring at the door with my dad's old gun in my hand. When I heard they were all dead... I honestly didn't know what to think. Relief, which is a terrible thing to admit. For Mom and me. Then I started wondering who'd do that to the Quayles, who were the scariest motherfuckers I ever met—present company excepted—and if the killer figured out I had some of the money from the bank heist, then maybe I was next. That's when I gave mom the sleeping pill and started packing. Please don't turn me in, Grady. If I go to jail, I'll have even less than I have now."

Grady gripped his old friend by the front of his shirt and shook him. "You have a roof over your head and a mother who loves you. You have friends and, except for the injured leg, you're in good health."

"Please don't have me arrested." Saul started crying then. "I'm sorry. Sorry I ever tried this."

Grady felt emotions of his own surfacing. Neither of them had had many opportunities growing up. Grady had taken the ones he'd been given and run. Saul had been left to flounder.

Grady took a breath. Thing was, he believed the story Saul was telling. It was too complex for Saul to have made it up. The guy had never been particularly imaginative.

"I can't let you go, but I can do one thing for you. Turn yourself in. Things will go a lot easier for you if you do that, and I doubt you'll serve time. Tell Darrell how you went out to the Quayles for some lumber to fix the front steps that are rotting through. While you were there, you recognized Colin from the robbery. Colin threatened you when he realized you recognized him. Then they tried to buy you off with cash. You were scared and didn't know what to do at first, so you accepted the money, but you planned to come into the Sheriff's Department this morning and tell them everything. Then you heard about the killings and became worried he might think it was you that murdered the Quayles. That's why it took a few hours for you to come forward. Unpack that suitcase of yours. Bring every stolen dollar to the sheriff's department, and tell your story to everyone who'll listen, not just Darrell."

Grady used the knife in his boot to cut the zip tie. "Tell them all that and you might just stay out of prison. Try to escape with the cash, and I'll make sure the FBI hunts you down and puts you away for a long time. Understand?"

Hope and defeat warred in Saul's eyes. "Okay. Okay. I'll do that. Exactly that. Thank you."

Grady's cell phone rang.

It was Cowboy.

Grady stepped away from Saul. "I need to take this. Call dispatch and ask for an appointment with Darrell before I finish this phone conversation. Then unpack. Then get the hell over there ASAP."

"What are you going to do?"

The cell stopped ringing. Dammit. "I don't have time to be detained again. You never saw me, understood?"

Saul's eyes widened and then narrowed. "You're not really suspended, are you?"

Grady didn't answer.

Saul laughed. "Oh man, Darrell's finally gonna get what he deserves, isn't he?"

Grady gathered up Murphy's leash and stuffed Saul's 1911 in the back of his running pants. He'd already written up his report about this morning's violent arrest and submitted it to Novak to go with the photographs. "Call the Sheriff's Department, and turn yourself in. Maybe you'll luck out and get a front row seat to the rest of the show."

He walked out the back door, realized he had another missed called from Brynn. He needed to talk to Cowboy first.

He dialed his friend. "S'up?"

55

Ryan was bringing Grady up to speed when there was movement on the boat. Ryan tensed as the Russian woman walked out onto the deck of the yacht. She was ducking under the crime scene tape when their gazes locked.

"Busted." He ignored Grady and stuffed the cell in his pocket.

A car pulled up along the wharf as Donnelly started heading across the road toward the entrance of the marina.

Where was the man? Where was Lushko?

"Howdy, ma'am." He tipped his hat as they'd met a couple of times now. "Didn't know you were a sailor." Perhaps he could bluff his way out of this. But something must have given him away. Maybe the hand he kept hidden from view, sliding around his weapon.

The woman fished into the plastic bag she carried and pulled out the perfume bottle he'd spotted last night. Dread filled him. Donnelly reached the other end of the narrow walkway. The woman knew she was trapped.

"Do you know what's in this?" Her accent was thicker now. Her brown eyes accurately read his lack of surprise. "I did wonder if Sergei was being overly paranoid when he insisted you and your ditsy girlfriend were more than a couple of dumb tourists, but obviously his instincts were correct. More his field than mine, I suppose."

"And what's your field, ma'am?"

"Me?" She took a few steps toward him.

"You need to stay where you are, ma'am. Why don't you tell me what's in the bottle?" He cast a worried eye at Donnelly. She was directly in the line of fire should a bullet go through the woman or should he, by some unimaginable twist of fate, miss his target. He was restricted in his options. Donnelly needed to *move*.

"My field and what's in the bottle are connected." The Russian stared at the perfume bottle. "I'm a chemist by trade. Top Secret stuff." She gave a wild little laugh, but it sounded fake to him. This woman knew exactly what she was doing.

"Where's your partner? Where's Lushko?" Out of the corner of his eyes he watched the car idling and realized the driver was waiting for someone. Could it be Lushko, picking this woman up? The timing fit. Or was the old KGB agent hiding in the boat, getting a bead on him while the guy in the car was some innocent bystander?

When the Russian woman took another step toward him, he dropped the politeness.

He pulled his weapon. "FBI. Down on your knees. Down on your knees and place the bottle carefully at your feet, or I will shoot you."

She smiled at him then removed the cap. *Fuck*. Ryan couldn't get a clean shot because Donnelly was right fucking *there*. Then the Russian sprayed her wrist before throwing the bottle onto the walkway toward him where it smashed a few feet from where he'd been standing.

Ryan was already slicing through the icy water.

He heard gunfire and felt an even deeper fear spear through him. He powered quickly toward the shore, staying under for as long as possible. Saw Donnelly in a firing stance as someone shot at her. When she went down, his heart stuttered.

Ryan couldn't explain the terror that gripped every part of him with glass-shard fingernails, but he knew he'd felt it before.

Motherfucker.

He surfaced again and returned fire while holding onto a nearby trawler. His fine motor skills might have been reduced, but he could still hit the side of a car at twenty yards. The vehicle peeled away with a screech of tires. Ryan fast crawled to the ladder closest to Donnelly and climbed out even though his hands and legs were completely numb.

The relief he felt when he saw Donnelly wasn't dead of a bullet wound or poisoned to death was like a tidal wave of emotion.

He caught her by the arm and dragged her as far as they could get from that broken bottle of death.

"I slipped on a patch of ice. I can't believe I let him get away."

"We need the cops to cordon off this area and get the license plate of that vehicle to the team."

His teeth chattered, and his body was a wall of pain. They staggered across the street and he braced his arms against the wall while she made the call. People started to come out of their doors or on deck to see what was happening.

He pushed away. "Keep back. There's poison on the marina. FBI. Keep clear."

People looked at him like he was out of his mind, but no one tried to help the woman who lay on the walkway. She was already dead. From the poison and the fact Donnelly had nailed her with two to the chest. Probably a mercy under the circumstances.

"You need to get dry," said Donnelly.

He turned his eyes to her as fury washed over him. "I couldn't shoot her because you were in my line of fire."

"I was blocking her escape."

"I know. Fuck, I know. But you should have moved to one side. I had her, I fucking had her but I…*fuck*." He gasped for air and for a moment they both froze with dread. Then he swallowed and held up his hand. "It's okay. Just my balls in my throat. Not deadly nerve poison."

"You hope."

"I do fucking hope." He heard the team arrive and strode over to explain what had happened and to tell them where the potential Novichok spill was. They needed their biohazard gear before they even attempted to check the woman and investigate the boat.

He put out of his mind the absolute terror he'd experienced when he'd seen Donnelly go down. He'd been reminded of a very valuable lesson today. He wasn't going through that again. No way. He'd rather take a sniff of the Russian's lethal perfume.

Time to get this weird obsession for Donnelly out of his damn head.

She was his teammate. Nothing more. Nothing less.

Time to remember that.

————

Something was going on down at the harbor. Brynn was pretty sure she'd heard gunshots a few minutes ago. Now there were men in black running around with face masks. The big cowboy who'd dragged his girlfriend out of here had taken a plunge in the harbor.

She knew exactly how cold he must be and contemplated taking a pot of coffee and a blanket down there for him. Except, before she could hustle, he climbed into an SUV and took off. The girlfriend stayed behind and…was now pulling on a black suit over her clothes before placing a gas mask over her face.

"I think we've been invaded by aliens," Brynn said in a daze.

Linda, Angus, and Jackie stood beside her, gawping at the show.

"It's better than TV." Jackie blinked rapidly.

"Except it looks as if someone is hurt," Brynn said softly. It was hard to tell from here, but she thought it was the female tourist. The men in black approached her carefully.

What had she been doing down there? Had she and her

husband been illegally staying on Milton Bodurek's boat? Had they killed Milton?

Two people entered the sailboat. One of the black-clad men checked the prone figure for a pulse but obviously didn't find one.

Rather than waiting on the sheriff or Medical Examiner, two people placed the body into a body bag and then slid that first bag into a second.

Another person left a weird-looking canister on the walkway. Then they tossed some substance down onto the wood.

Brynn shuddered. This whole thing was surreal.

Their three remaining customers, Fancy Lucette, Mayor Brian Gesbriecht and his wife, Shannon, were also standing and staring out the big picture window.

"I bet it's the FBI," Linda stated thoughtfully. "Some sort of trafficking ring. That hot cowboy and his girl were undercover FBI agents who ran out of this café to take down the bad guys."

"That doesn't make any sense." Brynn turned away from the window. "Grady would have recognized them."

Angus huffed out a rough laugh. "There are thousands of FBI agents, Brynn." He looked thoughtful, though. "Unless Grady is undercover, too."

Brynn stared hard at the scene. "Why would he be undercover?"

"Grady Steel is a disgrace. Maybe they're here to investigate him." The mayor shot her a look full of malice.

"Grady Steel is a nice young man who has served his country well. Maybe he's investigating white collar crimes. Corruption?" Fancy raised her silver brows in a guileless smile that fooled no one.

The mayor's expression shut down. "He'll find himself in jail again before the end of the day, you mark my words."

"I don't think so, Mayor." Brynn turned to the man. "You seem to have forgotten I was with Grady last night, and there's no way he killed the Quayles, so why would he end up in jail?"

The mayor raised his nose in the air. "Can't be a coincidence he arrived the same night Milton died."

Brynn felt sick at the implication. She shook her head to try to clear it. She wanted to kick the guy out, but at this rate she'd be banning everyone in town and her parents would have no customers left. Still, she didn't have to listen to his sly gossip either. Not when it impugned her reputation as well as Grady's.

The mayor wasn't done. "He comes from bad stock—"

Fancy drew herself up on an indrawn breath. "I've known Grady Steel since he was a small boy and, while his father might be a poor example of humanity, the rest of his family are good people and some of the founders of this town. His bloodline has been here for centuries, and you should have a little more respect." She wasn't finished. "Grady Steel understandably struggled as a child because of a violent parent he didn't choose and the tragic early death of his mother."

The mayor opened his mouth to say something, but Fancy cut him off. "You're quite happy to give one of his teenage partners in trouble another chance as sheriff. Why are you so afraid of Grady?"

The mayor sputtered. "I'm not afraid—"

Fancy cut him off. "Maybe it's because he's part of one of the world's most elite tactical law enforcement units and doesn't let wrongs slide." Her sharp eyes cut to Brynn. "He was a late bloomer, but it was more than worth the wait to see what he made of himself given the slimmest of opportunities."

Brynn smiled at the woman, understanding the seal of approval from at least one of the town elders.

"You know," Brynn rubbed her hands together, "I have no clue what's going on down there, but it feels like a sign. I'm sorry but we're closing early. I can give you all to-go cups for the drinks."

The mayor's wife scowled, but Fancy smiled and started pulling on her coat.

"I'll throw in a couple of chocolate brownies or a muffin each for the inconvenience."

The mayor's wife looked slightly mollified although her

mouth was still sour. It was always sour.

Damn. Brynn didn't want to turn out like that. Comfortably wealthy but a total bitch. She'd rather be poor and happy.

"Don't let the door hit you on the way out, *Brian*," Linda muttered under her breath.

"You three head home," Brynn told her staff as the customers shuffled their way out of the door. "I've got this. Don't forget to take your soup and goodies from out of the fridge, and I'll see you on Thursday."

It took another five minutes to wipe down the tables one last time and give the kitchen a final once-over. She checked the thermostat, although she could control it from her cell phone if needed.

Then she pulled on her jacket and hat and opened the fridge to grab her own food. She stopped short in surprise. Her father had forgotten to take his bag of chowder and rolls and other treats. She rolled her eyes. It was so like him.

She grabbed both packages before going out the back and onto the deck. The wind stole her breath, but the snow really wasn't that bad yet.

People were rushing around down at the harbor, and Brynn knew something bad had happened. Maybe they'd found the person responsible for all this. Maybe it was over.

She hoped so. She really hoped so.

She was supposed to call Grady when she was done, but it was still light out, so she figured she'd quickly run this stuff over to her mom and dad first. She'd still be home hours before she'd told Grady she'd finish work. Or, if he was back at the house maybe he could come with her for the drive. The idea of him meeting her parents, even for five minutes, didn't completely terrify her.

What was with that?

She stifled a yawn. Or maybe she'd slip into his bed and wait for him there, wearing nothing but a smile.

A girl could dream.

56

Grady dropped Murphy at the house, grabbed his vehicle, and drove to the harbor so fast the Jeep skidded on the slick roads. He pulled up to the edge of the harbor road, a hundred yards from where Milton's boat bobbed in the water.

Grady hung his creds around his neck and, as he did so, felt a measure of peace settle over him. He didn't have to pretend any more.

He strode past two deputies and whirled when one guy grabbed his arm. He twisted free and raised the creds to eye level.

"FBI. Touch me again and I'll break your arm." He stared hard into the wild eyes of one of the deputies who'd held on to him this morning as Darrell York had plowed his fist into his face.

Understanding slowly dawned and the guy stuttered, "B-but you're not working for the FBI anymore."

Grady allowed himself a mean smile. "I was always working for the FBI, asshole."

He shook the guy off and strode toward Novak who stood at the mouth of the narrow alley that led to Brynn's café. None of the guys wore breathing units so it must have been deemed safe at this distance.

Grady looked up at the café but the lights were off, save for the cheery fairy lights strung around the window.

Had Brynn closed early?

He hoped so.

He hoped she was back at the house now, safe and sound. Maybe catching some sleep because he had plans for them both as soon as he was done here tonight. Hopefully, after he'd told her the truth about why he was really here so there would be no more lies between them.

"What happened?" he asked when he was close enough not to raise his voice.

"Cowboy was at the end of the marina walkway when the woman came on deck. She caught him checking out the boat." Novak's brows drew together. "A car drove up around the same time. The woman spoke to Ryan and mentioned Sergei by name. Then she tossed the perfume bottle at Cowboy. It smashed on the wood, but Ryan was already in the water. Donnelly shot the suspect dead."

Grady nodded at Donnelly, who looked pale. Taking a life could do that to a person.

"Ryan okay?" Grady asked.

"He seemed fine afterward. Was in the water before the bottle hit the dock."

Grady nodded, relieved. The thought of losing another of his friends was gut wrenching.

"He was pretty pissed." Donnelly's lips were pinched.

Novak pressed his into a matching thin line. "Medic assessed him back at the hotel. His quick action saved his life."

Donnelly looked upset. "I messed up. I was in his line of fire. He couldn't shoot her without risking hitting me."

"Seems to me one of you had to move, and you're the one who had her contained." Grady shrugged even though Ryan had come perilously close to death—assuming the perfume bottle did, indeed, contain poison and not eau de cologne. "If you feel that bad about making him go in for a dip, you can jump in when this is over."

Her smile trembled. "Not sure I feel that bad. It looks freezing in there."

"It is," Grady agreed. "No one else was injured?"

"All the boats on that pier were thankfully empty. Nash checked with the hand-held radar. There was one guy on one of the fishing boats but we were able to get him off to safety in a mask and biohazard suit—as a precaution." Novak looked up at the thick clouds. "The offshore wind and poor weather conditions worked in our favor. And thanks to Cowboy and Donnelly's scouting yesterday, we had the neutralizing agent flown in last night and deployed it near and over the spillage. Military wants to send a unit out of Fort Detrick to work with the WMD team coming up from headquarters. They'll likely remove all the wooden planks and probably take the boat for testing, although the Russians appear to have been living onboard without any mask or gloves, so we're presuming it's clean. We took samples for analysis, and the field test confirmed it was likely some form of nerve agent."

"Lushko wanted the world to know who killed Kane if and when he found him," said Grady.

"Or the Russians ordered the hit. Not like they'd ever admit it anyway, so their denials mean nothing." Novak hunched his shoulders against the wind. "Maybe using Lushko gives them plausible deniability—they can say he acted alone. However it shakes out, he and his partner had a supply of deadly Russian nerve agent. Someone must be held accountable for that."

Grady was extra glad he wasn't a spook.

"Nash did the preliminary examination of the boat with a camera in full biohazard gear and is currently being scrubbed down in our portable decontamination unit by Keeme and Griffin, even though he didn't detect anything onboard. The air seems to be free of the toxin. We were very, very lucky no one else was hurt today."

Grady saw Ryan Sullivan loping down the alley.

Ryan's hair was damp, but he was wearing dry clothes, black tactical pants, shirt, and vest, plus a dark raid jacket with FBI stenciled on the back in yellow. He was fully geared up, too. "Any word?"

Novak shook his head.

Grady looked around and caught Darrell York's angry gaze where he stood talking to deputies on the opposite side of the harbor. "I guess the undercover part of the operation is officially over?"

Novak nodded. "Ropero and Dobson are at the hotel coordinating our next step, but this is an FBI crime scene. I've requested as many agents as possible from the three nearest satellite offices, assuming the weather permits travel." He checked his wristwatch. "Lushko is in the wind. We have a make and model of the vehicle he was last seen driving, a silver Subaru Forrester sporting bullet holes in the driver and passenger doors."

"He might be injured?"

Ryan nodded. "We did our best but shooting and swimming at the same time is hard."

"Slacker." Grady grinned.

"Can we trust the locals to guard the scene while we brainstorm the next move?" Novak asked him.

"Not sure we have much choice until we can get other agents down here. The possibility of a bioterrorism attack should be enough to garner their full cooperation. The Medical Examiner knows what they're dealing with?" Grady asked.

Safety of personnel was paramount.

"Yeah. They know the drill. We double bagged the body and decontaminated between bags," Novak replied, then strode over to ask Sheriff York for his department's assistance.

The less Grady had to do with the guy the better. Could Darrell be working with Kane? Grady didn't know.

Grady's cell rang. He checked it and felt a bolt of disappointment it wasn't Brynn. He wanted to talk to her even though he didn't have a lot of time to explain the details. "Grady."

It was Ropero. "Hey, those cigarette butts you picked up outside the café the night you had your head bashed in?"

Grady grunted. He'd forgotten all about them.

"One of them was Kane."

"*What*?" Grady strode up the alleyway until he reached the gate where he'd been attacked. His blood was still on the ground.

Ryan followed him. Grady looked around. "He'd have had a clear view of the harbor from here."

"The harbor *and* the café." Ryan narrowed his eyes at the back of the building.

Grady felt something niggling at him. "Who do we have left on our list of suspects with safe deposit boxes?" he asked Ropero.

"Angus Hubner, Kent Callow, Allan Grogan, and Mayor Brian Gesbriecht. We haven't found anything to definitively eliminate any of them yet."

The café's chef, the waitress's husband, his sister's father-in-law, and the town mayor. If the FBI brought any one of them in for questioning Grady's popularity in town was going to further plummet. Not that it mattered.

"Can we get eyes on all four of them? Or warrants to set up some sort of surveillance?"

"Not sure a judge will go for surveilling all four of them on so little circumstantial evidence." She blew out a long breath. "This storm is about to shut everything down. I think we should ask the locals to cordon off the area and leave a patrol unit there. We reconvene at the hotel and go through the data again. Maybe bring the sheriff in on the investigation but monitor him."

"You dig up *anything* on him or any of the others?"

"I'm still digging. Sheriff looks clean but his daddy has those dubious financial transactions in his past."

"He isn't Kane though. He was first elected before Kane went AWOL."

"Of the others, all four came to live in town *after* Kane disappeared. All married after Kane disappeared except for Angus Hubner, who is a bachelor."

Grady didn't like the fact that two of the suspects had close ties to Brynn. "I'm gonna call Brynn and check on her. She closed the café early today. I want to tell her some of the truth. It's not as if everyone isn't going to find out in the next thirty minutes thanks to the dead Russian woman lying in the harbor and the emergence of a bunch of FBI HRT tactical operators out of nowhere."

"That reminds me." Ropero's voice dropped lower. "There's zero activity on credit cards, cell phone, passport, tax filings, and social security after the husband disappeared two years ago. I mean *zero* activity."

Grady stared toward where the dead woman's shrouded form was slowly being covered in snow. "You think Brynn's husband is deceased?"

"I didn't say that, but if he's alive he's living deep under the radar. Deep, deep. She divorced him in absentia." There was a long pause. "Be careful, okay."

That Ropero thought Brynn might be involved in her husband's death was ridiculous but then, she didn't know Brynn the way he did.

Grady remembered Saul. "Shit, I almost forgot. I spoke to someone today who told me it was the Quayles who hit the bank. Source said they were visiting the Catfish Crossing compound yesterday afternoon. Said the Russians went walkabout on the Quayle property and one of the Quayles warned them off with a shotgun."

"DNA came back on the unknown Quayle. He isn't Kane, but the Russians wouldn't know that." Ropero spoke thoughtfully. "Who was the source of information, Brynn Webster?"

He bristled at her tone. "No. Saul Jones." He braced himself to lie to a fellow agent and wondered if Saul was worth it. "He figured out yesterday that the Quayles robbed the bank and when he confronted them, they gave him money to buy his silence. He had a change of heart when he spoke to me about an hour ago."

Ropero snorted. "I bet he did."

"I persuaded him to turn himself in," Grady conceded. "If he doesn't, he won't be hard to find."

"Okay. Do we think the Russians killed the Quayles? Why?"

Grady shook his head. "No fucking idea."

"Still doesn't feel right, unless he chickened out of killing the woman and kid at the last minute," Cowboy added, listening in to the conversation.

Grady shivered. Why would Kane be standing here in this spot in the recent past?

Suddenly Edith's words came back to him.

"Hey, you know we cleared Brynn's father based on her DNA."

"DNA you provided," Ropero reminded him.

He bit his lip. It felt like a betrayal of Brynn but what if…

"I spoke to Edith Bodurek about an hour ago. She told me Brynn and her father were at the bank not long before the robbery, changing documents for the business so Brynn was a signatory. Their box is on the side where the print was found."

"Yeah?" Ropero obviously sensed the same something that was beginning to niggle at his mind.

"Brynn told me something I hadn't realized the other day. She wasn't born here. They moved here when she was two. Do me a favor. See if you can find out any more information about—"

"Wait. Wait. I have it." Ropero sounded excited now. "We pulled her birth certificate as part of the deeper dive, but I hadn't gotten to it yet. I was looking at the ex, not at her. I haven't had time with everything happening so fast."

She swore.

"Tell me," Grady demanded, feeling as if he was about to get stabbed in the heart.

"Her father isn't listed on the birth certificate."

He frowned. That was weird. He had the horrible feeling he knew why. "Did Paul Webster adopt her?"

"Not as far as I can tell. But he definitely isn't named… Get back here while I take a look into Paul Webster."

"No." Grady held Ryan's gaze. "No. I'm going to find Brynn."

"Grady—"

"I'm going to find Brynn. I won't tell her about Kane. Track her phone. Then do a deep dive into the Websters." He gave Ropero Brynn's cell number as he strode down the alley back to his Jeep. Ryan stuck to his shoulder, also on the phone with Novak.

This was it. This was the lead they'd been waiting for, and it was his fault they'd missed it earlier. His over confidence.

"Paul Webster is Kane. I'm sure of it."

Could he be wrong about Brynn, too? No. He didn't believe that.

He sped back to his house and even though he wanted to burst inside, he and Ryan went in cautiously, guns drawn.

If Paul Webster was Eli Kane and the Russian figured it out, Sergei Lushko would want Brynn in order to hurt the other man the same way he'd been hurt.

Even if she wasn't Kane's biological daughter, she was Kane's kid just the same.

Grady felt his heart drumming and forced the feeling away. He went back to his training and treated this like a drill so he could think clearly and not dissolve into a mess of worry.

Fear helped no one, so, even though it clung to his bones, he put it aside.

He searched her apartment first, then the rest of the house, room by room, stroking Murphy's ears along the way.

The house felt empty, but they searched methodically regardless.

He stopped in his bedroom and quickly changed from running stuff into his tactical gear.

"Found a note in the kitchen." Cowboy eyed him like he was a grenade missing the pin. "Says she was going to drop some food from the café off at her parents' house and she'll be back soon."

Grady strapped on his ballistics vest, checked his weapons, and grabbed his cold weather jacket. "I know you don't like her—"

"That's not it," Cowboy interrupted. "But you are my friend and teammate, and you're the one *I'm* going to look after and protect."

Shit. Grady blew out a breath. Hard to argue with a man who'd just basically told him he loved him.

"She's not part of this, Ryan." He'd bet his life on it. "Let's go."

"You don't wanna wait for the others?"

Grady shook his head. "I'm not waiting. If we're right about Webster and Lushko finds him, Brynn's going to become a pawn in their revenge-fest." He checked Murphy's food and water supply before heading out the door.

"Pity we don't have a sniper team on site." Grady jumped in the Jeep, aware his neighbors were staring out of their windows in the gathering dusk.

He wanted to raise his hand. *This is who I am. This is who I really am. Not the guy in handcuffs dragged from his grandmother's house. Not his asshole father. A dedicated FBI Agent.* But worry for Brynn trumped every other consideration.

"Novak has a long gun with him," Cowboy said.

"Tell him to bring it."

"If you're wrong about this, we're pouring all our resources into one place."

Meaning Kane and Lushko could both get away.

"And it will be one hell of a 'meet the parents,'" Cowboy added wryly.

Grady clenched his fingers around the wheel grateful for the gloves he now wore. "If I'm wrong, Brynn is probably never gonna speak to me again. But rather that than her end up dead."

He picked up his phone and called her, but still she didn't pick up. He pressed his foot on the accelerator and gunned the engine.

57

Brynn held tight to the steering wheel, her teeth clenched as she drove. The wind was a lot stronger the higher she climbed. The snow thicker. She almost turned around, but she was only two minutes away from her parents' property now, and maybe she'd borrow her father's pickup that had its own little plow on the front, to drive back to town.

She turned into the driveway, noticing her dad had already done one sweep with the plow as the snow was thinner on the ground here.

She pulled up beside the truck that was parked in front of the house, idling.

Her dad must be going out again. Maybe taking a turn around the neighbors like he usually did.

She picked up the large paper bag out of the footwell and fought her way out of the car as the wind tried to rip the door out of her hand. She struggled out and slammed the door, held onto the bag of goodies. She doubted her parents would hear her arrival with the howling wind.

She tucked her head down and headed inside.

She stomped her boots and called out. "Mom? Dad? You forgot your food. Mind if I—" She looked up and came to a shocked halt in the kitchen. Her dad stood there, holding a lethal-looking black pistol.

"Dad? What's going on?"

His eyes darted outside and then settled on the bag she carried.

"You didn't really come out here during a blizzard because I forgot the chowder, did you?" Her dad looked behind her and lowered the weapon.

"Mom's favorite." She put the bag into the refrigerator.

The murders were making everyone nervous, and she wished her own gun hadn't been confiscated by the sheriff. He hadn't returned it yet. Probably figured he'd wait for her temper to cool first.

"Didn't seem so bad in town. But I'm not staying. I was going to ask if I could borrow the truck to go home but I should be fine in the sedan. I'll say a quick 'Hi' to mom first." She walked toward him, and his lips tightened as she kissed him on the cheek.

Her mother sat on the sofa in the living room. Brynn went over and kissed her. Her color was pale, skin stretched tight over the bone. A suitcase sat near the door. A photo album sat beside it.

The radio was playing. Brynn winced. "I can't stay long, but I guess you heard?"

"Oh," her mother held onto her forearms, "I heard. Are you all right?"

Brynn forced a smile. "I'm fine. Tired. What's all this?" She pointed at the suitcase.

Her parents exchanged a look.

"We decided to drive into the city. Stay closer to the hospital, so we don't miss a treatment session." Her father looked as if he were holding back tears.

Her mother's thin fingers gripped hers painfully tight. "We'll call you when we get settled."

"Okay. I love you." Brynn crouched by her mother's side. "I'm gonna head back to town. Don't worry about a thing, but I want you to promise to call me if…" She swallowed and then forced it out, "If you start to feel worse, okay?"

Her mother's eyes shone as she ran a hand over Brynn's hair. "I will. You go back now and spend some time with your new boyfriend."

Brynn opened her mouth to argue when her mother laughed.

"The things I heard from Linda this morning made me laugh and want to punch Darrell York in the face all at the same time. I'd like to sue the pants off that guy."

"Yeah, but the only people who win from legal action are the lawyers." Brynn climbed to her feet and took a step back.

"Such a cynic." Her mother's bottom lip trembled.

"I guess we raised you right in the end." Her father smiled as he came over and took his wife's hand.

Brynn smiled. "I guess."

The music on the radio was abruptly cut off by a breaking news announcement.

"The police have issued a shelter-in-place alert while they search for a dangerous fugitive who is believed to be in the area. Former FBI agent Eli Kane disappeared twenty-seven years ago after brutally slaying his wife and two young children."

Brynn frowned. *FBI?* Was that connected to what had happened down at the harbor? Had to be.

"Kane is also a suspect in a series of murders that have rocked the small Maine community of Deception Cove. Police advise everyone to stay inside and keep your doors locked. Another person died at the harbor there today in a related incident. The FBI are investigating."

Brynn shuddered. "Well, that's scary."

Grady was probably upset he was missing out on all the action. He'd be glad when he was cleared for duty again, but at least the two of them had the opportunity to get to know one another better. A lot better.

Her parents exchanged another worried glance.

Her cell rang, and she dragged it out of her pocket.

"Don't answer that," her father said sharply.

"But…" She gaped when he snatched her cell out of her hand and popped the sim card, then smashed the cell against the coffee table.

"Dad? That's my phone. What the heck has gotten into you?"

He looked away and swallowed, breathing heavily. "We need to go, Gwen. Now."

Her mom held out her hand to him. "Tell her, Paul. *Tell her*. She has a right to know."

"If we don't get out of here soon—"

"I have a right to know what?" Suspicion began to seep through Brynn's body in a chilled wave. "Do you know this person the cops are looking for?"

"You could say that," her mother's tone was wry.

"Is he after you for some reason?" She hugged herself, afraid of what her gut was suddenly telling her even though it was ridiculous.

"He's not after us," her father bit out impatiently. "Eli Kane is not a danger to anyone."

The FBI obviously thought otherwise. "Dad?"

Her father looked away.

Realization settled like a stone in her stomach. "Please tell me this is not what I think this is."

Her father squared his shoulders, and a sad smile touched his handsome features. "I'm sorry, Brynn. I'm afraid I am the person they are looking for. I used to be Eli Kane."

58

Brynn couldn't believe what was happening.

"That's not funny." Her voice quavered as she tried to take it in.

Her dad's eyes crinkled in a familiar expression of amusement. "Why would I lie?"

"I don't know!" Brynn exploded as she clasped her hands to her head. "I don't know, but that makes no sense. Eli Kane killed his family. The FBI think he killed..." She trailed off not wanting to believe what they were telling her.

Her dad stood there staring at her. Her mom gripped his leg.

Brynn looked from one to the other.

"But just today you said you never lied to Mom before she was diagnosed..."

"I said I'd lied more to her in the past six months than in our entire marriage."

"Don't play semantics with me," Brynn snapped, her voice sharp enough to have him drawing back. "Don't bullshit me anymore. I want the truth."

Gwen leaned forward. "He never lied to me about who he was. Never. I knew it all along." Her voice was fierce with emotion.

Shock made it hard for Brynn to catch her breath. Discovering that her parents had deceived her for her entire life was like getting punched in the face all over again. But this pain was longer lasting and all-consuming.

"We met when I was a waitress in a diner he came to regularly in Bethesda." She smiled at him, love shining in her eyes. "One night that spring, when it was quiet, I hit on him, but he said he was a married man. He didn't sound happy about the fact, though."

Brynn couldn't believe what she was hearing.

"I sat down and started talking to him. He was still working for the FBI then. Still a G-man, just like your Grady."

Her Grady?

Brynn felt sick.

The guy wouldn't want anything to do with her now, and she couldn't blame him. She closed her eyes and swallowed. When she opened them again, her world was still in ashes.

"I knew he was FBI because I saw his sidearm one time and was a little freaked out. He noticed and calmly showed me his badge. That gave me an unexpected little shiver." Her mother's voice spoke of fond memories. "Our chats went on for months, always platonic, usually late at night when the diner was at its quietest. Then, one day, he told me everything. Blurted it out as to why we didn't have a hope of being together and that he had to go. Leave me and never come back. I told him I'd die if he did that. I couldn't have borne it."

Brynn was trembling. Her mother was describing a romance, but the little Brynn knew suggested Kane had been the villain not the hero.

"I didn't think she'd believe me. The fact I was being set up as a stooge by the KGB sounded like some crime thriller. I wanted to stop the feelings we had for one another before I hurt her too badly or made her a target." He folded her mother's fingers over and kissed them. "I figured I was going to prison for treason regardless. I didn't want to drag Gwen down with me."

"But I did believe him. Every word. It made all the pieces of him click perfectly together." Her mom closed her eyes, sadness etching her gaunt features as she clutched his hand. "We were the love part of the story. The doomed lovers, except we refused to simply give up." When she opened her eyes, they were a vivid blue.

Paul Webster leaned down and gently hugged his wife's shoulders. "I should never have told you. I put you in danger. I'm still putting you in danger, and we *need* to go."

Her mom laughed and shook her head. "There was never a time in our story where you wouldn't have told me everything, eventually. And you know it." She looked at her husband and Brynn's eyes burned at the depth of feeling she saw there. "I loved you from the very first moment I saw you even though you had a wedding ring on your finger and I knew it was wrong because you already had a wife."

"That bitch was never my wife."

Brynn flinched. She'd never heard her father talk about a woman that way before.

"I wanted to be with you whether you were married or not. I didn't care. But…" Then her mom looked at her and Brynn realized she hadn't heard the worst. "I had you to consider."

Shock rocked Brynn so hard her knees went from under her, and she dropped to the nearest chair. "I don't understand."

Pity filled Gwen's gaze. Not sorrow. Pity.

"We never told you that Paul wasn't your biological father for several reasons, not least the fact he was on the run from the FBI and the KGB and using a false identity." Her mother laughed a little but she was obviously in pain. "Being part of a family rather than being a lone male was a much better disguise for him."

Yippee. He was wanted for familicide not tax evasion. "Happy that my existence provided good cover for a fugitive."

And yet, this man had raised her with absolute love.

Brynn's thoughts were tangled, and she couldn't make sense of any of this.

"Who is my biological father?"

They exchanged a look and her dad—Paul, Eli, whatever his name was—nodded.

She watched her mother brace herself to tell her something worse. Something worse than the fact the man they both loved had killed his previous wife and children in cold blood.

"I was raped one night in college." Gwen's voice trembled.

Brynn flinched.

"I didn't tell anyone. It was my great shame. I was drinking in a bar, having a good time. Society thinks I asked for it, deserved it even. All the 'me too' in the world and that hasn't really changed over the years." The bitterness was still there, ripe with anger. "I guess it was instilled deeply enough that I thought the same myself. Blamed myself and my own behavior. I never told anyone that I was forced. Blocked out the consequences until it was too late."

The consequences.

Her.

Brynn wanted to throw up.

"I dropped out of college. Then when my parents found out I was pregnant, they kicked me out of the house." She sucked in her bottom lip and her eyes shimmered. "Just like that, they kicked me out."

"Mom," Brynn said softly.

"A charity for young, single mothers helped me get on my feet and find work after you were born. I found a job that paid enough for me to get a room in a shared house. There was another single mom there, and she took care of you when I was at work." She turned to her husband and for the first time, guilt stretched across her features. "Or when I was with Eli." She straightened her shoulders. "It was my suggestion to kill his wife."

Brynn's world was rocked again, and she wasn't sure she could take much more.

"I'd already thought of it. You knew that." Her father argued.

Brynn's mouth went dry. "And the children?"

Gwen's lips trembled and she looked away.

"That was my decision. Your mother had nothing to do with that." Paul spoke loudly. Maybe he was worried he was being recorded or something. He blinked and Brynn was relieved to see his eyes were damp with tears. At least he wasn't the psychopath the media portrayed. "I'm not proud of what I did. It was monstrous. But I did it. I'm not denying it, but they weren't my kids."

Brynn's stomach rolled. *They were innocents.*

"Lisa had a KGB lover. They were his. They were both his. She married me only to compromise me. She never loved me. I was a mark, a patsy."

Brynn shivered. She was so cold now.

"If she hadn't decided to destroy me, she wouldn't be dead. She gave me no choice. She laughed at me. Taunted me. I snapped."

Her father came across the room and sat beside her. She wanted to draw away, but she couldn't. She'd loved this man with her entire being for as long as she could remember. His beloved face was close to hers. His hands cradled her icy ones in his.

She flinched.

"I made mistakes. I did terrible things, Brynn. I know you think there can be no justification, but the soviets put me in the situation and at the time I could think of no other way to escape."

Numbly, she shook her head. She couldn't accept that.

"Lisa put those children in the line of fire the day she decided to go along with the KGB's plan to seduce me and play me for a fool."

"You're saying your then wife,"—*the one you murdered*—"married you specifically to compromise you. Had children that she passed off as yours, that she was going to let you raise as your own?"

"I only figured it out after I discovered I was infertile. That's the first moment I even considered she'd been lying to me. I was such a fool, Brynn. She'd have lied to me for a lifetime, wasting her life and mine at the same time, destroying me for the goddamned Kremlin."

It hit her like a brick that this was why Grady was really here. He was undercover, looking for Eli Kane. *Her father*.

Did he know? Did he think she was complicit? If he didn't, he would when the truth came out. How could someone grow up with these people and not know, not even suspect?

"I asked Lisa for a divorce. Told her I didn't love her anymore, but she refused. Not long after that was the first time anyone from the KGB approached me directly. They told me if I wanted certain parts of my life not to become public then I'd better not make waves. Looking back, I suspect they were setting her up for something bigger after they bled me dry and probably killed me, making it look like an accident or suicide." He gave a bitter laugh. "At least with their compatriots they don't bother to hide it anymore. They chuck the poor bastard out of the nearest window and bleat 'accidental death' even though the entire world knows it's a hit job." He sent her a look that froze her insides.

It was a look she'd never seen on him before. Cold. Assessing.

"Why do you have to run? Mom can't go anywhere."

"We have to." Bitterness twisted his features. "I made a stupid error. Got sloppy. Or my luck simply ran out." He raised his head to look at her. "Remember that trip we took to the bank to add you as signatory to the business accounts when you came home?"

She nodded. It had been a few days before the robbery.

"After the robbery the cops gathered fingerprint evidence even though the robber wore gloves. Sheriff Darrell York's stupidity for once working for the benefit of law enforcement."

He rolled a shoulder. She realized then he wore a weapon's holster under his jacket. "I held my breath and hoped it wouldn't come to this. When I heard Milton had been murdered, I was pretty sure the Russians had found the scent. Same when Grady Steel *just happened* to be back in town." He gave a bitter little laugh.

"Mom told me to sleep with him. Were you trying to set him up?" The thought shot horror through her core.

Her mother laughed weakly. "No. I didn't know your dad was worried then. I have a soft spot for FBI agents and liked the smile on your face when I mentioned him. You need more fun in your life."

Brynn couldn't even look at her mother without bile rising up in her throat.

Her dad glanced outside the window clearly anxious to be gone. But the wind had gotten up again, and it was almost whiteout conditions now. "I would have left immediately after someone killed Milton, except I had to arrange somewhere for your mother to continue her treatment. Somewhere that wouldn't ask any questions." He checked his watch. "We must leave *now*. Come with us," he urged.

Brynn stiffened in shock. "Come with you? I can't just *come with you*. I have a life—"

"You can build a new life. I can help you create a whole new identity."

A new life?

The idea was like barbed wire pressing against the inside of her skin. Did they really believe she could forgive them? It was inconceivable. And the thought of leaving Grady behind when she'd finally met someone she really liked, maybe more than liked... But Grady wouldn't believe she knew nothing about her father's past. He'd think she'd lied to him.

Except she hadn't. She'd been clueless. This whole thing was like being trapped in a terrible nightmare.

"I don't want to go on the run."

Her mother sank back against the cushions, watching her intently. "I recognize that expression. She's in love."

Her father stared at the ceiling and rolled his eyes. "She's only known him a few days."

"I knew the moment I saw you."

"This isn't about me," Brynn protested. But she had the horrible dawning realization they might be right.

"Remember the last time she fell for someone? That prick she married." Her father's mouth tightened.

"Well, your first choice wasn't exactly a prize now, was she?" Gwen said pointedly.

Her dad shot her mom a look, and they both laughed.

Brynn stared at them aghast. It was like they truly didn't understand the enormity of what they'd done.

"Grady will never believe I didn't know the truth about any of this. You need to stop this madness. Mom needs to go to the hospital. Turn yourself in. Face up to it. Tell the truth about everything that happened."

"No one will ever accept what I did."

Because you murdered two innocents.

"But they might understand it a little better. You get the chance to tell your side of the story."

"I'll be dead in days if they arrest me," her father declared. "The Russians are even more keen than the US government to see me pay—some of them at least."

"Why did you have to kill the boys, Dad?" Brynn's voice broke. "That's what I don't understand. That's what no one will ever understand. Why not simply run away?" *Why turn yourself into a fiend?*

"I needed lead time."

"You could have left them somewhere they'd be safe."

Her father stood and paced. Her mother looked brittle, as if she might shatter at any moment.

Brynn's hands curled into fists in her lap. She was appalled by her mother's confession but also terrified at the thought of losing her.

"I had to buy enough time to clear the house of anything that either side might use to find me while they all thought I was on vacation. DNA techniques were just becoming reliable enough to use in court. I wiped down every surface, washed every sheet in bleach. Never expected them to exhume my bloody parents to get a familial match. Nothing I could do about that. They had my fingerprints on file. Ironic that's what got me in the end."

Gwen started coughing, and Paul strode over to rub her back.

Tears blurred Brynn's vision. "You killed two little boys to buy time?"

"I didn't have a choice." The answer held a bite of anger now. "Are you coming with us or not?"

"You cannot seriously be thinking about going on the run in a blizzard with Mom in her condition."

"It'll be fine. It'll keep everyone else off the road. I have the plow on the truck. We'll get through."

Her mother smiled weakly.

"Is this what you want, Mom?" Brynn threw herself at her mother's feet.

Gwen ran her fingers over Brynn's head. "I know you don't understand. We don't want to leave you, baby, but I need to go with your father now. I don't have long left."

"*Don't* say that," Brynn and her father said in unison.

"I'm not letting you go, Mom. This is insanity." Brynn felt the tears flow now, hot ribbons down her cheeks.

Then she stood and threw her arms around her father's waist. He was a murderer and a wanted man and someone she'd spent her entire life loving with every atom of her being. "Please. I don't want to lose you. You are two of the most important people in my life."

He kissed her hair. "I know. And maybe it's time to change that. Say goodbye to your mother now. I'll make sure she's comfortable on our journey and as soon as she's feeling better, we'll contact you."

But he'd already proven she couldn't trust a word he said.

Had he acted like a loving parent to the two young children he'd raised and then murdered? Dread wound through her bones like ivy. Would he hurt her? She'd be naive to think she was immune from danger.

Brynn hugged her mom, who felt fragile as spun glass in her arms. She stepped away and picked up her jacket. She'd drive back to town and find Grady. Tell him everything. He would think she was bonkers but whatever. She'd never imagined she'd one day want to see her father arrested for murder, but it was time he faced up to his actions. Told the world the truth. And, while she doubted it would change his sentence, it might help her be able to live with herself.

The images of two little boys flashed through her mind.

Her mouth went dry and she tried to swallow. What her father had done was unforgivable. It was impossible to reconcile those evil acts with the man she knew.

"Be happy, love," her mother told her. "Nothing we did reflects on you. We both love you more than either of us can ever say. You've made us so proud over the years."

Brynn nodded and stumbled away. She couldn't speak. She headed out to the kitchen, her father on her heels.

Despite everything, she didn't expect to be pushed up against the wall and to have her arms pulled behind her back. She felt something circle her wrists and cinch tight.

Restraints.

Her father had put her in restraints and slapped his hand over her mouth so she couldn't scream.

59

G rady was forced to slow down or risk going off the road.

"Ropero says Brynn's cell signal went dead." Cowboy had his phone to his ear.

"Where?"

"At her parents' house. Grady—"

"Don't say it."

"She could be in on it. This could be the escape plan. She might have known about her dad this whole time."

"No." He refused to believe it.

And yet, what did he know? Maybe she'd been faking her attraction to him. Keeping him close the way you kept the enemy close. Maybe she'd known exactly why he was here this whole time and had played him like a damn fool.

It made sense. A woman like her hooking up with a guy like him.

And yet...

And yet, it hadn't felt fake. Not a single second since he'd seen her again had felt fake.

He'd spent his life pushing emotions away but not since he'd met Brynn. He was alive with feelings. Electric with possibility. Petrified by self-doubt.

She made him feel as if he were a good person. Him. Not the HRT Operator. The man.

He realized with sudden insight that his job was a shield he hid behind to prove to everyone he was a decent human being.

It was the label he pulled out if his integrity was questioned. The institution whose values he both upheld and embodied.

Fidelity, Bravery, Integrity.

As long as he followed the rules, his job wouldn't leave him. It wouldn't die. He was in control—as much as any person could be in control of their life—which was why Ropero's stunt last Friday had shaken him to his core.

That was why he was so invested in it. Yes, he loved his teammates, but his job was the center of his universe simply because it was the only thing about himself he was proud of.

His job *proved* he wasn't like his father, but then so did his character…

He shared so much with his old man—DNA, similar backgrounds, temperament, looks—he'd always worried he was irredeemably flawed. But Grady saw now that he'd taken those fundamental characteristics and shaped them into what he'd wanted them to be. He'd taken all the potentially bad traits and followed a different path. He'd *chosen* to be a better man than his father. He'd chosen to be one of the good guys. And Brynn had seen that, recognized that, when very few others in this town had bothered even to give him a chance.

"Look, I know you like her." Cowboy shifted to face him.

Grady didn't know what the hell he felt for Brynn, but it wasn't as simple as "like."

"But think about the ex—"

"She didn't kill her ex."

"Someone did," Cowboy stated baldly.

"If he's dead, then Kane killed him." Grady didn't look away from the road, but he knew his friend's expression was skeptical. "It makes sense. Maybe the guy recognized him. Or maybe it was because the asshole hurt her…" He risked a quick glance at his friend. "Shit. Maybe Kane killed the Quayles because Caleb punched Brynn in the face yesterday. And the others robbed the bank and brought all this shit down on his head. But he couldn't kill the woman and the little girl. He's mellowed. Gone soft."

"I don't think knifing five grown men in retaliation for punching your kid in the face is 'going soft,'" Cowboy argued.

"What's Ropero think of my theory?" She was still listening in on Cowboy's cell.

"She's torn between thinking you're a genius and a complete idiot."

"Join the club." He was approaching the Webster property. "Where are the others?"

"About a mile behind us."

Grady drove past the entrance but noted the house wasn't directly visible from the road. Instead, it was shielded by a series of tall evergreens.

He noted a vehicle track going into the woods and decided to follow.

"Well, my guess is that silver Subaru up ahead belongs to a certain, supposedly long-dead, Russian agent." Cowboy pulled his H&K 416 carbine from behind the seat along with a couple of spare magazines.

Lushko was nowhere in sight.

———

"I'm sorry I have to do this, Brynn. So sorry."

Her dad forced her through to her bedroom and pushed her onto the bed on her front and sat on her legs while he zip-tied her ankles together. She fought him, but he was stronger than she'd imagined.

"I guess I should be glad you simply didn't shoot me, huh."

"Trust me," he said grimly. "Way you're acting, I'm thinking about it."

Stark fear filled her. He'd murdered those two little boys. Was she next?

He left her for a moment. Came back with a roll of duct tape.

"You can't be serious." Her voice shook.

"I'm completely serious. I know how resourceful you are."

"You did teach me everything I know."

"You'll be fine here. I'll contact someone as soon as we get somewhere safe. It'll be a day at most. Sergei hasn't figured out my new identity yet. You'll be safe here, out of the blizzard." He ripped off a strip of tape.

Had he killed the Quayles? A shiver of apprehension ran down her spine. This man was a cold-blooded killer. "Dad, wait. Dad, *please*."

He paused, but she saw the resolve in his eyes.

"You can't run forever."

"I don't plan to. Just until your mom…" He swallowed repeatedly and looked away.

Even now he couldn't face the awful reality of what was bearing down on them in the form of her mother's disease. Gwendolyn Webster was involved in heinous crimes, and Paul was a monster hiding beneath a meek and mild mask, but the love they shared was probably the one honest thing about them.

"I'd take you with us if I thought you wouldn't give us away at the first opportunity."

"I won't be complicit." Fear rose up. She didn't want to lose her parents, but then again she already had. Right now, she couldn't afford to piss off this man or provoke him into silencing her permanently. "Don't hurt anyone else. At least promise me that."

He hesitated then nodded. "Unless it's unavoidable."

"Dammit, Dad." She wiggled her head from side to side. She didn't want to be gagged. "Do not hurt Grady. If anything happens to him, I'll…"

"Hell. Your mother was right. You are in love with him."

She was caught off guard when he pressed the long sticky strip over her mouth and from ear to ear.

He kissed her brow, the way he had a million times when she'd been a kid growing up in this very room. Soothing her hurts, smothering her with so much love she'd never once questioned that he'd been hers.

"I love you, Brynn. You've always been my little girl. Sorry about everything." He hesitated at the doorway. "I'm especially sorry about Aiden." And then he closed the door and was gone.

60

Grady and Cowboy jumped out of the Jeep, sinking knee deep in snow. Fuck.

They approached in formation, scanning a full 360-degrees in case someone flanked them and attacked from behind. The driver's door of the Subaru that had been at the harbor earlier was open, and a trail of rapidly disappearing crimson droplets marred the pristine snow.

"He's hit."

Cowboy nodded.

They paused to insert earpieces and pulled their face masks down to cut out the chilling effects of the wind.

"Tell Ropero we're cutting northeast of the property to get a visual on the house. Lushko's vehicle has been spotted. He's here."

Grady didn't wait for his teammate to update the other agent. If Lushko was here, Brynn was in danger.

Servare vitas.

To Save Lives.

That was HRT's motto.

He needed to save Brynn more than he needed to breathe. It was his ability to do his job that he needed to draw upon now.

He forced the fear out of his blood and found the zone he needed to operate at his best. The gray zone he'd discovered by training over and over and over again.

He couldn't afford to think of Brynn as anything except a faceless hostage. No matter how his heart argued otherwise. He shut down his emotions and tried to see beyond the blowing snow. Beyond his limited senses.

———

Paul Webster helped his beloved wife walk across the living room toward the kitchen and another new life.

"Is Brynn okay?" Gwen gasped.

"She's upset. Of course, she's upset. She found out the man who raised her is a cold-blooded killer and her biological father is a rapist. On top of that, I'm stealing her mother away from her and tied her up to do so."

"I'll talk to her after you're safe."

Paul buried his nose in his wife's hair as she paused to catch her breath. "Only you would be more worried about other people right now."

Gunfire shattered the glass in the conservatory.

He swore.

Gwen gripped him hard even as he laid her down out of the line of fire. "Brynn!"

"She'll be okay. Her room's behind the original brick walls. Don't draw attention to her. He won't even know she's here."

"Are you sure?"

"Yeah, I'm sure." He laughed when he really wanted to cry. All he'd ever wanted was in this house, and he was certain the person outside would destroy them both the first chance he got—unless Paul got to him first.

"Crawl with me." He urged during a gap in the barrage. "Crawl into the kitchen with me." It was also built of brick and more protected. "Then I'll go get rid of this bastard."

She looked up at him, pain crinkling her forehead as she reached up and touched the side of his face. "I can't. I can't go any farther."

"You have to, Gwen." His voice cracked. He laid his forehead against hers. "You have to."

"I can't."

Another volley of bullets smashed every piece of glass he'd so painstakingly installed in their conservatory.

"I'm sorry. I'm so sorry." He broke then. After all these years, he finally broke. "This is my fault." Tears streamed down his face. "He's destroying your favorite place, and it's all my fault."

She shook her head and stared at him with those vividly blue eyes that had seen through him from the very start. "*You* are my favorite place. My whole life you're the only one who ever really saw me, except Brynn." She touched his face, ignoring the noise and the danger. "It's too late for him to destroy anything of mine, except you and Brynn. I don't care about me. I'm almost done with this life, but Brynn. She deserves the chance of happiness. Promise me you'll try to give her that if you can."

He wanted to deny her words. Tell her she'd live for years if he could get her to the right doctors. But she needed this promise. "I won't do anything to get in the way of her happiness."

Paul closed his eyes. The bullets weren't letting up, but they would soon. Only so many rounds Sergei Lushko could carry through that much snow. The woman who'd been with him in town was apparently dead. The guy was on his own.

"We're getting out of here. You and me. That's how we make sure Brynn stays safe. We'll draw him away."

She smiled faintly, as if they were lying on soft pillows rather than the rough carpet. "You were always the dreamer, Paul. I'm so sorry they picked you."

"I'm not." He wiped the moisture from his cheek. "Without them, I'd never have found you."

"Oh, we'd have found each other. Star-crossed lovers destined to meet throughout the ages."

He shook his head as bullets hit the watercolor painting they'd bought in Boston a couple of years ago on a rare road trip. They'd driven down to console Brynn after her jerk of a husband had "disappeared."

A couple of weeks prior, Aiden had come here without Brynn and tried to shake him down for cash. Threatened Gwen with jail.

Gwen hadn't known.

Aiden had ordered a replacement birth certificate for Brynn because the idiot had lost the originals. He hadn't wanted Brynn to know she needed a passport as he'd planned to surprise her with a trip to Belize. A trip Paul and Gwen were supposed to pay for, apparently.

Paul had never quite figured out how the weasel had made the leap from him not being Brynn's natural father to him being Eli Kane, but Aiden had been a damn fool to think it would earn him anything except a bullet in the head, especially after he threatened Gwen.

The gunfire stopped for a few moments, and Paul took his chance, scooped up his wife in his arms, and ran toward the kitchen. He sucked in an agonized breath as a bullet caught him square in the back and he tumbled to the floor.

———

When the shooting started, Brynn rolled off the bed and onto the floor.

It had taken a few seconds to realize the bullets were shaking the wall but not piercing it. Who the hell was shooting? The FBI? The *Russians*? The whole thing felt surreal.

It didn't matter. She expected one bullet felt very much like another.

Lying on her bedroom carpet, she'd spotted a pair of scissors on her bookshelves and wriggled over the floor like an ungainly caterpillar to get to them. She stabbed herself with the sharp end before she managed to saw through the ties on her wrist. Once her hands were free it was easy to release her feet. She dragged the duct tape off her face with a silent curse at the man who'd raised her. Tossed it on the floor.

She went to the window and tried to open it, but it was locked.

No wonder her dad had always been tight on security, even out here in the boonies.

Not that it was doing them much good right now.

She could break the glass and climb out, but where was the shooter? How many of them were there? Impossible to see with the blizzard now.

She thought she saw an armed figure moving outside and ducked out of sight. Her heart pounded. She didn't want to die.

What about her parents? Were they still here?

Paul Webster was the only father she'd ever known. She loved the man she'd thought he'd been, but she wasn't convinced he wouldn't shoot her on the spot if she got in his way.

Her dad kept a handgun in the kitchen cupboard. If she could get that, she had a chance of defending herself—assuming her father hadn't taken it.

She braced herself and slowly eased out of the bedroom into the hallway.

———

Grady and Cowboy hauled ass behind a large tree as the shooter laid down automatic weapon fire aimed at the Webster house and, inadvertently, straight at them.

"I think we're at the right place." Cowboy grinned.

Grady couldn't joke. Not about this.

"Brynn's in there." He'd spotted her car as they'd followed the trail.

The barrage paused for a few seconds. They set off trying to get around the building so they could get eyeballs on the shooter, but the building was a large L-shaped construction, and the snow was deeper here, slowing them down.

"How do you know if you're in love?" asked Grady.

"You've only known her a few days," Cowboy growled.

They sheltered behind a wide trunk as they both caught their breath.

"How quickly did you know?"

Cowboy brushed the snow off his weapon. "With Becky? I knew the moment I saw her." He met his stare. "I wouldn't wish that on anyone, Grade."

"I'm not gonna lose her, Ryan." He looked up and swore he saw the drapes move in one of the rooms. He thought he caught a flash of red hair before the shooting started again and the person —he was pretty sure it was Brynn—fell to the floor.

"I'm going in."

"Fuck it, Grady. At least let me get around the other side and put down some cover fire."

"You've got sixty seconds." He met Cowboy's gaze.

The guy nodded. "Let's wait until he runs out of ammo—"

Grady heard Ryan swear, but he wasn't waiting that long, not while Brynn was in danger. Grady moved closer, finding another tree to wait behind, then realized the bullets weren't exiting this section of the house.

He ran toward the building, head down, not allowing himself to think about the danger as he crept along the wall and peeked through the window. Disappointed filled him. The room was empty.

61

The automatic gunfire had stopped now, and Brynn listened to the howling wind fill the silence, hyperaware of every sound in this nightmare her life had suddenly become.

Crawling on her hands and knees, she reached the kitchen and saw her parents sprawled on the floor, her father lying half-across her mother, a dark crimson stain saturating his back.

"Dad. Mom." She hurried beside them.

She checked them both for a pulse and found they were still alive, but unconscious.

Thank God.

Her hands shook as she dug through her father's pockets for his cell and turned it on.

She called 911, unsure if the call would go through in these conditions.

The sound of crunching glass beneath heavy boots had her sliding the phone into her jeans pocket with the call still connected.

She rose to her feet and lunged for the cupboard where, for years, her father had kept a weapon—for *bears*, he'd said. She knew exactly what nationality these bears were now.

Damn.

The gun was gone.

Her father probably had it on him, but she'd run out of time. She swallowed uneasily as she turned to face the man she'd served food to and who she'd stopped to help on the road a couple of days ago. He stood there, staring at her with dark brown eyes and a dissatisfied expression carved into the deep folds of his face. He was bleeding heavily from a wound in his side.

"Is he dead?" He jerked his head toward her father.

She shifted to one side, but there was nowhere to run to. "Yes."

He smacked his lips together a couple of times. "Too bad. I wanted them both to see this." He raised a handgun and pointed it at her.

"Wait! I never asked to be part of this," she said quickly. "I discovered who my dad was and learned about your vendetta about five minutes ago."

"My boys didn't know either." He stared out the window for a moment. Swallowed a grief that looked as fresh today as it must have been all those years ago. "They didn't even know me. They were innocent."

"*You* placed them into a dangerous game. *You* made them players in a war no one else wanted to play."

"Not me." His face twisted. "My bosses. KGB. Always fucking KGB."

"I thought *you* were KGB?" Brynn was trembling so hard she was sure he could hear it. She didn't want to die. She'd just found something to live for.

"I was." He sneered. "You think I had a choice about Lisa or our children?"

"I honestly don't know anything about that world, but it seems cold and cruel."

"Kane lived in the same world as I, little girl. Played the same games. But he was a fool. If you want to blame someone for this, blame him." He spat the last with vitriol.

She did blame him. She blamed them both. And she blamed her mother and Lisa for putting those children in harm's way.

The former KGB officer was pissed. He might consider Eli Kane to be a fool, but Kane had beaten this man and the system for nearly three decades.

She needed to stall or reason with the guy, although why? No one was coming to her rescue. Emergency services would never get here in time. Still, she had to try. "Who was the woman you were with at the café?"

"Alana Petrokova." His mouth firmed. "She was a chemical engineer with, let's say, *special* skills. She was also Lisa's sister. Lisa was sent to the US with her parents. Alana and her brother were considered too old and were raised by the State. I contacted her many years ago and told her the truth about her family. The State had told her they'd died in an accident. She was happy to come here. She wanted revenge on the government that had lied to her and the man who'd killed her sister and nephews. We planned a very special something for Eli when we found him. An excruciating death that could have started a war"—he laughed— "but the FBI became involved. This will have to do."

He raised his pistol again. She was going to die.

"I'm sorry for what he did, although I suspect you were both as bad as each other. I want you to know my mother had nothing to do with it. And I was a baby." It might be a lie about her mom, but Brynn didn't care. Maybe he'd leave without checking to make sure her mom was actually dead.

He smiled at her sadly. It touched his eyes, but she saw only weariness and resolve in their depths. Not pity. Not rage. "It doesn't matter. It's the principle of the thing."

She almost laughed at his talk of principles. "He won't even know."

The man gave her a tired look, his face pale and drawn. "But I will."

Brynn was sick of being used by people—Aiden, her parents. Now this stranger. She wasn't about to stand here and let him kill her without a fight. She wasn't some mindless pawn in their time-worn game. She launched herself at him and shoved his arm into the air before he could fire. Suddenly, she was knocked down. She rolled to one side as another figure wrestled with the Russian.

Grady.

Oh, god. The person in black was Grady, here to rescue her. She sprang to her feet.

The gun went off, and she froze, but Grady reared back and headbutted the other man hard enough to knock him out cold.

Grady staggered back and raised his arms, wrapping them around Brynn and holding on so tight she could barely breathe.

"Grady. Grady. Oh my god. Thank you. I'm so grateful you came."

She drew away and realized with alarm she had blood on her. She stared at the smear of red for a shocked moment before raising her gaze to Grady's.

He sagged to his knees.

Brynn screamed. "Grady! Grady's been shot. Send the emergency services." She dragged out the phone from her pocket. "We need an ambulance. Quickly. An air ambulance. An FBI agent has been shot. Get here as fast as you can. Pike's Turning." She looked at her parents and the old Russian KGB agent. "Lots of people injured. We need emergency help. Please."

She dropped to her knees beside him. "You can't be hurt. Not because of me." He started to sway.

She wrapped her arms around him to keep him upright.

"Please, please, please, I have never begged before, but dear God, don't die." She held his shoulders and stared into his perfect sky-blue eyes. "I think I love you, Grady Steel. Please don't go and die on me. Even if you don't feel the same way. Stay alive so you can laugh at me later and tell me I was just some undercover op. I don't care, as long as you don't die."

62

Footsteps sounded behind her and she braced herself for danger as she looked over her shoulder. She wasn't even surprised when she spotted the cowboy from the café carrying a lethal-looking assault rifle.

She didn't have time for questions. "Help me, quickly. Grady's been shot."

The man rushed forward with a quick glance around the kitchen. He zip-tied the Russian and her father before kneeling beside her. He ripped off Grady's ballistics vest and she stared in horror at the tiny round hole at the top of his thigh.

She covered her mouth. "I had 911 on the line, but I don't know how fast they'll be here. I don't know if they believed me that it was urgent."

"Do you have medical supplies in the house?"

Brynn nodded. "In the cupboard. Let me get them."

She staggered to her feet and rushed to the cabinet her dad always kept well-stocked with emergency supplies.

Now she knew why.

She pulled out the large red box and hurried back to Grady. She knew she should take care of her parents, but she had to help Grady first.

His skin was pale and clammy, but he caught her hand and smiled. "You okay?"

"Yes, yes, I'm okay. But I'm so *sorry*."

"How long have you known your father was on the FBI Ten Most Wanted Fugitives list for killing his wife and their two kids?" The cowboy asked with bite.

"About as long as I've known he wasn't my biological father. Ten minutes and counting."

She gripped Grady's hand and squeezed. "I was bringing them some soup, and I found them on the verge of leaving. Oh, my god. None of this would have happened if I'd just stayed home like I should have."

Tears threatened, but she blinked them away. She didn't have time to cry. "I should have stayed home."

"Then a dangerous fugitive might have escaped," the cowboy said with a stony inflection.

"Give her a break, Ryan." Grady's grip on her hand tightened as the Russian started coming around. "She's had a rough day."

"*She's* had a rough day?" the cowboy sputtered. "You've been shot, and I jumped into the harbor to avoid being killed with freaking *Novichok*."

Brynn felt her eyes bug. That's what the Russian had meant when he'd said they'd "planned a very special something." "That's why you went in the water?"

"Well, it wasn't for fun, lady."

Brynn flinched and started to back away. Grady's grip tightened.

"Leave her alone."

"Grady, I had no idea about any of this. I promise. I don't expect you to believe me, but I didn't know. I didn't know any of it. Please don't die. I really like you."

"You said *love* earlier."

"Earlier I didn't have Mr. Grumpy staring me down," she muttered with a watery smile.

"He's not so bad. Hey, I think I'm falling in love with you, too. Never said that before to anyone, ever."

She watched in dismay as his eyes rolled, and he passed out. "No. Stay with me, Grady. Grady."

The Russian cracked his eyes open a slit. "Perhaps watching you watch your lover die at my hand will be satisfaction enough."

"Shut the fuck up, asshole." Ryan pressed a pad to the wound on Grady's upper leg then checked the back of Grady's thigh. "No exit wound. The bullet's still in there."

He laid him back down.

"He's not going to die." Brynn swore as she spotted the bruises on Grady's ribcage.

"Courtesy of your pal, the sheriff." The cowboy's expression was stern.

"Not my pal," she protested. This man didn't like her at all even though the only thing she'd ever done to him was serve him good food.

This was why the FBI was here…Eli Kane. Had they been watching her? Did they all know about what had happened in the shower that morning with Grady? Had it been part of the plan?

Did she even care?

No. Not if it had been real. Grady had said he thought he was falling in love with her… She didn't care about anything except this man being okay.

"Hold the pad while I tape it in place. Keep applying pressure."

Brynn did as she was told. "I don't think an ambulance will be able to get through. We can use Dad's truck to get to the emergency room in Blue Hill."

Ryan looked around at the scattered bodies.

"It's a double cab with a plow on the front. Best option we have."

The sound of more people arriving had Brynn tensing.

"Don't worry," Grady said waking up.

Thank goodness. She leaned over him to hear properly.

"S' just the guys."

"Okay." She kissed his cheek. She wanted to be with him. The idea of losing him sat like a lead weight in her stomach but she knew this was probably the last time she'd have with him. He was FBI, and she knew he loved his job. She was about to become a national pariah.

She checked her mother's and father's pulse again. Both were alive but barely. The Russian watched her through narrowed eyes.

"He's not dead, is he?" He started laughing maniacally. "Just my luck. I waited so many years for my revenge, but Kane's still not dead, and his bitch of a daughter lied to me."

Black-clad FBI agents streamed inside and despite her clinging to Grady's hand, she was forced to let go. Her mouth went dry as she was cuffed for the second time that day.

Worse, they were rushing Grady away from her, and she had no idea if he'd be okay or not.

Her mother groaned.

She tried to go to her but was held back. "My mother has stage-4 cancer. Please be gentle with her."

Tears filled Brynn's eyes at the insurmountable mess her life had become. It wasn't self-pity. It was the fact every single person she loved was in danger of dying and she couldn't do a damn thing about it. If Grady died, she'd never forgive herself. Never.

But rather than helping, she got to stand uselessly, wearing handcuffs while a blizzard blew through her parents' ruined home. And wasn't that the perfect metaphor for what her life had become?

"Miss Webster?" A short, serious-looking blonde woman in a black parka walked up to her. "Agent Kelly Ropero. We need to ask you some questions."

———

Grady's teammates carried him to the back seat of a truck and laid him down flat. They'd attached a field IV with some sort of painkiller because he didn't hurt anymore. That, or he was dying.

Nash sat beside him, keeping a check on his pulse.

"Where's Brynn?"

"Being questioned, Grade, you know that. She'll be fine."

Grady cursed as he stared at the dark trees rushing past a pale gray backdrop. The blizzard was intensifying. The forecasters had gotten it right for a change.

"None of this is her fault. She's finding this shit out for the first time herself."

"How do you know?" Donnelly asked from the driver's seat.

"I just know." He'd never been surer of anything in his entire life, and he didn't make decisions lightly. When he started to float, he heard the panicked words of his teammates, but he didn't have the strength to speak. He'd lost too much blood. Fuck knows what that bullet had hit on the inside.

He started to float higher, and all he could think about was that he was going to miss his chance. Not that he'd miss his job or his teammates, though he would. But he was going to die and miss his one chance at love.

Man, if that didn't piss him off.

63

Brynn was handcuffed in the back of an SUV, following a couple of ambulances and a snowplow headed toward the nearest ER. Grady had been taken ahead of them in her father's truck. She shivered despite her coat and the heater being on full blast.

Shock had turned to grief. Grief to anger. Anger to red-hot fury which morphed slowly back to grief. It was a vicious circle.

She couldn't quite believe any of what had happened was real.

But the burn on her wrist was raw against the unforgiving metal of the cuffs, and Grady's blood stained her clothes.

"Any news on Grady? Is he okay?"

The blonde agent turned in the passenger seat to face her. Another man drove. "I'm afraid I can't disclose any information about Operator Steel except to close relatives."

That felt like a shot to the chest.

"Seriously? You can tell his sister who hates his guts about how he's doing, but not me?" Her voice broke. "Whatever you do, don't give her power of attorney. Give it to one of his friends or something."

Fear at the possible implications rushed through her.

She glanced at the big man sitting beside her. He was dressed in black and armed for all-out warfare, much like Grady had been.

"I'm serious. Crystal Grogan would turn off anything that kept him alive if it meant she could get her hands on his property. Please," she implored them all. "Talk to the hospital staff, and tell them Grady's sister is not to be trusted with decisions about his health care."

"But you are?"

Brynn didn't miss the skeptical note in the man's voice.

"Yes, actually. I am to be trusted. I'm an honest person, and I want Grady to be okay." *And to love me.*

She kept those words locked down. No matter what he'd said to her, she couldn't imagine him wanting to know her when this was all over and the truth became public.

"We'll watch out for Grady," the man beside her promised.

"Okay. Good. My parents? Can you tell me anything about them?"

The female agent hesitated. "Medics say your mother is very sick."

Brynn felt the lump fill her throat. "Can I be with her when we get to the hospital?"

"I need to ask you some questions first."

Brynn's fingers gripped one another. "And if she dies while you're asking me these questions, the answers to which will be, no, I didn't know my supposed father was a notorious fugitive on the run from the FBI and the Russians—what then?"

"Maybe the questions revolve more around your ex-husband."

"My ex?" Brynn expelled a rush of air. "If Aiden keeps me from being with my mom on her deathbed, I'm going to track him down and kill the bastard."

"That's the point." The agent held her gaze. "We can't track him down. We suspect he's already dead."

Brynn opened her mouth but no words came out. She could hear her heartbeat suddenly rushing in her ears. "I don't understand. Aiden went off with another woman."

"There are no records of him."

"Where did you look?"

"Everywhere."

Pain began to throb behind her eyes as she remembered what her father had said after he'd restrained her in her bedroom. That he'd been especially sorry about Aiden.

At the time, she'd thought he'd meant about the fact the bastard had hurt her but now...

"I want to talk to my father."

The agent shook her head.

"You can put a wire on me. I don't care about you hearing anything that might incriminate me. I have nothing to hide. I want to know what my father had to do with Aiden, if anything. He'll talk to me. He won't talk to you. Afterward I want to sit with my mom." She swallowed tightly. "And I'd like an update of Operator Steel's condition. I might not be family but I...I need to know he's okay." She wanted so much more than that but was in no position to ask.

The agent stared at her with distrust in her eyes. Then she nodded. "Deal."

———

Brynn forced the worry out of her mind as she walked into the hospital room and stared at the figure lying quietly in the bed. He'd gone through surgery but his heart beat steadily if the monitor was to be believed.

Was he asleep?

A slight smile curved his lips as she approached.

"I thought I'd lost you. Are you okay?" her father asked.

"Am I okay?" she asked, incredulous. "*Okay*? I discover you're on the FBI's Most Wanted list accused of multiple murders. I was threatened by an ex-KGB operative who wanted us all dead. And the man I've fallen for was shot while rescuing me. Let's add the fact you lied to me my entire life and compounded that by tying me up and dumping me in my bedroom like a kidnap victim—"

"For your own good."

"Yeah, right. I don't think you get to determine that anymore. In fact, you don't get to have a say in my life ever again." Exhaustion wanted to tear her down, but she had to push through this. "On top of that, Mom's not doing well."

The smile dropped and a frown creased his brow. "Is she here?"

She took his hand, forcefully reminded of their new reality by the metal bracelets that secured him to the hospital bed. At least they'd removed her cuffs. For now.

"Yes. She's hanging in there, but they won't let me stay with her. Because of you." She swallowed noisily. "I don't think she has long."

His grip tightened. "I want to be with her."

"That's not up to me." She looked around for a chair, uncomfortably aware of the listening device in her pocket. "The FBI thinks I was in on your schemes."

"I'm sorry for that." His blue eyes were surprisingly clear for someone who'd recently undergone surgery. "I'm not sorry for most of it, but I am sorry for that. We decided early on that the less you knew the better. Telling you would make you an accessory, and neither of us wanted that—plus, we were trying to forget that part of our lives ever happened. How's your young man holding up?"

The sound out of her mouth was a cross between a laugh and a sob. "He's not mine." Although, he'd said he might love her? *Christ, what a mess.* "I don't know. He was shot when the Russian came in to finish us all off in the kitchen. You were unconscious."

"Sergei Lushko." His words were bitter with suppressed rage. "First time I ever met him in person he drugged and raped me at an orgy that Lisa magically got us invited to. I was completely wasted. Consent wasn't a big issue back then, especially in that sort of arena and, if I'm honest," he gave a bitter twist of lips, "I was too proud to admit I'd been violated. And exactly who was I going to tell?" He laughed. "I was such a goddamned fool."

Her father looked away. "I'm sorry."

"Don't be." His expression hardened. "I did the same to him at the next party minus the drugs—I wanted him to know exactly what was happening. And then I did much, much worse."

Revulsion filled her. God. It really was all true. Brynn still couldn't believe it. Maybe it was lack of sleep, but she felt as if she was floating between two worlds, one of which was Hell.

"I wish I'd found a way to kill him back then, too." He huffed out a quiet laugh. He spoke of murder with the same ease he'd talked about building a chicken coop. "Apparently, they chose me because I was arrogant. I guess I showed them exactly how arrogant I was in the end."

For Eli Kane, she realized, it had been a deadly game. Brynn stared at this person and tried to reconcile him with the man who'd raised her.

Couldn't.

"You wouldn't believe the people who attended those parties, Brynn. Not that you want to imagine your old man having sex, I know."

"Technically, you are not my parent, but you're right. I don't want to picture you at a sex party."

He squeezed her fingers hard enough to hurt. "I am the only damn father you've ever known, and I was good at it, wasn't I, Brynn? I was a good dad."

She exhaled loudly. "Yeah. Yeah, you were. I loved you."

His eyes were fierce. "I love you. Always. That was never a lie."

How could she trust him?

"I don't know what to believe anymore." She wanted to ask if he'd have killed her too if she'd gotten in his way. But, right now, she couldn't deal with the answer. Instead, she asked another question that was burning through her brain like caustic acid.

"You mentioned something about Aiden when you tied me up in my bedroom…"

His face twisted into a grimace, and she knew her ex-husband was dead.

"What happened?"

He sighed. Then he raised his voice. "If anyone's listening, I'll tell you everything you want to know as long as I can be in the same room as my wife. I'll sing like a goddamned canary, but only as long as I can be with my Gwendolyn. She doesn't have long, and if she passes…" He shook his head. "Then it'll go with me to my grave. Every damn thing. Bring me to her or her to me, and I'll tell you everything you want to know. I just," his voice stumbled, "I need to hold her hand."

Brynn looked up when the blonde agent walked inside. "If we bring her in here you have to start talking immediately. I'm not risking you reneging on your promise if she dies and you haven't finished your confession. We want to know everything, otherwise it's no deal."

Her father's eyes were glassy with tears as he raised his head to stare at the agent. "Deal." He smiled grimly. "How did you enjoy Australia, Agent Ropero?"

Ropero swore and left the room.

"You went to Australia?"

He shot her a wink. "No. But she thought I did."

Brynn recoiled, then climbed stiffly to her feet, unable to joke about this mess. "I'll be back in a moment."

She handed the listening device to an agent outside the door and headed down the corridor to a glass window where she could see several black-clad operators milling around outside.

It must be Grady's room. They'd refused to tell her much about his condition, only that he needed surgery.

Several honed gazes latched onto her as she walked toward them.

The large man she'd sat beside in the SUV blocked her way.

She looked up. "Is he okay?"

He pressed his lips into a thin line and nodded, eyes assessing. "Can I see him?"

After a few seconds, he moved aside and let her pass. She stood at the window and pressed her hand against the cool glass.

Grady lay in bed, asleep. He looked incredibly pale. His chest was bare, showing off the bruises and small burns he'd accumulated over the past few days. The monitors showed a slow and steady heartbeat.

"How's he doing?" she asked the assembled group at large.

The dark-haired woman—the one she'd served in the café that day—opened her mouth to say something but the tall cowboy spoke over her.

"He lost a lot of blood. It was touch and go for a while." The guy stepped closer and leaned down to whisper close to her ear. "Look, lady. I hate to be the one to break this to you, but his fiancée is due here any moment. Might be best if she didn't find out that his undercover role crossed a certain line. Know what I mean?"

Brynn's eyes widened in shock.

Grady was engaged?

Her heart shattered inside her chest. Rattled around like broken glass. She'd figured he'd been undercover, but she'd foolishly assumed that the interactions between them had been real. Hadn't he told her he was falling for her while bleeding from a bullet wound in her parents' ruined kitchen?

Perhaps he'd simply been caught up in the moment or still acting undercover in case the authorities worried she wasn't telling the truth.

She raised her chin and swallowed.

Of course, he'd lied to her. Like everyone else in her life. She'd been foolish to believe him. But how could she ever trust her own judgment when it seemed everyone she cared about set out to deceive her?

A *fiancée*?

"Oh." Tears blurred her vision but she blinked them away. "Wow."

Her mouth opened and closed because she didn't know what to say. She hadn't been physically injured but inside she felt utterly destroyed.

She stepped away. Cleared her throat. "Perhaps someone could get word to me about his condition later?"

She kept her chin high. They all knew what she and Grady had done together, and shame bloomed inside that she'd been foolish enough to fall for it.

"I'll see to it," the big man with cool but curious blue eyes said.

She suppressed the emotion that wanted to drive her into a fetal ball and walked away. She increased her pace when she saw her mother being wheeled in a bed into her father's room.

She needed to concentrate on her mom now. Brynn might not be a doctor, but she could tell from the pallor of her mom's skull-tight skin that Gwen Webster didn't have long to live.

"Mom." She found a seat beside her mother as her parents were reunited, probably for the last time. Brynn couldn't think about Grady. He had his own life. A real life.

Her heart felt pulverized, but there was only so much she could deal with before she broke. She needed to forget about Grady Steel. Forget everything except untangling the mess her life had become.

Her father closed his fingers around her mom's hand. And then Paul Webster/Eli Kane started talking.

64

FEBRUARY 1

Mon., 8:00 a.m. FBI HRT morning briefing

It had been almost a week since Grady had been shot. He leaned back in one of the hard plastic chairs with his arms crossed as the big boss debriefed the teams about last week's op in Maine.

He knew what had happened. He'd been on the ground. Ropero had filled him in on some of the missing pieces of the puzzle. Gold Team had been lucky overall. No deaths. No serious injuries except for a bullet in his upper thigh, which had been removed and, aside from blood loss, thankfully, hadn't done any serious internal damage.

No—that had come from having his heart ripped out of his chest.

He'd been released from the hospital and flown back here on Saturday.

Brynn hadn't contacted him.

He was alive. He was recovering quickly. He had his dream job where jumping out of helicopters and blowing things up was all part of a day's work. He was fortunate—and it was no longer enough.

At first, he'd given her a little space. He'd been unconscious for the first twenty-four hours. She had a lot going on. Her mother had died. Her father was in custody. Her childhood home was being taken apart brick by brick to see what secrets it contained. She'd just discovered her ex-husband had not dumped her but had, in fact, been murdered by her non-biological father after the guy had foolishly tried to blackmail Kane.

Add to that, she'd discovered that her beloved father had murdered five men and set fire to the animal clinic in an effort to get Grady arrested and out of the way when bashing him over the head hadn't worked.

Maybe it was flattering to have been considered such a dire threat, but it went to prove, no matter Paul Webster's gentle demeanor, he remained a vicious killer.

And her natural father had apparently been a rapist.

That had to do a number on a person.

So, he'd given her some space.

She'd told him she loved him, and he'd told her he felt the same way. He'd stepped back and let the FBI do their thing, trusting the system, safe in the glow that although everything was shit right now, it would be okay. *She loved him.*

And after three days of almost climbing the walls, he'd finally texted her.

But she didn't reply.

He'd checked with Ropero and made sure she had access to a new phone as her father had destroyed her old one. He'd texted her again only to discover she'd blocked his number.

Then he'd found out Brynn had been released from custody. She wasn't being held. She was free to come see him.

But she hadn't.

She didn't.

Reality had taken a long time to drop.

She didn't want to see him. She'd figured out he was under-cover and that ultimately, he'd been responsible for tearing her family to pieces. What was some sort of fledgling romantic love compared to that enormity?

Ackers was winding up.

Grady felt the eyes of his worried teammates on him but refused to show the wound inside him that festered.

Love made people stupid.

He should be happy. Gold Team had helped capture Eli Kane. Eli *fucking* Kane. Not to mention contain a nerve agent that could have killed a lot of people and further exacerbated relations with the Kremlin. HRT had more than proved their worth. *He'd* more than proved himself. But inside he was numb.

He'd spent his whole life working toward this feeling of acceptance and belonging, but it felt hollow. Worthless.

Ironic that Brynn had told him what being dumped by someone you loved felt like that night in the bar—like being eviscerated. He knew now.

Donnelly stared at him. Concern in her brown eyes.

Daniel Ackers cleared his throat. "Operator Steel, I'm putting you forward for the FBI Medal of Valor."

A shocked silence rang around the room. A week ago, Grady would've been as proud as hell. Now he was simply numb.

"I don't need a medal for doing my job, sir." Not when the alternative would have been watching Brynn die.

"Nevertheless." Ackers inclined his head. "I'm also putting Operator Livingstone forward for the FBI Medal for Meritorious Achievement for his work last month, and SSA Montana forward for the FBI Shield of Bravery." His moustache quivered. "It seems unlikely we'll be able to recover Kurt's body for burial, but the family is planning a memorial service for later this month. I've also put in for the FBI Memorial Star on behalf of both Operator Monteith's and SSA Montana's families."

The mood dipped in the room. Losing two members of the team had hit them all hard. Medals didn't replace them. It only made the loss more tangible.

"One last thing." Ackers paused and stared pointedly at Grady. "Don't forget to schedule those psych appointments."

Grady nodded reluctantly, but the idea of a shrink crawling around inside his head was as appealing as drinking that Russian perfume.

Sergei Lushko was being held at some secret location. Grady suspected the guy would ultimately be offered immunity and a new identity if he turned on his homeland and fed them all the dirty secrets.

The FBI better make sure he never went near Brynn again else Grady would prove exactly how like his old man he really was.

"Good work, everyone." Ackers left.

Operators started heading out to do a day's work. Grady sat there staring into space.

"Coming?" Shane Livingstone kicked his chair.

The guy was out of his cast and training full time on the team again. It was Grady's turn to observe from the sidelines.

He was staying in Grace's spare room while he recovered. Murphy had been a big hit and was so good with the kids that Grady wasn't sure he'd have the heart to take the dog away again when he moved back to his cold, empty apartment.

Cowboy muttered something impatiently under his breath.

Donnelly bared her teeth and gave Ryan a shove. "Perhaps if you hadn't told Brynn that Grady was engaged to someone else, he wouldn't be sitting there looking like someone shot his damn puppy."

Grady's head whipped around. "You did *what*?"

Novak raised his head. "That's what you said to her at the hospital?"

Cowboy rolled his shoulders. "I figured it would be better for everyone if Brynn gave Grady a little space in the aftermath."

In a flash, Grady had his friend against the wall and his forearm across his jugular. "You told her I had a fiancée? Even though you knew what she meant to me?"

Cowboy didn't try to defend himself. "At the time, her

involvement was still unknown. I wanted to give you time to think about things."

"Time to think about things?" Grady pressed harder against Cowboy's neck and felt the indrawn breath of everyone watching. "Time to think about how life feels like it is no longer worth living? Time to think about how the one woman I've allowed myself to have feelings for, ever, had changed her mind about me? Probably because I helped destroy her entire world? Or time to think about how awful it must be for her right now? How fucking bleak and terrible to have everything you thought you knew ripped away from you in front of the entire world? Is that what you wanted me to think about?"

Cowboy held his gaze with a mutinous thrust of his jaw. "I wanted you to think about how shitty it feels when it all falls apart."

"*Ryan*, for fuck's sake." Grady wanted to punch the guy but instead shoved him away. "I know you had your heart broken. We all know. And it must suck." He ran his hand over the thick scab on his scalp, another reminder of Eli Kane's ruthlessness. "I can't imagine what you went through—except, yes, I fucking can, because you decided to drag me through the mire for *days* and, now I have to beg and grovel to the woman I love and pray she forgives me."

"Want a ride to the airport?" Livingstone asked.

"I'll put in the paperwork to extend medical leave. It was too early for you to be back at work anyway." Novak stared at Cowboy like he planned to beat the shit out of him. He was going to have to get in line. But first, Grady had somewhere he needed to be.

65

Brynn parked near the hotel as there were no spaces on the street and walked to the Sea Spray Café. The FBI had thankfully released her car from evidence so at least she had her own transportation. She saw a couple of locals, but no one met her gaze.

She lifted her chin. What did she care?

The snow from the most recent blizzard had been cleared and was piled high between the sidewalk and the road. They'd had a good twelve inches in town and twenty-plus in the interior. Another storm was on the horizon. Hopefully, she'd be gone before it hit.

The café had been searched by the FBI in case her father, or the man she'd always considered to be her father, had hidden anything there.

Apparently, there had been a cubby in the storeroom, hidden behind a sheet of drywall that had at one point contained money and passports for them all. Paul Webster had been trying to retrieve them the night he'd hit Grady on the back of the head.

So much for slipping on ice.

Her father had brutally attacked the guy. *Her father* had been the one to send her the warning text after seeing the two of them walk home together after their drink in the bar.

Her father had killed the Quayles in revenge for robbing the bank and, in his words, fucking up his life, and also as punishment for Caleb punching Brynn. Of course, he'd also killed them and set fire to the vet clinic so that Grady would be the main suspect in the murders, tying him up in jail and, presumably, slowing down the FBI's investigation into Eli Kane's whereabouts.

The ends had justified the means in her father's self-centered world.

It was difficult to be mad with Grady for lying, knowing what he'd really been doing here. Her father had committed despicable crimes and conned everyone for years. He deserved to be arrested. Deserved to spend the rest of his life in prison.

He'd been holding her mom's hand when she'd passed. They both had. Brynn was glad she'd been able to do that but now she had to navigate her grief in an ocean of unfamiliar feelings that kept crashing into one another. Part of her hated her mother for allowing herself to fall in love with Eli Kane. Part of her was still in denial that the woman she'd adored had been involved in such vile atrocities. Part of her wanted to throw up whenever she thought about the fate of those two little boys.

She sniffed and hoped her red eyes and blotchy nose looked less like weeping and more about this cold weather that still gripped the state. Frankly, she had a lot to be miserable about, but she didn't want the world to know the depth of her pain. Her father had done a lot of damage. She doubted anyone would believe she'd never, for a moment, suspected the truth.

Aiden had been murdered to protect her father's identity. Paul Webster had first set Aiden up with a prostitute and then arranged the emails and postcard to be sent remotely. He was a resourceful man, this Paul Webster/Eli Kane hybrid.

The pain of that betrayal was almost too much to bear. Her father had watched her fall apart when she'd believed Aiden had left her without a word. It had crushed her, yet, the truth was so much worse.

All this time she'd been a widow. She'd divorced a dead man, and her father had let her. Showering her with sympathy and gentle hugs while telling her he'd never been good enough for her anyway.

Her father hadn't told them what he'd done with Aiden's body. Maybe he was holding back details for his plea deal. He had confessed that he'd emptied their joint bank accounts to make Aiden's leaving more believable. Her father had placed the money in a new account at the Savings & Loan and had planned to gift it back to her at some point.

Generous of him.

Brynn grieved for Aiden, and it was so much worse than when she'd believed he'd left her. Her father had murdered her husband, and she was now trying to figure out what had been true about her marriage and what had sprung from the false narrative that her husband had left her for another woman.

It was a raw, guilt-ridden ache, made worse by the realization she'd already fallen in love with someone else.

But he was taken.

And maybe he'd never really existed—not the man she thought he'd been.

She'd deleted his text without reading it and blocked his number because she couldn't stand to hear him explain or ratio-nalize or *apologize*.

She got it.

She understood.

It hurt, but he'd been doing his job, an important job. The two of them had gotten carried away in the moment.

The passion had been real. Despite everything, she believed that one thing had been genuine—genuine enough to make him forget he had a fiancée back home.

But no matter how *right* it had felt between them, they were an impossible combination, and he already had someone in his life. She wasn't going to ruin that for him.

She shuddered at the parallel between her situation and her mother's—falling for a guy who was already with another woman.

Gwendolyn Webster had meant everything to her, and Brynn grieved at the reminder of her death, coming as it had, so abruptly in the end, leaving so many unanswered questions behind. Brynn would carry that anguish with her for the rest of her life, even as she struggled to come to terms with all the dark secrets her family had concealed.

No way would Brynn knowingly become involved with a man who was married or engaged. She deserved someone who wanted her for herself. From Darrell to her parents to Grady, they'd all tried to use her for something.

She deserved better.

The only good news in this whole freaking nightmare was that her father hadn't murdered Milton Bodurek. Apparently, that had been Sergei and Alana, searching for her dad.

A shiver skipped down her spine. She hoped they locked the Russian up forever. She had no doubt they'd lock her father up for life. She hoped they didn't execute him for his crimes. Despite everything, she'd felt pity when he'd told his story. Revulsion for his actions—pity for the man who'd somehow convinced himself that cold-blooded murder was his only way out.

He'd been wrong. But he'd believed it.

Brynn and Agent Ropero had formed a reluctant kind of respect for one another. Brynn hadn't put up any barriers to the investigation and had helped fill in as many gaps as she'd been able.

She'd stayed in Bangor because the FBI had wanted her close-by, but Ropero had called this morning to say the café had been cleared for her to reopen. As had her rental apartment.

It was a relief because however much she dreaded coming

back here, at least she could now do something to move forward and finish this thing.

She decided to clean up whatever mess the FBI had made in the café and then ask her staff to come in for a difficult conversation tomorrow. She planned to sell. Live in a cave on Mars somewhere.

First, it was time to face the town. Let them get their hits in before she moved away for good. They deserved the opportunity. Kalpa and her partner, Muriel, had dropped off a care package for her, which she'd very much appreciated. Not everyone hated her.

Funny how her and Grady's reputations had been reversed. She didn't begrudge him that. He deserved the praise and recognition. The guy was a true hero.

A big white SUV rolled up beside her.

She gave it the side-eye and reluctantly stopped. Turned to face Darrell York as he wound down the window.

"Sheriff."

"Brynn." He dropped his shades to the end of his nose.

"What do you want?"

His lips tightened at her less than polite tone. "Thought I'd let you know I cleared off the reporters from outside your apartment again."

"I appreciate that. Enjoy the day." She turned to walk away.

"Brynn."

She inhaled a deep breath as she mentally counted to three.

"I hear the FBI released you."

Technically, she'd never been arrested, only questioned.

"I have a bunch more questions—" His gaze drifted along the street. "Oh, looks like the Feds aren't quite done with you yet."

He was enjoying this.

She gritted her teeth.

Sure enough, agents Ropero and Dobson were climbing out of their black SUV, along with another two deputies who Brynn didn't recognize.

Her shoulders slumped.

What now?

The lawmen bypassed her.

"Darrell York, you need to step out of the vehicle." Ropero flashed her badge and opened his door.

"What the hell is going on?" asked Darrell.

One of the deputies held up a piece of paper.

"That's a directive from the Governor." Ropero cuffed the sheriff and removed his sidearm. "Darrell York, you're being detained on charges of assault and battery, and various other abuses of power. You have been removed from your elected position as Montrose County Sheriff by the Governor of the State of Maine."

"This is bullshit. I'm going to sue the shit out of you, lady."

"That's Agent Ropero to you."

Darrell struggled, but Ropero easily controlled him.

Brynn laughed.

Darrell swung to face her. "Oh, you won't be laughing after I finish telling the FBI that your precious Grady Steel only got into the sheriff's department after he blackmailed my father and therefore lied on his FBI application. He'll be out on his ass."

Ropero arched a brow. "Blackmailed him with what, Darrell?"

Sweat slicked Darrell's forehead now. His expression turned mulish. "That's between me and my lawyer."

"Perhaps"—Ropero was clearly enjoying herself—"it was the time he took the blame for crashing a vehicle into an outbuilding and doing major property damage because you, apparently, the real driver, were way over the legal blood alcohol limit?"

"Grady was driving, and I wasn't drunk. He lied."

"In which case, how exactly did Grady Steel *blackmail* your father for a job as a deputy?"

Darrell blustered. "Grady's a goddamn serial liar. I bet his application was full of them."

"Yeah, funny thing that. In his original application, Grady laid out an entire story how, as a juvenile, he made a false statement. He and his buddy, Saul Jones, followed you on his dirt bike one night because they were concerned about you driving in such a state. Grady explained how he came upon the scene of the accident and called nine-one-one. Then he called Sheriff Temple York, who turned up and personally took control of the scene. Thankfully, you weren't hurt. Just shaken. The sheriff took Grady aside and made him an offer to save your drunken ass. Take responsibility for the wreck, and the sheriff would give Grady a job when he graduated high school. But when time came to make good on his promise, your daddy reneged. Grady, being a mistrustful young soul, used the existence of the nine-one-one recording along with an interview with the property owner that he recorded the day after the accident, to *persuade* your daddy to keep his promise."

"Bullshit." Darrell's words lacked energy.

Brynn shook her head. She wasn't surprised. It was probably one of many things Grady had been blamed for that he hadn't actually done.

"The FBI knew the truth all along—even when you applied. I'm surprised they let you set foot in the academy. You have the right to remain silent..." Ropero met Brynn's gaze across the hood and sent her a wink. Then Ropero carried on reciting the Miranda warning as she marched Darrell to her SUV and placed him in the back seat. One of the deputies jumped into Darrell's vehicle, and they all drove away.

Brynn blinked after them.

That was the best thing she'd seen in days and yet it barely dented her despondency.

She reached the café. The blinds were drawn, which was unusual, but the FBI wouldn't have wanted witnesses to their work, and reporters had been swarming the town for days. She noticed a flyer stuck to the window and smiled. It was for a tea party and tombola at the Church hall—raising money in aid of Kalpa's veterinary practice. Brynn would be sure to make a hefty donation as soon as she had access to the bank accounts, considering it was her father who'd torched the place.

She made her way cautiously around the back of the building. Someone had cleared the snow and spread sand so it wasn't slippery. The scene reminded her of standing beside Grady and looking down at the harbor the morning after Milton had been murdered.

A *hiss* had her clutching her heart with a gasp. The ginger tomcat sat on the nearby fence and flashed his teeth.

"Survived the storm I see. Good." She needed to talk to Kalpa about catching the stray and finding him a good home.

She let herself in the back door and stopped short.

"Brynn." Linda climbed to her feet from where she'd been on her hands and knees scrubbing the floor.

Angus was in the kitchen, putting his pots and pans back in order.

Jackie turned from where she was wiping dirty smudges off the walls and light switches.

"What are you all doing here?" asked Brynn.

Undercurrents swirled around the room like a riptide.

"Cleaning up so we can open on time tomorrow," Linda said firmly.

"Why are you helping after everything my family did?"

"Because we want to help *you*," Angus said carefully from the kitchen.

Brynn sat heavily at the nearest table. "I thought you'd hate them. Hate me."

Linda came over and pulled her into a hug. It was the first time anyone beside law enforcement had touched her in days.

"Silly goose. How are you to blame for something your parents did?" Linda's mouth was pinched with tiredness. "They were my best friends, and I didn't know. Does that mean I'm to blame, too?"

Brynn shook her head. "Mom loved you."

Linda flicked her hair out of her face and, although her eyes were shiny, she didn't cry. "I loved her, too. I tried to visit, but they wouldn't let me in. They wouldn't let anyone in."

"She went quickly in the end." The lump in Brynn's throat was like a wedge of iron. "I don't think she wanted to face what had happened, especially what would happen to Dad now."

Linda squeezed her shoulders. "They loved one another. Anyone could see that." She tucked a piece of hair behind Brynn's ear. "They loved you, too."

"I'm going to sell." Her voice was scratchy.

Linda nodded. "If that's what you want. But this place is going to take off after this. Just you watch."

Brynn shrugged out of her coat. "I'm not sure I'm Machiavellian enough to capitalize on the notoriety."

"If you don't, someone else will. At least that way you control the narrative."

Brynn looked around at her mother's beloved café. Shook her head. "I can't do it, but if you guys want to buy me out or manage the place, I'm open to it. It doesn't feel the same anymore."

Linda pressed her lips together. "Let's show the town what we're made of. And any potential buyers that this place is a thriving business."

"We won't need to hire a real estate agent. I'll mention it to one of the incessant reporters following me around, and it'll be all over the news."

Jackie came over. "What happened to Grady?"

Her heart knocked hollowly against her sternum at the reminder. "He's gone." She didn't know when the pain would stop, but she couldn't think about it now. "It wasn't real. I was a job to him."

She didn't miss the angry glance the three of them exchanged.

"It's okay. Not like I'm a prime catch, especially for an FBI agent." She forced a laugh. "It's fine. I'll be fine. I didn't even really know him that well anyway."

The words echoed emptily around the café and fooled no one. They were veritably dripping with self-pity.

But it was better to keep her misery to herself than drag

everyone else down with her. It was better to keep busy than to sit around moping.

Angus started noisily banging his pots around in the kitchen. Linda placed a cloth in her hand and pointed her toward the refrigerators, which all needed wiping down. Brynn forced the longing and the loneliness aside.

66

G rady rented a car in Bangor and drove straight to the café. It was dark by the time he arrived, and the lights were all out, even the fairy lights around the picture window.

He didn't know why that made him feel so sad, but it did.

His cell rang. He answered it, hoping it was Brynn, but it was Edith.

"Agent Steel."

He found himself smiling despite everything. "Mrs. Bodurek."

"I wanted to thank you." She sounded tired. "I was able to bury Milton today, and that's due in large part to you keeping your promise."

"I was simply doing my job, ma'am."

"Nonsense. Very few people keep their word these days, but you kept yours. And you helped rid us of that incompetent sheriff."

Ropero had texted him earlier that the order from the Governor had come through. He hadn't realized she'd already confronted Darrell.

"Next time make sure you vote for someone better qualified."

"Indeed. I had wondered if you might be available to take up the position. I'd give you my backing and financially support your campaign."

Grady hadn't thought much could shock him anymore, but this did. "I'm flattered, but I'm happy where I am."

"Well, think about it for when you retire from the FBI. My offer will stand for as long as I'm still around."

"Edith…" He didn't know what to say. He'd waited a long time for acceptance in this community, and he wasn't quite sure how to deal with it now that it had arrived. "I'm glad you found out what happened to Milton and we were able to detain his killer."

"Me, too, more than I can ever say. And I'm grateful to be able to get to know and aid our new veterinarian. It's given me new purpose. Kalpa already has me fostering a poodle who was being bred in a puppy mill. Poor thing." She hesitated. "I heard Brynn Webster was back in town today."

Grady set his teeth. If anyone bad-mouthed Brynn—

"I expect she could do with a friend. I hope you won't hold her parents' actions against her."

Grady scratched his jaw. "I'm more worried she's going to hold my part in this against me."

Edith laughed. "Then you'll have to persuade her otherwise, won't you?"

He smiled. "Wish me luck."

"Good luck, young man. Come visit me when you have time."

"I will." He'd drop by tomorrow to surprise her. Assuming he'd found Brynn by then.

They said goodbye, and he drove to his house. The house he'd grown up in. The house his mother had grown up in and where his grandmother had died.

He wasn't sure what he was going to do if Brynn wasn't there, or if she didn't want him. The thought of that rejection was almost enough for him to turn around and learn to live with the pain of being alone. But he'd seen what that did to someone. Ryan Sullivan, for all his wicked charm and string of women, was probably the loneliest human Grady had ever met.

He pulled into the driveway and got out. He inhaled a deep, fortifying breath and walked to Brynn's door. Even though he had a key he knocked and waited. Nothing happened.

Shit.

It looked dark downstairs but hard to tell with the thick drapes drawn closed on the small windows. There were lights on upstairs though.

He headed up the front steps, let himself inside, and came face-to-face with his sister, who was vacuuming the living room.

She jumped and pressed a hand against her breastbone. "You scared me."

"I didn't mean to." He looked around. "Did you rent it out again?"

She turned the vacuum off. "No. I was going to call you about that."

He didn't want to talk about it right now. He needed to find Brynn.

"A few of your FBI colleagues stayed here when they searched downstairs and the café. I wanted to clean up after they left. I didn't think you'd mind." At his expression she added, "I didn't charge them."

"Okay." He went to touch her arm, to reassure her, but she flinched. He sighed. He forced himself to ask her calmly, "My whole life you've treated me like something to be scraped from the bottom of your shoe. I know I was a little shit, but I don't remember doing anything truly terrible to you. But if I did, I'm sorry. Maybe we can start over?"

She unplugged the cord and started winding it up. "You didn't do anything terrible to me."

"Then why? Why do you hate me so much?"

Her blue eyes shot to his in surprise, and he thought she was going to deny it.

"Because you look just like him." She put her fisted hand against her mouth.

He frowned. "Like Dad, you mean? That piece of shit sperm donor of ours?"

"I know it's not fair. I know it isn't your fault. But you were always this mini version of him." She sucked in her lips. "You were a toddler when he was arrested, but I was older. He used to hit me and shout at me. I was a little kid, Grady. Mom always took his side. Just like Gran always took yours." Bitterness leaked out again.

"I'm sorry, Crys. So sorry."

Crystal blew her nose. "I know. And I know it wasn't your fault. Not looking like him. Not Gran choosing you over me." She drew up her shoulders. "I'm ashamed of the fact I've always been mean to you." Some of her blonde hair fell out of its ponytail, and she pushed it back. "I need to say that I'm sorry. I tried before, but I'm terrified of admitting all of this. It is so much easier to hate."

"You're terrified?" he said skeptically. "The scariest person I know is terrified?"

"Yes." She laughed. Braced herself. "I'm sorry I've been such a horrible sister all these years." She raised her head. "I've been avoiding all my own trauma and taking it out on you instead. That's not fair." She gathered her stuff together and pulled on her coat. "You're not like him. Not where it matters. Inside. I won't bother you again, but if you'd like to come by the house before you leave town, I've some things I kept for you. You'd be welcome. More than welcome." She smiled. The first genuine smile he'd seen on her face in years. "And I don't want Gran's house."

"Liar," he joked tentatively.

She shook her head. "No, it's true. Bob and I made a tidy income, but it always felt wrong. It *was* wrong."

"I'm grateful you took care of the place and Gran shouldn't have left it all to me. She was wrong to do that, Crys."

"It was hers to do with as she wanted." Crystal shrugged

unhappily. "It doesn't matter anymore. The house is yours to deal with. Keep it or sell it. Bob and I have already made an offer on another place. We're going to gut it and renovate." She stood there awkwardly. "You have my number."

He hugged her stiff frame, and she placed a quick kiss on his cheek.

"Brynn's downstairs. She hasn't stopped crying since she came home from the café earlier. I can hear her through the floorboards. Poor thing."

The pity in her voice seemed genuine.

The ache in his chest intensified and at the same time he settled. She was here.

He locked the front door after his sister left and opened the door to the basement.

Music was playing but someone was definitely crying.

He headed down the stairs, not trying to be quiet.

"Crystal, I already told you." Brynn's tone was upset and held a warning note. "I don't want to talk about—"

She stopped speaking when she caught sight of him. Hope bloomed in her eyes for a moment before her expression became stricken. She whirled around and dove for a box of tissues.

He walked slowly toward her.

She blew her nose and knuckled away her tears. "Sorry. I didn't realize you were back." Her gaze ran over his body to where he'd been shot then rose to meet his. "Are you okay?"

He shook his head. "Not really."

"I thought they'd released you. Sit down. I thought the wound wasn't as serious as first feared. That's what Agent Ropero told me." She took a step forward and then moved away again, as if circling a dangerous animal, or like Murphy had after living scared and lonely on the streets.

He settled further. He knew what he wanted now. Knew what he needed. This was not a woman who didn't care about him. Even if she never forgave him, she cared. "The bullet wound is healing fine."

Three little lines formed between her brows. "I don't understand."

He hated seeing the uncertainty in her eyes.

"Going somewhere?" He indicated the suitcase and box of food on the kitchen counter.

"Yeah. I'm leaving tomorrow. The FBI said it was okay."

He winced at the defensiveness in her tone.

"Linda's going to run the café until I find a buyer. I figured I'd head down to Boston. Talk to the person subletting my apartment. Either sell it or rent it out longer term."

He grimaced a little as he lowered himself onto her couch. "Where will you go?"

"I haven't decided yet." Her gray-green eyes shone with uncertainty. "It depends a little what happens to Dad. Legal stuff."

He nodded.

She cleared her throat. "I didn't get the opportunity to apologize to you—"

"Yeah, you did. In your parents' kitchen when I was shot. Around the same time you said you thought you loved me."

She clutched her hands together and turned away from him.

"I'm sorry about that, too. I shouldn't have said that. I guess it was the pressure of the situation."

"Do you remember what I said back?"

She nodded. "But you don't have to pretend or let me down easy. Your friend told me about your fiancée. I hope I didn't cause you any trouble."

She was so stiff and formal and proper.

"I told you that I thought I was falling in love with you, and that I'd never said that to anyone before."

She tossed her tissue into the garbage and pulled another one. "I figured you were keeping in character to get more information out of me."

He shook his head, incredulous. "I'm not that good an actor."

He watched emotions crash over her features. Heartbreak. Hope. Confusion.

"Are you saying you don't love your fiancée?"

He would have laughed at the ridiculous notion if he couldn't see her obvious pain. "No, I don't love that fickle bitch, but I appreciate how your mind works."

She tilted her head. "I really don't understand."

"Ryan, my so-called friend, lied to you."

"What?" Hurt soaked her voice.

"He lied. I don't have a fiancée. I'm not engaged to anyone. I never have been."

She took a few steps away. Began pacing. "He must really hate me."

Grady held out his hand. "No, but he doesn't want me to get hurt."

"Why would you be hurt?" She looked at his hand like it might bite.

"Because I'm in love with you, Brynn. I know it's true because I've never been more miserable in my entire life—like I've been eviscerated. When you didn't come to see me in the hospital and then blocked my number—that hurt more than any bullet."

Her lip wobbled but her expression was less devastated, as if she was finally starting to believe his feelings for her might be real. "I came to see you. Just after you came out of surgery. That's when, when…"

When Ryan had broken her heart the way Grady worried she might now break his.

"I need to apologize." The words knotted in his throat. What if he messed this up? Ruined his chance with her completely? "Not only for Ryan being an asshole, but for everything. I couldn't tell you why I was in town. I was supposed to be deep undercover. The FBI had been after Kane for so many years we couldn't risk telling anyone outside the immediate 'need-to-know' circle."

The copper in her hair caught the light as she looked up.

"But I should never have started something with you with those untruths between us."

"*Untruths.*" She huffed out a disgruntled laugh, but she refused to meet his gaze. "Funny how many untruths have shaped my life without me realizing it. Can I ask you one thing?"

"I'll tell you anything that I'm able."

She raised her chin and met his gaze. "Did you get close to me *because* you suspected my father?"

"No. No. Definitely not." He blew out a big breath knowing he had to tell her everything even though it might make her hate him even more. "I took your coffee mug from the café that first morning and had your DNA compared to what we had on record for Kane. I only allowed myself to act on the feelings I'd begun to have for your *after* I thought I'd proven you couldn't be related to Kane."

"Paul Webster not being my biological parent came as a pretty big shock to me, too." She injected humor into the words, but he knew this was another thing that had devastated her.

"I should never have kissed you." She gripped the edge of her cardigan like it was a lifeline.

He hated her saying that or blaming herself. Those kisses had made him come alive.

"You didn't know I was lying about my reasons for being in town. You were acting openly and honestly on what was happening between us. I'm the one who screwed up by kissing you back." It was true. He'd crossed a line. "And I definitely shouldn't have had sex with you."

Her eyes widened with hurt.

"But I couldn't seem to stop myself. My job is important to me, and I'm good at it, but"—he shook his head—"the things I felt for you were completely out of my scope of experience, and they kept growing until suddenly I realized it was love. For the first time in my life, I was in love, but I still couldn't tell you the truth about why I was in town." Emotion clawed at his throat. "Instead, I helped to destroy your family. The one person in this town who saw me for who I really am, beyond my father, beyond my teenage transgressions. The one person who believed I was one of the good guys without needing any damn proof." His eyes were damp, but he held her gaze. "I'm so sorry, Brynn."

She tugged her cardigan tighter around herself, flimsy armor against a world of hurt.

"I'll understand if you can't forgive me or don't want me anymore, but I needed you to know what we had was real."

"How can I ever trust you?" She burst out. "How can I ever trust myself?"

His mouth went dry because they'd done this to her. Destroyed her self-confidence. "You're a smart woman. If you've been made to feel otherwise, it was by master manipulators playing games with your life that we had no right to play. And look at how we all fell in love with you while we were doing it, whether we liked it or not—even a stone-cold killer like Eli Kane."

She squeezed her eyes closed against tears, and he used her distraction, leaning forward to snag her hand and tug her onto the couch beside him.

"I love you, Brynn. I have no experience in how I'm supposed to act or feel, and I'll probably screw it all up." He brushed a silky tress of her hair behind one ear. "I love you. I want to start over. Give me a chance to prove myself. Give us a chance…"

"No." She pulled back, crushing his heart with that two-letter word. "Being with me would kill your career, Grady."

The tension drained away from him. "No, it won't."

"It will. I can't abandon my father. I'm all he has left. I will go visit him. I know he's a monster, but he's still the man who raised me. I hate him for the evil things he's done, but I also love him on some level. It's all a confusing mess in my head, and I need time to figure it out." She looked ashamed by the admission.

"I'm not going to judge you for loving your dad any more than I expect you to judge me for not loving mine."

"But your bosses…"

He leaned forward despite the discomfort in his hip and kissed her.

Her lips melted against his, but then she pulled away again. "I can't mess up your career, Grady. I know how important it is to you."

He cupped her jaw. "You won't. Seriously, you won't. And if the FBI can't deal with it,"—he leaned his forehead against hers—"then I'll quit and buy a boat. Start running those whale-watching tours."

Her eyes bugged wide. Then she laughed as he'd hoped. "You're serious?"

"I have never been more serious about anything in my entire life." He felt his pulse kick up a notch in apprehension. Give him an armed hostage situation any day. He didn't know what he'd do if she said no again.

"Do you really think we have a hope together?" Her stormy eyes were clear now, hope beginning to take a hold.

"I don't think it. I know it."

She knelt beside him, kissed him tenderly. Inside, he wanted to cheer, open champagne, and let off party poppers. Instead, he kissed her, pouring every ounce of emotion into that heartfelt caress.

She pulled back. "I thought I'd lost you. Over and over again, I thought I'd lost you. I'm scared of believing again. I'm scared this is a dream and when I wake up, I'm going to be alone…"

"I won't let you down, Brynn."

Her eyes filled. "You didn't let me down, Grady. You never let anyone down."

He pulled her in for another kiss, heat surging between them until tears were forgotten, their breath becoming short.

She sat back on her heels. Smiled. "To think I was bemoaning the lack of excitement in my life not that long ago."

"I wish I could promise it will always be exciting, but my job means long periods of me being away from home. I have to live near Quantico to deploy at a moment's notice."

"It's okay." She sighed. "Excitement is overrated."

He rested his head against the back of the couch. "It would be nice if I had someone to come home to…"

She blinked rapidly. Her brow crinkled. "Are you asking me to move to Virginia?"

He pulled her against him. "I'm asking you to *live with me*."

Her expression was pensive. She'd been through a lot this past week and maybe this was too much, too fast.

"But only if you want to. We could find a new place somewhere. Something with a yard for Murphy." The fact he was trying to sweeten the deal with a dog revealed his desperation. "See how we fit together in the real world."

She ran her hands gently through his short hair and down the sides of his face to cup his jaw. "Well, I already know you make great coffee and are an excellent kisser—*amongst other things*."

He grinned, but she wasn't done.

"I know you're kind to old ladies and animals, even the ones that try to peck you to death." She bit her lip. "You're brave and honorable, fair even when you've been treated unfairly. But you did say you can't cook…"

"I can learn to cook. I can learn to be a goddamn gourmet and bake chocolate ganache cake you don't have to sell your soul for." He cupped the back of her head and grinned as she kissed him. Quiet tastes that were driving him slowly mindless with lust.

It wasn't going to be easy to make love with his wounded thigh, but he hoped he got the opportunity to give it a try. Soon.

"What do you think?" he murmured against her throat.

"I think I'd like to move to Virginia and be with you and your dog. I think I love you." She looked as if she might cry again, but at least she was smiling this time.

"I love you, Brynn Webster." It felt good to say it when he wasn't delirious with pain. He wanted to practice saying it every day of his life, with words and actions. Make it so she'd never doubt him again, or herself.

He'd found his happiness, finally, and he intended to take care of it.

He had everything he'd ever wanted, along with the sneaky suspicion his grandma would be delighted he'd hooked up with a local girl, even if neither of them had any intention of staying in Deception Cove.

———

Thank you for reading *Cold Snap*. I hope you enjoyed Grady and Brynn's story. Ready for the next installment of the Cold Justice® - Most Wanted series?

Read *Cold Fury*...the next Romantic Thriller from *New York Times* and *USA Today* bestselling author Toni Anderson.

Have you read the book that started it all? *A Cold Dark Place* is the first book in the Cold Justice® world.

With over five thousand ⭐⭐⭐⭐⭐ *reviews on Goodreads!*

When a series of brutal murders links to a cold case that is intensely personal for one FBI agent, she seeks help from a cybercrime expert with a secret identity in the hunt for a vicious killer—in this award-winning Romantic Thriller from *New York Times* bestselling author Toni Anderson.

FBI agent Mallory Rooney spent the last eighteen years searching for her identical twin sister's abductor. With a serial killer carving her sister's initials into the bodies of his victims, Mallory thinks she may finally have found him.

Former soldier Alex Parker is a highly decorated but damaged war hero with a secret—he's a covert government assassin who hunts predators. Now he's looking into the murders too.

When danger starts to circle Mallory, Alex is forced out of the shadows to protect her and they must race against the clock to find the killer. But the lies and betrayals that define Alex's life threaten to destroy them both—especially when the man who stole her sister all those years ago, makes Mallory his next target.

Winner of the New England Readers' Choice Award and the Aspen Gold. Available in digital, print, and audiobook format.

USEFUL ACRONYM DEFINITIONS FOR TONI'S BOOKS

ADA: Assistant District Attorney
AG: Attorney General
ASAC: Assistant Special-Agent-in-Charge
ASC: Assistant Section Chief
ATF: Alcohol, Tobacco, and Firearms
BAU: Behavioral Analysis Unit
BOLO: Be on the Lookout
BORTAC: US Border Patrol Tactical Unit
BUCAR: Bureau Car
CBP: US Customs and Border Patrol
CBT: Cognitive Behavioral Therapy
CD: Counterintelligence Division
CIRG: Critical Incident Response Group
CMU: Crisis Management Unit
CN: Crisis Negotiator
CNU: Crisis Negotiation Unit
CO: Commanding Officer
CODIS: Combined DNA Index System

CP: Command Post
CQB: Close-Quarters Battle
DA: District Attorney
DEA: Drug Enforcement Administration
DEVGRU: Naval Special Warfare Development Group
DIA: Defense Intelligence Agency
DHS: Department of Homeland Security
DOB: Date of Birth
DOD: Department of Defense
DOJ: Department of Justice
DS: Diplomatic Security
DSS: US Diplomatic Security Service
DVI: Disaster Victim Identification
EMDR: Eye Movement Desensitization & Reprocessing
EMT: Emergency Medical Technician
ERT: Evidence Response Team
FOA: First-Office Assignment
FBI: Federal Bureau of Investigation
FNG: Fucking New Guy
FO: Field Office
FWO: Federal Wildlife Officer
IB: Intelligence Branch
IC: Incident Commander
IC: Intelligence Community
ICE: US Immigration and Customs Enforcement
HAHO: High Altitude High Opening (parachute jump)
HRT: Hostage Rescue Team
HT: Hostage-Taker
JEH: J. Edgar Hoover Building (FBI Headquarters)
K&R: Kidnap and Ransom
LAPD: Los Angeles Police Department
LEO: Law Enforcement Officer
LZ: Landing Zone
ME: Medical Examiner

MO: Modus Operandi
NAT: New Agent Trainee
NCAVC: National Center for Analysis of Violent Crime
NCIC: National Crime Information Center
NFT: Non-Fungible Token
NOTS: New Operator Training School
NPS: National Park Service
NYFO: New York Field Office
OC: Organized Crime
OCU: Organized Crime Unit
OPR: Office of Professional Responsibility
POTUS: President of the United States
PT: Physiology Technician
PTSD: Post-Traumatic Stress Disorder
RA: Resident Agency
RCMP: Royal Canadian Mounted Police
RSO: Senior Regional Security Officer from the US Diplomatic Service
SA: Special Agent
SAC: Special Agent-in-Charge
SANE: Sexual Assault Nurse Examiners
SAS: Special Air Squadron (British Special Forces unit)
SD: Secure Digital
SIOC: Strategic Information & Operations
SF: Special Forces
SSA: Supervisory Special Agent
SWAT: Special Weapons and Tactics
TC: Tactical Commander
TDY: Temporary Duty Yonder
TEDAC: Terrorist Explosive Device Analytical Center
TOD: Time of Death
UAF: University of Alaska, Fairbanks
UBC: Undocumented Border Crosser
UNSUB: Unknown Subject

USSS: United States Secret Service
ViCAP: Violent Criminal Apprehension Program
VIN: Vehicle Identification Number
WFO: Washington Field Office
WMD: Weapons of Mass Destruction

COLD JUSTICE WORLD OVERVIEW

ALL BOOKS CAN BE READ AS STANDALONE STORIES.

COLD JUSTICE® SERIES

A Cold Dark Place (Book #1)

Cold Pursuit (Book #2)

Cold Light of Day (Book #3)

Cold Fear (Book #4)

Cold in The Shadows (Book #5)

Cold Hearted (Book #6)

Cold Secrets (Book #7)

Cold Malice (Book #8)

A Cold Dark Promise (Book #9~A Wedding Novella)

Cold Blooded (Book #10)

COLD JUSTICE® – THE NEGOTIATORS

Cold & Deadly (Book #1)

Colder Than Sin (Book #2)

Cold Wicked Lies (Book #3)

Cold Cruel Kiss (Book #4)

Cold as Ice (Book #5)

COLD JUSTICE® – MOST WANTED

Cold Silence (Book #1)

Cold Deceit (Book #2)

Cold Snap (Book #3)

Cold Fury (Book #4)- Coming soon

The Cold Justice® series books are also available as audiobooks narrated by Eric Dove, and in various ebook box set compilations.

Check out all Toni's books on her website (www.toniandersonauthor.com/books-2) and find exclusive swag on her new store.

ACKNOWLEDGMENTS

As always I want to thank my longstanding critique partner Kathy Altman. She's my first reader and the only person to ever see my books naked. I did have a major panic attack at the end of the first draft and Kathy talked me down. Since then, I have fallen in love with this book and the lost souls within.

Thanks to Rachel Grant and Jenn Stark for great beta reads. You guys are the best to tackle a 123K word manuscript with smiles and grace. I love you!

I put together a fresh editorial team for *Cold Snap*. So, thanks to my amazing new developmental editor Lindsey Faber, my stalwart copy editor Joan at JRT Editing, and the ridiculously talented Pamela Clare who provided a fabulous proofread.

Thanks to the Public Affairs Specialists of the FBI's National Press and Operations Unit for assisting me with some details regarding FBI procedure. Any mistakes are my own, either in blissful ignorance or in the pursuit of good fiction.

I'm so grateful to have assembled such an amazing group of people to help me produce and package my books. Huge appreciation to my assistant Jill Glass, my brilliant cover designer Regina Wamba, and my awesome audiobook narrator Eric G. Dove.

I'm so thankful for my family, especially Gary, the love of my life, and my dazzling daughter and wonderful son. This is the first book I've written in more than a decade without my beautiful rescue dog Holly by my side, *sniff*, but I'm so happy to have Fergus, my goofy Black Lab, who makes every day a good day.

ABOUT THE AUTHOR

Toni Anderson writes gritty, sexy, FBI Romantic Thrillers, and is a *New York Times* and a *USA Today* bestselling author. Her books have won the Daphne du Maurier Award for Excellence in Mystery and Suspense, Readers' Choice, Aspen Gold, Book Buyers' Best, Golden Quill, National Excellence in Story Telling Contest, and National Excellence in Romance Fiction awards. She's been a finalist in both the Vivian Contest and the RITA Award from the Romance Writers of America, and shortlisted for The Jackie Collins Award for Romantic Thrillers in the Romantic Novel Awards. Toni's books have been translated into five different languages and more than three million copies of her books have been downloaded.

Best known for her Cold Justice® books perhaps it's not surprising to discover Toni lives in one of the most extreme climates on earth—Manitoba, Canada. Formerly a Marine Biologist, Toni still misses the ocean, but is lucky enough to travel for research purposes. In late 2015, she visited FBI Headquarters in Washington DC, including a tour of the Strategic Information and Operations Center. She hopes not to get arrested for her Google searches.

Sign up for Toni Anderson's newsletter:
www.toniandersonauthor.com/newsletter-signup
See Toni Anderson's current book list:
www.toniandersonauthor.com/books-2

Made in the USA
Columbia, SC
01 May 2024